WISH UPON A STAR

By the same author

OLIVIA GOLDSMITH

Wish Upon a Star

HarperCollins*Publishers*

HarperCollins*Publishers*
77–85 Fulham Palace Road,
Hammersmith, London W6 8JB

www.harpercollins.co.uk

This paperback edition 2004
4
First published by HarperCollins Publishers 2004

This novel is entirely a work of fiction. The names,
characters and incidents portrayed in it are the work
of the author's imagination. Any resemblance to actual
persons, living or dead, events or localities
is entirely coincidental.

A catalogue record for this book
is available from the British Library

ISBN 0 00 713338 3

Set in Sabon by Palimpsest Book Production Limited,
Polmont, Stirlingshire

Printed and bound in Great Britain by
Clays Ltd, St Ives plc

For Millie Mohammad
and her dear friend
Rose W. Ravid

. . . leaves all decisions up to us, including whether we wish to make any at all. It is up to us whether we wish to make any application to our life from a fairy tale, or simply enjoy the fantastic events it tells about. Our enjoyment is what induces us to respond in our own good time to hidden meanings as they may relate to our life experience and present state of personal development.

BRUNO BETTELHEIM
The Uses of Enchantment
The Meaning and Importance of Fairy Tales

ONE

Once upon a time in a magical city called New York a girl under a spell lived on an island.

It was Staten Island. And to get to work in Manhattan, Claire Amelia Bilsop had to commute almost two hours each way. She took a train from Tottenville, then a short walk to the ferry slip, then the ferry to Manhattan. She did it with her friend Tina and today was no different from most other days.

'Oh, c'mon,' Tina said. 'Come with us. You never go anywhere and you've never done anything.'

Claire looked down at her knitting and frowned. When the ferry bumped against the pilings she had dropped a stitch. 'That's not true,' she said, though in fact it pretty much was. She thought of her trips to the library, the video store, the wool department of Kelsey's, all on Broad Street in Tottenville. 'I have traveled broadly,' Claire retorted, 'and I come into Manhattan every day. Last summer I went to Long Beach Island.'

'Long Beach, for god's sake! In Jersey! And you went with your mother and that douchebag boyfriend of hers.'

Claire winced. Tina's heart was in the right place but her mouth was in the gutter. 'I prefer to think of him as a windbag,' Claire said.

'Douche, wind, whatever.' Tina stuffed her magazine into her purse, fished out her sunglasses and stood up.

Claire stood beside her. 'Put that wool away, Granny,' Tina told her and looked at her watch. Claire sighed. The ferry had docked and, as always, they had twenty minutes to walk up Water Street, get coffee and bagels from their regular street vendor, then be upstairs on the thirty-eighth floor of the Crayden Smithers Alliance Building. They had plenty of time but Tina always behaved like a child at a birthday party, afraid she wouldn't get the last seat in musical chairs. As if anyone else would want their seats at Crayden Smithers. Claire picked up the dropped stitch, wrapped up her knitting, slipped into her coat and joined Tina and the crowd jostling to get off the boat.

As Tina pushed to the head of the line she pulled Claire in her wake. 'Jersey, for Christ's sake!'

'I went to the Poconos,' Claire murmured. People were looking at them angrily. Even in Manhattan, a city fabled for pushers, Tina stood out.

'The Poconos!' Tina almost spat as they stepped off the ferry. 'That's one step *lower* than Jersey.' She shook her head and her big hair trembled. 'And you went with that yutz. You didn't even have sex with him.'

Claire colored. She looked around but the crowd paid no attention, busy dispersing to buses, subways, and a new day of boredom or aggravation. Claire's sex life – or lack of it – meant nothing to them. 'I slept with him,' she protested. She wouldn't admit to Tina that it had been mostly sleeping. Bob had not been an Italian stallion, as Tina always claimed her fiancé, Anthony, to be.

'That's even more pathetic,' Tina said. 'Sleeping with Bob. Fah!' They stepped out of the terminal and the wind off the bay battered them. 'Jesus, it's cold,' Tina complained. 'It's March, for god's sake. When's it gonna warm up?' Claire knew Tina didn't expect an answer so she didn't venture one, letting Tina continue her ongoing monologue and possibly well-meaning harassment. 'It's warm in San Juan, Claire. Beaches. Casinos. Bars.'

The trouble was that Claire didn't really like any of those things. She burned in the sun, she'd never gambled – not even on a Lotto ticket – and she hated bars. Though Tina had been her friend since they'd grown up on the same street in Tottenville, there wasn't much that Tina enjoyed doing that didn't make Claire bored or uncomfortable or both. People who lived in Manhattan referred to people like Tina as one of the 'bridge and tunnel crowd'. Though they didn't take a bridge or a tunnel to get to Manhattan from Staten Island, Claire felt this technicality wouldn't affect Tina's status. She was parochial, and not just because of her Catholic school upbringing. Claire hid a smile.

She often thought what a strange, ill-matched pair they made. Tina was tiny and dark, with big breasts she liked to be noticed and she wore bright, tight fitting tops. Her skin was olive and her make-up was dramatic. Claire was tall and, though fifteen pounds overweight, her chest was almost embarrassingly small – god must be a man because a woman god would not let all the weight she put on go to her hips. She had pale, fine skin and eyes that were somewhere between gray and green (but if she was honest – and she always was – closer to gray). Her light brown hair hung straight, cut below the chin in a simple bob. Aside from some pink lip gloss and an occasional (inept) wave of a brown mascara wand, she wore no make-up at all. Now the cold made her lick her lips and wish she'd brought the lip gloss with her.

The buildings on either side of them made a wind tunnel and Claire felt like Dorothy about to be battered by the tornado. Except, of course, there was no Oz. 'If it's about the money, hey, I got a few extra bucks,' Tina offered. Claire blushed. She regretted telling Tina recently that her mother had begun charging rent. 'Just for you to stay in the room you've slept in since you were four years old?' Tina had demanded, outraged. Claire had nodded. Since Jerry had moved in, her mother seemed more short of cash than ever,

3

though his contribution and the insurance money from her father's death should have been more than enough for her mother to live on.

'Ya know, it's a sin the way your mom treats you. My uncle says if your dad left the house to you, you shouldn't be payin' no rent.' Claire neither pointed out the double negative nor the fact that it was none of Tina's uncle's business. Of course, it sometimes seemed that Tina's uncle – some of her other male relatives too – didn't have a business. And their wives spent lots of cash and discussed everyone's. But Claire never criticized – she knew what could happen to people who criticized Tony Brunetti. But if Tina was bossy, judgmental and a gossip, she did have a generous heart. 'So, you want a loan?' she asked.

'No. It's not that,' Claire told Tina. They were only a block from the office but the chill was piercing. She tucked her chin down against the wind and tried to adjust her muffler – one she'd knit for herself – so that none of her throat was exposed. At least when they turned the corner, in sight of Sy's pushcart, the wind abated.

'Hello, ladies,' Sy called out over the heads of the other customers on line for their morning caffeine and carbohydrate fix.

'Hey, Sy!' Tina replied. 'Wanna go to Puerto Rico with me?'

'Nah,' Sy said. 'I'd rather stand here in the cold, freezing my nuts off and doling out coffee to rich, cheap bastards.'

The rich cheap bastards on line were too busy reading the *Journal* headlines or talking on their cell phones to react, but Claire smiled.

'Yeah. You got the life,' Tina agreed. When she and Claire got to the front of the line Sy, without needing to be told, put their regular orders into two little bags. He handed them over to the girls with a flourish.

'Tell ya what,' he said. 'I'll ask my wife's permission. But screw Puerto Rico. If she says yes we're going to Aruba.'

'If she says yes, I'll *buy* Aruba,' Tina wisecracked. 'Then I'll sell you the Brooklyn Bridge.'

'Been there, done that. That's why I'm pushing this cart,' Sy said. He turned to Claire. 'But maybe a cutie like you could sell me the Williamsburg.' He winked.

Tina was rooting around in her gigantic purse. She looked up. 'Geez, I barely have enough money for Danish and coffee. Hey, Claire, can you lend me a twenty till Friday?'

Sy, still looking at Claire, shook his head. 'Same shit, 'nother day,' he smiled.

Claire nodded, opened her backpack and handed the bill to Tina. 'Thanks,' Tina said, and handed the twenty to Sy. 'My treat.'

Claire smiled. That was so Tina. Always there with her hand out but always willing to share. She'd give you the blouse off her back – but she'd probably already borrowed your money to buy the blouse. Claire was the kind of person who always had money saved to lend to Tina – who was the kind of person who always needed to borrow some. Claire wasn't old or experienced enough to know the whole world was divided into those two kinds of people, one never happy with the other. She just smiled at her friend as Tina handed Claire the bag of black coffee and a buttered bagel. As they walked from the cart, though, Claire did idly wonder why she was more comfortable lending than borrowing. It certainly wasn't her mother's influence. Her mother owed money not only to Claire but also to most of Tottenville. But neither did Claire remember her late father being open-handed with money. Perhaps she didn't take after either one of them. Despite genetics she had always seemed completely unlike her parents or her brother Fred.

'My brothers and Anthony went out last night and got hammered,' Tina said. 'Boy, were they hung this morning. They said they missed Fred. How is he?'

The truth was Claire had no idea how her brother was. He had joined the Army and had been shipped off to

Germany. Claire had written to him dutifully for the first six or eight months after he left but he had rarely responded and when he did it was only with a brief postcard (no picture). As her letters became more and more difficult to write, Claire had admitted to herself that she and Fred never had much in common. So her letters had petered out. That didn't mean that her guilt did. Aside from Fred and her mom she had no relatives she associated with. There was an aunt on her father's side, but Claire had been told that the Bilsops had disowned her forever.

Tina, on the contrary, lived amidst scores of complex ongoing relationships: cousins, second cousins, their wives or husbands, godmothers, goddaughters, and dozens of courtesy aunts and uncles where no blood relationship existed at all. Sometimes Claire was turned off by Tina and her boisterous clan, but now and then she was envious of their closeness and even their feuds. You had to care about somebody to bother to fight with them. Now Fred was away, she only had her mother and Jerry, her mom's repulsive boyfriend.

'I guess Fred's okay,' Claire told Tina. 'My mother got a card from Dusseldorf.'

'Dusseldorf? Who's he?'

Claire just shrugged. She'd decided long ago that educating Tina was not her job.

They arrived at the enormous glass doors to their office building with the usual couple of minutes to get upstairs. The lobby was crowded and the elevator was, as usual, jammed. The ride in the elevator was Claire's least favorite part of the day. She had told herself over and over that it was only ninety seconds but she still dreaded it. In the summer people's sweaty bodies were oppressive and in the winter the smell of wet wool was equally unpleasant. But it probably wasn't the smell as much as the crush. All those strangers' bodies rubbing. At that very moment Claire felt the breasts and belly of a large woman pushing against her back while in front, inches from her, she faced the wall of a man's black coat, almost touching it with her nose. Her coffee had to be cradled directly against the tall man's back. She was waiting for the day when the bag broke.

She was always relieved when the doors opened on the thirty-eighth floor and she could make her way out of what she thought of as 'the aluminum sauna'. But her relief was almost immediately replaced by dismay as she remembered her next challenge: Once she had said goodbye to Tina she would have to scuttle down the rows of secretarial desks lined up outside the windowed offices which were ranged around the edge of the floor. Then she would have to turn and make her way down the windowless hallway that led to an even deeper corridor. It, in turn, would bring her to the interior room she shared with half a dozen other 'analysts', lorded over by Joan, a woman who proved that a little authority could make one a petty tyrant. Another day, another ninety-two dollars take-home Claire thought.

As they filed out of the elevator Claire hunched her shoulders in her habitual way but Tina, beside her, was jaunty, queen of the floor. How could she be so cheery? Maybe it was because Tina worked for Michael Wainwright, otherwise known as 'Mr Wonderful'. Claire repressed a sigh at the thought of him. All the girls in the office talked about him. He was thirty-one, single, gorgeous, successful, and deeply in love . . . with himself. He had a hot- and cold-running stream of women, all of them financial executives in size six Prada suits. That wasn't mentioning the shoes they wore, which cost more than Claire earned in a week. Michael dated them serially, replacing an investment banker with a broker with a fund manager. Secretaries like Tina and analysts like Claire were not his style. Many of them hated him, many admired him, but Claire was the only one who was in love with him. Of course, she wasn't stupid enough to betray that information to any of her coworkers, not even Tina.

Michael Wainwright had spoken to Claire exactly four times in the eighteen months she'd worked at Crayden Smithers. The first time he'd asked, 'Would you make five copies of this right away, please?' The second time he'd said, 'I need these numbers crunched by this evening.' The third time – Claire's favorite – was when she'd delivered a report to his office and he'd said, 'Thanks. Nice dress.' The last time was a little over two weeks ago when he had brushed against her on his way out to lunch and said, 'Oh, sorry.'

They got to Tina's desk. Claire glanced at the office behind her but couldn't see Michael Wainwright. 'I'm meetin' Anthony tonight,' Tina said. 'We're goin' to the bridal registry at Macy's. You wanna go?'

Claire doubted that even Anthony wanted to go. Was the choice that or garroting (something Tina's uncle might know about)? She just shook her head. 'No. I want to get home. I have a book to finish.'

Tina shrugged. 'You and the books.'

Claire shrugged back and refrained from saying 'You and QVC.' Then she began the unpleasant route which made her disappear down the corridor like Alice down the rabbit hole.

TWO

'He ain't gonna get away with it. Someone should tell him ta get ovah himself,' Michelle D'annunzio said.

'Yeah,' Marie Two agreed, then laughed. 'But he thinks he's so big he'd need to mountain climb to get ovah Mr Michael Wainwright.'

Michelle, Joan and Marie Two giggled. Marie One shook her head.

There were three Maries in the office – four if you counted Marie LaPierre, but nobody counted her – so the Maries were called One, Two and Three to avoid confusion. Two of them, along with Joan, Michelle, Tina and Claire, were having their lunch together. It was interesting to Claire to watch how the secretaries' status was a reflection of whom they worked for. Marie One worked for Mr Bataglia who was middle management – nothing much – and she didn't get much attention or respect. Marie Two worked for Mr Crayden, Junior who was one of the Craydens of Crayden Smithers. That meant Marie Two was considered much more important than Marie One or almost anyone else. Tina's work for Mr Wonderful, the golden boy of the firm for the last few years, made her number two or three with a bullet. Michelle worked for the semi-retired David Smithers who was more a phantom than a physical presence. Everyone, it seemed, was more important than Claire, who only worked for Joan. It was a race Claire didn't mind losing. She actually enjoyed watching the sudden shifts in power that change at the top wreaked on those at the bottom.

'I don't think he's goin' to get away with it this time,' Marie One said. She put down her salami and egg sandwich. Then she picked up her Diet Coke and took a slug right from the can. Why, Claire wondered, did people who ate two thousand calories for lunch bother with diet sodas? Marie was still as large as the day that Claire first entered this lunchroom.

'No. He ain't,' Michelle said, then took a bite of her triple-decker sandwich, followed by a potato chip. She didn't have a problem with weight – she always had all the carbohydrates she desired and never put on an ounce.

'Sure he will,' Tina told them. She pushed some of her dark hair back over one ear and took a bite of her turkey club. 'Hey, his social life is as busy as Grand Central Station, but I'm a great conductor. I keep all the different trains on separate tracks. They never crash into each other.'

Claire didn't bother to point out that that wasn't a conductor's job. Actually, she thought the conductor analogy was an apt one but she would have used the metaphor of a symphony orchestra, not a commuter station. Michael Wainwright had a complicated and splendid private life that, without his knowledge, was public to all of the clerical women on the thirty-eighth floor.

Marie Two gave Tina a sour look. 'Hey. Tell Mike Engineer that someday two of those engines will crash. And we'll all be readin' about it in the *Wall Street Journal*.'

Joan, the head of the analysts and – aside from Claire – the only woman at the table who wasn't either a secretary or Italian-American, shook her head. She was a divorced single mother in her mid-thirties and, in Claire's opinion, justifiably bitter. 'From your lips to god's ears,' Joan said. 'The bastard deserves it.'

But Claire didn't think that was fair. Though Michael

Wainwright certainly played fast and loose, he could afford to. It wasn't just the looks, brains and schooling. He was also socially connected. Claire, via Tina, had an almost daily update on whom he was seeing, whom he was about to drop, whom he was adding to his conquest list, and where he was taking his latest date. Claire's mental calendar, empty of engagements, was full of Mr Wonderful's life. She wasn't sure if Tina's ongoing conversation was good or bad for her private obsession, but she certainly couldn't ask Tina to stop talking without raising Tina's always-acute suspicions when it came to romance. And it wasn't as if Claire even dreamed of any real connection to Michael Wainwright. She knew he traveled in a world of money, entitlement, and the natural aristocracy of beauty and that she didn't belong in any of those categories. Michael Wainwright was not a romantic possibility and she had no illusions otherwise. But it didn't mean that she didn't have feelings. She just kept them to herself. Her interest, she thought, was a kind of hobby – like bird watching.

Tina put down her sandwich and angrily wiped her mouth with a Subway paper napkin. 'Why does he deserve it?' she demanded of Joan. 'He never promises any of them anything. They're big girls. They can take care of themselves.' Claire smiled. In public Tina was loyal to Michael but Claire knew that she sometimes warned him of the dating Armageddon that she so nimbly put off.

'It's time to get back,' Joan said primly and looked at Claire. Claire nodded and put her untouched apple back into her bag. Unlike the others, Claire didn't work for an investment banker. And reporting to Joan didn't always make life pleasant. She stood up and smiled at Tina, who flipped a bird behind Joan's back.

Claire's afternoon was spent doing what seemed like endless revisions to spreadsheets of figures. The worst part about her job was also the best. There were no changes, no surprises, no peaks and valleys. She knew that as soon as she completed an assignment, Joan would hand her another one. Unlike Tina and the three Maries, Claire didn't get to glimpse the drama going on in and around the windowed offices: she didn't see the clients arrive, the meetings held in the glass-enclosed conference rooms. She didn't witness the hirings and firings. But she heard all about them. Sometimes Claire felt her imagination was a better place to view the dramas than in reality. Tina was a kind of human radio – all Tina, all the time – and Claire saw the wins and losses, the corporate coups and the promotions and demotions more vividly in her imagination than if she had seen them in reality.

The problem was that she had time to daydream – too much time – and too many of her daydreams centered around Mr Wonderful. She wondered uncomfortably if it was becoming closer to an obsession than she admitted to herself.

While Claire had the title of 'analyst' she wasn't much more than an educated clerk. Of course none of the secretaries were called secretaries, either. They were 'Administrative Assistants' (though they all expected gifts and flowers on Secretaries' Day). But the two groups had something important in common: there was nowhere for either analysts or administrative assistants to advance to within Crayden Smithers. After a decade of service you weren't promoted to investment banker. At best, you might get Joan's job. Not that Claire wanted it. Joan was the sphincter muscle in the bowels of Crayden Smithers.

That evening at five to five she was almost finished compiling a statistical table – she hated typing statistics – and stayed until a quarter after to get it done. It was unusual because, unlike the secretaries, the analysts had scheduled hours and usually left on the dot of five. Only Joan had to stay on to complete paperwork and arrange for temps or overtime work.

Now, as Joan put on her coat, she eyed Claire. 'Don't stay past six,' she warned.

Claire smiled and nodded. The rule at Crayden Smithers was that an hour or more of overtime guaranteed a car service ride home. Of course, a ride to Tottenville meant going through Brooklyn, the Verrazano Narrows Bridge and half of Staten Island. It was a two-hundred-and-ten-dollar fare in a chauffeured Mercedes. 'We don't have the budget for that,' Joan told her as she walked out the door.

'I know,' Claire called after her. There, alone for the first time in more than eight hours, she took a deep breath. The commute this evening would be less brutal than at peak hours, though the wait would be longer. Getting to Tottenville after rush hour was the slow hour – or maybe two or three. Ferries, trains and buses didn't run frequently. Everyone in Tottenville called Manhattan 'The City' – even though Staten Island was part of New York. Staten Islanders felt forgotten and inferior to the other boroughs. They were always coming up with new resentments and plans to secede. Her father had always said the place was too small to be a city but too large to be an asylum. Despite the four hours a day, lots of people made the long commute because they wanted to live in what seemed like – and what had once been – a small, waterside town within the New York City boundaries. But for Claire it was all tiresome, with nothing much waiting for her at either end.

Now she decided she would stop in a diner near the ferry terminal, have a salad for dinner, and then, she thought guiltily, maybe pie à la mode. Well, with or without dessert she wouldn't go home until the rush was completely over. She was too tired to fight the crowd, for the long wait to board and perhaps having to stand for the whole ride. If she waited that would also mean she wouldn't have to eat with Jerry and her mother. Now she'd be able to read while she ate, another guilty pleasure. She looked down into her bag. She had her knitting, and beside it was *The Passion* by Jeanette Winterson. Claire was almost halfway through, at that delicious place where she felt compelled to go on reading yet didn't want the book to end. She felt herself looking forward to her modest evening, her little dinner, a special dessert (she would have the pie) and her book as company.

She sighed. She often wanted to read on the ferry but if she was with Tina – and she almost always was – it was impossible without offending her. That was one of the reasons she carried her knitting. Tina teased her, but it was something to do while Tina nattered on.

Claire finished the statistics, hit the print button and gathered up her belongings while the document rolled into the waiting basket. She was just putting on her new coat – a light green one that she thought complemented her eyes – when Mr Wonderful, Mr Michael Wonderful Wainwright himself, stepped into the room. It was a jolt because no matter how good he looked in her daydreams he was so much better in reality. He was slightly taller than Claire, his posture perfect, his chest broad and taut through his dress shirt. Mr Wonderful's light blond hair was shiny in the fluorescent light of the office. As he surveyed the room with his hazel-colored eyes he almost looked through her. Claire froze then reminded herself to continue putting her arm into the sleeve of her coat. 'Where's Joan?' he asked.

'Joan's left for the day,' she told him, sounding more calm than she felt. She was afraid she'd begun to blush. She looked away from him, down at her bag. She picked it up and placed it carefully on her chair. Something to do. Keep busy and her eyes to herself. She also had to change into her sneakers but was embarrassed to do it in front of him.

She figured he'd leave then, but was startled by a loud thumping noise. She looked up to see Mr Wonderful had hit Joan's desk with a thick document. 'Shit!' he said. Then he turned back to her and smiled. His smile was devastating, if not sincere. As irresistible as a frozen Mars bar in July and probably just as bad for her. 'You don't know where the Worthington numbers are, do you, Karen?'

'Yes,' she said. She went to the printer bin and held out the still-warm pages. 'They're here. And it's Claire.'

'Claire?' he asked and looked down at the report in her hands as if she was talking about the document.

'My name,' she said. 'Not Karen. It's Claire.'

He reached for the print-out then looked into her face as he took the pages from her. 'Of course. Claire,' he said. 'I was so panicked over this damn thing that I forgot. Excuse me.' The closest Michael Wainwright had come to panic, Claire thought, was probably the day he feared he wouldn't get into the right eating club at Yale. She just nodded and went back to her desk expecting him to go.

She picked up her tote bag, took out her sneakers and was about to sit down to put them on when she realized Mr Wonderful was still there. He was paging through the stats, then he looked right up at her. One of the shoes slipped out of Claire's hand and bounced on the floor.

'Look, Ka – uh, Claire,' Michael Wainwright said. 'I already know I've made a couple of mistakes in this thing. We're meeting on it tomorrow morning and I'll look like a total fuck-up if I don't have it right.' He paused. She was afraid to reach for her dropped shoe so she just stood there, waiting for the other shoe to drop.

Michael Wainwright walked over to her, bent gracefully to the floor and, with the report in one hand and her sneaker in the other, offered her the shoe with a princely flourish. She reached for it and he, as if in return for the favor, raised his eyebrows in a faux pleading look. 'Do you think you could stay just a little while longer and make a couple of corrections for me?'

Of course. Some prince. But her hand actually tingled,

15

holding the old sneaker that his hand had touched. She told herself she was a very foolish girl, then nodded her head because her neck seemed to work, though her tongue didn't.

'You will?' he said in a voice that sounded less than surprised. 'That's great.' He turned and shuffled a few pages, scribbling with a red pen. Claire struggled out of her coat and stowed her purse – along with the errant shoe – under her desk. She glanced up at the clock. It was already five-forty and she doubted she'd be out by six but she wouldn't forget Joan's directive about the car service. Claire wondered if it had gotten a lot colder, and how often the buses from the ferry ran after seven.

'Hey,' Michael Wainwright said. 'Take a look.' She stood beside him and looked at the papers spread in front of her. 'Here are my corrections,' he said, pointing to more than a dozen pages slashed with red. 'And could you check my tabulations and change this to a bar chart?' To her concern the changes looked like the kind of statistical work which was painstakingly slow to correct. And if she changed the layout of the chart, it would need reformatting. And that would probably alter the pagination of the rest of the report. Then she'd have to page preview the entire thing before she printed it out, just to be sure there were no widows or orphans.

'Can you do it?' he asked, and it was, of course, impossible to say no. Unfortunately it was equally impossible to say yes, since she couldn't speak. She was close enough to him to smell his scent – some kind of soap and perhaps just a hint of a clean cologne as well as something that smelled like . . . like fresh starch. How, she wondered, could he still smell fresh at six o'clock? He was pointing to one of the changes and she noticed that his cuff was whiter even than the printer paper. Yeah. And her sneakers smelled. 'Will it take long?' he asked, interrupting her self-loathing.

Claire shook her head and then managed to find her tongue. 'About two hours, I think,' she told him.

'Great!' he said. 'You're a lifesaver.' He gathered up the pile of papers and handed them to her. 'Thanks,' he said. 'I'll wait in my office. And let me buy you dinner.'

THREE

Not counting the time Claire spent nearly fainting, then the dance she did around the room, it still took her a little longer to finish the Worthington revisions than it should have because she kept forgetting formatting codes and her fingers trembled for a long while after Michael Wainwright left the room. She also couldn't stop herself from imagining what it would be like sitting across from that face for an hour. Would he ask her questions about herself or talk about his own life? What in the world would she say? Somehow she doubted he was interested in the kitchner stitch. Perhaps, she thought, Cinderella would get to go to the ball. Of course, she told herself, Michael Wainwright wasn't interested in her, but even if the shoe didn't fit she could wear it for one night.

She was hungry and tired by the time she was through, but she was also elated by the prospect of dinner with Mr Wonderful. She proofread the pages twice just to be sure that there wasn't a single typo then printed the final draft out on high rag content bond. Ready to run it in to him she stopped her frantic activity, uncertain for a moment. Should she put on her coat and meet him ready to go out to eat, or just bring the document over then go back for her things? Perhaps she should call him. She knew his extension number was just one digit different than Tina's, so she took a deep breath, sat down and dialed. He answered on the first ring. 'It's . . . it's Claire,' she said. 'I'm finished.'

'Terrific. Do you mind bringing it to my office?'

'Not at all,' Claire said and heard how stiff it sounded. 'Sure,' she added. 'Right away.'

She emptied her bulky bag of her knitting, her sneakers, her book and her muffler. She put on her new green coat, smoothed it and checked the pocket for tissue since she was starting to get the sniffles. Then she quickly ran a brush through her hair and wished she'd remembered her lip gloss. But she was flushed with exhilaration, and as she glanced at herself in the mirror hidden behind the supply closet door, she was actually pleased with what she saw. She regretted not having the silk scarf she'd bought to go with the coat but it had been far too cold this morning to wear that. Oh well. Her muffler would do.

She walked out of the windowless maze and over to Tina's desk. The office behind it had a single light on and in the shadowy room she could see Michael Wainwright at his PC, apparently still working. We've been working together, she thought and smiled. That and her new coat gave her the courage to enter his lair with a bit of confidence. 'Here it is,' she said, walking up to his desk. He continued working at his keyboard. She put the report down in front of him.

'Thank god!' a voice behind her said. Claire spun around. A slim, dark woman was sitting on the sofa behind her. Her legs, up on the coffee table, were crossed neatly at the ankles. Even though the light in that corner was dim, Claire could see the elegance of the cut of her hair and her gray suit. Claire didn't know all the female investment bankers on the floor by name but she certainly would have noticed this chic woman. Was she a client from Worthington? 'I'm absolutely famished,' the woman said. Her voice was clear, her accent as polished as her obviously costly heels.

'Me, too,' Michael Wainwright agreed. Then he turned

from the PC and looked up at Claire. For a panicked moment she thought he might invite the woman along for dinner. But perhaps Ms Chic just wanted the report and would be off to some elegant penthouse or spacious loft to study it overnight. Claire fervently hoped so. Mr Wonderful picked up the document, slipped it into his briefcase and stood up. 'Ready to go?' he asked.

Claire nodded, grateful she had worn her new coat. She could see that in comparison with the other woman's clothes it was a cheap and shoddy thing but at least it was a hell of a lot better than her old one. 'I'm all ready,' she said.

Michael Wainwright and Ms Chic rose together. They both grabbed their own coats. Claire was ushered out the door in front of them and, to her dismay they walked as a trio to the elevator. In the fluorescent light of the hallway Claire could see the woman was about her age, with perfect skin, a size eight figure and the long legs of a fashion model. The shoes were spectacular, very sexy in contrast to the restraint of the suit. Claire hoped the woman would break a slender ankle.

'Thanks a lot for doing this for me,' Michael Wainwright said as they got into the elevator.

'I can't believe it took so long,' Ms Chic complained.

'I'm sorry,' Claire apologized, then wanted to bite her tongue.

To make it worse the woman smiled at her. 'It's not your fault. It's Michael's,' she said, dismissing Claire and focusing on Michael Wainwright's face. She was not only much thinner but a little taller than Claire, and now she gave Mr Wonderful a look over Claire's head. 'You're so inconsiderate,' she told him.

Claire didn't like her tone: it was provocative in the same way her shoes were.

'Jesus, Kate, give it a rest,' Michael Wainwright told her. When the elevator opened he allowed the two women to precede him into the deserted lobby, Ms Chic's heels tap-tapping on the marble floor. At the huge glass doors of the building entrance a uniformed guard rushed up.

'Let me unlock it for you, Mr Wainwright,' he offered. Claire looked out into the dark. It was raining ferociously, but Claire was delighted to see a black sedan waiting at the curbside. She only realized the implication of a single car as the door was unlocked. Was this Kate going to go to dinner with them after all? Claire should have known not to get her hopes up or expect too much. She sighed.

Hearing her, Michael looked down at the top of her head. 'You must be exhausted,' he said. 'Should I have Gus here call you a car?'

For a moment Claire was completely confused. He seemed to be looking at her but was he asking this Kate woman the question? Claire said nothing. Michael continued to look at her. Did he want to take two cars? Did he still have business to discuss with Kate before their dinner? What should she do? Now she felt both Gus's and Kate's eyes on her.

'No, thank you,' she said and hoped it was the right answer. What was going on?

Michael shrugged. 'Okay. Well, thanks again.' He turned then paused and put his hand into his pocket. He drew out his wallet and turned back to her. 'I almost forgot,' he told Claire. 'I'm buying you dinner.' He took out a crisp hundred-dollar bill and handed it to Claire. In her embarrassment and horror she accepted it. She felt tears rising, her throat closing.

'Have a nice evening,' Michael Wainwright said. 'Good night, Gus.' He took the chic Kate's arm and the two of them stepped out the door, almost running through the freezing downpour to the warm waiting car.

'What a great guy,' Gus said.

'He's the best.' Claire sighed and Gus missed her disappointment and sarcasm.

FOUR

'Yeah,' Tina said. 'Katherine Rensselaer. She's new. She works for the Ford Foundation.' Claire wondered why only the rich worked for philanthropists. She doubted there was one Hispanic single mother from the Bronx in charge of giving out charity. 'He hasn't dropped Blaire, but Kate is moving up fast. And Courtney is over. She just doesn't know it yet.'

Claire sneezed. The weather had turned warm again and the sunlight glanced off the water of New York harbor. But the beautiful light only hurt Claire's watering eyes.

'Want a tissue?' Tina offered.

Claire shook her head. 'I brought some. I knew I was coming down with this cold yesterday.'

She had left the lobby humiliated, too embarrassed to go back upstairs for her sneakers, knitting or book. She'd gone out into the downpour without an umbrella and her muffler was drenched before she got to the corner. It had been hideously dark, no cabs in sight and, despite her hunger, she'd been too sick to her stomach to consider eating. Anyway, eating alone with nothing to read was no treat. In fact, on her wet and lonely walk to the ferry it had struck her as pathetic to eat alone at all.

Now she fished in her purse, pulled out a tissue, and blew her nose. She pinched her nostrils hard, but it wasn't just because they were streaming. She wanted to pinch herself, to remind herself not to be so stupid ever, ever again. Her watery eyes cleared a little as two tears ran down her cheeks.

'That's some cold! You know, a beach would bake it right out of you. I'm getting our tickets today. It's your last chance,' Tina coaxed.

'No thanks.' Despite Claire's intentions, tears continued to rise in and then fall from her eyes. She blindly reached for another tissue and pulled out what she thought was a crumpled one only to find it was actually the damp hundred-dollar bill. She'd gripped it in her hand last night until, after more than an hour, she'd realized it was there. Then she'd thrown it angrily into her bag. Now, of course, Tina spotted it.

'Where'd you get that, just before pay day?' Tina asked. 'Did your mother finally feel guilty and decide to do the right thing?'

Claire pushed the money into her pocket, though she would have preferred to throw it over the side of the ferry. She sniffed. Despite her lack of Kleenex, she couldn't stop her nose from running or her tears from escaping. She felt as if her whole head was leaking. 'I'm going to run to the ladies' room before we get to Manhattan,' Claire said, ignoring Tina's question.

In the ferry's dim, gray-painted head she had a long cry in a stall. For a few moments she wished she were under the hull, down at the bottom of the harbor. Was it possible to cry under water? The thought made her stop and she got up and began to clean herself up at the sink. But the dented metal mirror over it gave her something else to cry about. She looked awful. She was actually grateful to her cold for giving her an excuse for the swollen eyes, the pink nose, the pallor, and the chapped, cracked lips she'd been biting since last night. As she looked at her image, the memory of Katherine Rensselaer's came to her unbidden: the perfect skin, the understated clothes that discreetly announced big money, the well-cut glossy hair. Even her name was distinguished. Wasn't there a city named Rensselaer in Connecticut or Pennsylvania?

Claire pulled out a comb and tried to give her hair some order while she wondered what it would be like to have your name on a place. Claire Amelia Tottenville. Ha! Even considering the dump her hometown was the name sounded more important. At least more important than Claire Amelia Bilsop.

As she was putting the comb away she felt the ferry bump gently. They were docking. How long had she been in here? Tina would be furious, waiting on the other side of the gangplank for her, angrily tapping her foot as the hordes of other commuters barreled past. As if Sy would give away her buttered roll. Claire, in the hold, knew all of the top and main deck would have to clear before she had a chance to get off and Tina would berate her along Water Street. Claire began to tear up again. She wasn't sure she could stand it, or stand Joan's questions about the Worthington work, or stand to look through her wet, tired eyes at today's page of meaningless numbers until they blurred. The enclosed space of the toilet was unpleasant, but Claire realized that she felt safer there than she would feel once she was out. She wasn't sure how she would make it through the day. But since she didn't have a choice she shouldered her purse and stepped out to find Tina, waiting in exactly the attitude that Claire had predicted.

Claire kept her head down, literally and figuratively, during the walk to work, the stop for coffee, the entry into the lobby, the more-than-usually ghastly ride up in the elevator, and her scurry to her desk. She stowed her bag and hung her coat, and continued to hang her head. She didn't know whose gaze she was avoiding; she almost never saw Michael Wainwright, and the Kate woman certainly wouldn't be around. Gus, the guard, must be on the night shift. Nobody else had witnessed the event. In fact, it had been a non-event to Mr Wonderful and his woman of the day.

Yet, as she signed on, Claire realized the non-event had caused some seismic activity within her psyche, some significant rift. And the exposed subterranean gap seemed so horrifically visible to Claire that, somehow, she thought it must be visible to everyone.

As she sat at her desk and opened the bag holding her coffee and bagel, she realized that a belief she'd always held about herself might not be true. She had always ascribed her lack of passion to her own nature – reserved, introverted, shy, whatever. And she had never taken the crush that she had on Mr Wonderful seriously. She looked at it as a kind of avocation, not something you made a life's work or took too seriously. But when he – as she had mistakenly thought – invited her to dinner, something had happened. Some feeling had burst through the scrim of her emotional life and flooded her with an undeniable joy. It had felt so intense, so complete, that to deny it would be a kind of sin. It had filled her to her very borders. In that hour or two of anticipation she had felt all of herself alive and knew how big she was capable of being, how much larger her repertoire of feelings was. Now, her limited life, her few outlets restricted her and she felt pain. It was as if she was a brilliant concert pianist who had always been forced to play with only one hand. Last night, for a few precious hours, both of her hands had been freed. This morning, knowing that she had to go back to living with a single hand, the future didn't seem bleak – it seemed impossible.

She looked down at the keyboard in front of her, placing her hands on the home keys. A tear dropped onto her thumb but she wiped it away quickly. She spread out the work Joan had already assigned her and began. But she had trouble. Each dull line of figures was followed by yet another dull line followed by yet another . . . it seemed as if reading them or typing them into her consciousness and then onto the screen was building her into a prison, line by line, number by number.

She couldn't imagine how to recover from this. Perhaps if she went out, had lunch alone, got an ice cream sundae and licked the spoon while she licked her wounds, she'd feel better. Something sweet with butterscotch sauce would be so . . . so soothing. But Tina wouldn't stand for it unless she came too and that would spoil everything.

The odd thing was that even without telling Tina, with no one at all – even chic Kate or Mr Wonderful – knowing about her foolish misconstrual, Claire was experiencing such deep shame that it felt unbearable. She realized she had never known what that word meant until now, for, bearing the shame, she could hardly lift her head or her shoulders. No beast should be asked to carry such a burden.

Her cold gave her the pretext for her pink eyes and her posture. Luckily, there was a lot of work and no time for anyone else to notice her, at least not until eleven when Marie Two came in and started some kind of argument with Joan. Marie Two worked for Mr Crayden, Junior, and she was very particular about the research done for him. She often asked specifically for Claire but that was against Joan's policy. Not that Marie Two believed in any policy but her own. Claire ignored their conversation until the volume rose. And she heard her name. Then Joan and Marie were standing at her desk. 'She's already working on . . .' Joan was saying.

'I don't give a shit what she's working on. Mr Crayden needs this and Boynton's stuff can wait.'

'You can't just come in here . . .'

'Watch me.' Claire lifted her head. Marie Two was standing before her with a thick sheaf of papers. 'God, you look sick,' Marie Two said.

'I've caught a cold.'

'No shit, Sherlock. You shouldn't be here with that. A,

you should be in bed. And B, you'll get everyone else here sick, too.'

'I'm sorry,' Claire apologized.

'*Madonne!* What's wrong with you, Joan?' Marie Two asked, glad to use any excuse against her enemy. 'Can't you see you should send her home?'

Suddenly the idea of her bed, her pillows and the puffy quilt over her seemed not only irresistible but imperative to Claire. Her mother and Jerry would be out of the house. There would be silence and comfort. A cup of hot, hot tea. Then a nap. And maybe, after that, some soup with buttered toast. She could eat and drink and read in bed without her mother accusing her of being antisocial. And if she used up an entire box of tissues from mopping her brimming eyes, she had an excuse: she was sick.

'Do you think you have a fever?' Marie Two asked and, like the practiced mother she was, placed a hand on Claire's forehead. 'You're burning up,' she said. 'Joan, call the car service.'

'She lives all the way in Staten Island. And I don't have a client to charge it to. Boynton's over budget,' Joan protested.

'Oh, charge it to Cigna. Mr Lymington puts his Cuban cigars on their expense sheet. What the hell will one taxi ride matter?'

Claire sat there passively as if they weren't talking about her. She felt light-headed and distant, as if she was already slowly moving away from them in a vehicle. Donna, the apprehensive analyst who sat beside her, was looking from Marie Two to Joan. So, Claire finally noticed, were the rest of the analysts in the room. Her shame and misery would be complete, if she could feel anything. But she was beyond that.

'She'll get us all sick,' Donna said. 'There's no air circulation in here.'

A buzz of conversation began but Joan put a stop to it

by raising the phone to her ear. 'I'm sending you home,' she told Claire, as if the idea had come to her spontaneously.

The rest was a blur. A car was called. Marie Two bundled Claire into her coat, Donna carried her purse and knitting bag and they took her to the elevator. 'Car number 317,' Donna said. 'That bitch Joan didn't want to do it,' she whispered. 'Like it's her money.'

The elevator arrived. Claire wobbled as she got into it. 'You okay?' Marie Two asked. 'I gotta get back to Mr Crayden or he'll pitch a fit. Just go outside. The car will be right there.' Claire nodded as the doors slid closed. In the still moment before the elevator began its descent Claire began to cry again. Oddly, the unexpected kindness of people – in movies, on television or in books – always made her cry and now, as the actual recipient of the concern, she began to sob again. It wasn't just about her cold, or the miserable scene the night before, or the collapse of her small hope. Her entire life, suddenly, felt pitiable. In that moment, in the elevator, she had a glimpse of herself as others probably saw her: a single, slightly overweight woman still living at home and working in a dead-end job. No profession, no romantic prospects, and nothing likely to change.

The elevator continued its downward trip as Claire's feelings continued to sink. Why, she asked herself, didn't she have an ambition, a goal? Why was this good enough for her? She had run out of energy. Worse, as the elevator reached the lobby she realized she'd run out of Kleenex again. There was no way she could be seen in this condition, but though she scrabbled through her purse and pockets she had nothing at all to absorb her tears and smears. All pride gone, just as the doors opened on the lobby, she wiped her nose and her eyes on the cuff of her new green coat, now so despised that it didn't matter to her at all.

Then, as she stepped out onto the marble floor of the lobby she was almost pushed over by Michael Wonderful Wainwright. He grabbed her arm – the snot-free one – and steadied her. 'Sorry,' he said then looked at her for another moment. 'Claire? Is that you?' She was beyond face-saving, beyond artifice, beyond caring.

'Yes.'

'Are you sick?'

'Yes,' she repeated. He probably expected some sort of minimizing explanation, one that would make him feel better. That she was mildly flu-ish, not to worry, it was just allergies/sinus/pneumonia/SARS/plague and he shouldn't be concerned. The cancer of hope was in remission.

'I'm sorry,' he said. She wondered idly how many times he'd already said that word to her.

'I'm going home,' she told him and pulled her arm away.

'Okay. Well, I hope you feel better. And thanks for that work last night. It really saved my ass.'

She just looked at him for another moment and told herself to remember forever that men like Mr Wonderful did not ask women like Claire out for dinner. They asked them for favors, for notice, for admiration. They asked them to balance their checkbook, to juggle their love life, to pick up their tuxedo from the dry cleaners, to shop for a gift for their client, mother, or lover. They had them order out, order flowers, order supplies. Then they gave them a hundred bucks. She'd been stupid and deluded and ridiculous to think otherwise.

'I have to go,' she said and tried to turn and walk away with a shred of dignity. Impossible when you were holding a knitting bag and had a runny nose.

It was only when she walked out of the lobby that she recalled she still had the hundred-dollar bill in her pocket. She wished she had remembered that before so she could have given it back to him. The car was waiting. Claire sank into the back, more grateful for the shelter than she ever had been for anything.

'Tottenville?' the driver asked. 'Staten Island, yes?' Claire nodded, put her head down and closed her swollen eyes.

Perhaps she slept. Perhaps she dreamed something. She wasn't sure. When the car pulled up to her house she roused herself. The long ride was over. Claire, feverish and achy, reached into her purse, took out the hundred and handed the bill to the driver. 'But is paid for,' he protested.

'It's a tip.'

'But tip is paid, too.'

'Keep it,' she said. 'I don't need it.'

Almost tipsy, she got out of the car and slammed the door. If only it was that easy to get Mr Wonderful out of her life.

FIVE

Claire was in bed for five days. It was, after the first twenty-four hours, only a mild cold. Once she managed to stop crying she only had to put up with a runny nose for another day or two. She felt weak all over and the indignity of a nose that glowed from chafing was unpleasant. But it was the pain in her chest, which wasn't bronchitis, that took longer to heal.

After surprising the car service driver with the outrageous tip Claire slept away all of the afternoon and most of the night. The next day she napped fitfully and was up until the small hours. She didn't eat or bathe. When she woke she, mercifully, couldn't remember the exact details of her dreams but she knew that in each one she had been humiliated. Michael Wainwright's face had appeared at least once, but it had been twisted in malicious laughter. The evening of the second day, her mother brought her up a plate of meatloaf and macaroni and cheese – two of Jerry's favorites – but Claire merely shook her head and her mother took it away. The act of going down to the kitchen and making toast and tea felt overwhelmingly difficult, and swallowing it was impossible. She couldn't even manage to hold a book up to read. Claire went back to sleep.

When Claire woke at three that morning she took out her knitting. She was just binding off a waistcoat she had made for Tina's dad. Tina had picked the yarn and the pattern. It was a variegated worsted, Claire's least favorite yarn, in a profusion of browns and oranges, colors that Claire didn't much care for either. She was grateful that the pattern was a one-piece so she didn't have to sew it together. Finishing it wasn't particularly satisfying, but neither was Claire's life, she reflected.

At a little before four she put down the circular needle and got out of bed to lay out the garment on her bureau. She felt light-headed and empty, but it was the middle of the night so she didn't want to go downstairs to the kitchen. She'd once run into Jerry, standing nude in front of the open refrigerator, illuminated by its light. Instead of taking the chance of letting that happen she opened the bottom drawer of her bureau and looked at the treasures inside.

Whenever Claire was sad or bored or lonely she made her way to one of the many knitting stores she knew and let herself be tempted by the beautiful colors, the delicious textures, and the promises that all the seductive yarn whispered to her. Now, spread in front of her, were the spoils from those frequent jaunts. Despite her misery Claire was moved, as she always was, by the colorful chaos. She took out her favorite, a costly and luxurious cashmere, in a color that was somewhere between blush and the inside of a shell. It was a very fine ply, and Claire had decided long ago to knit a sweater of it for herself in a tiny and complex cable pattern. She laid the skeins on her bed, then – after long consideration – fetched a pair of size three wooden needles from her knitting basket. She had saved the directions for the sweater though she thought she could do it without following the pattern.

With a cable sweater she only had to resort to the pattern for the first full cable. Once she'd cast that on and knew the number of rows in between the cable twists she very seldom needed the pattern again. She got back into bed. It was windy, and she could hear the bare tree branches being whipped against the house by the wind. She felt cozy, tucked under her blankets, the cashmere on her lap. As she began to work she found that she would have to be certain to check the position of the twist and not forget to alternate between the front and back with the cable holder. With her state of mind now, she knew she'd welcome the concentration this project would require. As her fingers manipulated the needles she was especially attentive to what she was doing.

She spent the next couple of days knitting, reading, sleeping, watching a few television programs and licking her wounds. She wished she had her own VCR so she could watch tapes up in her room because she didn't want to go downstairs to her mother's TV in the evenings. When Jerry came in he wanted to watch *Cops* or *Junkyard Wars*. Instead she stayed upstairs and finished the Jeanette Winterson book. Crying over it helped put things into perspective. Her life could be worse.

Tina was concerned. When she came over for a visit, Claire pretended to be truly ill and kept the visits short. But she knew the retreat couldn't last forever.

Finally, on Sunday, she was over it. She had decided her silly idea that a man like Michael Wainwright could possibly have been interested in her – even for a moment – was not painful as much as ridiculous. She forced herself to remember who she was, where she lived and the small pleasures that she had. She would find more of them, go to some theater, buy her own VCR. She'd register at a gym. Since graduation her size kept creeping up and the desk job had helped her waist and hips spread. But a benefit of her illness was that she'd lost weight. She'd work out. Not, of course, that that was a pleasure nor that it was easy – she wasn't comfortable in the expensive, high class gyms in lower Manhattan and she was tired from her commute when she came back to Tottenville. But she would do it and, she decided, she'd let Tina's mother – a hairdresser – streak her hair.

But those things wouldn't change much and the Worthington incident – as she was now calling it – had showed her the sheer smallness of her life. And Claire knew that reading, knitting and watching television, no matter how uplifting the program, would alter nothing.

Yet she couldn't think of an alteration she could make. She wasn't a badly cut pair of trousers. She was simply a rather timid young woman with solitary interests. She didn't know if she read and knit because she had never been social, or if her social failures had driven her to her isolated life. And what could she do to change it? Go out with Tina's cousins and in-laws and the brothers of her friends, all men she had nothing in common with and who saw her as a plain brown wren? What was the point?

Go back to school? How would she pay for it? Travel? Alone? And to where? Join a club? A book circle? Go online to find friends, or even a soul mate?

Claire cringed at the thought of all of it. She simply wasn't a joiner. She crawled back into her bed. Even if she did put herself 'out there' the same thing would happen as always had. If a local hitter approached her she'd be bored, and if someone intelligent and attractive (by a miracle) spoke to her she'd freeze tighter than a jammed photocopier. No one would notice her and she would stand – or sit – on the fringes with nothing to do or say. She even considered, but only briefly, taking Tina up on her invitation to go on vacation but quickly – really quickly – got over that. She might have had a fever but she wasn't delirious. What she did instead was call Tina and ask if her mom would do her hair. 'Come right the fuck over,' Tina said.

'Tonight?' Claire asked. 'It's late.'

'Hey, you're only about five years late. My mom figured we'd have to wait until you went gray before she could do you.'

So Claire dressed and went over. Tina and Annamarie, her mom, fussed over her. 'Worst haircut I ever saw,'

Annamarie said. 'It's like three cuts on one head.' So, mostly out of wounded pride, Claire let them cut and streak her hair.

She was surprised by the result. Instead of the brassy colors that Annamarie – the queen of Big Hair – usually favored, she used subtle honey blondes that blended with Claire's natural light brown. And the feathering gave her fine hair some body. 'The secret to this cut is Product,' Annamarie told her as she held up a mirror. 'You need a conditioner, a thickener, and a finishing gel.' Claire couldn't imagine putting more things on her head than she had members in her family but, looking in the mirror, she was pleased.

Monday morning she was dressed and composed when Tina came by to go to work.

'You look much better. The haircut, and I think you lost a little weight in your face from the flu,' Tina reported.

It was an unseasonably warm day, and the two of them were sitting in the sun on the benches on the side of the ferry protected from the wind. Claire had her knitting out but it lay, untouched, on her lap. She felt as weak as a convalescent and held her face up to the sun as if she needed to drink in vitamins.

'Though you sure could use a little color,' Tina added. 'Last chance for Puerto Rico.'

Claire couldn't withhold a sigh. Gone for a week, but the conversation continued without a stitch dropped. She closed her eyes and remained silent wondering, not for the first time, why Tina wouldn't want to be alone with Anthony. Claire couldn't imagine wanting to take Tina away on a trip with a lover – if she ever had the chance to make such a trip. She wondered if that made her a less loyal friend or less co-dependent. Or, perhaps, both.

'So guess what happened with my boss?' Tina asked. Claire was grateful she had her eyes closed. It made it easier to keep her face blank.

'He's at that ultimatum stage again,' Tina was saying. 'He wants to keep Katherine around but she's found out about the on-again-off-again with Blaire and she's insisting he break it off with Blaire or else.'

'And will he?' Claire asked, her tone neutral.

'Get a grip,' Tina said and laughed. 'And even if he did, he's obstinate and doesn't like to be told what to do. If it wasn't Blaire it would be someone else. His big mistake is being honest with them when they ask and theirs is asking.' She shook her head. 'Courtney hung onto him for almost a year because she never asked him what he was doin' on the nights and weekends he didn't spend with her.' Tina shrugged. 'But he ditched her anyway, in the end.'

'That's the fate of all his women, isn't it?'

'Yeah,' Tina agreed. 'He's the bomb. The only difference is how long they last and whether or not there's a scene at the end.'

'Speaking of the end, we're about to dock,' Claire said and rose.

'God, I'm hungry!' Tina said, as always moving like clockwork to the next item on the agenda. 'I hope Sy saves the biggest Danish for me.'

Claire gave her a forced smile and filed down the gangplank with everyone else, and they made their walk up Water Street along with a portion of the crowd. A helicopter hovered overhead and Claire imagined from that height all of them must look like ants purposefully streaming into their anthills.

Claire sighed. After her week off, the commute and the job seemed more oppressive than ever. She thought again about going back to college, getting a BA in library science, but what was the point? Libraries were closing down every day in New York. Her own Staten Island branch was only open three days a week – and only in the mornings on Saturday. She simply had to face the fact that she was a caterpillar – albeit a thinner one than she had been – and wouldn't even graduate to moth, much less butterfly. Claire Bilsop, the social caterpillar.

And now she no longer had her pathetic, secret little crush to dream about, to keep her from loneliness. Nor would she let herself take on a new one, not that she admired any of the other swaggering investment bankers. What was the point? She would deceive and distract herself no longer.

So in a way, the incident with Mr Wonderful had had a salutary effect. It had been a kind of vaccination. A little bit of deadly Mr Wonderful in her blood stream had had its toxic effect, but after a brief illness she had built up Mr Wonderful antibodies.

As they all sat over the lunch table later that day, the conversation drifted back and forth in its usual desultory way. When Tina contributed anything about her boss, Claire was relieved to find herself no longer hungrily grabbing at each syllable, filing it away for future contemplation. She blocked it.

'Jeez, you look skinny,' Marie One said to Claire. 'It must be the new cut.' They had, of course, focused on Claire's new hairstyle and everybody approved, except Joan, which made Claire feel certain that it suited her. She didn't welcome the attention, but she had expected it. She had borrowed a dress and matching jacket from her mother – a black knit with flecks of beige. She felt that after her absence she might as well look good, but Joan narrowed her eyes as if she suspected Claire had never been ill at all.

'Hey. She was sick. Lay off,' Tina said.

'You want some liverwurst?' Marie Two asked. 'I got plenty.'

'Now that would make her puke,' Michelle said, to be rewarded with a look from Marie Two. Michelle always felt she was better than Marie Two because she had worked for Smithers longer than Marie had for Crayden.

'Like you can cook,' Tina replied.

The talk moved to recipes and Claire was glad she was no longer the focus. She was concentrating on chewing and swallowing her egg salad sandwich, though it tasted like sawdust.

'Vic wants us to go to Vegas, but I said fagetaboutit,' Marie One said. 'Last time we went to Atlantic City he dropped six hundred bucks cash,' she continued as she nervously twirled her diamond ring around her tiny finger. 'I didn't know it, but he also got cash advances on our Visa and MasterCard.'

'I don't believe in gambling,' Joan said. 'Not even the lottery.'

'Then you won't get a share of mine when I win,' Michelle assured her.

'The odds are better in a casino,' Marie Two said.

'They got casinos in Puerto Rico, but that's not what me and Anthony are going there to do,' Tina offered.

'Me, I say Disney World,' Michelle said. 'The Magic Kingdom is great for the kids and Epcot is good for the grownups.'

'Epcot sucks,' said Marie One. 'I was never so bored in my life.'

Speaking of bored, Claire could barely stand it. She was suddenly so tired of these tedious repetitions of the obvious that she was ready to throw down her sandwich – or possibly throw it up. Then, oddly, the conversation became riveting.

'Mr Crayden, Senior is spending the next month in London doing some new business deal,' Marie Two announced. 'He may take Abigail with him.' Abigail Samuels was Mr Crayden's secretary of almost thirty years. Unmarried, tall and ultra-efficient, she was an office wife and handled every detail of Mr Crayden's business, as well as a significant part of his social plans. She never lunched with any of the other secretaries. She was a haughty white-haired patrician with better things to do. Claire had seen her, once or twice, eating lunch alone in local coffee shops reading Balzac in the original French. Claire was impressed and awed by her.

'Lucky Abigail,' said Michelle sarcastically. 'She gets to travel. Too bad she doesn't have a husband or a life.'

Marie Two ignored Michelle, as she often did. 'Well, Mr Crayden, Junior may also go for part of that time, and if he does, guess who's invited?' A series of surprised coos and ooohs circulated the table.

'Your husband would shit a brick,' Marie One said.

'Like that matters,' Marie Two said. 'Crayden asks, I go. I never been there.'

Claire felt the hair on the back of her neck rise. She had never traveled much, but if she could go to London! If she *had* to go to London, so that she wouldn't be nervous or tempted to cancel. If she were going there to work, so there would be some people she knew, some familiarity . . . well, she would never get the chance. Analysts were not invited to London.

Tina put down her pastrami sandwich and raised her heavily penciled brows. 'Hey, maybe that's got something to do with Michael Wainwright going,' Tina said. 'I just booked him a couple of tickets for next Thursday.'

'You goin' too?' Marie One asked.

'Nah. He's only stayin' till the end of the weekend. And he's taking Katherine. His new one.'

Claire forced herself to take the last bite of her egg salad sandwich, wiped her mouth with a paper napkin and put it and the other trash in her lunch bag. 'I have to run out to Duane Reade,' she said. 'Does anybody need anything?' Nobody did, but Joan was quick to remind her she only had twenty minutes until she was due back in the department. Claire nodded, and freed herself.

She didn't need to shop. She just needed some air. She walked up to City Hall and paced the small park in front of it. What was she doing? Why did she spend her days in a windowless room, and her nights at home alone reading?

She had sequestered herself from life; she may as well have been cloistered. But the fact was she knew she was nothing like a nun. She wanted to travel. She wanted an exciting job. She wanted to do new things and meet new people. She just didn't know how. She sat, for a moment, on a bench. It had turned cold, but in the sun, with her coat wrapped tightly around her, she managed not to shiver. The thought of going back to Crayden Smithers and Joan made her shudder. Even out here, wind from the harbor on her face, she felt as if she were jailed.

Manhattan was clearly the answer but it intimidated her. How could she manage to afford it and would she find a roommate? Other people did it, she reminded herself, but she didn't feel like other people. In fact, she'd always felt different from everyone she had known. Worse yet, as best she could objectively see, everyone else agreed with her. No wonder she felt so lonely.

I could sign up for a trip, some kind of tour group she told herself. I could go to Europe, if I had a guide. Then the idea of traveling with a bunch of strangers, winding up with Marie One and Michelle – or their equivalent – traipsing through Paris seemed ridiculous.

Perhaps, she told herself, there might be an Abigail Samuels or even a well-read man. She had read all of *The Human Comedy*, and Jean Rhys and Collette. She felt as if she had already been to France and couldn't bear to go for real as a stupid tourist, unable to speak the language, wearing the wrong clothes and going to the wrong places.

The fact was, she was not only a coward but she was also a snob. A secret snob, the worst kind. She sat at lunch and felt superior to and amused by everyone. But who was she to feel that way? At least Michelle and Tina and the Maries – and even Joan – went places and did things and slept with men. She would have to change, she decided, and stood up. She would have to change because not doing so, living as she was living, had become impossible.

Claire looked at her watch. She would be late getting back to work and Joan would punish her by giving her the most onerous jobs for the rest of the afternoon. She wouldn't mind because she had decided something important. She wasn't sure if she could transform into a butterfly, but she'd transform herself into something. She had a new resolve: despite the obstacles, she was going to change.

The problem was she didn't know what she was going to change into.

SIX

The next day the women were sitting, as usual, at lunch
and gossiping the usual gossip – the television of the night
before, or the latest movie – when Tina came charging into
the room all excited. 'You're not going to believe what just
happened!' She looked around the table to make sure she
had everyone's attention. 'A minute ago, Katherine walks
right past me into his office. I mean, I try to stop her but
it's like I'm totally invisible. He's on the phone, but when
he sees her, he's like "gotta go". Once he hangs up she
says, "I don't know who you think you are but I'm sure
as hell not who you think I am!"'

'She goes!' said Marie One.

Tina nodded. 'She goes, but she ain't goin'.'

'Goin' where?' Michelle asked.

'To London. She blew the trip.'

'No shit,' Marie Two said. Then she paused. 'Did she
tell him to stuff the trip up his ass or did he tell her that?'

'No ass-stuffing was involved,' Tina sniffed. 'They didn't
swear once. She called him "a narcissistic self-parody" and
he . . .' she narrowed her eyes as if trying to remember Mr
Not-So-Wonderful's exact phraseology. 'I think he asked
her to keep her psychological profiles to herself until he
requested one. Then Michael came out to me and ordered
me to hold the second airline ticket.'

Then without a beat, Tina moved on to drop a new

conversational grenade about a confrontation – almost a scene – in the outer office, between two of the other traders.

'Well, I think a "go fuck yourself" wouldn't have been inappropriate,' Michelle said. Just then Abigail Samuels walked in, in time to hear the vulgarity. Claire hung her head. She was in the company of these people and surely perceived as one of them by everyone but herself. Still, she wished she hadn't been there when the remote, educated Abigail – who was probably a virgin – heard the conversation.

Abigail, however, moved serenely by them to the re-frigerator, took out a yogurt and turned to go. At the door, as a kind of after-thought, she turned back to the now-silent group. 'Claire,' she said. 'Would you be free to photocopy some important documents for me?'

Every eye at the table turned from Abigail Samuels to Claire. Claire looked first to Abigail, then to Joan. Joan shrugged and nodded. 'She can do it,' Joan said.

'We know she can,' Abigail Samuels said, and Claire, most probably, was the only one who realized Joan's grammar was being corrected. 'The question I asked was if she was available.'

'She's available,' Joan said after a moment's pause. Claire stood up and wordlessly followed Abigail out of the lunch room.

They were along the row of executive offices, almost to Michael Wainwright's, when Abigail turned to Claire. 'You seem like a girl who keeps herself to herself,' she said. 'This is a job that I want to be kept exactly where it belongs.'

Claire nodded, and Abigail seemed to feel that was enough. They reached her office outside of Mr Crayden's. 'You'll use the photocopier in the executive supply room.' She lifted a pile of documents and handed them to Claire. 'I'd prefer you don't read them, but I don't insist.'

Claire was shown through a door she had never noticed. The room was small but paneled, and leather-jacketed pads of paper, engraved personal letterhead and all manner of high-end office supplies were carefully placed on shelves behind glass cabinet doors. A photocopier, a shredder and a fax were built into mahogany cabinetry as well.

'Do you know how the machine works?' Abigail asked. Claire nodded. 'It doesn't have a collator and I'll need two copies of everything. Can you keep them in order?'

'Yes,' Claire managed.

'I thought you could.' Abigail smiled. 'If you have any questions, just call.'

Claire began the work. It was dull, but it made a break in her usual day. Anything that kept her away from Joan was a good thing, but she had a feeling that, just like in high school, there would be a price to pay for being singled out.

Feeding the first page in, she only glanced at the contents to make sure she wasn't going to be a participant in grand larceny or fraud. Crayden Smithers was one of the few firms that hadn't been involved in a nineties stock scandal but you couldn't be too careful. Once she realized that the work was only employment contracts, and sensitive because of the salaries and bonuses involved, she didn't look any further and simply did the job.

There was a certain repetitive comfort in lifting the flap of the copier, placing each page just so and removing the two copies and separating them. It was a task that required no thinking, but after she had organized it and gotten used to the robotic rhythm she had set for herself, having time to think was not necessarily a good thing. She didn't want to remember the conversation at lunch, nor think about Michael Wainwright's business trips or the companions he took on them. She wanted to get her work done, look out at the skyline on her ferry ride home and then finish her cable sweater. That idea pleased her. It was going to be a lovely garment and, though the purchase of the cashmere had been extravagant, she was glad she had done it. She was also glad that she was going to keep it for herself.

The small room was getting warm. Claire tucked her hair behind her ears and bent over the machine. She felt her face flush from the heat. She wondered if there was a fan, though she doubted anyone often used the room for this volume of copying. The noise of the machine and her concentration on the task kept her from hearing the door open and close behind her.

SEVEN

'Hi, Claire,' Mr Wonderful said.

'Hello.' Claire jerked her head up, trying to keep her surprise from showing and her tone cordial but nothing more.

'I didn't know you were in here.' He looked her up and down and gave her an oddly shy smile. She didn't know how becoming the color in her face and the new haircut looked. She was glad she had worn her mother's dress again today, and hoped it wasn't too tight across her backside. Then she told herself sternly that it didn't matter how she looked. If she had any pride at all she would be, if not nasty, at least abrupt with him.

'Why would you?' Claire asked.

Michael Wainwright paused for a moment then shrugged. 'No reason, I guess.' He looked down at the paper he was carrying. 'I have to fax these to Catwallider, Wickersham, and Taft right away.'

Claire looked at him calmly and didn't offer to help. Abigail's work for Mr Crayden, Senior out-ranked Michael Wainwright's work. Not offering gave Claire a tiny bit of satisfaction. He moved over to the fax and, in passing her, had to sidle around her. She steeled herself to feel nothing, but she couldn't help listening to him as he fumbled with punching in the fax number before loading the document he wanted to send. The machine whistled, asking for the start button to be pushed but he didn't push it. Claire, though she knew what he needed to do, didn't offer any guidance.

'God, I'm a complete idiot. How the hell do you do this?' he asked her at last.

She knew that was malespeak for 'Do this for me'. Jerry used that all the time on Claire's mother: 'How do you turn the washing machine on? How do you stack the dishes in the racks? How do you boil an egg? How the hell do you do this?' Claire shrugged and was grateful for the three stacks of paper in front of her. 'Where's Tina?' she asked, by way of answer.

'That's what I'd like to know.'

He didn't sound really irritated, but the idea that Tina might be loafing somewhere and getting in trouble was enough to force Claire to place the two copies on the appropriate stacks and leave off her task. 'Here,' she said, taking the sheets of paper from his hand. She didn't bother to show him where to place them, or explain that the paper should be face down, or that you had to hit the start button once the connection with the receiving fax was made. What was the point? The Michael Wainwrights of the world were not born to spend time in little rooms like this. And now, looking down, she fed another sheet into the fax machine and watched it slowly be devoured. She could see Mr Wonderful's loafers and felt certain they would move away. He'd leave her in here and go back to his wall of windows. Perhaps she'd get a thank you, because he was always polite. But instead of walking away his shoes stayed in front of her own feet until she was forced to look up.

He narrowed his eyes. 'Has something changed?' he asked. And she wanted to answer 'Yes. I hate you now.' But of course she didn't. 'You're really very pretty. Do you know that?' he asked her. Claire couldn't have been more surprised if he'd hit her in the face with a dead fish. She felt herself flush again, but it was with anger, not pleasure or embarrassment. Who did he think he was? Wainwright or not, he had no right to play with people's feelings to no purpose but to kill a little time or gratify his overblown ego.

'Do you want strangers to comment on your looks?' she asked. 'I'd be willing to if you want a summary.' Her voice was steady, and there wasn't a bit of the hurt or anger she felt in it. He blinked, then straightened up a little and looked at her, this time with something closer to real interest.

'I'm sorry. Was that condescending?' he asked.

She decided to ignore the question. She'd let him work out the math. 'Is there something else you want me to do?' she asked. 'I'm working for Mr Crayden, Senior. It will take me another twenty minutes to finish this copying.' She handed the originals to him and turned back to her job. 'If you need help maybe you should ask Joan.'

He smiled. 'Joan can't help me. But maybe you will.'

She knew it. What grunt work was he going to grace her with? What tedious job was she to receive as if it were a land grant from a monarch? She fed another page into the copier then looked back at him, silent. She'd do the work, but she'd be damned if she'd be charmed or act grateful for it.

'I wondered if you were free next Thursday?' he asked.

She tried to register his question but couldn't quite see what he was asking. 'When on Thursday?'

'All day, actually. Starting Wednesday night.'

'I don't understand.'

'I just . . . I just wondered if you'd like to go to London with me for a long weekend. I have to leave Wednesday night and work Thursday and Friday, but there are the evenings and I'm staying the weekend.'

'What?' she asked. There seemed to be some kind of disconnect between her ears and her brain. She thought she'd heard him say . . .

Just then the regular sound of the copier stopped and it

began to beep. Confused by what he was saying, she was determined there would be no further misunderstandings on her part when it came to Michael Wainwright. The beep continued and she looked down, saw the light that indicated a paper jam and bent to pull out the trapped page. She couldn't manage. 'Can I help?' he asked. Her brain jammed and she felt as trapped as the paper seemed to be. She pulled at it ineffectively. Disbelief, embarrassment and confusion fought for supremacy in her completely overwhelmed consciousness.

'Here. Let me.' He leaned down and touched a button at the side of the copier. It released the entire top of the paper feed. If he touched her, Claire thought her whole head would pop off too. 'I've fought this baby more nights than I like to remember,' he said and, pushing another switch, freed the document. He handed the page to her and smiled. 'So, would you like to go to London with me?' he said.

Now her mind beeped a warning more frantic than the copier had. All of the gossip she'd tried to ignore replayed in Claire's head: The working trip Marie Two might be going on, the new business activity in the UK, Tina's blow-by-blow about Michael Wainwright's difficulties in lining up a woman for this latest escapade. She tried to see where the trap was, where humiliation was waiting. Perhaps he needed secretarial help. That must be it. She sighed with relief. Of course . . .

'Can't Tina help you?' she asked.

'Help me what?' he asked in return.

'With typing or . . .'

He laughed and Claire felt herself blush. He was laughing at her, and she had tried so hard to avoid that, to forget him, dismiss him, and yet . . .

'Claire, I'd like you to spend a long weekend with me in London. Not for work. For fun. As my . . . guest.'

And then he put his left arm around her. She felt his

hand warm – almost hot – through the clothes on her back and then he was pulling her toward him and he lifted her chin with his other hand and put his mouth on hers.

Claire was so surprised she didn't have time to stiffen or think. It all had a dream-like quality, as if she was in some story she had read long ago – *Snow White* or *Sleeping Beauty* – one of those passive young women who waited for years for a kiss to awaken them. She could feel every tiny place of contact she had with him – each finger between her shoulder blades, his palm against her cheek, and his lips against her lips – as if her skin there had never been touched before. Her surprise fought with a surge of feeling both sensual and emotional.

When he moved away from her Claire was struck speechless. In a hundred fantasies she'd imagined – well, nothing as good as this. She literally held her breath and couldn't – wouldn't – say a word.

But after a brief pause, he wet his lips with the tip of his tongue. She remained silent because she couldn't make a sound. He took a step back and she could see that for a moment doubt rearranged his face. 'I'd certainly understand if you thought that was inappropriate of me . . .' He seemed to stumble for a moment, '. . . or if you feel it's politically incorrect. Or even harassment. Please don't. I mean we don't actually work together. Just in the same place.'

Claire still couldn't speak. By chance, her silence had allowed her to see a moment of Michael Wainwright's uncertainty, a rare bit of, well, insecurity, or something that looked like it. Somehow it made him more alive, more accessible. Her eyes actually clouded. She had to blink.

'Okay. Sorry. It just occurred to me that we might enjoy it. But whatever.'

Claire held onto the photocopy machine and tried to remember how to make her tongue capable of speech and her eyes capable of focusing. She was looking at Mr

Wonderful, but she was having trouble seeing him. Still, what she was most afraid of was that she wasn't hearing him properly.

He had turned and was going to leave. Do something, she told herself. But where had this invitation come from? Why her? She remembered the conversation at lunch, the one she had tried not to listen to, and realized he had most likely run out of women available at short notice. 'Wait,' Claire heard herself say. He turned. 'I'd really like to go,' she told him.

EIGHT

'Are you out of your friggin' mind?' Tina asked Claire the next morning, her voice shrill enough to be heard above the engine of the ferry and not only by Claire but by another dozen people sitting nearby.

Claire moved the yarn from the back of the needle to the front so that she could knit the next three stitches, then slipped them off her cable holder and onto the main needle. She knit those stitches to finish the back twist of the cable while calmly shaking her head at Tina. She would wear this lovely sweater in London.

'For god's sake, Claire. You don't even know him.' Tina crossed her arms in front of her chest. 'And it's not as if you don't know what he's like with women. If Katherine Rensselaer couldn't handle him, how do you expect . . .'

Claire carefully put the knitting into her bag. Even Katherine Rensselaer couldn't have a cashmere sweater this lovely, this fine. 'I don't expect anything,' she admitted calmly.

'Well *he* will! You think he'll just take you across the Atlantic because he wants a roommate?' Tina shook her head and it occurred to Claire that she was more angry than concerned. 'You think this is the start of some love affair? Sometimes you're like a kid.'

'No, I'm not!' Claire protested. 'I'm planning to sleep with him. I want to. But I don't expect anything else.'

Tina laughed but it was one of her sarcastic ones. 'Yeah, right. I know you. Claire, I'm warning you. You think you'll come back and start going around New York with Michael Wainwright and you can fagetaboutit.'

'I don't have to forget about it because I'm not even thinking of it,' Claire told Tina. Then, to her relief, the ferry gently bumped against the pilings and the motor reversed. Soon they'd be off.

But there was no respite. 'So what *are* you thinkin' of?' Tina asked, putting her hand on the damp rail of the ferry and tossing her hair back. 'You thinkin' about how to make yourself more miserable? You thinkin' about how you can become the laughin' stock of the office?'

And all at once Claire realized she didn't like Tina's attitude or tone. And that she didn't have to listen to it. She stood up. 'I'm thinking that I've never been further away from Staten Island than to Boston. That I've read about London since *Mary Poppins* and I've never been there. That no man ever invited me anywhere.' She paused and reined in her temper. She looked Tina directly in the eye. 'I'm also thinking that I don't need any more advice.'

Tina's face tightened. Then she shrugged. 'Suit yourself,' she said and they didn't speak on the walk to the office.

'Do you have a good suitcase?' Marie Two asked. 'You can't travel with a backpack, you know.' Claire hadn't thought about it. The news of her trip had, via Tina, moved through the human circuits faster than e-mail on electronic ones. She'd already received everything from a high-five from Marie One to a congratulatory note from Michelle, passed surreptitiously to her folded up like a note passed in study hall. It seemed to Claire as if the working class had risen up and were proud; as if their team had scored some kind of touchdown. The irony was that while Claire knew she wasn't patrician, she had never felt at one with the 'girls'. Perhaps that was why she didn't react to Joan's fish-eye response. In fact the odd thing was that Claire realized that she didn't care about what the others might think. A sea-change had taken place in her own emotional landscape since Michael Wainwright's invitation. She simultaneously felt more a part of the business harem while more detached. Now, over the lunch table, where even Marie Three had joined them, her trip was the major topic of discussion yet Claire didn't feel the slightest bit self-conscious.

'And you aren't goin' to use one of those little wheelie things? Dufus bags,' Marie Two continued. 'These guys fly First Class. The hotel porters will sneer if you don't have decent luggage.'

'Oh, fuck the porters,' Marie One said. 'It isn't about the luggage. I mean, what's going to happen at the hotel?'

'I think we all know the answer to that,' Joan said.

No one responded to her judgmental tone. 'What hotel?' Michelle asked.

'He's booked a suite at the Berkeley,' Tina announced. She'd been angry all morning and still didn't look at Claire. 'Ya know. It's not like he isn't a gentleman. He is. And the suite's got three rooms. The sofa in the living room is right there, waiting for her, if Claire doesn't like what's goin' down in the bedroom.'

'Goin' down?' Marie Three said, being her usual obnoxious self. Claire, for once, didn't blush and no one laughed.

'She's got a round-trip ticket,' Tina added. 'If she can afford the taxi fare she can come back whenevah she wants to.'

'I'd never come back,' Marie One said.

'What about Vic?' Marie Three asked.

'Screw Vic. Then I wouldn't have to,' Marie One said and they all laughed.

'Look, ya don't hafta do anything ya don't wanna do,' Marie Two reminded Claire. 'And what goes on in the bedroom is none of our business,' she told the rest of the table, though Claire knew Marie Two was always eager to listen to stories of sexual dysfunction, romps and betrayals.

The truth was, Claire was just as curious to find out what might go on in the bedroom as she was to see London. The idea of Michael Wainwright choosing her, actually wanting her, even if only by default, was astonishing as well as exciting. She could hardly believe she was going to get on an airplane with a man she'd only been kissed by once, fly to London and sleep with him. She thought again of his hand on hers and had to close her eyes for a moment to contain the thrill. If such a small gesture, such minimal contact, had that effect on her how would she react to his body on hers? Claire shivered.

'What will you take to wear?' Michelle asked. 'Do they wear hats, like Princess Di used to?' She sighed. 'I loved her hats.'

'Forget hats and bags,' Tina said. 'Claire, do you even have a passport? You can't go to Europe without one.'

For the first time since she'd made her decision Claire felt her optimism and hope begin to disappear as slowly but surely as the Cheshire Cat did – but leaving no smile behind. In fact, her vision got blurry with tears. She didn't have a passport and – worse – she didn't even know how to get one. She looked at Tina, trying to keep the panic out of her eyes. 'I can get one.'

'Ha! You're screwed,' said Joan. 'And not in a good way. I've been to the passport office. Forget it. You hafta get your birth certificate and photos and go to the post office, fill in a form and wait six weeks.'

Claire felt the walls suddenly contract, as if she was on the morning's elevator ride. She should have realized that escape, that a real adventure, couldn't happen to her. She wasn't the kind of person who had a passport sitting in her top bureau drawer. No. She had knitting needles. She wouldn't be able to go. She clenched her fist hard, so that the physical pain of her nails biting into her soft palm distracted her from the other agony she was experiencing.

'Six weeks?' Michelle asked. 'Always?'

'Always,' Joan said.

'Nonsense.' They all turned to see Abigail Samuels in the doorway. She ignored everyone but Claire. 'You can get it in a few hours. You just bring your birth certificate, your application and a letter on our letterhead saying you must go for business.' Abigail smiled at Claire. 'And bring your ticket. Or do what our executives do. For fifty dollars an expediting service will take care of it all. And in two hours. You should know that, Tina.' They all turned to Tina, who said nothing.

'Thank you,' Claire told Abigail Samuels, her voice shaky.

'You're welcome.' She smiled at Claire again, her small, even teeth as white as her hair. Then her mouth snapped into a thin, straight line. She looked at Joan but continued speaking to Claire. 'If you have any difficulty getting a letter from the firm, come to me and I'll give you one signed by Mr Crayden, Senior.' She eyed them all, then turned to go. But before she moved down the hall she looked at Claire. 'And if you need to borrow a trunk, I'd be happy to lend you one of mine.'

The table was silent for at least a moment after Abigail Samuels left. Then 'Holy shit!' Marie One whispered.

'She family?' Marie Three asked.

'Fagetabout family,' Marie Two said. 'Has she got this table bugged? Because if she does, we're all in deep yogurt.'

Tina looked over at Claire. 'You tell her?' she asked. 'Because if word gets out among the executives about this . . . I mean they might not like it.'

Claire shook her head. Before the day Abigail Samuels had specifically requested her help, Claire had never spoken to the woman. And in helping her she hadn't spoken much either. There was a social order at Crayden Smithers that was as unbreachable as Fort Sumter had been. Secretaries, administrative assistants, analysts, bookkeepers and all the so-called 'support staff' were working-class people. They lived in far-flown suburbs – never in Manhattan. They all said 'the city' when they meant Manhattan, even if they lived in Queens or Brooklyn or Staten Island – all a part of the city. They wore clothes from discount stores, cheap chains and factory outlets. Their hair never looked right, not the way hair looked in fashion magazines or on the heads of women professionals. And the inside of their heads had been educated in public schools, never the tony private ones. If they'd gone to college they hadn't graduated, or if they'd graduated it had been from a junior college or a state school, never from the Ivy Leagues. They were an underclass and, though none of them would admit it, they either resented the elite professionals (as Joan did) or – worse to Claire's way of thinking – basked in the reflected glory of the professional they worked for.

The one exception was Abigail Samuels. She'd probably been a secretary for fifty years. She'd gone to the best schools, dressed in the best conservative clothes and looked like a wife of one of the elderly partners. But Abigail Samuels had 'gone to business' back in the days when secretaries wore hats and gloves and women didn't even think of law or business school. Her class separated her from the secretaries and her job separated her from the professional staff. Claire had always thought she must be the loneliest person at Crayden Smithers.

Claire had no idea how Abigail knew about the trip. She was also surprised that, knowing, she didn't seem to disapprove. The thought that Abigail Samuels would be interested in anything that Claire did – besides photocopying – was as surprising to Claire as it was to the rest of the table. That Abigail knew about her trip, that she'd volunteered not only the information about the passport expeditor but actually threatened Joan on Claire's behalf and then offered to lend Claire a bag was . . .

'Fuckin' amazin',' said Marie One.

Claire saw all the faces turn to her, and recognized the faint tinge of suspicion on each face. In this hen house, when anyone changed the pecking order feathers were ruffled.

'She must like you,' Marie Two said.

Curious and curiouser, Claire thought, but was wise enough not to quote Lewis Carroll at that table.

NINE

After work on Friday, Claire decided she'd better go get money for her trip. She had a little over nine hundred dollars in her account. A pathetic amount to travel with, but it was highly unlikely that her mother would be paying back her 'loans' anytime soon. She carefully counted the bills, then put them in an envelope and hid the envelope inside a beach bag in the bottom drawer of her bureau. And what exactly could Claire say to her mother as an excuse for going away? It was too early for a bachelorette party for Tina and it certainly wouldn't require that many days. Claire would just come up with a plan at the last minute. Now she had more important things to worry about.

She began to sort through her closet. In less than half an hour she had a big pile of garments on her bed. Way too much stuff. It was only four days, she reminded herself sternly, but somehow it felt as if she needed everything she had and yet none of it was right. She was a little thinner than usual – not much – so while the size twelve tops fit, size fourteen slacks and skirts were a little looser than usual. But not loose enough. She sighed. Perhaps her problem wasn't that her butt was too big, but that her tits were too small. She wondered if there was a scientific ratio to determine that. She thought of Katherine Rensselaer and her perfect body in her perfectly cut clothes. Claire's best jacket came from Ann Taylor. Katherine Rensselaer had probably never been in there, just as Claire had never been in Prada. She would definitely have to shop, not that she had the money for that. She looked at the pile of clothes on the bed, shrugged and then smiled. She might have fat thighs and second-rate clothes, but it was she, not Katherine Rensselaer, who was going to London with Mr Wonderful.

Claire spent Saturday morning trying on almost every decent garment she owned. By lunchtime she was exhausted. She had decided on a pair of black slacks from a pantsuit (but not the jacket), a beige sweater set from BCBG, a black and tan tweed A-line skirt and not much else. There was also the possibility of a navy dress she'd worn to a wedding, but it was floor length, which wouldn't work.

'Where you been all morning?' her mother asked when Claire, rumpled and tired, walked down the stairs and into the kitchen. 'You've been so quiet. More knitting?'

'No. I finished the sweater.' And she had. It had come out beautifully and Claire would definitely take it with her. The thought made her smile.

'So what were you up to?'

'Just doing some spring cleaning,' Claire told her mother. 'Do you have any navy thread? I have to fix a hem.'

'Look in the bottom drawer. I think so.'

Claire rummaged in the kitchen drawer full of old ice cream scoops and dull knives. She found thread, all of it in a tangle, and pinking shears that might or might not cut. Meanwhile, her mother got a can of beer and a diet Pepsi from the fridge and wandered out. Claire was hungry, but she wanted the skirt and pants to fit. So she made herself a tuna salad, poured an iced tea (without sugar) and took them back upstairs.

She ate lunch then tried on the navy dress. It was a sleeveless boat neck, a simple full-length sheath. If she cut it short, above knee-length, it might look nice. But before she began cutting she took out a pad, sat at her desk and began a list. Despite the piles of things she'd tried she really had no other clothes up to the mark. She'd need a nice black T-shirt and a good blouse – white or beige silk – along with a pair of shoes; maybe strappy heels. She had comfortable shoes for walking, but – she almost blushed – she'd definitely need some nicer underwear and a good nightgown.

Claire didn't really enjoy shopping. Perhaps if she was a size ten she might, but she always found it dispiriting to hopefully pick out a size twelve, have trouble getting her thighs into it, go back for a fourteen and just barely fit. And then her taste was so different from everyone she knew. Claire didn't read women's fashion magazines and she was too modest to realize that she possessed style, though it was a simple, classic one. She just thought, as Tina so often told her, that 'she dressed boring'. That reminded her that Tina would be over in an hour. She would prefer not to do the shopping with Tina, but that was absolutely impossible.

When Tina arrived, she was apparently over her sulking and was now acting as if the whole plan was her idea. 'Victoria's Secret, here we come!' she yelled as they stepped out of the door.

'I'm not sure I want to go there,' Claire said.

'But you said you need panties and a bra. And a sexy nightgown. I saw a red lace robe and nightie that . . .'

'I want to go up to Saks.'

'Saks Fifth Avenue? You're crazy! It's so expensive.' The wind whipped the two of them as they stood out on the street.

'But I have a Saks card,' Claire said. It actually was her mother's, but at this point she owed Claire something over a couple of thousand dollars. And Claire would pay the bill when it came in.

'Well, that's different!' Tina said. She lived on her credit cards. 'Let's go.'

Two hours later, after cruising the third and fourth floors at Saks, Claire had on a cream silk blouse she was at last ready to buy, despite the price tag of two hundred and ten dollars. 'You're nuts!' Tina told her. 'This was thirty-nine dollars. On sale at Banana Republic.' She pointed to her own top and Claire looked at the two of them in the three-way mirror. That decided her. The blouse she had on looked as if it cost five hundred dollars more than Tina's. It was something Katherine Rensselaer might wear.

Getting the black T-shirt, thank god, was easy and so were shoes. In fact, two pairs. It was pleasant in the shoe department, a relief to be sitting down, to be served by a polite older man and easy to give him her size without blushing. She didn't have to fight a zipper to get into a high heel. She selected backless black ones with beige stitching that were comfortable enough for walking and a pair of navy courts with a little leather bow – in the back. 'They are something,' Tina admitted. 'And everyone's wearing heels with pants now.'

'Really?'

'Absolutely!' Tina assured her. Though Claire didn't totally trust Tina's taste, a mannequin near the shoe department was dressed in narrow slacks and four-inch spikes. That inspired her to go back to the fourth floor and get a pair of navy pants with side slits to show off the shoes. To her delight, she fit into an eight.

'They run a little big,' the saleswoman told them.

'So does her ass,' Tina said.

Claire ignored the laughter and bought the slacks, though the wisecrack made her think about getting undressed in front of Mr Wonderful.

Next, Claire and Tina went to the lingerie department. As Claire had feared, Tina kept managing to find the few things that were trampy or in bad taste or both. 'I can't picture myself in that,' Claire told her as she held up a black lace bodysuit with underwire cups and a minuscule thong string.

'It's not what *you* picture,' Tina said. 'It's what *he* pictures. And sees.' She waggled her fingers through the crotch of the transparent lace.

After the remark about her butt, Claire certainly wasn't wearing a thong. She just shook her head and finally selected a blush pink satin nightgown with lace across the bodice. It could be seen through but only just. 'And you might want the matching robe,' the saleslady suggested. Claire did.

It was only when they got to the raincoats that she had a crisis. Most of them were six or seven hundred dollars. She looked at her mother's card and simply couldn't do it. She'd have to wear her green coat, though now it seemed tacky and wrong. She sighed. 'These are ugly anyway,' Tina said.

On the ground floor, on the way out, Claire's eye was caught by a string of irregularly shaped pearls. They weren't real, but the luster was beautiful and they were strung on a gold cord with space in between each one. 'Oh no!' Tina said. 'Why don't we just go to Tiffany's?'

'Because they sell real pearls and these are just fakes.'

'What's the diff? You can't afford this stuff either,' Tina told her. But though they were a hundred and five dollars, Claire decided she could, along with the matching earrings.

'But they're so plain,' Tina complained. 'Everything you got is beige. Are you a beige person?'

'I guess so,' Claire said as she took the cute little bag from the sales clerk.

'They do look lovely against your skin,' the clerk said. 'Enjoy them.' Claire promised her she would.

As she and Tina walked through the thinning crowd on their way to the subway Claire refused to think about the total she'd spent. 'What will you wear on the plane?' Tina asked.

'I guess whatever I wear to work on Wednesday. I'll dress up.'

Tina shook her head. 'People dress down for the red-eye. You know, you sleep on it, so you don't want to wear your best outfit.'

Claire hadn't known that. 'What does . . .' she couldn't bring herself to call him Michael, though she would have to try. 'What does he wear?'

'Jeans, usually. Sometimes with a T-shirt and blazer. Sometimes just a sweater. He changes at the office.'

Claire was surprised and mentally began revising her plan. She'd bring her Levi's to work and she'd wear them along with the sweater she'd knit. 'I still need a raincoat,' Claire told Tina.

'Century Twenty-one,' Tina suggested. 'You can go on your lunch hour, Monday.'

'No. I have to get my passport.' Claire shivered. It wasn't just the March wind. If her passport didn't come through, all this preparation, all the excitement and money spent was wasted and foolish.

'Well, you only have to go and drop off your documents at Rockefeller Center. After that I can send up a messenger for it,' Tina said airily. 'We do it all the time. So I say after your drop-off we meet at Century Twenty-one.'

Claire knew all the women from Crayden Smithers shopped at the discount store but she could never stand the hustle or the hassle. Still, she knew the green coat simply wouldn't do. She doubted that the classy, perfect, sophisticated raincoat she pictured would be hanging on the seventy per cent off rack in Century Twenty-one. But she might as well give it a try. She shrugged. She couldn't spin straw into gold but maybe she could find a needle in a haystack! 'Meet you there,' she promised.

TEN

On Monday Claire took the morning off work, went straight up to the passport expeditor, dropped off her documents and took the subway back downtown for shopping with Tina. The store was as jammed as it always was at lunch hour and just walking in made Claire feel dizzy. But she had forgotten that she was with a pro. Before Claire even had a chance to register the racks and racks of men's sports jackets, the display of dozens of scarves, bins with hundreds of sweaters – all at sixty per cent off – Tina had put a clamp on her shoulder and directed Claire 'to the back, up the stairs, and to the right on the mezzanine'.

Claire pushed her way up the steps through the crowd of women with bags, umbrellas, purses, and other armor.

They were in a section with two rows – at least a hundred feet long – all lined with coats. 'What size are you?' Tina asked. 'A ten? A twelve? Or bigger?' Claire thought she heard contempt in Tina's size-eight voice. 'Will you wear a sweater under it?'

Before Claire could answer, Tina had turned away and, with an expression of intense concentration, began to click through the rack in front of her, the extra inch or two between garments used to push the rejected coats further away and give the next candidate a moment of breath. Tina surveyed each, then, heartlessly, clicked it beside the previous reject before Claire could even get a look. Soon, Tina had gone through ten feet of coats and had pulled three out. 'Here. Want a slicka?'

It was a yellow plastic, exactly the color police wore when they directed traffic. Claire didn't even respond. 'I didn't think so,' Tina laughed. 'How about this?'

It was black, with more straps, buckles, epaulettes, and pockets than any uniform the French Legionnaires had ever imagined. 'No, I want . . .'

'. . . beige,' they said simultaneously and to Claire's complete amazement Tina flourished a decent-looking light tan raincoat.

'Ta-da!' Tina said. 'Looks like your style. Really boring.'

But when Claire began to unbutton it she saw the label and the lining. It was Aquascutum. And though Claire didn't know anything about fashion she knew it was a label on the coats that the people with the windowed offices wore.

She slipped into it. The lining was soft and the color was more a light gray than a tan. 'Hey. That looks good,' Tina said as if truly surprised. She pushed Claire in front of a mirror and Claire had to agree. It did look good. The shoulders were slightly built up to enhance Claire's narrow ones. But it flared enough to camouflage her hips. It hung from a raglan sleeve in a simple drape without a belt or extra gimmicks. 'It's a little plain,' Tina pointed out. She held up the black one. 'You get more for your money with this.'

But Claire continued to survey herself in the mirror. She thought of Katherine Rensselaer on the rainy night. She was wearing a raincoat similar to this one. 'I want it,' Claire said and only then looked at the price-tag. *Reduced*. But it was still three hundred dollars!

'Get outta here!' Tina said when Claire showed her the tag. She turned and checked the rack, checked the signs above and gave Claire the moderately good news, 'Twenty per cent extra off any coat bought today.'

'But it's already reduced,' Claire said. It was true. The original price was just a little under a thousand dollars.

'So? It's twenty per cent more off the three hundred. At least you save sixty dollars.' She looked back at the black coat. 'This one's only a hundred and forty,' she said.

But Claire had made up her mind. She looked at herself in the mirror. Somehow, in this coat, she could imagine herself on a London street looking up at Big Ben.

On Tuesday night Tina came over to 'help with the packing' though Claire suspected she actually wanted to snoop and report back to the lunch table, if not all of Tottenville. Claire knew that even if she asked Tina not to tell anyone, it would be far beyond her capabilities. Let's hope, Claire thought, she doesn't say anything to my mother.

'Hello, Mrs Bilsop,' Tina said, her voice sing-song with secret.

'Hi, Christine,' Claire's mother responded, luckily – as usual – not interested. 'What's up?'

'Nothin' much.' Then Tina silently mouthed, 'Did you tell her yet?' in an exaggerated, cartoon way. Claire shook her head. Luckily, her mom's back was turned.

'We're going upstairs,' Claire said and, as she led Tina up the steps, she rolled her eyes. 'Shut up.' Subtlety was not Tina's stock-in-trade.

In her own room, the door closed, Claire felt comfortable enough to take out her passport and her suitcase. She had decided not to embarrass herself with Abigail Samuels by borrowing her luggage. The passport was an adorable little booklet. What thrilled Claire the most about it was that behind the picture page there were another dozen pages of *Entries/Entrees* and *Departures/Sorties*. Her pages, of course, were blank but soon there would be a departure and an arrival. And a book to fill.

She wondered for another moment how many entries Michael Wainwright or Katherine Rensselaer had in their passports. She shook her head. She was twenty-four and she had never even managed to get this far.

Meanwhile Tina looked over at the bag. 'Is that all ya bringin'?' she asked before the suitcase was even open.

'Well, I'm not quite packed,' Claire admitted. 'Oh, there's my new sweater.' She took it from the top of the packed pile of clothes and unwrapped the tissue paper. She slipped out of her T-shirt and pulled the sweater over her head.

'Wow!' Tina said. 'Nice.' She came over and fingered the delicate cables. 'Feels good. Angora?'

Claire felt a moment of contempt. Angora was as much like cashmere as burlap was to silk but 'Cashmere,' was all she said.

Tina looked into the suitcase. 'You're the queen of beige. You sure you don't want to jazz it up a little?' she asked. 'Hot pink or a little turquoise? I have a new tube top I think would fit you.'

Claire smiled. It was March, pink and turquoise were not her colors, and she didn't have the anatomy necessary to hold a tube top up but, she reminded herself, Tina didn't notice details about other people unless they made good gossip.

Tina, bored with the contents of the bag as well as the contents of Claire's room, walked over to the desk and picked up an old framed photo taken at their high school graduation party. She smiled at it, put it down, turned and looked over at Claire.

'Look, you know I don't mean to hurt your feelin's when I say this, but you do know it isn't goin' to last longer than the weekend. It's nothin' personal,' she added. 'It's just the way Mr Wonderful operates.'

'I know.'

'And bitches like Joan are just goin' to be thrilled to watch you fall to pieces when – I mean, if – you know, if Michael doesn't . . .'

'You mean when he drops me,' Claire said calmly, folding her new nightgown carefully. Then she looked at Tina. 'It's not all about Michael,' she said, forcing herself to use his name. 'I mean I like him, but I like the adventure more. London! I can't even imagine it.' She gestured to the half-packed bag on her bed. 'I don't expect anything. I can hardly believe I'm going at all.'

Tina waggled her head in a dismissive gesture she used. 'Yeah, yeah, yeah. That's what ya say now. But afta ya spend a romantic weekend with the guy, ya may get othah ideas. He's very good at what he does.' She winked broadly.

Claire folded the silk robe and carefully stowed it in the bag along with the nightgown. 'I know. He's the star of the department.'

'I don't just mean his work. I mean everythin'. You should see the e-mails some of the women he's slept with send him.'

'How have you seen them?' Claire asked.

'Oh, it's not like I don't know his password,' Tina said and then, for the first time Claire could remember, she actually blushed. She got up off the side of the bureau she was perched on and crossed to the bed. 'Look, Claire, what I'm tryin' to say is that people like Michael Wainwright, they're not like us. It isn't like I wouldn't want to find a guy like him. But guys like him, they don't go with girls like us. That's why I'm with Anthony. He has a good job, a pension plan. He thinks I'm gorgeous and sexy. And his family loves me. You'd never even get to meet Michael's family and if he saw this place . . .' she gestured, her fingers with their long, painted nails wiggling at the tiny room, the wallpaper curling away from the wall under the window, the worn nylon carpeting.

And instead of shame, or gratitude, Claire was suddenly filled with such rage that she had to turn her back so that Tina couldn't see it. She knew Tina didn't 'mean anything by it' but for once Claire didn't need to hear about how she wasn't good enough, that she shouldn't expect too much, and wasn't going to get it even if she did. She knew all of that already.

Claire calmed herself enough to look at Tina. She was careful to control her voice so that it was neither loud nor shaky. 'I'm not stupid, Tina. I know there's nothing like what you'd call a "future" with Michael. I don't have a real future. And I don't even have a past. There's no Anthony taking me to Puerto Rico, and there's no wedding that I'm saving up for. And anyway that's not what I want. But just because I can't settle for some guy from around here doesn't mean I'm going to make a fool of myself over Michael Wainwright. I'm going to have an adventure.'

As soon as she had spoken, she could tell by Tina's tightened mouth and her body language how offended she was. Claire bit her lip, picked up the new blouse and began to fold it.

'All I'm sayin' is to be careful,' Tina said. 'I don't want to see ya get hurt.'

Claire couldn't bear to look at her. She just put the blouse in her suitcase and went to the closet. 'I know,' she said. Then, looking at the empty hangers and the rejected clothes – clothes she realized she never wanted to wear again – the thought came to her that Tina might be jealous.

In all the years that they had been friends, Tina was the one who did things, who went places, who had boyfriends. She was the one with the big family and lots of family parties. She'd had a sweet sixteen, an engagement celebration, and a string of rejected suitors. Claire had an aunt she never met, never had anything that Tina wanted, not even her good grades. Tina didn't care about school. And, oddly, Tina would never believe that Claire didn't want any of the things that Tina had.

Now, it struck Claire almost like a blow to the head that, for the first time, Tina might be envious, and that she felt Claire had also dissed her and Anthony. And with that knowledge Claire felt fear. But it was too late. Claire shrugged. 'Is there anything in here you want?' she asked.

Without moving, Tina snorted then shook her head. 'Hey,

it's not like ya movin' away or dyin',' she said. 'It's just four days.'

Claire nodded. Her bag was almost full. She just reached down beside her bed and picked up her knitting and two extra skeins of wool.

'What are ya doin'? You're not takin' your knittin'?'

'Why not?' Claire asked.

'Are ya crazy? Men don't like to sleep with their grandmas.'

'Tina, I'm not planning to sit in bed and knit. But he's working on Thursday and Friday and if I have nothing to do . . .'

'. . . you'll shop. Or have a facial. There's a spa on the top floor of the Berkeley. There's a pool on the roof.'

'A pool?' Claire asked amazed. Somehow a rooftop pool in rainy London wasn't part of her mental landscape.

'Yes, a pool. Ya know, the kind ya swim in. Bring your suit.'

'Really?' Claire didn't want to bring a swimsuit. She didn't have a nice one and she didn't want to go swimming with Michael – she needed to show him her thighs like she needed a spinal tap. But she felt Tina's eye on her. She walked to the dresser, took out her old blue maillot, put it in the suitcase and closed the lid. She reminded herself to take it out once Tina had gone. 'Well,' she said, turning back to her friend, 'I think that's about it.' She looked at Tina.

Tina shrugged. 'Well, I better be gettin' home.' Claire nodded and the two of them silently walked down the stairs. Behind her Claire heard the sitcom, Jerry's snore and her mother's chuckle over some television joke. 'Bye, Mrs Bilsop,' Tina called.

'Bye-bye,' Claire's mother called back.

'Okay, see ya tomorrow,' Tina said, raising her voice as if it was important for Mrs Bilsop to hear. Claire stood, holding the screen door open, while Tina walked down the back steps. When she reached the walkway, she turned back to look at Claire. 'Ya know, I love Anthony.'

Claire nodded. 'Of course you do,' she said.

'No. I mean it. I really love him. More than I could ever love someone like Michael Wainwright.' Claire nodded again. It occurred to Claire that she might not be the only one with an unrealistic crush on Mr Wonderful. She looked at Tina for a moment, then looked away for fear of embarrassing her. We all have our secrets, Claire thought. And our blind spots. 'Well, have a good night,' she said. She didn't know what else to say.

Tina shrugged, walked off and Claire stood there alone, listening to the tippy taps of Tina's heels against the Tottenville sidewalk. She realized that something in their friendship, such as it was, had ended. Something was very amiss when Claire's life was more interesting than Tina's.

Claire went back to the door and stuck her head inside. 'Mom, I'm going for a little walk,' she announced.

'Better take a sweater or something. You don't want another cold, do you?' her mother called back.

Claire reached in and took a sweatshirt off the chair by the entrance, quietly closed the door and shrugged into the garment.

Tina was out of sight now so Claire went off in the same direction and made her way down Ottavio Promenade, where a lot of the big new – and in Claire's opinion – ugly houses were located. They were mostly huge fake Colonials with lots of brick, columns and concrete balustrades. Her father would have hated them, but now they cost a million dollars to buy. The same thing had happened on Hyland Boulevard. There used to be nothing but a woods with little cottages there but since Claire was in kindergarten all that had changed. The area below it, once a dump, was now filled with mansions along the waterfront, each one larger and gaudier than the one next to it.

Claire preferred her neighborhood. On Amboy Road she

turned onto Main Street. Egger's Ice Cream Parlor was closed and so was the Tottenville Bakery. But as she passed it, a heavenly smell of baking cookies enveloped her. No bakery anywhere was better than Tottenville's, Claire was sure of that. Hungry, she quickened her steps and walked past the bank building and the beautiful public library.

She was home with perfect timing – her mother and Jerry were still distracted by the television. Claire looked around. The house was a big one, and had probably once been elegant. But that would have been a long time ago. For as long as Claire could remember it had been in disrepair, and though her father had been proud of it, he had never been proud enough to accomplish any renovation. But he did, with Claire's help, take great care of the front yard and side gardens. Now, it was the only house on the street that hadn't been bought by rich young couples and spruced up. Claire, like her father, had always loved the house and the old apple orchard behind it. But her mother and Fred had only complained about its run-down nature, though it would be too complicated to move.

Claire turned, closed the door behind her and walked up the stairs to her room. Once in her room, she went to look out the window at the overgrown front yard – since her father's death, Claire had lost her enthusiasm for gardening, perhaps because it made her miss him. The fence around the house had long ago peeled its paint the way a snake shed its skin. The house was still called 'The Old Bilsop Place' and Claire had wondered what it had looked like when it was 'The New Bilsop Place'. But that would probably have been before they had cameras, and if they did, they didn't waste photographs on houses. Her father had always talked about his family as if they were important, but aside from the house, another grander one called 'The Bilsop Homestead' and an old sea chest that had once belonged to the family and was now in the town museum, there didn't seem to be much evidence of that. Her father had talked about a fight with his own dad, and his sister Gertrude who had weaseled the family fortune away from him, but Gertrude had left Tottenville years before Claire was born – if, indeed, she ever existed, and wasn't just one of her dad's fairy tales. She looked up at the night sky and took a gamble and made a wish upon a star.

She turned back to her bed, opened the suitcase, took out the bathing suit and threw it into the wastepaper basket under her desk. Then she picked up the discarded knitting and placed it where the bathing suit had been. She added a third skein of wool, a lovely yellow. She, like the girl in the fairy tale, would knit straw into gold.

ELEVEN

It was Wednesday, the day she was going to London. Claire left home later than usual, just after her mother went to the hospital where she worked as a nurse's aide, and before Jerry woke up, so neither of them saw her negotiating the heavy luggage. She rolled the black suitcase onto the ferry, off it and up to the office. She had a feeling as she made her way to her work station that all eyes were on her but she told herself it couldn't possibly be true. She stored the case in the closet behind Joan's desk, sat down at her own and tried not to think about how this was the most exciting day of her life. She told herself there was still a chance that Michael would cancel, but at ten-fifteen Tina called her and told her he was running late because he had to pack.

Claire hung up the phone and wasn't quite sure if she was feeling relief or dread at the news. Maybe some of both. Where had she read that reality was the leading cause of stress – for those who are in touch with it? She doubted she was in touch with hers. Wild imaginings – way more unrealistic than her daydreams – kept running through her mind. She tried to keep her eyes on the screen and her hands on the keyboard. She actually felt the sweat in the palms of her hands running to the ends of her fingers. Twice she stopped typing to be sure that she had her passport in her purse, along with the ticket. She did. She also had her money. She wondered whether she should change it into English money now. She decided that at lunchtime she would go out and see if she could find a bank that could help her.

She looked back at the ticket. She was seated in 2B. She wondered if it were an aisle or a window and if there would be someone else in their row. If Michael sat next to her would there be someone between them or at the end? And what would they serve? The flight took off at nine. Should she have a sandwich beforehand? Would they show a movie? They were flying British Airways, so would it be a British movie?

At a quarter to twelve, Claire having done very little work, Tina called again. 'I've just confirmed with the limo service. They're picking you up here at a quarter to seven. Mike has a six o'clock meeting so he'll probably be late. But it looks like you're ready to join the Mile High Club,' Tina chuckled. 'We're all going to meet for lunch a little bit early,' she added.

'Oh, I thought I'd just run out and do some errands,' Claire told her.

'Fagetaboutit,' Tina told her. 'We've got something special in mind; you can't miss lunch today. And if you have to run out to Duane Reade for some condoms or something, Joan will let you or Marie Two will tell her to fuck herself. Which, by the way, would be something I'd like to see her try.'

Claire didn't react, thinking instead about the teasing and innuendo that would probably go on over lunch. 'Rubbers' would be mentioned at least as often as in a B.F. Goodrich tires board meeting. She sighed. 'Okay,' she said. 'See you in ten minutes.'

When she entered the lounge, everyone was already there. Claire had brought a bologna sandwich but knew she couldn't manage to choke it down. When she got closer to the table, she saw that a chair in the middle had been reserved for her and – to her complete astonishment – there was a cake in the center of the table. On it, in blue and yellow icing, *Bon Voyage Claire* was written in melting script. 'Oh. Oh my. Thank you,' she said and took her place.

There were more than the usual lunchers. Even Marie Four, Marie LaPierre, was there. After some joking people opened their sandwiches and Marie Three brought out a bottle of champagne. Tina and Michelle passed out plastic cups and everyone had a sip.

'Look, we got a little something for you,' Marie Two said. All the women at the table looked at each other and then Marie Two handed Claire an envelope.

'Oh, no,' Claire said. 'I hope you didn't . . .'

'Hey, no bullshit,' Tina said.

'Yeah. Ya gave us all gifts for baby showers, bridal showers and . . . well, this is for you, from all of us.'

'Except Joan,' Tina added.

'She didn't have no dentist appointment today. She just didn't want to see anyone happy. Screw Joan,' Michelle said.

'Yeah. Screw her,' Marie Four agreed.

'Shut up,' Marie Two told her. 'Whadda you know about Joan?'

'Thank you,' Claire said. She was really touched. She began to put the envelope in her purse. She felt as if all of them were rooting for her; the representative of their underclass.

'Whaddaya, crazy?' Marie One asked. 'Don't you wanna see the map we got ya?' Everyone around the table laughed. And Claire opened the envelope. It was a card, and a paper champagne bottle with sparkle confetti popped up when it was opened. All the women had signed it, and they'd also added cash. Three crisp hundred-dollar bills and three twenties.

'Mad money,' Michelle said.

'I'll say. I'm mad I ain't goin',' said Marie One.

'Be sure to do everythin' Joan wouldn't do,' Marie Two said and snickered.

They cut the cake and all of them had a couple of pieces except for Claire who could barely take a bite. She returned to her desk and it was difficult – almost impossible – to believe that in only six hours she'd be on her way to the airport with Mr Wonderful. She told herself sternly that she'd have to stop thinking of him in that way but couldn't quite manage it yet. 'Michael,' she whispered. 'Michael.' She thought that Joan glanced at her but she ignored it.

At a little after three, she got a call. To her complete surprise it was Abigail Samuels. 'I wonder if you could come to my office for a moment?' Abigail asked. Claire agreed, hung up the phone and her heart sank. Of course, there would be some policy or other that this was breaking and she wouldn't be allowed to make the trip. She should have known.

She told Joan that she'd been called to Miss Samuels's office, got up and walked down the hall. Joan's face, never pleasant, now had a pinched look around the mouth and there was a vertical line on her forehead, slightly off-center, that humped her left brow. Claire could see Joan hadn't been born ugly, but by fifty she'd have the face she deserved. She supposed she would, too.

As she crossed the reception area Michael Wainwright was walking in from what Claire figured was a long lunch. 'Hey,' he said, a big smile crossing his face and his voice bright and cheery. 'I meant to call you, but I've had the morning from hell and the lunch that matched.'

Claire felt the eyes of the receptionist, Maggie, on her back and had no idea what to say. She just smiled.

'You all ready?'

Claire nodded.

'Great. I figured we leave at about seven. Why don't you wait in my office?'

'Sure,' Claire said. 'I have to go now,' she added. 'I was called to Mr Crayden, Senior's office.'

Michael Wainwright raised his eyebrows. 'Movin' up in the world,' he said and smiled before he turned in the opposite direction.

On her walk down the corridor, Claire wondered at his completely casual greeting. She was flustered, embarrassed, tongue-tied and her heart was racing. To him, it seemed, this was business as usual. And it is, she told herself. He goes off on trips with different women all the time. Remember that. She calmed herself down and got to the corner office. Abigail Samuels's door was open. But Claire knocked on it before she put her head in.

'Oh, come in,' Abigail said and stood. Her office was small but, being next to Mr Crayden, Senior's, it had a windowed wall and even a small sofa. 'You're leaving tonight, I think,' Abigail said.

Claire nodded. She felt as if every single person in the office was spending their day thinking about her night.

'Well, I just wanted to wish you well and give you this.' Abigail took a small wrapped parcel out of her top drawer and handed it to Claire. 'It's a guidebook to London,' Abigail explained. 'It's one of my favorite cities. I took the liberty of marking and underlining the places you should be sure to see; some of them are a bit off the beaten track but they're well worth while.'

Claire looked at the older woman. She couldn't imagine why Abigail was doing this, but she was touched and deeply grateful.

'I used to go to London very often with Mr Crayden.' Abigail's face softened, and Claire, for a moment, saw the much younger woman hidden behind the soft jowls and the crow's feet. 'We had some lovely times there.'

Claire realized the import of what she had just heard and tried not to show surprise. Abigail Samuels and Mr Crayden, Senior had . . . 'Thank you very much,' she said. 'I'll really treasure this.'

Abigail smiled. 'I thought you might also want this,' she

said. 'It's just a few pounds that I had left on my last visit but it might come in handy.' She held up a little mesh bag, pretty in itself, and put it down on the desk. 'Do you know pounds sterling?' she asked. 'Of course, the English haven't changed over to Euros yet.' Claire nodded.

Abigail opened the change purse and took out some bills and coins. 'They're well organized,' Abigail said. 'The smaller amounts are printed on smaller paper. And they're different colors so you can't confuse a single with a twenty.' She looked up and smiled at Claire. 'Of course, they don't have singles anymore. All of their one-pound notes are gone. They've been replaced by these.'

She placed a small but chunky coin in Claire's palm. 'When you give a cab driver a twenty and get seven of these back in change they really weigh your pockets down,' Abigail smiled. She emptied the purse and pointed out the other, lower denomination coins. Then she folded the bills back into the bag and poured the coins in too. She handed it all to Claire. 'Enjoy,' she said.

Claire looked at her in surprise and shock. 'Oh, I couldn't.'

'Of course you can,' Abigail said.

'Well, you must at least let me pay you.'

Abigail shook her head. 'Don't worry about it, dear. It was my per diem money.'

'Well, thank you,' Claire told her. 'Thank you for everything.'

Abigail just nodded and Claire turned to go. But when she got to the door Abigail cleared her throat and Claire, of course, turned around.

'Be sure to keep your dignity when you come back,' Abigail said. 'Don't have any illusions about the future, even if Wainwright isn't married.' And, as Claire looked at the much older woman, she saw something in the fine face, the large eyes that showed her what Abigail Samuels must have looked like thirty years ago. She had been very beautiful, Claire could see and, just as clearly, Claire could also see that she had loved Mr Crayden, Senior back then. She probably still did. Claire wondered at the strangeness of time passing. Abigail had been a girl, just like her. And she must have had many adventures. Claire wondered if Abigail had ever had any illusions, but she thought not. Still, it didn't mean that she hadn't had her heart broken though she seemed so even and calm.

As if Abigail could read her thoughts, she looked directly into Claire's face. 'Things were different then,' Abigail said. 'In a way I think they were easier. People knew exactly where they stood. Men didn't leave their wives. Women had lower expectations.' She looked away from Claire, turning to gaze at the view. 'Sometimes, even when it isn't appropriate, people find one another and simply can't be sensible. That hasn't changed.' She looked back at Claire. 'But don't become confused,' she told her. 'All of them have a different set of standards for their wives than they do for . . .'

Claire looked at her with compassion. But Abigail, a mystery who had revealed a great deal of herself, didn't want compassion. 'I didn't lose my dignity and I have no regrets,' she said.

'I won't either,' Claire promised.

TWELVE

Tina finally left Michael Wainwright's office a little after five-thirty, albeit reluctantly. Once she was there alone, Claire called her mother and told her she was off for a few days to Atlantic City. 'Wish it could be me,' her mom said. 'Tell Christine not to throw all her wedding money away.' Claire promised she would and felt a little guilty.

'I love you, Mom,' she said.

'Love you, too.' Then there was some background noise from Jerry. 'Oh, I gotta go,' said her mother, and hung up.

Now with nothing to do – Claire didn't want to be caught knitting by Mr Wonderful – she was tempted to snoop. Who was this man she was about to go overseas with? She was far too polite – and timid – to open the drawers of his desk or look in the credenza behind it, but she did start to examine the framed photos and the diplomas on the wall.

He had gone to Yale, and Claire wondered if he had been in Skull and Bones, the elite club that all of the insiders of the insiders were members of. He had also graduated from Wharton Business School, probably the best in the country. There was a silver-framed picture of a young boy with a good-looking older man's arm around his shoulder. They both held golf clubs.

Beside that was a photograph of Michael with three beautifully groomed women. The oldest must be his mother, because she looked just like Michael (although Claire reflected that, while Michael's looks were splendid in a man, they were not as appropriate on a woman). She assumed that the other two women, both of whom looked slightly older than Michael, were his sisters. All four were sitting on a damask sofa, two on the seat and one perched on each arm. Claire, despite her unschooled eye, could tell that this was not a snapshot. She wondered what it would be like to have professional photographers come into your home, instead of just setting the time on the Minolta and running into focus.

There was a photo that did look like a snapshot with a much younger Michael, kneeling on long grass, his arm around a Labrador retriever. Claire stared at the picture. She had always wanted a dog, but her mother had not allowed it. In the photo Michael was looking at the camera, but the dog was giving him a look of complete devotion. Claire reminded herself not to look like that when she and Michael were face to face.

Next to the dog picture there were a few awards for his charity work – Tina had told Claire about the boards he sat on – and tucked under a crystal one which had his name engraved on it there was a folded piece of blue paper. Claire picked it up. Then she saw it was a note, handwritten on heavy vellum paper, clearly with a fountain pen.

Michael,
After yesterday I have no idea what to feel about you. I believed, obviously incorrectly, that I was important to you and we each considered the other as central to our life. In case you don't know this, let me tell you that I value myself enough not just to be hurt by your continued involvement with another woman, but also to be both angry and strong enough to drop you as I would a toad that had somehow slipped into my hand.
I am dreadfully sorry that I lost my temper with

*you. It was merely the shock of what I consider
extremely bad behavior on your part. I won't
bother you with my recriminations again. In fact, I
and my circle will be sure to ignore you in the
future.*

*You may forget, Michael, that I was not just a
tennis champion but was also known for my good
sportsmanship. A gentleman should also play by
the rules and you are guilty of a double-fault. I
think you should, as on the court, reconsider
boundaries and your serve. I'm too good at my
game to bother to volley anymore.*

I just regret I kissed a toad.
Katherine

Claire looked up guiltily, folded the letter and put it back
under the crystal. It was quite a letter, and it must have
had some impact on Michael or else he surely would have
tossed it away. To stop herself from further predations on
Michael's personal life, Claire forced herself to sit down.
The letter, though, had sobered her. She reminded herself
she was only getting this opportunity because someone else
more entitled had dropped out. She wondered if life was
like that – you only got a slice of the cake when someone
else went without.

From her vantage point on the sofa she looked out at
the hallway and wondered how many more letters like that
Michael Wainwright had stored in the lateral files. Did Tina
read them all, the way she seemed to read his e-mail? Did
she keep them in a single folder? Did she label it, and
how? She couldn't imagine that Tina was good at filing
anything except her nails. But Tina had that easy-going
personality that could schedule meetings, briskly dismiss
the unwanted and pacify those that required it, make up
plausible excuses when necessary and juggle a raft of social
engagements and girlfriends.

All of the objects, photos and, most importantly, the note, had made her even more nervous. She was out of her depth and she knew she wasn't a good swimmer. One slip of the tongue, one cramp in her style and she'd go under. But, she reminded herself, she had no illusions about her relationship with Michael Wainwright. She was a convenience, a diversion, a temp. She had started her job there at Crayden Smithers as a temp and, if she found herself humiliated when she returned, she could easily leave. At her level in the business hierarchy it wasn't hard to find another poorly-paying job and perhaps she would go back to Staten Island, losing the commute and gaining a little self-confidence.

The longer she waited the more doubtful she felt about the whole plan. It wasn't too late, she told herself, to simply roll her little black suitcase out the door. She could put her ticket and a note on his desk but the thought of him, his smile, his jaunty walk, the ingratiating smile he used when he wanted to get his way, the memory of the feel of his hand on hers stopped her. And, she thought, she would never get to use her passport if she left now. She also wouldn't be able to face any of the women, not even Abigail Samuels.

Claire opened her purse once again and took out her passport. It was a lovely document and made her feel important. She stared at her own picture and at the pages and pages that were so-far empty. Michael's passport lay on his desk and, summoning up her nerve one more time, she went over and picked it up.

His face stared out at her neither smiling nor gloomy. It was a far more sophisticated expression than her goofy grin. But that wasn't what impressed her. It was the page upon page of stamps from immigration and visas. Bermuda. Italy. Germany. Hong Kong. There were stamps from places Claire had never heard of and the booklet was nearly full. She was surprised to see how the official seals were stamped helter skelter, one from the Netherlands stamped right over another from Thailand. She would have imagined it more like a postage stamp collection where each one would be carefully placed to be savored later. Michael's passport would expire in two more years. What happened if there was no more room in it before then? she wondered. She hurriedly put it down. She didn't want him to walk in and catch her snooping.

At seven thirty-four, when she was sure that they would miss the plane, Michael – she hoped she had practiced calling him by his first name enough – walked in. 'God, they talk and talk,' he said. 'We better get going.'

Claire stood up and grabbed her coat and the handle of her rolling case. 'Won't we miss the flight?' she asked. 'We need at least two hours for check-in.'

He smiled at her. 'Not with Special Services,' he said. He shouldered his own bag and took the handle of hers. His hand brushed hers and it was so warm against her cold one she nearly jumped. He didn't seem to notice. 'Come along,' he said.

The driver took their bags the moment they reached the lobby. Claire was a little surprised to see that the 'limo' was only a regular Mercedes sedan, but the seats were comfy and the driver was so skilled that they reached the airport in less than half an hour. Michael apologized when they got into the car because he had to look at a file for the next morning's meeting. 'Just let me get this over with and then we can have a drink and relax on the flight,' he said.

Claire nodded and spent the time looking out the window self-consciously, watching Queens fly by; the sad two-family houses, the ugly shaft of the Brooklyn Queens Expressway, the endless cemeteries and graffiti all depressing her. But as soon as they pulled up to the British Airways departures terminal at JFK everything changed. Porters greeted them, their bags were whisked away, they were escorted to a private elevator by a smiling aide and, when the keyed door rolled open, Claire was confronted with a vast, quiet, taupe-upholstered room with a view of the runways and the sound of the slight tinkle of ice in crystal glasses and the murmur of upper-class voices in discreet conversations.

They were settled on a love seat with a waitress beside them to take their drink order. Claire asked for an orange juice. Michael ordered a Scotch she'd never heard of 'And two glasses of water, otherwise we'll get really dehydrated.' Just as the drinks arrived the smiling aide returned with baggage tags, boarding passes and an apology. 'It's crowded right now at immigration,' she said. 'I'll be back to take you through Fast Track in about ten minutes. Your gate is the very last one.'

'It always is,' Michael smiled.

'Do you have any carry-on? I'd be happy to get a cart for it.'

Michael shook his head, picked up his drink and took a sip. 'We're just fine, aren't we?' he asked and looked at Claire for the first time.

She nodded. 'Perfectly fine,' she said and leaned back into the incredibly soft suede of the banquette. Michael leaned over and took her hand. 'Do you need something to read? It's your last chance to get a Hershey bar. They don't have the same candy in London.'

Claire smiled. 'No,' she told him. 'I think I have all I need.'

'Me, too,' Michael said, smiling back.

She turned away, embarrassed but flooded with happiness. This was the sort of adventure that Audrey Hepburn had in old movies. She could hardly believe she was here, with him. Outside, in the deep satin darkness, an enormous plane slid into a berth almost beside them. Michael spoke and she turned back to face him.

'Don't worry about a thing. I've ordered you a kosher meal so you should be all right,' Michael said.

For a moment Claire looked at him trying not to show her astonishment then she realized he was joking and giggled. 'Do I really seem Orthodox?' she asked.

He gave her a lopsided grin. 'Au contraire. I think you're very unorthodox. Lurking under that little librarian act is a world conqueror waiting to be set free. Don't think I missed that.'

Claire wasn't sure what she would have said, but it didn't matter because the smiling aide returned. 'Ready to go?' she asked.

And Michael took Claire's elbow and maneuvered her through the dim hushed lounge and out into the harsh fluorescent lights and crowded clattering mass of the terminal itself. At the gate the aide brought their passports to a desk, they were returned, and she ushered them down the jetway and onto the plane.

To Claire's surprise there was an attendant waiting. She escorted them, along with the aide, to a curtain on the right and into the very front of the plane. Claire knew it existed but she had never been in First Class. 'You're in the second row, Mr Wainwright. But if you'd like the bulkhead seat it's available. You might be more comfortable,' the flight attendant told him.

'No, the second row is fine.'

'Should I sit by the window?' Claire asked.

'Sure,' he told her. 'Not that there's much to see.'

He sat down beside her, took a blanket and a small box from the seat pocket in front of her, spread the blanket over her legs and took out one for himself. He handed her the box and she unzipped it. 'Don't bother. It has all the usual junk,' he said. 'Travel toothbrush, moisturizer, cologne, sleep mask, ear plugs.' Claire looked at the cunning little box. I'll keep it forever she thought.

The flight attendant was back, this time holding a silver tray of tall wine glasses. 'Champagne, water or orange juice?' she asked.

'One of each for me,' Michael said. He turned again to Claire. 'And for you?'

'The same,' she said, surprised and delighted.

'Here are tonight's menus. Please select whatever you like, and we do have the express meal. If you're planning to sleep through the flight, we can bring it to you right after take-off.'

'Thanks,' Michael said. 'I've got a meeting first thing tomorrow. I need all the sleep I can get.'

'I'm going to use the . . .'

'It's right over there, luv,' she was told.

She walked past the other passengers, trying not to stare, and opened the door to the lavatory.

That too was a surprise. There wasn't a tub or a shower, but it was an actual bathroom, twice the size of the tiny closets in the back of the plane and filled with all sorts of goodies. There was a glass vase, filled with fresh flowers, attached to the mirror. Small bottles of hand lotion, moisturizer, and eau de toilette, all of them a brand called Molton Brown, were there for her use. There were linen hand towels spread beautifully across the vanity and, once again, as in the cabin, the air smelled good.

When she got back, their seats had become beds and Michael had settled down in his. His jacket and tie were off, his sleeves were rolled up, his shoes had disappeared and she wasn't sure what he was wearing under the blanket that covered him from waist to toe. Did people in First Class put on pajamas? She gingerly lay down on her bed.

'Sorry I'm passing out,' Michael said. 'Tomorrow will be tough, but I promise I'll take you out for a great dinner after work.'

She smiled. 'That would be great.'

'I'll tell you what's great. You'll have all day to sleep.' He closed his eyes and grimaced. 'I'll be the one slogging through meeting after meeting while you have a massage and a pedicure,' he mock-complained.

She giggled at the thought. 'Highly unlikely,' she said.

'Well then, go shopping or see the sights.' He yawned. 'Good night,' he said and turned his face to the wall. Then he turned back to Claire and gave her hand a little squeeze. 'After this flight, I'll be able to say that I've slept with you,' he said.

THIRTEEN

At Heathrow they didn't have to wait to get through customs – there was a speed line for VIPs. Claire was thrilled to get her passport stamped but more thrilled to breathe British Air, not the airline, the real thing. And of course there was a driver – Terry, who apparently was Michael's regular chauffeur – who took their bags and ushered them into a Mercedes. Her first glimpses of London were through the rain on the back windows. Claire did her best to hide her excitement.

Though the day was dreary, the closer they got to London the more interesting the landscape became. First it was rows of connected houses. Then the houses got larger and they had front gardens. She was surprised to see so many flowers in bloom though it was only March. Daffodils waved their cups at her and her mood matched their sunny color. Then there was an entire block of houses with huge windows. They looked very old and the leaded glass and brickwork were complicated and beautiful. 'What are they?' she asked.

Michael shrugged. 'Just houses,' he said. 'I think they were once artists' studios.' He bent over and gave her a kiss on her forehead. 'Do you know how cute you are?' he asked and Claire blushed.

She couldn't help it. His eyes on her, approving, gave her a little rush. 'I think so. But I was going for glamorous.'

'For glamorous you need a hat,' he said and laughed.

She leaned back into the deep leather seat and, despite the driver, was brave enough to put her hand on Michael's. 'I'll remember that,' Claire told him and thought I can do this. It's fun. I can flirt. She turned back to the passing scene. A sign pointed to Hogarth's House, then on a raised highway they passed a modern glass building shaped like a lozenge.

'Ugly, huh?' Michael asked. 'They call it The Ark. It does look a little like a ship.'

'Have you been to London often?'

Michael shrugged. 'It depends on what you mean by often. A couple of dozen times?' A couple of dozen times! That was twenty-four or more visits and he didn't think that that was often. He shrugged again. 'Do you like London?'

Claire had known this moment would come, and though she had thought of other strategies, she had decided there was no option but the bare-faced truth. 'I've never been,' she said.

'Really?' He paused. 'How old are you? If you don't mind me asking.'

Claire knew he was thirty-one. The difference in age between them wouldn't account for twenty-four trips: unless he had made all his visits in the last seven years. 'I'm twenty-four,' she told him.

He smiled. 'You don't look a day over twenty three and a half.'

When the road lowered she nearly gasped at the view in front of her: this was the London she had expected, the one she had seen in movies. On the right there were Victorian buildings, most of them with signs advertising hotel rooms. On the left there was one monumental building after the other. She was dying to ask what they were but was far too shy. Luckily, Michael followed her gaze.

'That's the Natural History Museum. Never been there.

And this one's the Victoria and Albert. Big sucker. Full of furniture and musical instruments and decorative arts.' The traffic was heavier and so was the rain. 'That's Brompton Oratory,' he said. 'Pretty inside.'

Claire looked at the pillared building and had no idea what a Brompton or an oratory was but she didn't feel up to asking.

'We'll be at the hotel in another ten minutes, sir,' Terry said.

'Do you mind if I just change and run out on you?' Michael asked.

'No.'

'Thanks,' Michael said. 'My meeting today will be a ball-buster. They don't send me over here to play Mr Nice Guy. Except, of course, to you.'

Claire stood in the center of the room slowly turning around and trying to take it all in. It was spectacular, yet very restrained. How was it possible? she asked herself. It looked as if the walls were made of cloth and when she went over to touch one she found that they were, indeed, upholstered with a striped silk in beige and green. Where the fabric met the wooden paneling a silken cord divided them, the exact color of the green fabric stripe. There was a damask-covered sofa with a plethora of fringed throw pillows, an antique sideboard with a huge gilt mirror over it, and real paintings in carved frames. At the entry there was an alcove with a huge bunch of flowers in a Chinese vase, lit by a tiny light above. But most spectacular of all were the two windows that extended almost from the carpeted floor to the ceiling. They opened onto a tiny balcony that overlooked a beautiful, green park.

The curtains were green damask, like the sofa, but that was only the top layer. Underneath there was another pair made of filmy cream lace, and behind those there was a net curtain that let the light in. Claire was about to open the window and step out onto the balcony when there was a knock on the door. She jumped and before she could react there was another knock. She wasn't sure what to do but since Michael, in the shower, certainly couldn't hear she went to the door. A man in a blue uniform stood there, a brass luggage carrier behind him. 'I have your bags, miss,' he said.

'Oh, thank you. Bring them right in.'

One by one he carried each through the living room and into the bedroom, which was decorated in blue and white. She followed him. The noise of the shower here was louder and Claire became nervous that Michael might step out of the bathroom undressed. Luckily, he didn't.

'Shall I hang this up for you?' he asked holding Michael's shoulder bag. Claire had no idea and just nodded. He opened a door that was also upholstered in the blue and white fabric of the rest of the room and revealed a large closet with fabric-covered hangers, drawers, shoe racks, and – for all Claire knew – a little man who ironed clothes as part of the service. 'Shall I put your case on the luggage rack?' he asked. She nodded again and he pulled out a contraption that seemed to be made of four crossed sticks and some fabric bands. In a moment it opened into a kind of stand and he placed her bag on it. Then he opened the mahogany armoire against the wall. Claire figured it was another closet but instead there was a television, a fax, a stereo, a refrigerator, and a small bar stocked with crystal glasses, a bucket full of ice, and wine already cooling in it.

He handed her a remote control. 'Shall I show you how to operate it all, then?' he asked. Claire shook her head. She hadn't come to London to watch TV and she was sure Michael knew how to do it all. But she realized, with a kind of horror, that she would have to give a tip to this man. 'Is the temperature all right?' he asked. 'And would you like a fire?'

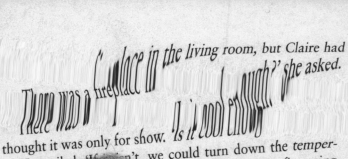

There was a fireplace in the living room, but Claire had thought it was only for show. *Is it cool enough?* she asked.

He smiled. 'If it isn't, we could turn down the temperature in here,' he said. 'Lots of our guests keep a fire going through their whole visit.'

Claire smiled. 'I would like one,' she said, 'if it's no trouble.'

'It's no trouble. I'll be back in a tick.'

He left and that gave Claire enough time to rummage through her purse to find the envelope that Abigail had given her. Should she give him a pound coin? Or two? A five-pound note and when he returned with an armful of logs and some newspaper she had it ready in her hand.

He kneeled at the hearth, looked up the chimney and put in two logs and some newspaper, laying the rest in a brass pot. 'I'll just put these here beside the fender.' Claire had no idea what a fender was but she nodded. When the bellman had lit the paper and flames were licking over the logs, he stood and dusted off his knees and smiled at her. 'Anything else you need, just call Housekeeping,' he said.

'I will,' she promised, though she couldn't imagine doing so. He walked to the door and was out in a moment. Then she realized she still had the five-pound note in her hand. She ran to the door. 'Oh! Please! Please sir.'

He heard her and turned around. Awkwardly she held out her hand with the money folded in it. 'For you,' she said and he smiled and didn't even look at the amount.

'That's very kind of you.'

Flustered, she closed the door and went back into the bedroom. She unzipped her suitcase to see whether everything had been crushed and wrinkled, but just then Michael emerged from the bathroom looking pink, shaved, refreshed and perfectly dressed. He walked over and put his hands on her shoulders, while his hazel eyes glimmered with mischief. 'There is nothing I'd like to do more than lie down on the bed right now with you,' he said. 'But work won't wait. I hope that you will.'

'Of course,' she said. 'When do you think you'll be finished?'

'With work or you?' he asked with a sly little grin. She blushed and looked away. Michael leaned over her. The heat from his shower or simply from his body seemed overwhelming. And when he put his hand on her chin, raised her face to his and kissed her – really kissed her – for the first time, she knew what the Victorians had meant when they wrote about 'swooning'.

'Ummm,' he said. 'Something to live for.' He let her go. 'See you around seven,' he said. 'Take a nap, have room service, order anything you want, Harvey Nicks is just a block away and Harrods is two streets beyond. That ought to keep you busy,' he smiled, and, throwing his raincoat over one arm, he picked up his attaché case and was gone.

Alone, Claire walked over to the bed. It was higher than beds in America, and covered with a fluffy quilt in the same blue print as the walls. There was also a kind of crown above the headboard with blue fabric that draped all the way down to the floor. Claire kicked off her shoes, climbed onto the bed and jumped. Up and down, up and down, three or four times until she was breathless and allowed herself to fall in a heap in the middle of the beautiful coverlet. She felt as if she was in the Princess and the Pea, but there was no lump in the bed. It was all unbelievably perfect, and far, far nicer than anything she could have imagined. She wanted to look at every picture, every ashtray, vase, and pillow. She wanted to take photographs so she would never forget any of it. But first she had to go to the bathroom.

That was a whole suite in itself. A counter at least ten feet long with two sinks in it had a silver framed mirror over it and an orchid in a low ceramic bowl. A marble shelf that seemed to float on the wall below the mirror had glass bottles of shampoo, conditioner, hand cream, body cream and shower gelée as well as glass jars with silver tops filled with cotton, Q-tips, make-up sponges, and – the best one – wrapped hard candies. Claire lifted the lid of that one, and read the bit of paper. *'Jermyne's Boiled Sweets'*, it said, and though that didn't sound very inviting she popped one into her mouth and it tasted exactly like an orange slice.

In the mirror she could see the glassed shower behind her. It was as large as the bathroom she shared with her mother and Jerry in their house in Staten Island. Next to it was the longest bathtub Claire had ever seen, with another host of little bottles of soaps and unguents. Lastly, there was the most adorable little kidney-shaped vanity table with a blue and white skirt and a bench that matched the bedroom fabric. A silver lamp, like a candlestick shaded by a pink silk shade, stood on either side, and across the back a three-way mirror reflected her mid section. Claire actually laughed out loud in delight.

She ran back to the bedroom, fumbled through her suitcase and found her cosmetics bag. It was only a Ziploc, but she took it back to the bathroom, laid out her brush and comb, her lipstick and blusher, her Oil of Olay, and her tubeless toothpaste. Then she sat at the vanity, looked in the mirror and brushed some color onto her face. She smiled at the three faces before her. 'Aren't we having fun?' she asked aloud. 'You're not in Kansas anymore.'

FOURTEEN

Claire walked purposefully toward the corner. In her bag
was the guide to London that Abigail had given her as well
as the pounds. She also had her dollars and needed to find
a bank to go to change them. She looked around her. Every
single thing was different. It wasn't like the hotel or the
flight: – it wasn't just rich people's air – but the air did
smell better, at least to her. Of course there were crowds –
almost as many as in the usual walk she made up Water
Street – but there wasn't the elbowing and rudeness. People
seemed to make their way out of the small streets and the
subway in a more orderly and polite fashion. She had asked
at the hotel front desk where she might get on a bus: she
didn't want to do the obvious tourist thing and be one of
those dumb groups she saw on Wall Street all the time,
gaping from a bus or running after some impossible woman
waving a red umbrella.

It was a little warmer here than in New York but the
sky was gray and the air had a promise of rain so she
buttoned her new coat and was grateful for it. She looked
around her and felt as if she looked close enough like everyone else. Now she was aiming for Knightsbridge and Sloane
Street. The man at the desk had told her, 'Walk out of the
door, turn right then left. You'll be on Knightsbridge. Look
for Sloane Street on the left and the bus stops are just there.'
But there didn't seem to be a bridge anywhere. She kept

walking but soon her attention was caught by a window display. She'd never seen anything quite like it. A swimsuit without a body was suspended in the air. At the end of it there was a huge scaly fish tail. On the other side, where the head should be, only a long blond wig, reaching to the bottom of the window and cascading across the sandy floor, stood in for the absent mermaid. Discreetly written in the sand was a message *Bathing costumes on two*. Claire had to stop and wonder what it meant.

She immediately realized there would be no problem in converting her money into sterling. There seemed to be little offices to change currency everywhere. The sign at the one she went into had little flags of every country with two columns beside each that were headed *We Buy* and *We Sell*. She changed a hundred dollars, feeling very sophisticated. She could do this, and all by herself.

At the next corner she found Sloane Street and a bus stop. She wasn't sure why – perhaps it was because she was so used to her long ferry trips every morning – but she felt as if she'd be safer and more comfortable on a bus. The sign explained not only the numbers and times but also which buses ran at night. There was a vast choice – it was a busy corner – but it didn't really matter to Claire which direction she went in. The first bus that came along was a twenty-two and, to her delight, it was a red double-decker. First, a wave of people got off the wide platform at the back then people beside her began to board and following them, she did too. Right in front of her was a small spiral staircase to the upper level. She began to climb up it then the bus lurched and she nearly fell down it. She grabbed at the railing and as the vehicle moved into the flow of traffic she climbed to the top.

She wasn't sure why, but on top the bus was virtually empty. Later she would learn that she was traveling in the opposite direction to most commuters, out to Putney where people lived and traveled into the center to work.

Unconscious of that she simply smiled at the opportunity literally before her – the front seats on both sides of the bus were available. She almost ran down the center aisle and nearly fell again when the bus pulled to an abrupt stop. But once she was in her seat she was thrilled. It seemed as if the bus had no motor: she was looking straight out at the traffic and the people who moved like powerful tides in front of her. And to each side were shop windows and above them glimpses into apartments with window boxes, terraces and a world's variety of curtains, blinds and shades.

Sloane Street was long, but at the end of it she was settled enough to enjoy looking down on Sloane Square and finding it on her map. King's Road seemed a bazaar of delights: clothing shops, cafés, restaurants, pubs (which looked so much more inviting than bars back home did) and a swiftly moving stream of pedestrians.

She had a few pages for notes at the back of the guide-book and began taking some. There was a stop called 'World's End' which seemed, actually, to be in the middle of everything.

When the conductor got to her she apologized. 'I don't have a token,' she told him. 'Or a Travelcard.'

'It's all right, luv. You c'n buy a ticket right 'ere from me. Where'd you get on, then?'

'Sloane Street up near Knightsbridge. *Is* there a bridge?'

He laughed, showing a gap between his front teeth. 'That's a good one,' he said but Claire had no idea what was funny. 'Where you gettin' off?' he asked.

'Well, I'd like to go to the end of the line,' she told him.

'Putney Bridge. You'll see a bridge there, me girl.'

'But I'd like to stay on and come back.'

'I'm afraid I can't 'elp you with that part. You'll 'ave to get off and get right on again. Regulations.'

She nodded. 'But will the bus go back?' she asked, nervous that she might be stranded.

'If not this one then another,' he told her. 'There'll be a

queue of them lined up, like as not. Fag break for the drivers.'

She blinked but asked no questions.

'It'll be one pound,' he told her. She rummaged through her change purse and remembered the chunky golden coins. She handed him one and he returned a ticket that he cranked out of a machine strapped around his waist. ''Old onto that, luv,' he told her. 'They're makin' us redundant, they are, and it will all be computer cards. You've got an antique of the future,' he said and laughed. 'I guess that's what I am.' He laughed again, turned and made his way down the aisle of the bus from handgrip to handgrip without even a lurch.

Claire looked out of the windows, fascinated. Everything, even the rare graffiti had charm, at least to her. When they turned a corner and she saw a pub with the sign outside declaring it the 'Slug and Lettuce' her delight was, even to her, almost unreasonable. Why it should make her so happy didn't matter. Though if she had thought of it, Claire might have ascribed it to the general glow she had because of her pleasure in Michael. But there are places that can be found by each of us, places we may have never been or never thought of that, in themselves, hold a mysterious key to our happiness.

FIFTEEN

Early that evening Claire stared at the hotel closet in complete confusion.

She had had a wonderful day so far. After the bus reached Putney Bridge she had walked over the bridge to Putney itself and explored that pleasant, residential area and its exotic – to her – stores. Then she had bought a sandwich at an Italian deli – this time, just like the ones at home – and eaten it on a bench in a pretty park back on the north side of the river. She decided to return to the hotel on foot, and found her way via the Fulham Road, where she was delighted by the windows and windows of antiques – all set as if they were tiny rooms. A diner table and chairs illuminated by a chandelier, a royal-blue sofa with golden sphinxes for arms and legs and two chairs flanking it. Best of all was a four-poster bed with enough purple hangings to drape a church.

She had hurried back to be in good time to get ready for her dinner date with Michael, but now here she was, with no idea where they were going and, even if she had, she wouldn't know what they wore there.

Of course, she didn't have a wide choice. She could wear the skirt along with her expensive silk blouse but perhaps a skirt wasn't formal enough. She decided to put off making the decision and instead did her hair, remembered Tina's advice to her and put on a little extra mascara, struggled into a pair of navy control top pantyhose and had just got the blouse and skirt on when she heard Michael in the living room. She snatched up her earrings and walked to the door. He was going through some papers at the desk and even as he stood there a fax came rattling through. But once the noise abated he looked up.

'Wow. You look good enough to eat,' he said. She felt a flush start at her chest and move to the roots of her hair. Now he'd looked back down at the fax. 'I'm starving,' he said. 'How about you?'

'I could eat,' she said.

'Great. Feel like Chinese? But Chinese like you've never had before.'

'How about English food, I mean, we are in London?'

He laughed. 'You must be joking,' he said. 'Roast beef and Yorkshire pudding? I don't think so. Simpson's is fine once but that trolley gets old fast.'

She didn't like to ask what he meant. 'I'll leave it up to you,' she said.

He nodded, looked at the fax again and picked up the phone. 'Can you confirm my booking at Mr Chow's?' he asked. 'Seven-thirty. We're eating unfashionably early.' He hung up the phone and smiled at her. 'We might have other things to do after dinner,' he said.

She looked away and put on her earrings. Was she as visibly nervous as she felt?

'Look,' he said, 'I've just gotten news that I'm going to have to go out to a business dinner on Saturday. Do you think you can amuse yourself?' She nodded. 'They have great room service here,' he continued. Just then the phone rang with their booking confirmation. He took the fax, tore it into strips and threw it into the wastepaper basket.

For a moment Claire wondered why, but supposed that there might be some business she shouldn't be privy to. He came from around the desk, took her arm and gave her a kiss on her temple. 'Umm. You smell good.' She realized she had forgotten to put on perfume, but her shampoo must have been good enough. 'Ready to go?' he asked. She nodded and the two of them walked out the door and to the elevator.

There he let go of her and then, facing her, put a hand on each of her hips and drew her to him. 'That feels good,' he said. He moved against her. 'A little appetizer,' he whispered. And just then the elevator doors opened to reveal three Japanese men in business suits. Michael was completely unruffled. 'Hooray,' he said, 'the gang's all here.' And he led her onto the elevator.

They walked to Knightsbridge, crossed the very busy road and Claire read the instructions painted on the street that told her to look right instead of left and left instead of right. She wondered how many Americans had been knocked over by buses before the reminder had been painted. They walked up a small but charming alley – everything seemed charming – and Michael opened a door that seemed to be a glass bubble. The restaurant front was very narrow. 'This place was the rage ten years ago,' he said. 'You couldn't get a seat no matter who you were. But you know how it goes: really exclusive, desirable hot spot, impossible to book, too much publicity, taken over by tourists, abandoned by the chic, and open to everyone.'

Two hostesses rushed forward and took Claire's raincoat. They were led up a spiral staircase to the main room. Each table had a light within that shone upward, making a circle through the tablecloth. Claire had never been to a restaurant that had gone through the cycle that Michael described. For a moment she wondered why he wasn't taking her to the kind of place that was 'a desirable hot spot'. Was it because he didn't want to be seen with her? She looked down at her outfit. It wasn't bad, but if it was a size ten instead of a size fourteen it certainly would look more stylish. Then she told herself to get a grip. She'd never been to a restaurant remotely like this. She should be grateful.

The place was mostly empty and they were given a table in the corner. As the waiter helped her into the banquette seat she knocked her head against the light fixture hanging from the low ceiling. She became flustered and horribly embarrassed but Michael laughed and shrugged. 'Everyone's been doing that for ten years,' he said. 'You'd think they'd fix the design.' He leaned forward and took her hand. She refrained from using the other one to rub her forehead and hoped that a lump didn't form.

Michael was talking and she tried to overcome her discomfort and focus on what he was saying. 'Chow started the whole movement. Before him there was no pan-Asian, no fusion. Not that his is really fusion. It's hard to define. Maybe Chinese crossed with French.'

It was only then that she realized he was talking food not politics. For a moment she thought of Katherine Rensselaer and how she would know exactly what kind of food Mr Chow's served, when they'd started serving it, where they had other restaurants, who had invested in them – and she had probably gone to school with Mr Chow as well.

The waiter came with menus. She looked at hers briefly. 'It all looks good,' she said.

'How about I order for us both?' he asked. 'We can share. You know, family style.'

Claire thought of eating with her family. For them it meant the food was served with resentment and eaten in silence. But she smiled. Sharing with Michael would be delightful, and thinking of what they would share later sent a little thrill from her chest to her . . .

'You have to try the gambei,' he said. 'They say that it's fried seaweed, but it isn't. People played guessing games about what it was for years. Whatever it is, it's sensational.'

The idea of fried seaweed made her not just nervous but queasy. She didn't like sushi and didn't want to get sick and spoil the evening. Perhaps she could just push it around on her plate. 'Then maybe the special chicken and I love his sweet beef. It sounds like a lot of meat but it isn't really. The portions are small. Does that sound okay?'

She nodded and knew she'd better speak soon even if she didn't know quite what to say. 'I do like vegetables.'

'Oh, they come along with the rice. Not too interesting but they'll do. And would you like wine?' She nodded, and he consulted with the waiter and the sommelier. There was a pause and Claire desperately thought of what she should say next. But he beat her to the punch. 'I think Tina told me you live nearby,' he said. 'I mean near to her.'

Claire nodded. 'Yes, we commute together every day.' Thinking of that long ride made her heart sink. 'I hate taking the train but the ferry ride is wonderful. It's different every day.'

'They take different routes?' he asked. 'Is it because of the weather?'

She laughed. 'No, it's the weather that makes it different.' She began to describe how the famous sight of the Battery and the New York skyline never ceased to amaze her. 'The light comes off the water in a hundred different ways,' she said. 'When the sky is really blue and cloudless the city looks . . . well, it's much better than Oz. And sometimes on the foggy days it disappears. That huge city with all the people just goes away and even when we pull into the slip there's no sign of it. That's my favorite. It's all like a ghost city.'

Michael was smiling at her. 'It's not quite enough for me to jump at a condo in Staten Island,' he said, 'but maybe a visit would be worthwhile.'

She smiled at the thought of him on the ferry with her and Tina. But the idea of him in her house was more than she could begin to imagine. 'Tottenville is a strange place,' she said. 'You know it's one of the earliest settlements in the harbor. My father's family lived there since before the Revolution. Or at least that's what he used to tell us.'

'My father's family had to run away during the Revolution,' Michael laughed. 'They backed the wrong side. That doesn't stop my mother from being a member of the DAR, though.'

Claire tried to imagine his mother, and thought just how dismayed she would be if Michael brought Claire home. Not that he would of course. He had all of those women whose mothers were also in the Daughters of the American Revolution, who weren't size fourteen, and who had gone to boarding school and the Seven Sisters and the Ivy League colleges and the elite business schools. She tried to think of movies like *Working Girl* and *Maid in Manhattan* and *Pretty Woman* where the classy hero falls in love with the plucky, beautiful plebeian. The problem was that of the three she was only plebeian.

'So what does your dad do?' Michael asked.

'He's dead.' The question had taken her by surprise and she realized the answer was too blunt.

'I'm sorry. My dad died when I was twelve.'

'I was nineteen,' Claire said, surprised that they had this to share. 'I miss him a lot. I guess I was his favorite.'

Michael smiled. 'I would imagine so,' he said. 'I can't say I was my dad's favorite. Actually, he didn't notice me much. He worked a lot and I wasn't very good in school so there wasn't much to brag about. My brother was the star.'

Claire looked at Mr Wonderful and thought perhaps things hadn't always been wonderful for him. She tried to imagine him as a neglected twelve-year-old but it was impossible. He was so self-assured and he always seemed not only to know just what he wanted but how to get it.

The food arrived then, served with a lot of ceremony by two waiters. So family style did not mean taking it from a platter on the table but having the servants share it out, Claire thought. She looked at the tiny green curls grouped beside the fragrant rice and promised herself that no matter how bad fried seaweed tasted she would manage to swallow it down. She was offered a pair of ivory chopsticks but shook her head. Michael accepted them and for a moment she wished she had too, but what was the point? She might be able to pick up pieces of chicken but certainly not the separate grains of rice and these tiny green whorls.

'*Bon appetit*,' Michael said and gestured for the waiter to fill her wine glass.

To her surprise everything was delicious. The crispy green stuff certainly didn't taste like seaweed, but melted in her mouth in a way that was both sweet and salty. The chicken and the beef were equally tasty and Claire realized that she was wolfing the food down. She forced herself to put down her fork and drink from her wine and water glasses instead.

Meanwhile, Michael regaled her with stories of his bad behavior in prep school, college, and grad school. It seemed as if his school life had been nothing but pranks and fun. She thought back to her dull days in Tottenville public schools and instead told him about her lunches with the Maries, Michelle, Tina and Joan. Somehow when she built up a little enthusiasm she became funny – or at least he laughed – and she began to play up the ridiculous aspects of all of the women and their lives. Michael asked questions and seemed fascinated. If he was slumming, or if she was betraying their trust, Claire didn't care. If she could find a way to entertain and charm Mr Wonderful she was going to do it.

By the time dinner was finished, Claire felt relaxed and happy. She managed to leave the table without banging her head, made her way unsteadily past the other tables and let Michael help her into her coat.

On the way back to the hotel she giggled a lot and at the corner, by a store called the Scotch House, he pulled her into a doorway and gave her a kiss that she melted into. 'There's something about you,' he said. 'You're adorable. You're not like anyone else I know.'

Claire was sure that was true. How many Bilsops from Tottenville had Michael Wainwright ever met? But she put her arms around his neck, held her face up to him and waited for him to kiss her again.

SIXTEEN

As Claire walked beside Michael along the hallway that led to suite 617, she felt almost overwhelmed by the possibilities of what would come next. The flight, her day in London, their dinner, all seemed to run together like a glorious dream. She actually felt dizzy. Maybe it's the jet-lag, she thought.

For Michael, she reminded herself, this was no big deal. He had done it before. He would no doubt do it again. Just then, Michael gently enclosed her hand with his own. 'I had a wonderful time,' he said.

'So did I,' she responded. And she had. But Claire couldn't help but think of Katherine Rensselaer and Blaire – Whatever-Her-Name. Had he sounded so sincere with them? Katherine had called him a toad, but he seemed – in so many ways – like a Prince Charming. She also knew that whatever happened between them during this trip probably wouldn't be remembered – at least by him – when they got back to the States, but . . . but she didn't care. She was charmed.

Michael released her hand so that he could fish in his pocket for the key and unlock the suite door. He held it open and ushered her in before him. As she entered the foyer, he put his arm around her waist. Claire melted, though she tried not to let it show. Should she stop him? Should she let it continue? She knew not to have sex on a first date but . . . this certainly wasn't that. He nuzzled her neck and then walked them through into the living room. Perhaps he wasn't going to do any more than this? Why did Claire feel so disturbed by that idea?

Instead Michael tightened his grip, cradled Claire in his arms and – at last – he kissed her again gently. 'You're very lovely,' he whispered. 'I'm not sure I noticed that before tonight.'

Claire didn't know what to say. She was momentarily shocked, not by his words, but his honesty. And how should she respond? She certainly didn't want to thank him. That would be ridiculous. She wasn't accustomed to anyone complimenting her, never mind taking hold of her and kissing her the way Michael just did. Luckily he kissed her again and she didn't have to think.

This kiss was deeper, and delicious, but Claire pulled away enough to look him in the face. Then, totally surprising herself, she said nothing, just pulled him back to her. She kissed him, hungry for his mouth. It was just as she had imagined it would be. He teased her with the tip of his tongue along the inner edge of her upper lip. It was . . . wonderful. She began to shiver. Michael left her mouth and kissed her cheek. 'Maybe we could get more comfortable. We don't have to stand here in the middle of the room.'

Of course not. But where to go? Claire felt a moment of real awkwardness. If she moved to the sofa was it coy? If she moved to the bed was she being forward or premature? The truth was that Claire was wild about Michael; she knew that she would do anything he asked. But she didn't have enough experience to know how cool or how eager she should be. And who does? Making love with anyone for the first time is almost always awkward. Even the most experienced man, the most confident woman, feels a little unsure. But Claire didn't know that and so she felt very unsure.

She also felt Michael's hands leave her hips and go up

her stomach, her rib cage and then lightly rub her breasts as he negotiated the buttons on the front of her blouse. Claire heard herself groan. She shivered again. He was pressed against her and, through their clothing, she could feel the intense heat of his body. She was paralysed against the wall; the only sense that seemed to be working was the sense of touch. And this felt so natural, and at the same time so unbelievable, so unexpected. She couldn't think. She shivered again. 'You're cold,' he said and he cupped her face in his hands. 'Let me warm you up.'

He pulled her to the sofa, and her awkwardness disappeared. Thank god she had not walked toward the bedroom! She'd try to relax and let him lead. Every motion he made was like a dancer, graceful and flowing. Now he helped Claire onto the cushion and as he did, his hands slid under the shoulders of her shirt and he pushed it gently down her arms revealing her new white lace bra. Michael bent down and his tongue glided from her neck down to the small cleavage that was created by the uncomfortable underwire. Claire wondered what he would think if he took it off and the cleavage went away. Then she told herself to relax. His tongue flicked against her skin and the sensation was so delicious that she couldn't contain the moan that escaped her lips. 'Oh, do you like that?' Mr Wonderful asked.

She couldn't speak. She only nodded. Michael maneuvered himself next to her and pulled her closer. She nestled her head against his chest. He took her hand and placed it on his shirt, indicating to her that she should help unbutton it. Claire, in her dreamlike state, still managed it without difficulty. His chest was flat and slightly furred, just in the middle, with soft straight down. The scent that came from his skin was dizzying. She closed her eyes as she breathed, then laid her cheek on his exposed skin. She took her index finger and slowly dragged it down to his stomach. She felt the smoothness and heat of his skin. 'Are you ticklish?' she asked.

'Tickling isn't what I've got in mind,' he replied. 'Unless that's a euphemism for making love to you.' He looked down at her. 'But I won't rush you. You tell me when.' He placed his hand behind her head and ever so slowly laid her on her back on the sofa, kissing her as she reclined. My god, Claire thought. This is so . . . magical.

She was surprised but grateful when he got off her and scooped her up and carried her into the bedroom. He placed her on the duvet and meticulously removed her shoes and then unzipped the back of her skirt. Claire was shaking from the chill and thrill. He then took the coverlet from the bottom of the bed and slid it over her body.

He took off the rest of his clothes, right down to his shorts, then sat on the edge of the bed and discreetly took off his underwear before he climbed in next to her. He wrapped his arms around her and for a silent moment they lay under the coverlet. Her heart was beating hard and she could feel each thump between her legs, an ancient drum beat. The bed felt so smooth, the sheets so cool and fine, the quilt so light. Claire held her breath. She felt Michael's hip press her thigh. His breathing slowed; then she realized he had adapted his to match her own. Without a word they rolled into one another and pressed hard against each other, kissing passionately.

'Are you still cold?' he asked, in between kisses.

She shook her head while still maintaining the connection of their lips.

'You're an angel,' he whispered.

Claire felt her muscles tighten. She had always wanted to hear these words but knew she shouldn't dare believe them. Yet the temptation was enormous. Michael pulled away from her to look in her eyes. She smiled and tried to put all thoughts out of her head. Michael caressed her cheek and she breathed a sigh of contentment. Here she was in the arms of Mr Wonderful. Better still in bed with Michael Wainwright.

He nudged her onto her back and then laid himself directly over her. She wasn't surprised by his skill but was by his strength and gentleness. Could it be because she was willing? His tenderness was genuine. He cradled her head with his hands and held her face to his and kissed her deeply. He stroked her hair. 'You're an angel,' he murmured again. He buried his face in the nape of her neck. 'Mmmm, you smell delicious.'

Claire kissed him passionately. She couldn't decide which use of his mouth she preferred: him speaking or him kissing. He was also very crafty with his hands. They moved effortlessly from her breasts to her thighs and up again to her mouth, each time becoming more probing, more intimate, more responsive.

Claire had only made love with Bob and that had been awkward and unsatisfying. But with Michael it was different. He registered the slightest shifting of her body, every change in her breath. He knew what she wanted without Claire having to say a word. Since she didn't like to ask for things, this was the best of all worlds. He was patient, precise and playful, but she also felt such an exchange of emotion that she lost herself. As they made love, Michael kept his lips on hers, and Claire thought he had a hundred variations of kissing, all of them in sync with all his movements as well as her own. He removed his lips only long enough to look at her or when he lowered himself to her nipples and down the length of her torso.

Michael brought her to climax first with his tongue and then his fingers. Claire couldn't breathe. This was a wonderful experience. She had never had any of this with Bob. Claire had no idea how much time had passed when he finally slipped inside her for the first time. He was such a powerhouse that she was entranced just watching his body moving over hers. His concentration, control and coordination were astounding.

At last, they both collapsed in sweaty exhaustion and he fell asleep with Claire still engulfed in his embrace. After a few moments of reveling in it all, she drifted off into a slumber deeper than Sleeping Beauty's.

In the morning, without an awakening kiss, Claire startled herself out of sleep. In the semi-darkness she had one of those moments of dislocation. Where was she? It wasn't her ceiling. Then she turned her head and saw Michael, still sleeping. The events of the night before flooded back. Claire smiled and felt herself blush.

While Michael slept, she simply looked at him; at his long arm lying on the sheet, his chest moving under the covers and how the light from the street was shining on his face. She felt safe, comfortable, happy. It was a feeling she wasn't accustomed to.

Claire sighed deeply soaking in the satisfaction of the feeling. Happiness this deep was something you could not hold onto, especially with Michael, and at least she was wise enough to realize it. She wasn't thinking about the sex, though it had been exquisite. It was simply looking at Michael, feeling the warmth, comfort and protectiveness that staring at him brought her. It was pure joy.

Slowly, so as not to wake him, she lifted her head to gaze at his sleeping face. Even without animation, his features had a beauty and liveliness that made Claire wonder. From their conversation the previous night she felt Michael Wainwright was not just another pretty face. After all, in his own way, Bob had been very handsome. But unlike Bob, to Claire's complete surprise, Michael seemed to have a depth of feeling, a sense of compassion and understanding that had been blocked in Bob.

As if feeling himself observed, Michael opened his eyes. 'Hello,' he said, his voice dipping somehow in the middle of the word, making it sound like a self-assured greeting. Claire felt herself blush again and this time it did embarrass her. She fell back on her pillow. Michael raised himself on one elbow, bent over her and kissed her. He lifted his head. 'Go back to sleep, angel,' he told Claire and tucked the sheet in on either side of her.

SEVENTEEN

When Claire opened her eyes again Michael was already dressed, his back to her as he loaded his pockets from the top of the bureau. He picked up the last two objects: the comb he tucked in the breast pocket of his jacket and the watch he strapped onto his left wrist. He was ready to leave!

She sat up suddenly and he must have seen her reflection in the mirror before him. She couldn't see herself but she could see his face, and the way it changed from concentration on his task to an open smile. 'Good morning,' he said. Surely he likes me, Claire thought. His smile was so warm. He didn't have to smile, she told herself.

Michael turned away from the mirror. As he came toward the bed he reached out for her hand, then kissed it quickly. 'I didn't want to wake you,' he said. 'I thought if I couldn't sleep until noon, at least one of us could.' He pushed some stray hair off his forehead. 'As they say over here, "I'm knackered."'

'What's that?'

'Tired. Exhausted.' He grinned.

Claire glanced at the clock beside the bed. 'Oh, I won't sleep very long,' she told him.

He turned to go, giving her advice over his shoulder. 'Well, change your plan. Sleep in. Then call down for breakfast, eat it in bed and then get your hair done.' Claire was about to ask him if he thought she needed 'doing' when

117

he turned back, but just to grab his raincoat and walk back to the door. 'Gotta go or I'll be late,' he said. 'I should be back before seven.'

She jumped out of bed, ran to the door and managed to get there before he was out. 'Bye-bye,' she said and gave him a quick kiss on the cheek. He smiled at her but she saw that he was already distracted, thinking of work.

'Bye,' he said and closed the door behind him.

She stood against the door and caught sight of herself in the mirror. From this distance she looked like a woman in a movie, or on TV. For a moment she wondered why the prepositions were different: you're in one and on the other. She smiled at the irrelevance. Michael had been both on and in her. That was obvious. Her hair was disheveled but in a sensual, luxurious way. And behind her the set was equally sensual and luxurious. The beautiful wood-work, the fabric on the wall, the soft carpet, the chair in the corner; it all looked like a scene from someone else's life, the kind of life she had not even imagined. But it is happening, Claire thought. It is happening to me. Because of him. Then, with a start she ran to the French doors and peeked out. If she opened them and stood just slightly outside, on the balcony but hidden by the curtain, she would be able to see Michael leave the hotel.

Below her a line of soberly-dressed business people stood beside the doorman. Cabs pulled up and devoured them in an orderly way. Claire counted three women in the line. No doubt each was as accomplished as Katherine Rensselaer but Claire felt a flash of pride and victory because those women were waiting for a car and a day of office work while she was waiting for Michael.

Of course Michael wasn't thinking of her. If he turns to look for me, it means he really likes me, she told herself. Then she was taken by a chill of fear. What if he didn't look up? She felt for a moment as if she was threatened. Just one look, she thought, and clutched the curtain. She wished the idea hadn't come to her but once it had she was forced to wait and watch. It seemed like hours, days, before she saw him striding out of the hotel. She watched as he ignored the line and made for Knightsbridge. He had told her that, despite the reduction in traffic brought about by the Mayor's new congestion charge, the underground was the only way to travel in London and she was proud of him, for some obscure reason, as he ignored the line waiting for the luxury of a taxi.

But she needed him to turn around, just for a second, and look up to where she stood. He was already across the street when, for a moment, his steps slowed and her heart felt as if it was actually about to move in her chest. She raised her hand, but saw that he had only paused to tap his back pocket, obviously checking for his wallet.

He kept walking and didn't turn around. Claire dropped her hand and after she saw him disappear around the corner, she came back into the bedroom. She told herself not to be stupid. There were no tests, there were no omens. She was foolish. She had been happy three minutes before – gloriously happy – and now she had made herself unhappy. It was ridiculous. She would not spoil one more moment of this precious time.

She went to the bed and, reflexively, began to make it. Then she realized the idiocy of what she was doing. The hotel must have a staff of ten to change the bed.

'I will take a bath,' she said aloud. She never began her day with a bath – she ended it that way. But the bathroom was so inviting and it was such a change and treat that she decided to do it. And while she was treating herself, she had the courage to pick up the phone and dial room service. 'May I have a cup of tea?' she asked.

'A cup or a pot, madam?' the room service voice asked.

Claire had never been called 'madam' before and she almost giggled. 'A pot,' she said. 'And some toast,' she added, amazed at her daring.

'Brown or white?' he asked.

The question made her smile. 'Brown bread,' she said, not that she preferred whole wheat, but because she wanted a chance to say 'brown bread'. It sounded so charming.

'Would you like a basket of breakfast rolls and croissants as well?' he asked.

She refused the offer but accepted one of a glass of fresh orange juice. Then she hung up and ran a bath, answered the knock on the door and directed the waiter to put the tray on the bed. Once he had done this and left, she carried her cup of tea into the bathroom. There she put it beside the marble tub, got into the bath and luxuriated in her surroundings. The warm tea inside her and the warm water surrounding her restored her sense of well-being. She was, she decided, the luckiest woman in London.

Lying in the bath she planned her day. She would try the underground, especially after Michael had recommended it, but she wasn't sure where she wanted to go. She had already glanced at Abigail's guidebook but didn't want to spend the day in museums. She wanted to be among people and watching the way they lived here.

When she was out of the bath and wrapped in the thick white hotel robe she picked at some breakfast, got back onto the bed, spread out her underground map, poured herself a second cup of tea and decided to just pick a stop. She was closest to the Knightsbridge stop on the Piccadilly Line. She let her eyes roam over the map. Clapham, Earls Court, South Kensington, then a word jumped out at her. 'Angel'. There was a stop on the underground called 'Angel'. How odd. She thought of Michael and his face when he had called her an angel. It gave her a shiver and she knew that whatever was there, at that stop on the subway, she was going to see it.

With a sense of destiny, she carefully dressed, put on her comfortable shoes, donned her raincoat and left the hotel. So many choices. But although she was a little nervous, the underground was easy. In fact, it was easier and much more pleasant than the New York subway. Her claustrophobia didn't appear at all. She went down one flight of steps to a big clean tiled station with machines to buy tickets as well as a ticket booth. Then she rode an enormously long escalator with interesting framed posters all along the way, down to the train. The majority of the crowd seemed to be moving in the opposite direction, but the different lines and tunnels were clearly marked and Claire easily got the right east-bound train and passed through Green Park, Piccadilly, Leicester Square and on to King's Cross, where she had worked out she had to change lines. All the stops seemed busy, but the people who filed in and out were neatly dressed and seemed far more polite and quiet than the ongoing cabaret and sense of danger she was used to in Manhattan trains.

She consulted her *A to Z* map and saw that the Angel was in Islington and was, in fact, named after a local pub. There was a main street, called Upper Street, and several small squares to the east of it. There was also a section marked Camden Passage. It sounded interesting and when she got out of the station she carefully followed the map.

Upper Street was busy with buses, shoppers and deliveries, but it seemed more like normal life, not the tourist life of Knightsbridge. Claire turned off the main road and came upon a tiny lane running parallel which was called, confusingly, Islington High Street. On it were a dozen antique stores – the city seemed crammed with antiques – and two pubs. As she walked by the first one she saw a signboard advertising 'Pub lunches'. Under that there were a few dishes listed including 'The Ploughman's Special'. She wondered what it could be, and decided she would lunch there and find out.

Then she began to wander up one street and across another. Everything seemed different from anything Claire had known before. Even the light had a special quality, a paleness that made even bright colors softer and more luminous.

She came to a square – not as manicured and perfect as the ones south of the hotel – but a little square with a church and an open common in the middle. There were some old trees and the grass was very green. Around it small houses, each attached to the one beside it, looked out to the shared park. An old woman carrying a heavy canvas bag made her way slowly along the sidewalk and a woman with two children crossed the street to the small playground beside the church. At that moment the sun broke through the clouds and a stream of watery sunshine played across the scene in front of her. Along with the light came a flood of joy. I'm here, Claire thought. I am part of this scene, the old woman, the children, the young mother, and me. We are all here. She smiled.

She walked until she was tired, and then made her way back toward the pub she had selected. But once there she felt shy. She pushed open the door timidly. Though it was one o'clock the place was almost empty. Two or three bar stools were occupied by older men. There were no other customers, though a few tables on the dark red carpet had empty glasses on them.

Claire picked a clean table in the corner. It was good to sit down. But after five minutes or so she wondered when – or if – the waitress would arrive. Leaving her bag on the seat she walked to the bar. 'Are you serving lunch?' she asked.

The drinkers turned to look at her. But the young man behind the bar didn't. 'You'll have to order it here. No table service on weekdays,' he said, his eyes on the mugs he was washing in a sink of gray water. Claire felt her courage draining as the water drained out of the sink, but she managed to stay in her place, though she couldn't bring herself to speak in front of these four men. 'So, what'll it be?' he asked.

'The ploughman,' she forced herself to say, as if she knew what she was ordering. If it were terrible – some nasty meat in brown sauce – she just wouldn't eat it.

'To drink?'

Claire hadn't a clue. 'Beer,' she said.

'Which one?' he asked.

'I don't know,' she admitted. They must have different brands here. She wasn't much of a beer drinker anyway but it seemed that one should have a beer in a pub.

Her ignorance worked in her favor. Two of the men at the bar smiled. ''Ave the bitter,' said the balding one with glasses.

'Bollocks,' said the older man wearing a cap. 'She's from the States. She won't like bitter.' He smiled more broadly. His eyes, under brows that were like furry caterpillars, were brilliant blue. 'Have a light ale.' He turned to the bartender. 'Give her a Courage, Mick. Half pint on me.'

'Oh, that's on you all right,' the first man said. 'A half pint. You're half measure all the way.'

'You're talkin' rubbish again,' Mick the bartender told the both of them. 'One more argument and both of you will be out of 'ere.'

The third man spoke for the first time. 'The lady is waiting for her lunch,' he said. 'Mick, I'm sure you're gentlemanly enough to take it over to her along with a half pint of Courage.'

The other two men laughed. Claire knew she was part of some long-standing drama, although it was certainly of the everyday variety. She looked at the third man, who looked pretty much like the other two. 'Thank you,' she said and was grateful to retire to her corner.

When the ploughman's came, handed to her along with a beer by the bored Mick, Claire was delighted by the plate. It was a strange lunch but one that suited her. Two large hunks – they were far bigger than slices – of bread, a lump of butter, a block of cheese, and some brown relish were arrayed with some lettuce and cucumber rather like a landscape on the plate. Claire broke off a piece of the bread, sliced some cheese, added some relish and took a bite. The flavors exploded in her mouth. The cheese was a cheddar, but much more savory than Tottenville cheddar. The bread had a chewy, yeasty consistency and the relish was wonderful – sweet and tart at the same time – and perfect with the cheese and bread. It was only the beer that Claire found unpleasant. It was warm and much stronger, at least in taste, than American beers. But she drank most of it out of courtesy and thanked the men at the bar profusely before she left. Why was it, she wondered, that everything here – even the simple things – seemed to have more flavor, more depth, more tang?

It was only then that she remembered the mysterious signs she had seen on the sides of buildings. 'TAKE COURAGE.' She had thought they were religious, or left over from the war. Now she realized they were beer advertisements! She smiled. Sometimes she felt like Dorothy wandering on the yellow brick road.

EIGHTEEN

Michael took Claire's arm as they walked out of the hotel that evening. She instinctively started to move to the right and onto Knightsbridge, but he steered her in the other direction. 'I'm taking you someplace special for dinner,' he said, as if every place that she had been to already wasn't special enough.

'What kind of place?' she asked.

'You'll see. It's just two streets and two centuries away.'

They made another left and then another. Claire found herself in a little lane that looked like a movie set. On the right was a wall of ivy and two small cottages. Beside them was the most adorable pub yet. A sign in the front declared it to be 'The Grenadier' and the charm of the small Tudor windows, the old brick stairs, the vines creeping up the side and the soft glow and noise that spilled out through the open door onto Wilton Row was indescribably inviting.

Michael stopped. Looked from it to her. 'Do you like it?' he asked. 'It's got better than usual pub food. No Cornish pasties or Ploughman's Specials here.'

'Great,' Claire said, and realized it sounded both too enthusiastic and too brief a response. 'It looks absolutely perfect,' she added.

Michael's face became more serious. He lifted her chin then kissed her very gently on the forehead, an exquisitely tender gesture. 'So are you,' Michael whispered and Claire had a moment of perfect happiness.

There were a few people standing outside, tall drinks in their hands. Michael led her through them and they entered the small, low-ceilinged foyer that opened to a dark bar on one side and a small dining room on the other. 'Table for two,' Michael told the tall young man at the dining room door.

'Have you booked?' the young man asked. Michael nodded. 'The name?'

'Wainwright.' Michael turned to smile at Claire and she smiled back, trying meanwhile to figure out the meaning of the conversation.

'Oh. Here. Booking for half-eight?' Claire quickly translated this into 'reservation for eight-thirty'. The young man looked up and smiled at the two of them. 'We've kept the table you requested.'

As they walked through the little dining room Claire wondered at the idea of asking for a particular table. Here, at the Grenadier, that would be especially complicated since it seemed as if none of the tables – or for that matter the chairs – matched. They were a collection of varied antiques, and so were some of the diners sitting at them. Beefy English faces along with younger refined ones were bent over their plates. The room wasn't large enough for more than six tables, but through a small door at the back there was another dining room, also small. Perhaps, she thought, there was an endless string of tiny dining rooms.

Once they were seated in the corner Claire had a chance to look around. Oddly, the first thing she noticed was the ceiling where it appeared that money – paper bank notes – from all over the world were glued along with greetings from the donators. The walls were painted a deep color somewhere between rose and rust. Dark oil paintings hung on the walls and the smell of cooking was delicious.

Michael, handing her the menu, smiled. 'They used to call these rooms "snugs",' he told her.

'Well, it is very small and cozy.'

'Actually, they weren't used so much for dining. They were the part of the pub that women were allowed into. No women at the bar.'

'There don't seem to be many there now,' she commented.

'They're famous for their game,' Michael told her.

As she looked at the menu she quickly realized he was talking about the meat. Because it wasn't just steaks and chicken on offer, there was venison and hare and boar and pheasant and grouse. Claire wasn't sure what kind of animal a grouse was but decided to avoid any of the game.

'The house pâté is very nice,' Michael said. Claire was sure it would be, but she would have asparagus and the chicken cooked in lemon and fennel. With chicken you were sure of what you were eating, and everyone always said that everything else 'tasted just like chicken', so she might as well. 'Shall I order the wine?' Michael asked. And Claire couldn't help it – she was so happy and excited that she laughed out loud.

'You'd better,' she said. 'Or else we might end up drinking Romanian red.'

'Not as bad as Wales white,' he told her.

'Is that like white Whales?' she asked.

'We will have no discussions of dicks here, not Moby ones or spotted ones,' Michael told her sternly.

'Spotted?'

He nodded. 'Take a look at the desserts.'

She ran her eye down the list and right after bread and butter pudding she saw spotted dick listed. 'Are they kidding?' she asked.

'Afraid not.' He leaned across the table to her and she thought he might tell her something risqué. 'It's just a pudding with raisins in it,' he explained. 'They're the spots.'

'Well, I'm not having it anyway,' she said.

'A wise idea. I have another suggestion for dessert.' He grinned at her and Claire felt her face as well as her chest redden at the thought of making love to him again. She told herself that she was getting greedy, and reminded herself that she had only a day and a half more of this before it was back to Crayden Smithers.

But even that couldn't dampen her spirits. Right now, right there, everything was perfect. She had an entire day tomorrow with Michael, another night, Sunday morning, a trip to the airport and the flight back. So many hours. So much time. It stretched out before her like one of Monet's beautiful meadows – endless, and dappled with sunlight and joyous poppies. When Michael ordered the rabbit she just decided not to think about it. The meal, with the Beaujolais he chose, was delicious.

During it they talked mostly about work and a little about their backgrounds. 'How long have you been at Crayden?' Michael asked.

'Just over a year. How about you?' She was becoming more clever and had realized it was best to ask him a question after she answered one.

'Oh, since college. I was a legacy at Yale and my dad went there with Jem Junior, so after Wharton it seemed like a fit.'

Sometimes Claire felt it wasn't only the English who spoke a different language. Claire, of course, knew what Yale was but she had no idea what a legacy would be and wasn't sure about Wharton except for Edith.

'I didn't expect to spend so long there. I figured it would just be my first job, you know, a stepping-stone. But they liked me.'

Claire nodded. 'Do you like them?' she asked.

'Oh, Jem Junior has been great.' Claire realized Jem Junior must be young Mr Crayden. His first name, like his father's was Jeremy. 'Pretty predictable, actually,' Michael said. 'The only unpredictable part is how well I've done.

My father never expected that.' Michael laughed though the laughter sounded a little bitter. 'What brought you to Crayden?'

'Tina. We've been friends since grade school.' Tina had gone to the Catholic school but after eighth grade had joined Claire at the high school. Claire's father had said, 'No member of the Bilsop family goes to a Catholic school.'

'Oh, you and your Bilsops,' Claire's mother had said. 'Get ovah it.'

Claire was brought out of her reverie by the sound of plates rattling next to her as a waiter struggled with a huge tray. 'I was studying library science but there are no jobs for librarians now. I got my associate's degree and before I went on Tina told me about the opening.' Claire put down her fork. 'After my father died there wasn't much money.' She laughed. 'Not that there was much before he died.'

Michael nodded his head. 'Yeah, my family was broke as well. We lived in Stamford but my mother always lied and told people it was in Darien. They could barely pay the country club bills each month. I worked as a caddy and she used to tell us, me and my brother, never to charge anything to the account.'

Claire finished her second glass of wine and nodded. She knew there was a big difference between her kind of money shortage and Michael's. With all her father's talk about the Bilsop family she was sure he never even dreamed of being a member of a country club. 'What's your brother doing now?' she asked.

Michael wiped his mouth carefully with the napkin. 'He's very busy being schizophrenic,' he told her. For a moment Claire thought he was joking, but he wasn't. 'He's living on the streets. He won't take his medication. The usual story.' Michael shrugged.

'I'm so sorry,' Claire told him. 'It must be awful for you and your parents.'

'We don't talk about it,' Michael said. 'It's more awful for Leigh, but he doesn't seem to want help.'

Claire didn't know what to say. She was ashamed of her inverted snobbery about the club. All families seemed to have tragedies and pain. Money couldn't cushion you from illness or death.

'Do you have siblings?' Michael asked.

'A younger brother. Fred. He's in the Army. He's some-where over here.'

'In the UK? He's stationed nearby?'

Claire shook her head. 'No. He's in Germany. Over here meant, well . . .' She stopped, flustered. 'Over here' meant across the Atlantic and Claire realized how unsophisticated it sounded.

Luckily, just then, the waiter returned with a menu for dessert. Michael looked at it. 'Mmmm, I think I'll have the apple tart. The lady will have spotted dick.' Claire looked at him and he gave her a wicked grin. She shook her head.

'Oh, no dick for you, dear?'

Claire shook her head again and, looking into Michael's eyes, told the waiter, 'I'll have what he's having.'

NINETEEN

To Claire's joy they made love again before going to sleep that night. It was wonderful, and before she drifted off she wondered if that was why Michael had a nickname and if any of the other women in the office . . .

She was woken by sun flooding the room. Michael was lying on his side; his back to her, and it was his voice, obviously speaking on the phone that had awakened her. 'Yes. Two pots of coffee, really hot please and two full English breakfasts. I'd like kippers as well.' He turned to her, saw that she was awake and smiled. 'Would you like kippers with breakfast?' he asked. Claire shook her head since she had no idea what kippers were. He turned back. 'And could you try to see that the toast is hot. No cooling racks, please. One order of brown bread and one white.' He hung up, but before he could turn to her she began to caress his back. It was such a perfect back. So broad and flat with just a hint of the muscles outlined under the skin. She ran her fingers up and down, and felt him move under them. 'Now, if you keep doing that, missy, I'll never be able to show you anything in London except the other side of these sheets.'

She giggled. He turned to her, kissed her on the forehead and ran one hand along her cheek. 'You're a very sweet girl,' he said. But for some reason Claire didn't like the compliment. She thought, suddenly, of Katherine

Rensselaer and the blue note. Michael would never call Katherine 'a very sweet girl' and Claire felt that he preferred women to girls – those who were not so sweet. But before she could think of any response he was on to planning their Saturday. 'I thought after breakfast we might go up to Portobello for a little while. It's such a nice day. And then maybe the London Eye? The National Portrait Gallery isn't too far from there. We could have a late lunch. And if you're willing to walk from Trafalgar Square to Westminster we could have tea with my friend Neville.'

Claire wondered at how simple it all seemed for him. An entire schedule, a whole day of pleasure, summarized in a moment. He was so fast, and she, well, she wasn't slow, exactly but she definitely wasn't knowing and confident and certain. 'It sounds perfect,' she said.

Michael smiled. 'You look beautiful right now,' he said. 'White suits you.' He tucked the top sheet over her shoulder and gave it a squeeze. 'Do you mind if I shower first?' he asked. She shook her head though she didn't want him to leave the bed. 'Will you get the door if breakfast arrives?' he asked on the way to the bathroom. 'Just sign for it. Oh, and don't forget I won't be able to have dinner with you tonight,' he told her before he closed the bathroom door. 'It's a pain in the ass, but they don't pay for the suite without demanding a pound of flesh.'

Claire tried not to let herself feel any disappointment. So, he wouldn't be having dinner with her. It wasn't a tragedy. There was all of London out the window waiting for her. And when she came back to the hotel he would be waiting as well. And they would make love again and he would hold her and . . .

There was a knock on the door. She threw on her robe but couldn't find the sash and went to the door clutching the peignoir closed at the throat.

It was the waiter, a man of about sixty, with what looked like an entire restaurant on a wheeled cart. There were coffee pots and creamers and a vase of flowers and flatware and plates. Everything but food. She wondered whether it was improper to greet him dressed like this, but he smiled cheerfully as if this was standard operating procedure and pushed the cart into the room.

'Would you prefer to eat here or in the bedroom?' he asked.

'In here,' Michael said from the door. He was in a hotel robe, a towel around his neck, his hair dripping.

'Very good, sir,' the older man said.

Claire wondered what it would feel like to serve breakfast to men half your age and call them 'sir' while you were doing it. But the waiter seemed perfectly happy.

'I'll just put it here, then, shall I?' He moved the cart beside the window and pulled up two wings, one on each side, turning it into a round table. He brought a chair from the desk and another from the seating area.

The mystery was where the food was, but Claire figured he'd go get it and return. Instead, he kneeled under the table. Claire couldn't help but take a peek. There seemed to be a safe built into the bottom of the cart that he opened. He took out two hot covered plates. Michael walked up to the table, lifted the silver cover on one plate and revealed eggs, beans, tomatoes, bacon, sausage – and shoelaces for all Claire could imagine. Then a plate of toast, a dish with small fish and a basket of croissants.

Claire loved the little pots of butter, the bowls of lump sugar, the tiny jars of jams and jellies. The food was good and though she was used to nothing more than a bagel for breakfast Claire ate an enormous amount.

Across from her, so did Michael. She tried the kippers and they were salty and buttery. The toast was warm and even the coffee was delicious. When they were finished, Michael picked up the *Financial Times* (a pink newspaper Claire had seen someone reading on the plane). She went into the bathroom, got washed and dressed.

Half an hour later, Terry returned with his Mercedes and took them through Hyde Park and somewhere northwest amidst streets of white painted houses. 'Shall I wait, sir?'

Michael nodded. 'It's a bitch getting a taxi out of here,' he told Claire.

She wondered how many times he'd been there to know such a detail but remembered his passport.

They got out at a corner and she found herself in the midst of hundreds, or maybe thousands, of people wandering up and down two streets where one shop after another seemed to be selling antiques and flea market finds. Michael took her arm and began to lead her along. 'Mostly crap,' he said. 'Lots of reproductions and tourist trade nonsense. But some of the arcades are good.'

He moved her through the throng and into a wide doorway where a corridor was lined on each side with tiny shop after tiny shop. Each one had a counter and shelves stuffed with old jewelry, porcelain, knick-knacks, carvings, clocks, silver and everything Claire could think of and many things she couldn't. They moved through one arcade after another and Claire was astonished by all the stuff. So much stuff. And so many people searching and buying it.

'Oh, look,' Michael said and pointed at a glass case sitting on the counter. 'A Battersea box.' He turned to the elderly dealer. 'May we see that?' he asked. She nodded and opened the case.

'Very good condition,' she said. 'It's a nice one.' She took out a tiny object and handed it to Michael who, in turn, handed it to Claire.

It was a little box made of tin or something like it and painted with some sort of enamel. The bottom was blue-and pink-striped and the top was pink with a blue oval surrounded by a wreath of minuscule roses and leaves. Within the oval in a perfect script was a motto: *When this you see, remember me*. 'Do you like it?' Michael asked her. 'They were souvenirs in the late seventeen hundreds.'

'This one is probably a little later,' said the dealer. She turned and looked at Claire. 'Some of them were snuff boxes, and others they used to keep beauty spots in. They glued them on their face to cover pockmarks. Then some like these were love tokens.' She smiled, revealing long, yellow teeth.

'It's pretty, isn't it?' Michael asked.

'It's lovely,' Claire answered.

'Best price?' Michael asked the dealer.

'Well, I could knock off forty pounds, but I couldn't do any better than that. These are quite desirable.'

Michael took it from Claire's hands. He looked it over. 'Four hundred,' he said.

The woman blinked, as if she was about to protest, then thought better of it. 'Cash?' she asked.

'Cash,' he told her. And when she nodded he had the money out of his pocket and into her hands in a moment.

'Might I just wrap it up for you, sir?' she said.

'Oh, it's not for me. It's for the lady.'

'Well, aren't you a lucky girl?' the old woman said. And Claire silently agreed.

TWENTY

The rest of the day was enchanted. Claire wouldn't let Michael carry her gift although he offered to several times. Instead she held it and wondered if their time together had begun to mean more to him than a weekend diversion. She tried to keep her mind off that and to listen instead to Terry's pleasant anecdotes about the tiny police station in the base of Marble Arch, the fact that the small green sheds scattered around town were canteens for taxi drivers and that to be an official 'cabbie' you had to take a three-year course and pass a test called 'the knowledge'.

While Claire recognized some of the sights they passed she was mostly confused, but Michael held her hand and it was enough to make her completely happy. He took her to lunch at the National Portrait Gallery, somehow getting them a table by the window. The restaurant on the top floor gave an incredible view of slate roofs, an overview of the National Gallery, the steeple of the church of St Martin-in-the-Field and the back of Admiral Nelson, standing on his column.

Claire couldn't help but think of *Mary Poppins*. She had once heard that no music lover was mature until he could hear the 'William Tell Overture' without thinking of the Lone Ranger and she supposed she would have to grow out of childhood clichés before she could appreciate London in a sophisticated way.

'It's not every day a person can eat their bruschetta while they look at Nelson's ass.' Claire laughed, and didn't even object when Michael ordered some white wine. At home she rarely drank at dinner much less at lunch.

After a delicious lunch, to her surprise Michael didn't even stop to look at the portraits of the kings and queens, the writers and statesmen that lined the walls. 'Forget it,' he said. 'Life is too short. Let's make our own history.' And he whisked her back into the car, through Whitehall, past Horse Guards where the sentries stood unnaturally still, over Westminster Bridge and to the other side of the Thames.

'If you liked that view, I've got a better one.' They were at an enormous Ferris wheel, but one like Claire had never seen before. Each gondola was enclosed, rather like a plastic egg and large enough for a group of people. It was right on the river and the structure seemed both fragile and far too tall. There was, of course, a long line of people waiting to get on but once again gracefully and unobtrusively, Michael managed to get them right to the front and they had a compartment of their own. She could see why it was called the Eye, it gave the most incredible view of the city she could ever imagine seeing. It reminded her of Wendy in *Peter Pan* flying away from the Darlings' nursery window and out into the London sky.

'I wish I had thought to bring binoculars,' Michael said.

'Isn't it funny how people like to go to high places to use binoculars to see things back on the ground?'

He looked at her for a moment. 'You are a funny thing,' he said. And she didn't mind that he said it because he gave her a kiss.

The circle the Eye made took almost half an hour, and between the sights Michael had his hands all over her and they kissed almost enough to satisfy her. But when he stretched out on one of the seats and asked her to join him she drew the line. Even so, when they stepped out of the compartment she was flushed and tousled. He took her hand and led her back to Terry. 'I'm sorry we can't have dinner together,' he said. 'You're absolutely delicious. An angel cake.'

Terry opened the door for them and Claire felt as if she were a precious package, a jewel set in a luxurious setting. When Michael joined her she nestled against his side. 'Time for tea,' he announced. 'We're going to have it with a business friend of mine. He's a little bit stuffy but he's an MP and we get terrace privileges.'

Claire was too shy to ask what an MP was. But when they pulled up past Big Ben and parked in front of the Houses of Parliament she figured it out. Neville Chanbley-Smythe was almost as large as his name, a portly man not much older than Michael but with a big paunch, a beefy red face and a large forehead where hair seemed to be replaced by tiny beads of sweat. And though he was decidedly unattractive, he was extremely pleasant and brought them through the Gothic hallways to an outdoor terrace set right on the river.

The sun was strong enough for Claire to take off her raincoat and while Neville and Michael talked about the Euro she devoured tiny sandwiches and equally small cakes. She surreptitiously unbuttoned the waistband of her slacks and told herself she had better stop eating. Between the huge breakfasts, the delicious lunches, the lovely teas and the dinners with pudding she would wind up a size sixteen before she got home.

After the table had been cleared and a late afternoon dampness was setting in they left Neville Chanbley-Smythe, MP, and got back into the waiting car. 'It's back to the hotel,' Michael told Terry. And though there was a lot of traffic along the way, Claire got to see Pimlico, Victoria Station, Eaton Place and Sloane Square before they pulled up to the hotel.

When they got back to the suite Michael took her face in his hands and gave her one more kiss. 'I wish I had time for a quickie but I don't believe in them.' He smiled and she smiled back. 'I'm gonna have to shower, shave and change,' he said. 'I'm sorry I have to abandon you. Will you be all right?'

'Of course.' Claire had never been so right in her whole life.

'You might want to have a swim up on the roof. It's glassed in and it's one of the most beautiful pools in the world. And you can have a massage while you're at it. Just charge it to the room,' he said.

Claire, of course, hadn't brought a bathing suit and the idea of getting naked in front of a stranger to have her skin rubbed didn't strike her as pleasant. 'I'll be fine,' she told him and stretched out on the bed while he bathed. She must have fallen asleep because the next thing she knew he was kissing her on the forehead.

'Gotta go,' he said. 'Call down for some dinner. I'll be back late.'

She nodded sleepily, turned over and must have dozed for another hour. It wasn't until housekeeping knocked on the door to turn down the bed that she roused herself.

But it was only half-past six and she had no intention of wasting an evening in a hotel room – no matter how luxurious it was. She changed into her other slacks, her sweater and a pair of more comfortable shoes. Then, with Abigail's guidebook in one pocket of her raincoat and her sterling safely in the other, she set out to explore a little bit of London at night.

She wasn't interested in clubs or discos. Instead she roamed the streets and squares on either side of Knightsbridge. There were blocks and blocks of red brick flats, each one perfectly kept, each balcony decked out with topiary trees or flower pots. Then there were older terraces of white townhouses, each with a set of columns placed at the entrance. And each with a perfectly manicured front yard not much bigger than a picnic blanket but where every blade of grass, rose bush, or stand of iris seemed perfectly placed and perfectly groomed.

The shops along Walton Street were closed, but each window glowed with seductive goods. Small paintings, cashmere sweaters, crocodile purses were displayed in still lives that made her crave them, though she knew she had absolutely no need of anything. The light was beginning to fade and fewer people were on the streets but Claire didn't feel the least bit nervous. Compared to New York, London felt safer than Tottenville.

After an hour or two, Claire had widened her circle of walking to Fulham Road and she realized she was hungry. She told herself there would be no starches, no salad dressing and no 'pudding' but she had to eat something. Just past the next corner an inviting glow of light on the sidewalk was the invitation to a little restaurant called 'The Stockpot'. Outside, a chalked board listed featured dishes and the prices seemed almost suspiciously modest. Claire peeked in the window and the place looked simple but clean.

She lingered over a dinner of poached plaice – a white fish – and peas, then refused even a look at the tempting dessert menu, had yet another cup of tea and took off again. She must have been tired because the walk back seemed very long. She hoped that she was walking off part of her dinner, or perhaps even a bit of her tea. No one was in the streets though it was only eleven o'clock. Still, she didn't mind, and walked through the dignified beauty of Eaton Square and Eaton Place without looking behind her even once.

She was greeted at the hotel by yet another attentive doorman. She realized she hadn't taken her key and told him so. 'Just get another one at the desk, madam.' She walked through the lobby to the front desk and marveled at how easy it was to correct a mistake when you were rich. The concierge was on the phone and motioned to her that he would be with her in a moment. As she stood there she longed to take her shoes off, but instead took a few steps backwards and sat in one of the barrel chairs in the lobby. She glanced to her right, through the large opened doors to the bar. Then her heart seemed to stop beating.

Michael was standing there, his back to her but his profile visible. He had his arm around a woman who was sitting on the stool beside him. Her legs were long and perfect, so were her feet and her shoes. It's just a business meeting, Claire told herself trying to get her heart to beat again. He told you he had a business meeting. She knew Michael was flirtatious and he certainly did business with women. But then, as if the gods despised denial, the woman put her arms around Michael and moved her hands down his back in the most suggestive way.

As if that wasn't enough she then put her head on his shoulder and from Claire's vantage point in the lobby she saw Katherine Rensselaer kiss Michael's neck. But how was it possible? Claire thought of the devastating note full in equal parts of Rensselaer pride and a relentless Wainwright character appraisal. How could a woman who had written such a note even consider returning to the man she had referred to more than once as a toad?

Then, in a visceral way Claire recalled Michael's love-making. Yes, she thought, it would be hard for a Rensselaer or any other woman to give that up forever. When he was smiling at you or kissing you or caressing your face or holding your hand Michael Wainwright was a prince. It was only when he turned his back on you that he became a toad.

His back was to her now, but Claire knew she couldn't linger. If he saw her she would die right there. She wondered for a moment why she felt so ashamed when it was his behavior that was so reprehensible? But she probably deserved it. She was so very, very stupid.

The concierge hung up the phone. 'How can I help you?' he asked.

Of course, her universe had changed since she had stood at his counter only a moment before. How could he help her? He could commit a double murder in the bar but she thought even a man with his dedication to service wouldn't do that. Perhaps, however, he could supply her with an overdose of sleeping pills. That might be more realistic. She sat there stunned and frozen. The concierge waited patiently. 'I've forgotten my key,' she said at last. And her voice had the old tone of shyness and defeat in it.

She imagined what Tina would say if she told her about this, and how, no matter how hard she begged, Tina would retell the story all over the office. Even if she didn't tell, Tina would watch Michael go back to Katherine Rensselaer and Claire would be put in her place. Flushed with shame, Claire took the key the concierge handed her and went to the elevator as quickly as she could. Worse than seeing Michael with Katherine would be having Katherine and Michael seeing her.

She couldn't get to the room fast enough. Once there she opened the closet, took out her bag and forced herself to carefully fold her clothes and her other belongings, stowing them all away. When she was done she zipped the bag up again and put it back in the closet. She took off the things she was wearing, folded them neatly over the chair and put on not only her nightgown but also her robe. She wondered if Michael would return at all, then figured that even if he and Katherine took a room at the hotel he would come back for his clothes if not for her.

She got into bed, making herself as small as possible, curling into a fetal position hugging the very edge of the mattress. The thought occurred to her that Michael might actually come back and want to make love. The idea was horrible, but as the minutes ticked away and became hours she knew she was safe. Broken in spirit, perhaps, but safe.

She cried a little but repeated over and over that she had expected nothing and had gotten something. And all the rest didn't matter.

Of course it did. And if only he had waited until he was back in New York before he returned to his women, she thought she would have been prepared to bear it. But this . . . this was too unexpected, too flagrant for her to swallow. She wondered if his business meetings on Thursday and Friday had included 'nooners' with Katherine. The idea sickened her. Michael Wainwright was free to sleep with anyone he wanted, but he wasn't free to go from them to her.

She was still awake when he came in but she feigned sleep. He undressed quietly and she had to use all her self-control not to cry out when he got into bed beside her. Soon, though, she heard his breathing deepen into sleep. She lay there, more humiliated and unhappy than she had ever been. For a while the misery was so heavy in her chest that she had to struggle with each breath. On the whole planet there was nobody who knew exactly where she was right now or how she was feeling, and she wasn't sure there was anybody who would understand or care. After what seemed like a long time in the dark a thought pierced her misery. Since nobody knew or cared about her unhappiness she might as well try to be happy. The tiny thought was like a small star of light in the darkness. Then, as dawn began to turn the sky gray over the roofs of London, the idea grew.

TWENTY-ONE

Claire was careful to get up, bathe and dress before Michael was awake. Somehow the thought of him seeing her naked or even partially undressed was intolerable. As she brushed her teeth she observed herself in the mirror. Her gray eyes looked sadly back at her, but other than that she seemed composed. 'You have no regrets,' she told her reflection.

And she didn't. Michael Wainwright had given her a precious gift. London had opened her eyes. It had made her aware that there were other worlds out there. And unlike with her reading, which had introduced her to many different locales and ways of life, this trip had inserted her into the picture in a way she never had been before. Lying beside Michael she had realized that she didn't have to go back. There was something exciting and at the same time deeply calming about London. She liked the street life, the pubs, the little cafés and the friendly transport system. The low rise buildings, the beautiful architecture and the wonderful parks made it . . . she searched for the word. Comfortable? No, it was more stimulating, although it was comfortable too. But it wasn't simply interesting, which many places might be. What it felt, when she was out in the streets or the markets or the shops, was . . . right. It felt right.

She heard movement outside the closed bathroom door. She put on a little lip gloss and some mascara and felt ready to face him. She packed her few cosmetics into her purse and, to her own surprise, she took a small bottle of bath gel. What could it hurt? She composed herself. There would be no confrontation, no accusation. Michael Wainwright owed her nothing, and he hadn't even lied to her. For all she knew, his meeting with Katherine Rensselaer was partly business. And he was free to do what he wanted.

She looked at herself one more time and felt pleased with what she saw. She was wearing the self-made armor of her sweater with the pearl earrings; her face had a very slight flush, either from the bath or her nerves, and she looked as good or better than she ever had. She felt as confident as Claire could feel. She joined Michael.

He was in his robe, on the telephone, holding a cup of coffee in his hand. He lifted his eyebrows and smiled at her as he gave her the nod that meant 'just one more minute'. She went over to her bedside table and checked the drawer again to make sure nothing was in it. She had been careful to pack everything, but might as well make sure.

'All right. Well, I'll take care of it,' Michael said into the mouthpiece. There was a pause. 'Yep, good talking to you too.' Claire idly wondered who he could be talking business with on a Sunday morning but internally shrugged. It truly was none of her business she reminded herself.

'I'll order breakfast,' Michael told her. 'What would you like?'

'I'm not hungry,' Claire told him.

'Are you sure? We probably won't eat until lunch on the plane. And we don't have much time. We have to leave by noon. You'll have to pack.'

'I'm already packed,' Claire told him.

'Oh. Good.' He put the coffee cup down and opened the closet door. He sighed. 'I hate packing,' he said. 'The worst part of travel. But going back isn't so bad. Everything's dirty, and you can just throw it all into your bag and pick up clean stuff at home.'

Claire thought about the neatly folded contents of her

bag and the absolute absence of anything she'd want to wear in the closet at home. Michael pulled out his suitcase and put it onto the bed.

'So you're all ready to go to the airport,' he said.

'I'm not going,' Claire told him.

He paused then turned around and looked at her. 'What do you mean?' he asked. 'We have to leave by noon.'

'No. I don't. I'm not going,' she repeated.

'What are you talking about? The flight leaves at three. As it is, I'm cutting it close.'

'I'm not going to be on the flight,' Claire said. 'But thank you very much.'

Michael sat down on the bed beside his open bag. He looked at her, really looked at her, for the first time that morning. If he had an inkling of what she'd been through overnight he didn't let it show. 'Are you all right?' he asked.

'I'm fine. But I'm not going back.'

'You're not going back today?'

Claire took her coat down out of the closet. It really was a good thing that she had bought it. She shrugged into it. 'I may not be going back ever,' she said. 'I'll have to see.'

'What are you talking about?' Michael asked, for the first time showing irritation, but Claire steeled herself. He might be a boss back in New York but he wasn't a boss here. She had nothing to fear from his moods she reminded herself. 'Claire, have you gone crazy?'

Claire shook her head. 'I've been crazy,' she told him. 'But now I'm quite sane, thank you.'

'Claire, you have a job to get back to.'

Claire smiled and shook her head. 'I'm not like you, Michael. It's not much of a job.'

He walked closer and put a hand on each of her shoulders. 'But you have family . . .'

'It isn't much of a family,' she told him with a shrug that described her feeling for them as well as freeing his hands.

His face changed – it was easy for her to read him – for a moment she saw the guilty little boy he might sometimes have been.

'Is this about last night?' he asked cautiously.

She would save what pride she could. 'What about last night?' she asked. And before he could go on she continued. 'You know there isn't anything real between us. It's been a lovely weekend. Thank you very, very much. I just think I'd like to stay on.'

She could see the relief on his face as he determined – wrongly – that he hadn't been busted. He crossed his arms over his chest and towered over her. 'I don't have time for this nonsense now,' he said. 'We can get something to eat at the airport.'

Claire went into the living room where her wheelie bag was waiting. She'd left the handle out for a quick getaway. Michael followed her. 'You don't understand,' she said. 'I'm staying on.'

A look of incredulity spread across his face. 'You can't stay,' he said. 'How much money have you got?'

'Seven hundred and eighteen dollars,' she told him.

'Christ. This suite costs more than that per night.'

'Well, I won't be staying here then, will I?' Claire heard the slightly nasty tone in her voice and pulled it back. She had to remember that she felt nothing but gratitude toward Michael. He had brought her here and she was grateful, and the fact that he didn't have a clue as to who she was, was not something for her to be nasty about.

'How will you live?' he asked.

'I'll work,' she said.

'You don't have a work visa. They're very difficult to get.'

Claire shrugged. 'Then I'll find a job that doesn't require one.' She smiled at him. 'I'm a lot lower on the financial food chain than you are.' Despite the smile, she was finding it difficult to keep a pleasant tone and his paternal arrogance did not sit well on him. 'I'll be all right,' she said. 'I want to thank you for everything. It's been wonderful.' She walked back and gave him a kiss on the cheek.

He blinked and almost flinched away. She was very close to his face, but that view receded as she used all her self-control to turn and walk down the hall, her bag squeaking behind her. 'Isn't it odd that we figured out how to build space shuttles before thinking of putting wheels on suitcases?' she asked, then turned the hallway corner and walked out of his life, she thought, forever.

TWENTY-TWO

Claire came out of the underground and pulled her wheelie bag down Camden High Street. In bed beside Michael she had realized that she did not have to go back with him. She could stay on and savor London. She didn't know how long her money would last or how long she could manage to stay but in the dark, at the hotel, the idea had been balm to her wounded self-worth. Sometime between getting on the tube, though, and getting off, her courage had deserted her. She felt foolish and lost, literally and figuratively. How would she get back? And where would she go back to? Perhaps like Hansel and Gretel, she should have left a trail of breadcrumbs behind her. But like the two of them she had a family that wouldn't welcome her back. What was ahead? Starvation in a witch's cage?

Michael's thoughtless discarding of her wasn't much different from the way her mother, Fred and even her father had behaved. Her mother didn't want her around, Fred went away and didn't bother to keep in touch and her father, for all the love he had professed, left her without any provision for the future.

Eventually she had realized that she had to get off the tube somewhere, and she'd read that Camden had a big Sunday market. She'd liked Portobello market, so she thought she'd give this one a try and then at least she'd have some entertainment while she decided what to do.

Now, for a few moments, Claire felt panic: Her act of false bravado was actually an act of idiocy. But the March sunlight warmed her face and the incredible bustle around her was impossible to ignore. After all, she was in a new place and it certainly didn't look like Staten Island, Manhattan, or even Portobello Road.

The street was jammed with shoppers and almost all of them were young. None of the middle-aged 'antiquers'. This was new merchandise. Hundreds, or more likely thousands of tourists and locals walked in throngs on the sidewalk and in the road. They wore leather and piercing, cashmere and silk, denim and flannel. She had never seen such a wide variety of ages, nationalities, styles, and types.

And the shops were – well, they were also like nothing Claire had ever seen. Many of them seemed to have half of their wares out on the High Street itself. Shoes, leather wares, backpacks, purses, new cheap clothes, vintage clothes, coats and jackets spilled out almost onto the road in racks, on tables, in boxes. As if all that wasn't a riotously confusing enough bazaar, the bizarre architecture, where each shop seemed to have some enormous representation of what they sold extending out from the upper floors and onto the street, added to the visual madness. Giant shoes, a pair of Levi's too big for Paul Bunyan, and a biker jacket that looked like a size XXXXL.

But the energy was great. The people walked along eating, laughing, talking, selling and buying in the liveliest way. Street hawkers yelled and joked and cajoled potential customers. If the English had a souk she supposed this would be what it was like and she was glad she was here. In fact, though she didn't have a place to stay that night, a way to earn a living, a bank account or any friends or family nearby that she could go to, she felt happier and more content than she could ever remember feeling. She would worry about all the rest of it later. For the moment, at least, it was enough for her to walk in the pale sunlight among all the colorful action and feel – for a change – as if she were a small part of the scene.

But, as usual, she was alone. She thought of Michael again, probably at the airport by now. She shouldn't miss him and she wouldn't miss him. He certainly wouldn't be missing her. Aside from his flash of anger, which was probably nothing more than surprise, she knew he felt nothing for her. Why should she feel anything for him? She buttoned the top of her raincoat and shrugged her shoulders. She felt cold, and her empty stomach gave a little nudge. It was stupid to think about Michael. She simply wouldn't allow it. She had made a choice. She was going to be glad that she did. Like Abigail Samuels, she had her dignity. And she had the opportunity for an adventure; this, she reminded herself, was a lot more than she usually had.

Claire found herself on a corner looking at a street sign. She was on Chalk Farm Road and the name alone made her smile. There was something about this city: its terminology, its quaintness mixed with its modernity that charmed her. She felt differently about being here in a crowd than she had about the crowds of New York, where she'd always felt excluded.

Well, she was hungry and decided she would walk until she found somewhere to get a breakfast or – she smiled to herself – perhaps a ploughman's special. She had done that without Michael and she had enjoyed it. As she walked along Chalk Farm Road she crossed a small bridge. Beneath it ran a little river. Looking more closely, Claire noticed a lock. Perhaps it was a canal. At any rate it was very pretty, edged with cobblestones and weeping willow trees. That nineteenth-century touch was delightful among the twenty-first-century crowds and noise.

From her perch on the bridge she could see a huge warehouse beside it, decked out on many levels with shops, terraces and people. She walked under a railway trestle and beyond the shops where leather jackets, sneakers and the like were being sold and into a far fancier area with some galleries, boutiques and several bistros.

There, at last, the crowd thinned. Perhaps half a mile from the underground she found just what she was looking for. The café looked like a working man's diner. Outside there was a triangular signboard on which was scrawled in chalk, the fact that breakfast was served all day. Tired and hungry but exhilarated, Claire opened the door, pulling her wheelie bag behind her.

The place was filled with men and they seemed to be very busy either just eating or eating and talking to one another. She could smell the bacon and her mouth watered. But, despite her hunger and her relief at being about to sit down, she hesitated. She looked around in some dismay. There were only four long tables, not individual ones and she would have to take her place beside one of these strangers. Too shy to do it, she turned to leave when she heard a woman's voice call out to her, 'Is it breakfast, then?'

She turned back to see a dumpy middle-aged blond wearing a pilled sweater and wrapped in a very dirty apron. She was gesturing to a seat and smiling. Because of the smile and Claire's hunger (and despite the woman's caked make-up and dirty hair) she sat where she was told. 'Move over, Burt,' the blond said to the small man in the chair beside the empty one. He was eating his breakfast with a spoon and had his arm protectively surrounding his plate. The waitress looked down at him. 'She won't touch your food, you silly bloke.' She looked up at Claire. 'Village idiot,' she said. 'Harmless when he takes his teeth out.' Half of the men in the café laughed. Burt picked his head up.

'Better to have shop-bought teeth than to be as long in the tooth as you are,' he said and there was more laughter.

'Oh, you.' The waitress looked back at Claire. 'They're a bad lot, all of them, but they don't mean no harm.'

Claire was relieved. The man wasn't impaired and it was

clearly safe to sit down. She thanked the waitress, who continued to stand over her. 'A slap-up breakfast?' she asked. Claire wasn't exactly sure what that was but she nodded her head. It had taken all of her courage to sit down and there didn't seem to be any menus, just another unreadable blackboard. 'Tea?' the waitress asked. Claire nodded again. 'With or without?'

Claire preferred her tea black with lemon, but didn't think slices of fruit would be available here. 'Without,' she said. Moments later she was surprised when the waitress put a cup of milky tea in front of her. Before she could object the waitress was gone, returning with a plate the size of a hubcap and filled almost to overflowing with two fried eggs, grilled tomatoes, thick slices of streaky bacon, fried mushrooms, French fries – and baked beans! Claire looked at the plate with dismay. If she began right then she wouldn't be able to finish eating until dinnertime. Then she realized that was a good thing. With her limited money she might be down to two meals a day in no time. She began to eat, avoiding the beans as best she could. Though incredibly greasy, everything was surprisingly good.

Perhaps I'm just born to be a peasant, she thought. Though the breakfasts at the Berkeley had been exquisite she actually preferred this. She wondered whether Michael had ever, or would ever, eat a meal in a place like this one. Probably not, she decided, though he might have done as a lark after some late night carousing at Wharton. She took a bite of the eggs and looked around her. The problem wasn't the food. Being without Michael and his privileges would not really bother her but being without Michael – or anyone – as a companion was hard. She felt self-conscious as the only woman – besides the buxom waitress – and the only American. Other people were alone but they did all seem to know one another, at least casually. She sighed. Why did it seem that her lot in life was to always be alone? If Michael had been there, unlikely as that thought was, she would have had someone to joke with, someone to point out the strange little man in the corner to. She sighed again and took a tentative mouthful of beans. Well, she told herself, she would have to start accepting her state. The men who liked her made her feel lonely, even when she was with them. And the men she liked were not likely to stay with her long – or at all.

She ate in silence for a while. Burt, next to her, was also silent and that was a relief. Around her there was some talk of Arsenal, and Claire listened to some argument about it. At her table there seemed to be some good-natured teasing between three men, one of whom they called 'Badger'. Claire wasn't sure if that was the man's first name, last name, an abbreviation for 'bachelor' or – probably unlikely – a reference to *The Wind in the Willows*. He was getting married – or had just been. Or perhaps had never been. She found it was difficult to understand their speech.

'Another tea?' the waitress asked, showing up at Claire's shoulder. Claire nodded then tried to work out how she could get it black. 'With or without?' the waitress asked again and Claire had the courage to ask.

'Without what?'

'Without sugar,' the woman said, as if only a simpleton would ask the question.

Claire picked up the cup. The china was as thick as her finger. 'I'd like it without sugar and without milk.'

'Without milk? Daft.' The waitress shrugged. 'Is that the way you all drink it?' Claire nodded. The waitress shook her head. 'No wonder you've picked such arses for presidents. You drink your tea all wrong.'

'Well, I have always wondered why we have fifty candidates for Miss America and only two for president,' Claire said. Most of the men as well as the waitress laughed.

She looked at Claire. 'You are from the States, then? You're not a Canadian or an Aussie?'

'No. I'm from New York.'

This started an entire flood of conversation. People's brothers, children, mothers, or friends had been to New York and to Orlando. Burt, who had cleaned the plate beside hers, smiled at her with his store-bought teeth. 'Me wife's been to Orlando. Went with her sister. Do you like it?'

'I've never been,' Claire told him. 'I live in New York.'

'Haven't been to Orlando? And you live right there?' He shook his head. 'How do you get to Disney World, then?'

'I've never been,' Claire repeated and decided that it was best not to add that she'd never wanted to go. But because Burt was eyeing her she smiled apologetically. 'I don't like Mickey.'

'She doesn't like Mickey Mouse!' he said aloud.

'I thought that was illegal in the States,' a younger man with red whiskers commented. There was some laughter, which made Claire's face flush.

'It is,' she said. 'I did a term in prison, but escaped. That's why I'm here. I'm wanted.'

This raised a lot of good-natured laughter. After that Claire kept her eye on her plate and was left alone, though a few men went on to chafe the ginger-haired man about something else she didn't comprehend. While they were clearly working men, Claire was surprised to hear that none of them used profanity. No one called anyone else a 'dumb mother-fucker', the way Jerry and his pals would have at the drop of a bean. And there were no fart jokes, which beans would have automatically introduced in Jerry's world back home. She wondered if the English knew 'beans, beans, the musical fruit', a favorite poem of Jerry's.

Claire finished as much of everything (but the musical beans) as she could. When the waitress came by asking if she wanted yet another cup she shook her head and was presented with a tiny piece of paper with some numbers scribbled on it. Her meal was surprisingly cheap. Less than five dollars, as close as Claire could figure it. She put down some money, including a big tip, and when the waitress came back to collect it Claire screwed up her courage and asked if the woman 'might know about an inexpensive guest house or hotel nearby'.

'Well, this isn't much of a tourist zone,' the waitress said. 'Not where people stay, anyway – they mostly just come to the market at the weekends.' She turned and faced the back. 'Hey, Jacko, do you know a good B & B nearby?'

There were several shouted suggestions but the waitress condemned whatever incomprehensible things were said. Then, when a deep voice issued out of the door to the back everyone stopped talking. 'Me brother's sister-in-law Madge has a place,' the voice – possibly Jacko's – said. 'She's cheese-paring. She don't do breakfasts, and I know she stews her tea, but she isn't a slut so things would be tidy enough.'

Claire wasn't warmed by the mention of the woman as a slut, but the waitress looked down at Claire and patted her shoulder. 'Interested?' she asked. 'I'll get you the address if you like.' Claire had no other choice so she nodded.

While the waitress was gone Claire surreptitiously added another coin to the stack for payment. Maybe she had found not only a place to eat but a place to sleep for the night. The waitress returned with another tiny piece of paper. An address, almost indecipherable, was scrawled there. *238A Chamberley Terrace*. Claire read it out loud to make sure she had it right.

'That's it, luv. See here. Her name is Mrs Watson.' Then the waitress – along with several of the customers – gave her directions, all of which seemed contradictory. Claire took out her *A to Z*, and Burt located Chamberley Terrace, which didn't seem to be too distant.

Claire thanked them all and set off again, this time with a full stomach and even more optimism. Who had told her that the British were reserved?

TWENTY-THREE

The farther Claire walked away from Camden Lock the less picturesque the surroundings became. Though the name sounded elegant, there were no window boxes or front yard plantings along Chamberley Terrace. There weren't even front gardens. Just a row of small houses with doors opening right on the street and an ugly, long new building on the other side. The houses were small brick ones, almost all of them with paint flaking off the window frames. Here and there, like a snaggle tooth in a row of dull smaller teeth was a larger but not necessarily better-kept house. When she found her destination, it wasn't very appealing.

Mrs Watson, Claire was relieved to see, was far too old to be a slut. Skinny and dry she looked more like a witch with permed hair. She answered Claire's knock, opened the door and hustled her into the dim foyer. Claire was amazed to find the house so much bigger than it had looked from the outside. The woman led her up three dim floors which Claire noticed had at least six rooms each, and finally they reached the tiny dark available room. Mrs Watson said she charged eighteen pounds a night, and that it was an enormous bargain, but 'Mind you, there are no accounts. Tea and toast are all in but not a cooked breakfast.' This confused Claire but she was suddenly so tired she nodded her head and handed Mrs Watson a twenty-pound note.

'Here you go.' Her new landlady fished into the pocket

of her apron (Claire hadn't seen an apron in New York in fifteen years and today she'd already seen two) and handed Claire one of those strange, gold-centered two-pound coins. Claire nodded her thanks and was left alone.

Claire unzipped her suitcase and then looked around the room. She was both thrilled and apprehensive. It certainly wasn't the Berkeley but it wasn't just a room, it was *her* room. The first place she'd ever rented on her own in her whole life. The room was tiny – with just enough space for the bed under the window and a wardrobe on the opposite wall. There wasn't even a bedside table. Instead, a kitchen chair with a small lamp stood beside the head of the bed. There was a small chipped sink, and a bathroom down the hall, apparently to be shared with three strangers from the other rooms. The view was rather dismal – a wall of ugly, new windows in an ugly glazed brick building.

She opened the wardrobe, empty except for a sad mixed flock of hangers. There were a couple of bent wire ones, a plastic one that seemed to be a child's, and three wooden ones, one of which had the name of a real hotel printed on it. There were two thin towels on the shelf above the hangers. Claire took them down, put them on the bed and began to unpack. She found the act very soothing. Her shoes went on the floor of the wardrobe. Above it her trousers, her single dress and her blouses hung in a little huddle together. She folded her sweaters and put them on the shelf above, along with her underwear, since there was no bureau or drawer to put them in. Her nightgown and robe she hung on the hook on the back of the door. Her bag was now empty, except for her cosmetics and toiletries, which she placed on the sink.

Then, before she stowed her case under the bed she saw the little package wrapped in newspaper. It was the enameled box from Michael. Slowly, almost reluctantly, she took it out and unwrapped it. The lovely colors and the two-hundred-year-old craftsmanship glowed in her hand, a spot of perfect beauty in the dingy room. *When this you see, remember me.* As if she could forget. How could she have thought, even for a moment, that Michael would think of her? By now he would be in the departure lounge, deeply involved in his workload for Monday, and she was most likely the farthest thing from his mind. Perhaps by now he already had a date lined up with Katherine or one of the half-dozen other women he had available to him. Claire's lips trembled.

To be fair, the little box was honest. What it said was that she should remember him, not that he would remember her. And, she firmly reminded herself, she never expected that he would remember her. She could choose to be bitter and miserable or she could choose to be glad for the spot of beauty and days of pleasure that she had received. She thought of Abigail then and Abigail's sound advice. She reminded herself that the only thing she had to be bitter about was that she was not a Katherine Rensselaer or anybody remotely like her. In good conscience she couldn't even be bitter that Michael had lied to her and made a 'business date' when it was clearly with a woman. For all she knew they might have talked business. Even if he had slept with her it was no business of Claire's. Michael hadn't indicated that he loved her or acted as if she was anything special to him. All he had done was invite her on a trip. He had only done so after his other possibilities had been tapped out. Claire reminded herself that she had absolutely nothing to be angry about.

Fact was that she was not, and would never be, in the same class as Katherine Rensselaer. Her dad had been a failure, her mother had never even read a novel, her brother was a private in the Army and she herself had not even finished college. Her clothes were inferior, her body inferior and her education inferior. If some of that wasn't her fault, some of it was. To think of herself with Michael was ridiculous.

She looked down at the little box. She would keep it. And, no doubt, whenever she did see it she would think of him. The fact that she was nowhere on his radar didn't change anything. But she wouldn't let herself be sentimental. It was a pretty box, she would enjoy looking at it and she would never confuse it with a love-token. She wrapped it up, put it in her suitcase and forced herself to smile.

Once the box was out of sight and she was settled in, Claire experienced a feeling of great accomplishment, almost as if she had built the room, not just rented it. She took her knitting and her book and placed them on the bed near the very flat pillow. Then she sat down, took off her shoes and considered her options.

She'd never done anything as mad as this, but somehow she no longer felt nervous or concerned. Instead of worrying, she just reached into her purse, took out her little notebook and began to do some arithmetic. If the room were eighteen pounds a night, and a good breakfast with tip was four pounds fifty, and she took a bus or the tube some place one way for a few pounds and later walked all the way back that would cost her almost twenty-four pounds per day. And that didn't include any other meals, laundry, admission fees to sights, and certainly no tea and scones on the House of Commons terrace. Claire smiled at the memory. But didn't allow herself to dwell on it. Not on the sex, not on the world of luxury and not on the humiliation. Right now Mr Wonderful was about to get on a plane, moving ever further away from her until, by this evening, they would be separated by more than three thousand miles. That was just fine. Because they were separated by more than that in social terms when they worked on the same floor at Crayden Smithers. Claire wouldn't allow herself to feel separated from Michael. They had never been together.

She looked back down at the pad and continued to work at the math. If she gave herself another four pounds a day for groceries and incidentals, that brought the total up to twenty-eight pounds. She took out her wallet and carefully counted her money. She had about nineteen days in which to find a job. The thought didn't daunt her. She wasn't afraid of working and she had always been able to work hard. She smiled to herself. Somehow, effortlessly, she had managed to do this thing and she felt more adventurous, more intrepid, than any Cortez could ever have felt. Because explorers were, by nature, brave while she, by her nature, was not. And yet she was doing this.

She thought for a moment about her mother. She had told her she was taking 'a few days off'. She said Atlantic City. After all, she still had her open return ticket tucked beside her passport in the pocket of her suitcase. With that thought, panic struck and she had to scrabble under the bed, pull out her wheelie bag and check to be sure the passport and ticket were there. Of course they were, and her heart stopped pumping at the ridiculous rate it had assumed. In twenty days, if everything went wrong, she could always go back. But, she told herself, things would not go wrong. Claire promised herself she was never going back to Crayden Smithers or Staten Island.

She knew it with as much certainty as she knew the passport and ticket were safely in her possession. But once she'd formed that thought she was compelled, despite the ridiculousness of it, to check once again to be sure she had both. She told herself that would be the last time she did it and, feeling delighted with and sure of herself, she decided to plan the rest of her day. On the way out the door she ran into – almost literally – a woman younger, paler and slimmer than she.

'Oh, I'm sorry,' the woman apologized, though it was clearly Claire's fault. 'Do you live here?' she asked. Claire nodded and introduced herself. 'Yer from the States, then?' the woman asked. Claire nodded again. 'I'm Maudie O'Connor. I'd love to go to the States.' Just then two children ran up the stairs and grabbed Maudie's slender legs.

'Do you baby-sit them?' Claire asked. Maudie O'Connor looked at her, clearly confused. Maybe they didn't say 'baby-sit' in London. 'Are you their nanny?'

'I'm their mammy,' Maudie said. Claire could hardly believe that a girl that young had two children. She smiled at both.

'Do you live here?'

Maudie nodded. 'Until we get thrown out, which is a bit of a snag,' she said. 'Shhh. Hush up, you scamps. Don't get up to any of your jiggery-pokery. Do you want that Watson witch down on us again?' She hustled the tow-haired boys down the hall. 'Nice to meet yer,' she called back. Claire nodded and went out to the street.

It had felt like a long walk to Chamberley Terrace but she had been pulling her wheelie bag, her stuffed purse and her canvas sack. She decided she would take the walk back to the market and look around. It seemed such a wild mix of people, goods, and foods and the setting looked like some abandoned Dickensian workhouse. She took her *A to Z*, consulted the streets she'd already walked, put the little book of maps in her canvas bag, just in case, and added her change purse and a lip gloss. That was all she needed to carry. She changed her shoes to the more comfortable pair and regretted, for a moment, that she hadn't brought her sneakers. But these would do fine and she was pleased to see that when she looked in the mirror built into the wardrobe she didn't quite look like a tourist. She didn't quite look like a native either. Well perhaps she could be a bit mysterious for the first time in her life.

Traveling light, she thought, must be the secret to happiness. Looking into the wardrobe with her few but more than adequate clothes was deeply satisfying. She didn't have one thing more than she needed and it felt liberating. She took her toiletries to the bathroom, which was rather grim and was literally what it was called – there was no shower – and then almost skipped down the short flight of steps and out the door.

She was very proud when she managed to get back to the bridge on Camden High Street without even looking at her *A to Z*. She'd gotten confused once where a bendy street had tempted her to go in the wrong direction but she had recognized a small grocery store and made the right choice by walking past it.

If anything now, at half-past two, the market was busier than ever. Claire felt a little tug in her stomach at the thought that Michael Wainwright would probably be boarding his flight and sitting down in First Class at this very moment, but she cheerfully reflected (in a phrase Tina frequently used) that she'd been there and done that and had never been here and done this.

From the bridge she could see a stairway from the street down to the lock and the willowed path that ran along it. Claire followed that first. The canal seemed to go on and on, a brick-bordered river that wound along between steep-sided warehouses. It seemed romantic and industrial at the same time – a cross between Venice and Pittsburgh (though Claire had been to neither one).

But as the path became deserted she became nervous. Anything could happen in this empty spot. How many bodies had turned up in the canal? Before she got morbid she turned back to the overabundant noise and crowds of the market. From the canal there were a dozen entrances into the courtyard and warehouse, each more inviting than the last. Some were up iron stairs, others through brick archways, and a couple of large ones led through gates that at one time must have enclosed the manufacturing yard. She went through an arched door in the wall and came out on a cobblestone ground where dozens – perhaps hundreds – of tables were set up with every conceivable kind of goods, and quite a few that seemed inconceivable to Claire. Tibetan jewelry covered a table beside another one where South American wooden bowls were stacked. A step further led her past African masks and sculpture to a table of T-shirts and next there was modern silver jewelry being sold by the designer.

She turned a corner and was hit with a scent-wall of incense, which was being sold by a couple who, between them, had more face piercings than Claire had seen on all of Staten Island. She tried not to stare, but the next table had vendors with multi-colored punked-out hair. And though they weren't pierced – at least not in a visible place – one had a spider-web tattoo across his face.

Here, however, in the sort of medieval market-day atmosphere, no one seemed particularly freaky or freaked out. The spider man was wrapping a purchase, handed a middle-aged lady in a crocheted hat a bag and her change and said, 'Thank you, luv.'

In fact, everyone seemed very polite. Whenever she was jostled, someone excused themselves. She did make sure to keep her bag tight under her arm but happily wandered from stall to stall examining everything from Peruvian sweaters (very loosely knit) to hand embroidered saris from Bengal.

After more than an hour she wandered out of the enclosure and on her way back along Chalk Farm Road she found an entirely separate entrance to a market even more interesting. It was in a far less tidy warehouse, and the interior was musty, filled with room after room of stalls. They had the sort of clutter that Claire used to see at Tina's school, Our Lady Help of the Christians, Christmas bazaar – ashtrays, vases, figurines, and dishes – but all of it seemed so much older and quainter. There were stalls that specialized in fifties memorabilia, ones with antique dolls and toys, tables and tables of old costume jewelry, then to Claire's surprise and delight she found a small table in one corner with nothing but old knitting bags, needles, and patterns. Thinking of her two skeins of wool and the needles back in her room made Claire feel comfortable, as if she had someone at home waiting for her. But these new, or rather old, needles were so tempting.

'They're vintage,' a young woman with her hair in a forties snood told her. 'The ones there are Bakelite. Collectors' items, really.'

Claire looked at the dozens of colorful needles – yellow, green, magenta, and baby blue – each with a different colored cap that had the needle size inscribed on it. It would be wonderful to have another pair or two, and when Claire thought of the hands that must have held these needles, knitting with them decades ago, she felt such a strong yearning to own some that . . .

'How much are they?' Claire was prepared to hear any number, not that she could have afforded much.

'Two pounds the pair,' the woman told her. 'I could do you three pairs for five pounds.'

Claire couldn't believe her good luck. Somehow it seemed like an omen. She fished in her purse, found five pounds in coins and handed it over. While the needles were being wrapped, she looked with longing at a cretonne knitting bag with a stand. But didn't allow herself to even think about another purchase.

'Are you a collector?' the woman asked. Claire smiled. The idea of collecting something as practical as knitting needles never occurred to her.

'No,' she said, 'I'm a knitter. Do you know where I could buy yarn?'

'Haven't a clue, I'm afraid,' the woman told her. She handed her the needles wrapped in a bag. 'Most people want them for their looks.' Then she turned to talk to another browser and Claire walked away to continue looking round the market.

But the day grew cooler and she became tired. She also felt the beginnings of hunger. Well, she would have to learn to feast her eyes instead of her stomach. She told herself, quite sternly, that she had spent enough money for the day. She would walk back to Chamberley Terrace.

It was twilight, and this time the walk seemed very tiring.

As the light waned so, again, did her courage. She had been with Michael Wainwright for such a short time, just a few days. But she had had the week of looking forward to going away with him and the year before that of fantasizing. Now, she realized she had nothing. For even the fantasy had been exposed as ridiculous. Any time Mr Wonderful had spent with her had merely been time that Katherine Rensselaer had denied him.

Alone in the twilight in a city she did not know, among strangers, Claire felt loneliness again engulf her, almost as physical as the cold damp that came up from the sidewalk. She shivered. For the first time she asked herself what in the world she had done. She had whimsically turned her back on everything that she knew. She looked around her at the darkened street, the houses with lights just going on. Nobody in the whole world knew where she was right now, and there wasn't a house anywhere with lights on and people waiting for her. What had she done?

Just then, and only twenty feet away, a door opened and two women, one of them pulling a little grocery trolley, walked out into the street. They were chattering and, though Claire couldn't hear what either of them were saying, she heard one of them laugh. Clearly, they were friends, and she reminded herself she could make friends too. She straightened up, fastened the top button of her raincoat and stepped into the darkness with the determination of making a new life for herself.

TWENTY-FOUR

Chance plays a large part in life and – though given lip service – is rarely acknowledged on a daily basis. The smallest thing – the change of a traffic light or the twitch of a muscle – can alter everything. The next morning Claire was greeted by the noise of wind rushing through the branches of the trees on Chamberley Terrace. Claire wondered if it was an east wind, the magical one that blew in Mary Poppins.

She dressed and felt both very hungry and very cheerful. Tired the evening before, she'd consulted Abigail's guide and already knew how she would spend the day. But it wasn't the scheduled sights that changed her life. It was a single glance.

Claire was walking down a charming street of shops and was about to pass a small doorway when the cat sitting in the window beside it caught her eye. Had the cat not swung its tail at that moment, Claire never would have met the man who became so important to her.

The store was a used bookshop and almost unnoticeable. Claire was by no means the only person who had walked by without registering its existence. The windows – for there were two – were on either side of the door that was several steps down from the sidewalk. Now Claire noticed a hand-lettered sign over the door that said 'Books For Sale' and so, partly because of the cat and partly

167

because she had nothing more to read, she stepped down into the gloom.

A little bell jingled as the door banged against it. It was a surprisingly large store with long shelves of books running from front to back but, oddly, there was no sales counter or register in the front. Claire wondered for a moment what would stop a shoplifter from picking up any of the volumes on offer, turning around and walking back up the stairs.

The shop was quite dark, but as she stood hesitantly a switch must have been flicked and one of the seven rows of books was lit. Claire thought of Mary Poppins and her visits with her charges to the strange and magical shops that disappeared when Jane and Michael came back alone to look for them.

'Hello,' a voice called and Claire was reassured enough to move down the dimly lit corridor of books to the back. There, Poppins-like, was a tiny living room of sorts. Two armchairs, a desk, a small table set for tea and a glass-fronted cabinet made a pleasant little room. The threadbare Persian rug was piled with books, but that only increased the charm for Claire.

Most charming of all was the long thin man standing at the table pouring tea out of a tarnished silver teapot. 'Oh, hello,' he said. 'Cup of tea?' He looked like a line drawing, perhaps by Modigliani: sloping shoulders, long arms, long legs, and a long but handsome face with a very long nose. If the Pied Piper ran a bookstore he would look like this. His hair, almost the sandy brown color of Claire's own, was fine as thread and cut in a surprising bowl shape that Claire hadn't seen on a child over the age of five. It was almost medieval. The haircut, however, suited him and under the bangs – which she was to learn was called a fringe – round eyes looked mildly at her as if she had been expected.

'Yes, please,' Claire said. There were four or five teacups on mismatched saucers on the tray. The colors and patterns fought madly amongst themselves, as if a small flock of hummingbirds were perched there. He surveyed her mildly then looked back at the cups and saucers, obviously selecting based on some formula known only to him. For a moment Claire was reminded of the Mad Hatter's tea party but this man looked far too gentle to be mad. And all the cups did look clean.

'Shall I be Mum?' he asked, a tone of irony in his voice. She couldn't imagine why he would want to be silent, so she didn't respond, though she thought perhaps it was best for her to simply shake her head and leave. But then he picked up the milk pitcher and poured out some milk into the cup. Claire wondered again what one had to do to get tea without cream, but it was obviously too late to ask for it now. He poured milk into a second cup and in a moment had added tea. He put a tiny silver spoon on each saucer and handed one to her. Then he folded his long legs into one of the chairs. 'Are you looking for something special?' he asked.

Claire looked down at the teacup. It was very beautiful. Birds holding garlands darted over an azure ground. On the saucer roses and lilies of the valley alternated up to the gold rim. 'Not really,' Claire said in response to his question.

'Wonderful. I hate people looking for one specific book, one author. There are thousands to peruse. It's not as if these are first editions.'

Claire, for lack of a better thing to do, took a sip of the tea. It was strong and hot. She realized it was not only dim but also musty in the shop. The shopkeeper wore a sweater and a sports coat over it along with fingerless gloves. She shivered, and wished she had her scarf finished.

'Do sit down,' he offered. She gingerly obeyed him, sitting at the edge of an old leather-covered armchair. Looking around she realized the ceilings were at least twelve foot high and shelves ran not only up and down the aisles but they also covered the walls right up to the ceiling.

'How do you organize these?' she asked, her library science-self coming to the fore.

'Rather casually, I'm afraid,' he told her, as he turned to the tray, picked up a little silver tongs and dropped a lump of sugar into his cup. 'I had a plan, and adhered to it quite religiously for years, but I seem to have lost my faith.' He gestured to the right with his long hands. 'Originally, it was fiction to the left and non-fiction to the right. Fiction by authors, and alphabetical. Non-fiction by subject. But that plan began to bore me. I admit the practical virtue of it, but consistency being a hobgoblin and all I decided that time should play a factor and reorganized by eras.'

'Errors?' Claire asked, doubting his sanity more than ever. Was he talking about some organization based on misprints? She glanced at the thousands of volumes again. How many misprints could there be?

He took another sip of tea. 'Yes. You know, Georgian, Victorian, Edwardian, Pre-World War One, Between the Wars . . .' He stopped.

She realized he had been talking about eras and was glad she hadn't spoken. She was finding that here in London her slight reticence served her well. She looked at the darling mismatched cup and saucer and then noticed that her tiny teaspoon was shaped like a palm tree with a monkey cunningly holding onto the top of the tree.

'Of course,' the man continued, 'I saw the flaw of that system almost immediately. I mean what about nationality? The Great War was seen very differently by the American expatriates in Paris and the English at home. And you couldn't consider Flaubert Victorian. So then I thought . . .' he paused. 'I'm so terribly sorry,' he said. 'Would you care for sugar? And am I boring you?'

'No and no,' she said. 'Actually, at one time I planned to be a librarian.' Expecting praise or at least some positive acknowledgment he surprised her by shuddering.

'Oh, that library science stuff. Dewey Decimal? Do we care? What monstrous nonsense that was,' he said. 'Absolute subjectivity posing as objectivity. Keeping and arranging books is an art, not a science. I have worked out several different schemes for my non-fiction, all much better than Thomas Dewey's. By the way, I'm Toby Stanton.' He put his teacup down and reached forward, putting out his hand.

'I'm Claire Bilsop,' she said and shook his half-clad hand.

'Bilsop? English name I think. But you're from the States. New York?'

'Yes,' Claire told him. 'I never liked the Dewey Decimal system in the Tottenville library,' she admitted. 'When they taught it to us in grade school they said it was scientific but even then I thought it was subjective.'

'A woman of sense!'

The more she looked at Toby, the more Claire liked what she saw. He wore long but shapeless corduroy trousers and had one leg casually crossed over the other, showing brown socks with what looked like little embroidered lines from the ankle up. His eyes were very blue and his cheeks and the end of his nose quite pink.

'But, of course, the problem with creating a new categorization is that none is perfect and, in the end, each becomes deeply personal and arbitrary.' He smiled, then sighed. 'I reckon no one could find a volume here unless they had either psychoanalysed me for decades or dissected my brain.'

'Both options seem rather extreme,' Claire said. 'Perhaps just a card catalog to begin.'

Toby laughed. 'Aah, a rationalist. I like that.' He looked around again. 'The problem is, I'm so busy trying to perfect the arrangement that I haven't time to catalog them. And then, of course, people buy them, and that can completely change the relationship between one book and the next on a shelf. Are you in London long?'

Claire was taken by surprise. She supposed it was not a personal question, as most people had a clear answer: a week for holiday, term at school, a short visit to family. 'I don't know,' she said. 'I've never been here before. I'm seeing if I like it.'

'And how long have you been here?' he asked.

'Five days,' she said.

'And how do you like it so far?'

'I love it,' Claire said. 'I can't think of one thing I don't like. At least not yet.'

'Ah. Well, that may change. But certainly you won't be bored.'

'Certainly not,' Claire agreed and told him some of the things she had already done and seen.

Toby nodded and smiled. 'Ah, well, at the risk of being too clichéd I quote Johnson, "When a man is tired of London, he's tired of life." Recently in *The Times* I saw it attributed to Oscar Wilde. Can you imagine? God knows he did say an awful lot of clever things, but he didn't say everything. Whenever anything clever is quoted people just assume Wilde said it. Drives me wild. More tea?' Claire wasn't thirsty but she was delighted with this man so she nodded her head. 'Who are you?' he asked. 'The Quiet American?'

Claire had read the book and seen the movie and got the joke. She just shook her head. 'No,' she added. 'And the cat doesn't have my tongue either. Although it was your cat that brought me in here.'

'Ah, yes. Therein lies my entire marketing budget. The cat. Do you fancy cats?'

Claire shook her head again then remembered she had better speak. 'It's not that I don't like them,' she told him, 'I simply don't feel, well, you know . . .'

'You don't feel articulate?'

It would have been insulting, but there was something rather delightful in the way he said it. 'Actually, I'm articulate enough; I just didn't want to offend you, since you obviously are a cat . . .' she paused. 'Fancier.' It was a funny term.

'Me? Oh, not at all. I mean there's nothing wrong with George, but it's not my cat – just wandered in one day and hasn't left.' As if responding to the sound of the name, George appeared and pressed first one cheek and then another against the side of Toby's leg. 'People think they do that in affection but they're actually only marking their territory. She thinks I belong to her.'

'She?' Then, very quickly it came to her. 'Oh. Named for George Eliot.'

'Oh, rather too perspicuous of me.' He filled her teacup. 'I try to be enigmatic whenever possible, which isn't easy when you come from Dorset.'

Claire wasn't exactly sure where Dorset was, but she couldn't remember ever being as charmed by a man as she was by this one. Of course, he wasn't Michael Wainwright and she wasn't sure she'd want to get physical – although there was something a little bit sexy about Toby's gangly arms and legs – but for charm, he probably couldn't be beat.

'I tell you what,' he said. 'Let's play my little divination game, if you'll indulge me.'

'I feel quite indulgent,' she told him.

'Okay, here's how it works. I catch your vibe, or see your aura, or touch your soul or any of that sort of mumbo jumbo. And then I pick out a book for you – not to worry, cost less than two pounds – and then you read it and see if it doesn't have a special meaning for you.'

Claire actually laughed. 'Will it tell my fortune?'

'No, no. Nothing as naff as that. Shall we?'

Claire nodded. She just wanted to be able to remain in this comfortable, warm spot, drink tea and look at and listen to this English Ichabod Crane.

He approached her, put his hands up about a foot away

from her head and waved them around making himself look even more ridiculous. 'Got it, my little lamb.' He walked to the aisle on the far right, pulled a hanging string and the light went on down the aisle. He went galloping away.

She heard him humming and decided to simply sit and enjoy this delightful little adventure. But he was back in just a moment and extended a book in her direction. 'Ta da! A good book, this,' he said and his smile was almost as wide as his extended arm was long. 'This is for you,' he said. The book was small, covered in red leather and more than a little tattered. It was essays by Charles Lamb. Claire didn't much like essays, but she certainly was not going to refuse the book. She reached for her purse. 'No, no,' he said. 'This one's on George Eliot.' The cat jumped into his lap as he sat down.

'Oh, I couldn't,' she said, really confused.

'Certainly you can,' Toby told her. 'You'll feel indebted and that will cause you to come back and then you'll have to buy something else. And it will all work out splendidly well.' He grinned at her. 'You're not the first,' he said.

'Well, thank you,' Claire said. How had all of this happened to her? She'd bought plenty of books in New York but she'd never had an adventure like this one. In fact, the bookstore clerks usually knew less about the stock than she did. She wondered if Toby might need an assistant, though it didn't look as though he had many customers. As if that thought created one, the bell tinkled.

'Hello,' Toby called out and threw a light switch on. It seemed he only illuminated when necessary. A portly man, stuffed into his tweed jacket and trousers, joined them.

'Hello, Stanton. Engaged with seducing the ladies again, are you?'

Toby smiled. 'In my small way,' he said.

Claire didn't know whether to be embarrassed or pleased and decided on both, though she didn't like to think of their little encounter as business as usual. She had to remember herself. She had probably overstayed her welcome. It wasn't anybody else's job to entertain her. This had been a charming diversion – very charming. But she must remember not to impose. The fact that she had nothing else to do did not mean that others were in the same situation. 'Oh,' she said, standing up, 'I must go.' She gathered her purse and closed her raincoat buttons.

'Come, take a seat, Harold,' Toby told the stout gentleman and Claire moved aside so he might take hers.

Toby rose. 'Don't forget your book,' he said to Claire.

'Yes. Yes thank you.' She tried to put it in her bag but the needles and yarn made it difficult to fit all the way inside. 'Thank you.' She would have liked to have taken a look at the other books, but felt too awkward now, it might look like she was trying to prolong his hospitality. The light in the aisle went off and all of the shelves of books were in semi-darkness. It must be on an automatic timing device. For a moment she did not know where to go but Toby hit the switch and the center aisle was illuminated.

'Come again soon,' he said. 'Let me know what you think of Charlie.'

For a moment Claire thought Toby was talking about the portly man but then she remembered he was Harold. 'I'll let you know,' she said and walked past all the delicious-looking old books, up the few steps and out the door.

Once on the street, just steps away, she was surrounded once again by the bustling, thrilling atmosphere of London. And she felt more a part of it than ever before. She had spoken with someone who loved books as much, or possibly more than she did. Someone at least as interesting as Michael Wainwright. And though he wasn't attractive in the same obvious, American good-teeth-Brad-Pitt way, he had . . . charm. He was . . . interesting looking and fun to talk to. For a moment, Claire was hit with an unexpected stab of pain, as she recalled the fun she had had with Mr Wonderful. But then she looked down at the book in her hand and smiled. It was hard to believe that the interval she had experienced was real. It really had been straight out of *Mary Poppins*. But it had happened. Still, she doubled back just to be sure the store was there and carefully wrote down the address in the front cover of her guidebook. She would certainly return.

She spent the rest of the day sightseeing and almost every sight delighted her. Of course, there were tourists everywhere but Claire had the satisfaction of thinking she was not just a tourist. She was traveling, and didn't know how long she might stay on. She wasn't in a tourist hotel and she wasn't taking tourist buses. She spent the day as an explorer might, charting her course on the underground and bus lines, following her map and looking everywhere. She decided not to bother with the Tower of London or Madame Tussaud's. She wanted instead to walk down normal streets, stop into normal shops and see how normal people lived. It was a long morning and afternoon. At last, sated, Claire made her way back toward Camden.

TWENTY-FIVE

Claire didn't realize how good all the walking would be for her spirit or her body. All she knew was that near the end of the day she was ravenous – the tea and biscuits from Toby's shop had hardly made a meal.

To conserve her money, she decided she would eat in her room. She remembered that close to Chamberley Terrace was a small, slightly dingy grocery. She decided to stop in. As she approached, she read a sign in the window: 'KEENEST PRICES IN CAMDEN.'

The store wasn't a delicatessen, nor was it a super-market, nor was it like the Korean stores in New York. It was long and narrow but instead of being neatly crammed with goods the way New York stores were, there seemed to be a little of this and a little of that. Claire walked up and down the three aisles, amusing herself with the different brand names, the small sizes of everything, and the odd placement of items. The cans all seemed tiny compared to American ones, and the juice and the soda were in what looked like miniature six-packs. It reminded Claire a bit of her favorite toy when she was young – a little grocery store with pretend boxes of soap and bottles of catsup and jars of pickles. Here, small portions of pickles came in a plastic wrap, like the way frankfurters were packed. And beside them, in the refrigerator, were sandwiches already made, sliced in triangles, and set in plastic containers exactly the right shape. She looked at the ingredients: tuna salad with corn, tomato and shredded cheese, sliced egg and cress. They all seemed odd. Claire felt as if she'd like to try them all anyway but decided that a homemade ploughman's would have to do. One loaf could last her for three or four dinners. She was delighted, however, when she found brown relish exactly like the kind she had had in the pub.

She continued looking and nearly laughed aloud at some of the juxtaposed positions of products. She wasn't sure if what she was looking at was typical, or unique to this little shop, but having the beans beside the detergents struck her as peculiar. After three trips up and down the aisles, Claire selected a small loaf of bread, the relish, a wheel of cheddar and a bottle of something that looked like a fizzy juice. While she browsed people had come in and gone back out, but when she got to the counter she was the only customer.

The woman behind the counter was small, compact and had a long braid of shiny black hair that reached below her middle. Above her head was a sign that read 'CASH POINT'. She wore a smock over a blue sari and peered through a pair of glasses at Claire. 'Will this be all?' she asked and though she was obviously from India, or someplace close to it, her English was perfect.

'Yes, thank you.'

'We have a special on bread. You'd do better with the Smith's loaf. It's organic as well.'

'Thank you,' Claire said and then had to ask where she would find it. Before she returned with the exchange a teenage girl with two children beside her came running out of the back of the store.

'Mummy, they won't take any notice of me,' she said.

Claire had to smile. The girl sounded exactly like Wendy in *Peter Pan*.

'That's very naughty of you,' the counter woman said to the smaller boy and girl. 'You must respect your sister.'

'But I want to watch the telly,' the little boy said.

'You'll have square eyes,' she said, shaking her head.

'Mummy, they haven't finished their homework.'

'What do I do with you?' their mother asked. 'If you don't do your lessons, there'll be no sweets.' The little boy began to object. 'You can't have the penny and the bun,' the woman scolded. She looked up at Claire. 'Do you see this? I am busy with my work and these children have no respect. They interrupt. I am most sorry.' Claire was about to tell her that it was perfectly all right when the woman turned back to her children. 'Do you see what you are doing? Apologize to the lady.'

'Oh, that's all right . . .' Claire began. But the children had already begun to sing-song an apology and their mother was shooing them back to the door.

She shook her head. 'Safta is studying for her GCSEs. She doesn't have time to muck about, but there's no one else to watch them in the evening.' Before she could think, Claire volunteered.

'I'd be happy to do it,' she said. The woman narrowed her eyes.

'Why?' she asked.

'Well, I'm new here and I thought, well, I like children.'

'You're American, aren't you?' the woman asked her. Claire nodded, not sure if that was a good thing or a bad thing. 'Why would an American girl want to work for me?'

'Oh, it doesn't have to be work,' Claire said. 'I mean, you don't have to pay me.'

The Indian woman's eyes narrowed further. 'What would a rich American want with my children?'

Claire blushed. 'I'm not rich,' she said. 'I just thought, well, they seem like such nice kids. And if you don't want to pay me, that's fine. Maybe I could look after them a bit and you could . . .' she paused and looked around. 'You could give me some groceries.' The woman looked at her with even greater interest.

'Are you hungry?' she asked.

Claire smiled. 'Well, just for a sandwich.' She took a deep breath. 'I'm not homeless or anything. My name is Claire Bilsop and I've just moved in on Chamberley Terrace and I need to get a job so . . .'

The woman stopped her. 'My name is Mrs Patel,' she said. 'Come back tomorrow at this time and perhaps we could talk.' She looked around. 'Would you be willing to sweep up?' she asked.

'Of course,' Claire said.

Mrs Patel regarded her for a moment, blinking behind her thick glasses. Then she rang up Claire's items. Claire handed her a note and took back the change. It was only after Mrs Patel put her groceries into a bag that Claire saw the swelling under her smock. Mrs Patel was obviously pregnant. Perhaps she really did need help. Claire could hardly believe her good luck.

Mrs Patel handed her the bag. 'See you tomorrow, then.' Claire nodded and walked out into the dark. She'd found a job, no matter that it was a very minor one. Certainly, she wasn't a tourist but when would she go home? She'd been in London five days and she knew she'd like to stay another five but she'd have to return sometime. Still, the richness of her days' adventures – the bookstore, her exploration and now this unexpected encounter – made her feel that five weeks, maybe even five months wouldn't be enough.

TWENTY-SIX

Claire sat in bed and in the dim light cast by Mrs Watson's lamp finished casting on the sixtieth stitch for a simple scarf and set down both needles on the chair beside her bed. Some people cast on with their hand, rather than the second needle, but Claire felt nothing but contempt for that. To keep the stitches uniform in spacing and tension it was much better to cast on with a needle, though it did take a little longer.

She had gotten home, made herself a frugal dinner and then bathed. She hadn't felt comfortable walking down the hallway to the bathroom in her nightgown and robe, but she had encountered no one since Maudie. Other guests must have been staying there however because she found their relics – soap slime in the tub and beard bristles inside the sink. She had to clean everything carefully before she was comfortable enough to get into the bathtub. As it was, it still felt odd to be bathing where a stranger had been. She and Fred had shared a bathroom at home and she had often had to clean up after him but somehow a stranger's leavings were a lot skeevier than a brother's. Still, the water was hot, and the little bottle of bath gel that she had taken from the hotel had filled the room with a scent of lilacs.

As most of us know, odors can be more evocative than anything, releasing memories with a sometimes-stunning strength. For Claire the smell brought back bathing in the beautiful bathroom at the Berkeley. She had felt so very pampered and so completely – and as it happened, unrealistically – happy. For a moment she could actually feel Michael's arms around her and hear his whispered 'angel'. Before tears could rise to her eyes she pushed the thought from her mind. Instead she thought of her encounter with Toby, then about poor little Maudie, and Mrs Patel and her children. Claire could go on without a liar like him.

Now, lying in bed, she found herself strangely contented. She would, she decided, use ribbing stitches on the ends of the scarf but run cable along the length of it and use one of her newly purchased slightly larger needles. A scarf knit in London, on English needles, by her, for her to wear when she took the tube or rode a double-decker bus. Claire smiled. She could not have imagined this moment a week ago, yet being in it seemed completely natural.

As she knit she tried to plan the next day. She had taken her guidebook into the bathroom and had looked through it while she soaked. She thought that she might begin by taking the tube to St Paul's, seeing the great dome and the crypt and then walking west to Leicester Square and through Mayfair. She shouldn't go to any museum that charged admission, at least not until she had some kind of job. But Claire was making an exception just this one time. But if she could work – even as a babysitter – she might be able to eke out just enough to stay on, at least for a while. And perhaps tomorrow she could look around and see if another job presented itself. She had surprised herself with the confidence she'd shown with Mrs Patel. Maybe she could do that again. After all, she had nothing to lose.

She put her knitting away and reached for the book Toby had given her. But since the bulb was so dim that her eyes had trouble adjusting to the light, she decided against trying to read the small, old print. Instead she took out the guidebook and continued from where she had left off after her bath. Tomorrow she thought she would have to get a plate and a knife. And she would also have to get a brighter bulb. The thought of spending the money made her a little nervous, but she had never owned her own dish and it might be fun to look through the tables and tables of them to select the one just right for her.

She looked around the room. The wardrobe door was open, and she realized that each thing, each object, each belonging was something she had selected and was perfect just for her: her shoes, the silk blouse, her few pieces of jewelry, even the raincoat. She had somehow collected these few, treasured objects and had dropped the dross behind her. She thought of her closet and drawers back home, filled with things she didn't want, didn't need, that didn't fit or didn't suit her. It felt so wonderful to know that she had just what she needed and could fit it all into the wheelie bag under the bed. I have to remember this, she thought. She thought of Tina's constant shopping and all the bags of 'bargains' that the women back at Crayden Smithers 'had to have'. Claire had never been guilty of that kind of shopping for sport, but somehow even she had gotten bogged down with more possessions than she needed – and the wrong ones.

She looked around again and pulled the thin blanket securely up around her shoulders. Hard to believe that the morning before she had woken up next to Michael Wainwright, on Egyptian cotton sheets in the most magnificent place she had ever slept in. And the thought of him wiped out the pleasure of her small adventures. How foolish of her to be so pleased about a cup of tea in a used bookstore and an opportunity to sweep up in a dirty grocery. In case she needed proof that she was humble, unimportant, all she had to do was imagine what he might be doing now and where he was. She wasn't envious of him – not exactly – but the thought of him made her and her life seem so very, very small.

But, she reminded herself, things had changed at least a little. She had done something different – very different from what she usually did. She had turned her back and walked away. Since then it seemed she had left her old life behind, along with Michael Wainwright. She had explored a new place and may have made a friend, and possibly even found a little job.

Crayden Smithers! The realization made Claire sit straight up in bed. She'd missed work – they'd expected her today – she had to let them know she was taking more of her vacation days. But whom would she call? She didn't want to speak to Joan, and it was inappropriate to leave the news with Tina. Claire looked around the room and at the sight of her guidebook she remembered Abigail Samuels. She could call Abigail.

Claire wrapped herself in her robe, grabbed the guidebook and walked quietly down the hall to the phone. She only hoped that Mrs Watson was tucked in bed so that Claire wouldn't be watched like a disobedient child. She flipped to the inside front cover to find where Abigail had written her home number, at least she hoped it was her number. She'd have to call collect, because she had no idea how to do otherwise. And the time difference – it was probably around five or six in the evening there, but she'd have to take the chance Abigail would be home from work. It took Claire a little while to find out how to do it, but at last Abigail's phone was ringing in New York.

'Hello?' a voice said. It was Abigail's.

'Miss Samuels? It's Claire. I'm sorry to bother you at home, but . . .'

'Actually, I'm quite relieved to hear from you. I thought the worst.'

'The worst?'

'Well, not the absolute worst. The fact that Mr Wainwright made it in to work, but you didn't, made me wonder and when they call a man a lady-killer it's for a reason. I didn't think Wainwright had actually killed you but, well, emotionally . . .'

'I'm fine,' Claire said and, at that moment she was. 'I just thought I'd stay on for a bit. London is wonderful.'

'Oh, good. I'm glad you can enjoy it.'

'Yes. I can. Tomorrow I'm going to tour and go to St Patrick's.'

'St Patrick's?'

'Oh, I mean St Paul's. Anyway, could you please put in for my vacation days? I know I should have called yesterday but –'

'Don't worry about a thing. You might enjoy that you're the talk of the office and take your time.'

'I'll probably be back next week. My money won't hold out too long but I have found a little place to stay.'

'Really? Give me the address, just in case.' Claire did and then Abigail Samuels said something very peculiar. 'I'm proud of you. Venture forth.'

Not knowing what else to say Claire simply said, 'Thank you. I will.' And they hung up. She tiptoed back to her room, carefully closed the door and got back into bed.

It was very hard to believe, but when Claire turned the light off and put her head down on the scratchy polyester pillowcase she smiled to herself in the dark. Tomorrow she looked forward to breakfast at the café, a long walk, a visit to the bookstore, and perhaps a way to earn money. She began to hum a song her father used to play on the piano that she had learned on the flute. And with that she fell asleep.

The next morning Claire woke up knowing that she had dreamed long and complicated dreams. But she couldn't remember them. It seemed to be cold and damp out, so she began her day with another hot bath, dressed in her black slacks, her new T-shirt and the sweater she had made. She looked at her knitting, decided to take it with her and – once she was out of doors – wished she had already finished the scarf. She buttoned her raincoat up to the neck and made her way toward the café and the tube station.

A soft protective grayness had settled on and around everything. She had read, of course, about London fog, but had always imagined it as dark. Wasn't it described as 'pea soup'? This was far more ephemeral. It was damp and wispy; it seemed to put a sheltering scrim over everything. With the gray of the stone buildings and the gray of the bark of the trees and the gray of the sidewalk Claire felt as if she might have walked into a Whistler painting.

By the time she got to the café all of the warmth from her bath had evaporated into the mist and she was chilled to the bone. A cup of tea and a big meal was exactly what she needed. Outside the café the window was obscured by steam. Claire entered and once again was in a world populated by working men. This time she waved to the waitress and wasn't afraid to take a seat without permission. When she ordered her breakfast she was careful to remember to ask them to hold the beans, but she ate her eggs and chips and the bacon, mushrooms and tomatoes. She sopped up whatever was left with brown bread and had three cups of tea before she was done.

'For a tiny thing like you, you can put it away, can't you?' the waitress said. Claire wiped her mouth and nodded. 'Did you find a place to stay?'

'Yes, thank you.'

'Hope it's not too bad.'

Claire shook her head. 'My name is Claire.' She held her hand out and the older woman shook it briefly.

'Well, good to see you again,' she said and turned back to her work.

Claire was a little disappointed that the waitress hadn't offered her name, but she paid her bill and went back out into the damp, feeling warm again.

The walk along Camden High Street was completely different today. It wasn't just the weather; most of the shops were closed and, aside from the car traffic, there was no one on the street. It seemed as if shopping days were only on the weekend. Claire tried to imagine the shops on Duane and Water Street shut down five days a week and simply couldn't.

She bought a ticket and took the underground, getting out a stop before St Paul's and walking the rest of the way. She was glad she did this because, although at first she found herself in a narrow street with large gray buildings closing in on each side, at the end, after a slight curve, the view of the rise of the hill with the dome of St Paul's above it was . . . well, it was stunning.

The mist was just beginning to evaporate, and the watery sunshine on the gold of the dome seemed to make it emerge from smoke the way a sun might dawn in a fairy tale. The cathedral was up a long set of stairs and Claire remembered that royal wedding processions had walked up these very steps. Now she, too, put her feet there and entered the cathedral.

To her surprise, it was very busy. In the center nave a service was being conducted. Though there were very few people in the congregation, there were large groups being guided through the sides of the church. Claire did not know if you had to pay to get a guide but by stealth she managed to go from one to another and hear bits and pieces about the building.

More important than the history though was standing under the vastness of the dome which arched over the very center of the church. She had read about the whispering gallery where the strange acoustics allowed a murmur to be heard two hundred feet away. For a moment she was sad as she watched other tourists try the trick. She had no one to whisper to her, but she watched as others delighted in the experience. The building was breathtaking. She had never seen anything remotely like it. She had, of course, been to St Patrick's Cathedral on Fifth Avenue in New York but it had none of the grandeur, none of the spectacular originality of this building.

The service ended, and Claire felt freer to walk around the center of the cathedral. The walls were dappled with memorial plaques, many with carved busts, or garlands of flowers, or what looked like Grecian ruins. Some of them were in Latin and many in an old English that was both charming and strange.

As she walked around the left side of the church she saw an inconspicuous modern sign that directed visitors *To the Crypt*. It sounded spooky but, nonetheless, she decided to descend the stairs. The crypt was only a basement, though a large and well-lit one. Here there were more memorials and she wandered around looking at names, dates and the sculpture. Then she turned a corner, past a pillar and fell in love.

A man was standing there. He was, without question, the most beautiful she had ever seen. His profile was breathtaking: a wide brow, a perfectly straight thin nose, rounded but still masculine lips and the most perfect jaw-line she had ever seen. His hair was pulled back into a small ponytail. She walked around to the front of the statue and looked him full in the face. He seemed to be staring off into some vast distance. Though he was carved of marble, the sculptor had managed to breathe life and tension into his creation, and the eighteenth-century uniform molded to his body did not conceal the muscles and sinews underneath that made him strain toward her.

Claire thought of the Pygmalion story. She had not created this statue, but she was in love with it nonetheless. He was standing on a platform, some sort of ship, and clearly about to sink and die. She looked at the name inscribed along the base – Captain Wentworth – and the date of his death. Tears filled her eyes. This beautiful man had died two hundred and sixteen years ago, in some unimaginable sea battle. What had his eyes seen before he died? His family, his wife or lover, even his dogs and horses – for he must have had them – would have been inconsolable. Claire stared at his lips and wished she could kiss them. If only that could breathe life back into him.

She thought of Michael, then, and his mouth. Michael, good-looking as he was, had never made a sacrifice for anyone, much less his country or his beliefs. Not only had he betrayed her with Katherine Rensselaer but he had betrayed Katherine Rensselaer by going up to the suite and lying beside Claire. It occurred to her that Katherine Rensselaer would have had to know that. She looked into the face of Captain Wentworth. Perhaps she was wrong, but she couldn't imagine that he would behave without standards or decency.

She didn't know how long she had been standing there transfixed by the statue and her thoughts, when a tour group came around the corner. Claire scurried away as quickly as she could. She knew she did not want to hear anything that would disturb her reverie.

She left the cathedral then, descended the stairs, gazed briefly at the stolid statue of Queen Anne and quickly walked down Ludgate Hill and on up Fleet Street. She knew this had been the home of many newspapers and that the press was still known by that name, though the newspapers had all relocated. But the thought of Captain Wentworth and the distressing feelings the memorial had brought up about Michael closed in on her, just as the narrow gray street did.

She walked on for a little while with her shoulders hunched. What was she doing here? she asked herself. This was madness. She was alone, friendless – and probably always would be. If she dropped down onto Fleet Street and died, how long would it take for anyone to know who she was? And who would mourn her? There certainly wouldn't be any statue put up by grieving relatives.

Fleet Street seemed to go on forever and suddenly Claire felt so tired that she would have liked to lie down. After what seemed like an endless trudge, the street opened and changed. She made a left, past a church that sat on its own little island in the middle of the road, and then she was on a much wider but less grim avenue. Eventually she found herself in a great open space. Pigeons rose and descended and lions – not real ones but huge statues – crouched at the foot of a tall monument with another statue at the very top of it. She recognized Nelson's column, and realized she was at Trafalgar Square, which she had seen in passing on her first Saturday in London. It looked exactly like a movie set. The difference was that she was in the picture. She was, suddenly, tremendously happy and filled with a spirit of adventure.

TWENTY-SEVEN

Claire found a bench at last and sat looking across at the pediment of the National Gallery and the front of the church of St Martin-in-the-Fields. She looked up at Admiral Nelson. For a moment she remembered how she and Michael had looked down on him from the National Portrait Gallery. Now, instead, she like everyone else could only look up at him. She would not allow herself to think about Michael. It was enough that she was here, even if she was alone. Back home it was – she looked at her watch – so early that right now Tina would just be stepping out of the shower and beginning the long process of getting her hair and face ready for the commute to work. Would she be wondering at Claire's absence? Had she asked Michael Wainwright anything? Soon she would be in the office and all of them, Tina, the Maries, Joan and even Abigail would discuss her absence. Tina would have called her house. Would Tina tell Claire's mother where she had really gone? She doubted it. Would her mother be concerned? Claire doubted that as well. Perhaps in another few days.

The idea that when she was back at Mrs Watson's after this day of astonishing sights and encounters the women at Crayden Smithers would be sitting down for another boring lunch gave her a chill despite the warming sunshine. The only difference her absence would make was that they would have a new subject to discuss – her. She smiled as her eyes followed a drift of pigeons that flew like a gray smear across the sky. She had never been the source of much entertainment before. Now even *American Idol* wouldn't push her off the lunch-table agenda as the most interesting event.

She stopped smiling when she thought of Mr Wonderful. He would be putting on his perfect suit jacket and reading the *Wall Street Journal*. When he showed up in the office Tina might give him a look, or even a wisecrack, but Claire doubted that he would otherwise give her a thought, except perhaps one of mild annoyance. She pushed Michael Wainwright out of her mind.

She stood up. She would go into the National Gallery, walk around and have another cup of tea. She was getting hungry, but she told herself sternly that she would neither eat lunch nor spend money on a bus. She would look around the museum, have a cup of tea and then walk 'home'. She'd been in London for less than a week and she'd already walked more than she did in a year in Tottenville. But somehow here the walking didn't feel like exercise. It felt like exploration.

And since she had left Michael in the hotel she had eaten less. There was no bagel from Sy, no Danish at her coffee break at eleven, no lunch after her big breakfast and very little for dinner. She thought of the loaf of bread and the cheese waiting for her in her room. She should have made a sandwich to take with her. Well, too late now. She would eat when she got home and then at eight she would go to Mrs Patel's little shop to see about a job. That would be her day.

The gallery was surprisingly crowded. Claire hadn't been to one in a long time and, standing amid the moving crowd, she realized that she didn't know how to look at a painting. She could see the Virgin Mary in the painting in front of her and the tiny ray of light with an angel floating in it but aside from the pretty colors, what did it mean? She decided to try and find out, so she sat down on a bench opposite *The Annunciation*. She waited patiently, staring at the picture, until a guide with a group of white-haired women stopped in front of it.

'This painting, executed in the fifteenth century, is a classic Annunciation. The Virgin is kneeling, hearing the news from the angel of the impending birth of Jesus. Now, what we see here is the iconography of the painters of the period. Because their audience was illiterate, they needed a way to tell them that this was the Virgin and not, say, Saint Anne or Saint Katherine. So they gave clues. Because she was going to bear the Christ – she was a vessel – we have the vase on the right. The lily is another symbol for the Virgin because she was without original sin, she was, like the lily, spotless in the eyes of god and man. Saint Katherine of Alexandria would be represented by the wheel on which she was martyred.' The woman smiled and looked at the group in front of her. 'They didn't have guides in those days, so explanations of the painting had to be right in the picture. Fra Filippo has done a far better job than I ever could,' she said and there was a small, polite murmur of dissent before the group moved on.

Claire continued to sit on the bench. She stared at the painting. There had been all of those clues and she hadn't known anything about them. The picture was still beautiful, but in her eyes it had completely changed. The gold vase now stood out, though she had not noticed it a few moments before. The lily, perfectly depicted, glowed. After a while she went through the whole medieval section looking at all the Annunciation paintings and noticing for the first time that there were, indeed, lilies and vases in almost every one. It wasn't so much that they were puzzles, Claire thought. It was more as if they were a different language. Next time she went to Toby's store she would buy a book about medieval art. She would learn the language. She left the museum determined to see the symbols not just in paintings but also those hidden away in everyday life.

It was an interesting but very long walk back to Mrs Watson's. Claire was so tired – both with the walk and perhaps lingering jet-lag – that when she got back to her room she had to lie down. She ate the rest of the bread and cheese, drank some water and then, despite her best intentions, fell asleep.

It was almost ten when she opened her eyes. For a moment she didn't know where she was and then, with a start she realized she was two hours late for Mrs Patel. She jumped up and didn't bother to change out of her wrinkled clothes. She nearly forgot to take her key she was so flustered. She ran down the stairs and out onto the street. She was in front of the little grocery store just as Mrs Patel came to the door.

'Well, there you are,' Mrs Patel said. Claire nodded, breathless from the run.

'I'm so sorry,' she said. 'I am . . .'

'You are late. Very, very late. I don't need any help now.'

Claire hung her head. It was probably useless to offer excuses. She was embarrassed and, surprisingly, tears rose to her eyes. It was silly, she told herself. It wasn't as if this was a good job, or even a certain one. She was about to turn away when, feeling stupid and guilty, she lifted her head. 'Could I just help you in any way at all – not for money,' she said and looked down at Mrs Patel's bulging belly.

'Well, you could pull down the grille,' Mrs Patel said and pointed to the iron gate rolled high above her head. 'But I'm not going to pay you.' Claire nodded and meekly did as she was told. 'Just half way,' Mrs Patel said sharply. 'And then you can follow me in.' Mrs Patel awkwardly ducked under the gate after she stabilized it and, once they were both inside, handed her a broom. 'Start at the back,' she said. 'And don't be hiding the dust under the shelves,' she added.

Claire took the broom, walked to the end of the first aisle and began. Within minutes she was sneezing and her eyes were watering. The floor clearly had not been swept in some time. Mrs Patel was at the front, doing something at the counter. Claire focused again on the sweeping but by the time she had gotten to the middle of the first aisle – and there were four to go – she had to go to ask, 'Do you have any water?'

'You are thirsty already?'

'No, no, not for me. I just need to sprinkle down the dust.'

Mrs Patel paused for a moment. 'All right then,' she said. She took a bucket out from under the counter. 'There's a slop sink in the back, next to the rubbish bin.' She looked at Claire who could feel her eyes watering and she became a little less starchy. 'The place is a bit of a tip,' she admitted, and though Claire wasn't sure what a tip was, she nodded.

As she worked she passed the refrigerated case and smiled at the sign, 'FROSTED FOOD', that hung over it. It took her almost forty minutes to finish the sweeping, and when she was done it took another ten minutes to pick up the dirt and wipe the floor. Claire was careful to put all the dirt in the bag Mrs Patel gave her.

'I suppose it could do with a wash,' Mrs Patel said, looking at the floor. Claire nodded, hoping it meant a little more work for the night.

'I'd be happy to,' she said. Perhaps she could win the woman over.

'Not tonight,' Mrs Patel said. 'It's too late.'

Once again, Claire felt flooded with guilt as well as the sadness of a missed opportunity. 'Where shall I put the broom?' she asked humbly.

'In the wardrobe in the back. When you come back tomorrow night you can use it again and give the floor a wash.' Mrs Patel raised her eyebrows. 'If you get here in good time.'

Claire smiled. She didn't know that when she did her pale radiance was almost irresistible to Mrs Patel. She also didn't know about the prejudice against 'Pakis', or the pain Mrs Patel felt when her children were harassed. The idea of an American kissing up to her gave Mrs Patel a little surge of pleasure.

'I'll be here,' Claire said. 'I'm actually quite responsible.'

'We'll see,' Mrs Patel said.

Claire washed her hands in the slop sink and made her way to the front of the store. The librarian in her felt frustrated as she walked by the cans and boxes arranged almost willy-nilly. She remembered a character in an Anne Tyler novel who arranged all of her canned goods alphabetically. The idea made her smile, and that's how Mrs Patel saw her as she emerged from the back. She must be simple, Mrs Patel thought, and Claire would have been hurt to know it. That or round the bend, Mrs Patel continued to herself. Why would an American girl be smiling over work that even an Untouchable didn't enjoy? 'Here,' she said and handed Claire a bag. Claire did not want to appear rude but she glanced into it. There was bread, some potato chips, cheese, two cans of Coca-Cola, and a box labeled biscuits. She started to thank Mrs Patel who waved her hand dismissively. 'Have you a fridge? Or a cooker?' Claire shook her head. 'Well, I was going to give you a packet of tea and a tin of fish but I wasn't sure if it would serve.' Mrs Patel pressed a button and looked at the till. She took a ten-pound note from the drawer and tried to hand it to Claire.

'No, no,' Claire said. 'I was late. I'm very sorry. I said I would work for nothing.'

'Nobody works for nothing,' Mrs Patel said.

'Well, I worked for this.' Claire patted the bag and before Mrs Patel could argue anymore she walked toward the door. 'Nothing else to do?' she asked.

'Well, you could chuck that into the dustbin. It's just outside.'

Claire picked up the heavy rubbish bag – now she knew not to call it garbage – ducked under the half-drawn security gate and managed to hold the groceries in one arm while she dumped the rubbish with the other.

When she got back to Mrs Watson's her landlady was waiting there. 'I'll need the money in advance,' she said, looking Claire over and seeming more and more witch-like. Claire blushed. She wasn't sure if she was allowed to bring food up to the rooms and she didn't want to be caught offending.

Now she put the grocery bag down between her feet and rummaged in her purse. She took out one of the twenty-pound notes and handed it to Mrs Watson who gave her two coins in return. 'So, then, how long will you be staying on?'

Claire smiled at her. 'I'm not sure,' she said. 'But I think for quite a while.'

TWENTY-EIGHT

When Claire woke up the next morning she felt as happy as a child on the first day of vacation – actually it was her seventh day. She jumped out of bed and saw the sun was actually shining through the window – it was the first sunny day she'd had. She bathed then dressed in her black slacks and the new T-shirt. She decided against the pearl necklace but she put the earrings on.

Then she sat at the side of her bed and took out her notebook. Mrs Patel had tried to give her ten pounds last night. If she gave her ten pounds every night, what did that mean? She did some calculations, and figured that if she was given groceries as well as ten pounds, she could almost double the length of her stay in this city. But one luxury she decided she couldn't do without was the cooked break-fast. That, with a hot cup of tea in the afternoon and then a high-carb-high-fat snack at night was enough to keep her going.

Today, however, she would make herself a sandwich and bring the potato chips for lunch. She packed the food with her knitting and noticed, for the first time that there was also the little 'packet' of cookies – labeled 'biscuits' – and put those in her bag as well. She thought she would take the underground to Piccadilly, walk up Regent Street, and through Mayfair. Abigail had underlined tea at Claridge's and written 'A Must!' in the margin. Claire wasn't sure what it would cost, but if she had time that would be her splurge of the day.

As she walked to the tube she thought about Toby. She hadn't even looked at the book that he had given her! Luckily, she had it in her purse and she would read some of it today. Of course, she felt drawn to the bookstore, but she told herself firmly that she might be unwelcome if she visited too often.

At Piccadilly she was amazed by the impossibility of getting across the streets because of all the fences, and at how insignificant the statue of Eros looked. The area was almost like a sideshow. She had never seen so many tourists. The Americans seemed underdressed, the Germans seemed overdressed, the Japanese were either too stylish or boring, and all the young people, whatever their nationality, were outfitted by Nike, Benetton, or The Gap.

Catching her own reflection in a Regent Street shop window, she realized that she looked more formal – or perhaps a little less flamboyant – than other people her age, but she also thought she seemed to fit in better with the people who lived here, and her haircut definitely looked stylish. For a moment she wondered if she herself could live here long term. That caused her to remember Tina, the office and her mother. She should call them, but she dreaded the experience and the expense. Just then, she passed a news-stand and saw bright racks of postcards. She had never sent a postcard in her life, perhaps because she had never been anywhere to send a postcard from. But now she was some-where. She looked at the racks. She immediately picked out a picture of a red double-decker bus, another of Trafalgar Square and a third showing Parliament and Big Ben with the London Eye looming behind. Despite her best inten-tions, Claire had to think of Michael and the wonderful trip up into the air. Although it had only happened a few days before, it already seemed a dream, or a fairy tale she had been told about a prince and a beggar girl.

Stop it, she told herself firmly. She was here and having an adventure and that was enough of a fairy tale. She looked back at the cards. She would send one to her mother, one to Tina at home, and one to Abigail at work.

She sighed. Abigail would keep their communication private but she had no doubt that whatever she wrote to Tina would be brought into the office and discussed. It made her think about the hours she had spent sitting at that table and listening to the gossip as it swirled around. It wasn't that any of them (except perhaps Joan) were really mean-spirited, but it seemed as if it had all been such a waste of her time. And now, since she'd gotten here to London, her time seemed incredibly valuable, though she didn't know why. It wasn't as if anybody else valued her more. She wasn't sure that her mother would care about her absence – after all, it gave her more time alone with Jerry. And certainly, while they might talk about her at Crayden Smithers she doubted any of them would miss her, not even Tina, though she might be wrong about that. And Mr Wonderful would get back to his busy life of work and his host of women and not think of her, most probably, ever again. She remembered the parting shrug he had made when he couldn't convince her to go back to the airport with him. No, she would not be missed. She wondered if she could live here as long as she had lived in New York without making the smallest impression on anyone.

Claire walked through Mayfair, a bustling business section with lots of fancy shops, and was surprised once again. With a name like that she had expected parks and trees and beautiful quiet streets. While the streets were beautiful most of the lovely houses had been turned into offices and the traffic everywhere was noisy. But perhaps, hundreds of years ago, there had been a fair here each May. Now it was Vanity Fair. The shops were astonishing: beautiful cashmere, gorgeous antiques, and men's clothes stores that were 'bespoke'. Though Claire did not know what, exactly, that was, she knew it was expensive and good.

She made her way through street after street until she came to Grosvenor Square. It was a lovely, tailored green space but one side was spoiled by a shockingly ugly concrete building. Claire walked that way, simply because she had to know what this dreadful place was. She was surprised to see a statue of President Eisenhower outside, an American president but as she crossed the square she read how he had helped win World War II. It was nice, she thought, for the British to put up a statue to him.

But then she got close to the ugly structure and had a shock. The building, of all things, was the American Embassy. Claire couldn't believe her eyes. How had this happened? It had to be the most hideous building in London. She took the time to walk around the building, though it was almost a whole block long. It did not get any better. She looked around to see if other people were staring at it in horror, but they didn't seem to be. Perhaps, she thought, they are averting their eyes. She felt personally responsible and, ridiculously, wanted to go up to any Londoner walking by to apologize. Of course, she didn't, but she had to do something. She was a citizen. It was her embassy. How had this architectural tragedy happened? She walked purposefully up the shallow stairs leading to the entrance.

But before she got even halfway up the stairs she was stopped by a young man in uniform. 'Ma'am, may I ask your name, your citizenship and the purpose of this visit?'

Claire was amazed, and even more angry. 'I'm an American,' she said. 'And I'd like to speak to someone at the embassy.'

'And what would be your business?'

How could she explain? She looked at the pleasant, square-jawed face of the soldier and thought of Fred. Fred would laugh at her. But she wouldn't let this man or anyone make her feel ridiculous or lose her sense of outrage. 'That's my business,' she told him. She thought she saw a glimmer of a smile.

'Well, that may be. But I will have to ask you for your passport.'

'But I've left it at home. I mean at my hotel,' she told him.

'I'm sorry. You can't enter without it, ma'am. You'll have to come back with it later.' He paused. 'I really am sorry. It's just security procedures. Are you in some kind of trouble?'

She shook her head then took a deep breath. He seemed like a nice guy and she would have been amused by his Texas twang if she wasn't so annoyed. 'Look, I just want to know who built this and when?'

'Who built what, ma'am?' he asked.

'This building,' she said, her irritation showing. 'This terrible building.'

He looked up and behind him as if he was seeing it for the first time. 'I don't know,' he shrugged. 'We did, I guess.'

'I didn't,' Claire told him. 'And if my tax money went into it, I want a refund. It's an embarrassment.'

He laughed, but not in a nasty way, not the way Fred would. 'Well, I never really thought of it that way,' he said looking around. 'But it's no Buckingham Palace.'

Claire relaxed. Perhaps she was overreacting. She blushed and had no idea how attractive a little color in her cheeks made her, or how lonely a young Texan far from home could be. 'Have you been here long? On a vacation?' he asked.

'I don't know,' she said and saw him look at her a little harder, as if she might actually be some kind of security risk. 'What I mean to say is, I'd like to stay on for as long as I can. At least till my money runs out.'

He smiled again. 'I can't wait to get back,' he said. 'Where you from?'

'New York, but not the city.' She told him about Staten Island.

'Sounds like a nice small town. Maybe that's why you remind me of home.' He paused and glanced around him to see if they were being overheard. Then he turned back to her. 'Say, why don't you and I get together and have a beer or somethin'? I know a place where we can get American Budweiser. And cold, too.'

Claire looked at him. He was attractive in a fresh-faced, All American way. But the last thing she was interested in was swilling beer with a good ole boy who wasn't aware of the very building where he worked. Of course, she told herself, she hadn't looked at much of the architecture in New York, but in New York there were no perfect squares with unbroken limestone and brick fronts. She hesitated.

He added coaxingly, 'We could go to a movie. And I might be able to get you invites to embassy parties.'

She didn't allow herself to snort. That was just about the last thing she wanted. But he seemed kind, and he had a nice smile. And – though she would never admit it, not even to herself – being asked out by a stranger made Claire feel good. 'I'm not interested in the parties,' she said. 'But a meal might be nice.'

'How can I get in touch with you?'

'Well, I don't have a phone but you could give me your number.'

'Will you call it?' he asked.

'Yes.' And as he scribbled it down and his name – Corporal Adam Tucker – she decided she would.

TWENTY-NINE

The day was so lovely that at one o'clock, as she passed the enormous black wrought-iron fence of Green Park, she decided to sit down. She'd read some of Toby's book and have her lunch. The day was warm and people seemed to be both strolling and sitting, some on the ground and some in lovely canvas chairs. At first she was struck by the fact that all of them seemed to have brought the same lovely but unwieldy chair. Was it the only one available in London? Then she realized that the chairs were provided by the park. She sat down in one and simply couldn't get over it. It was very comfortable and with her face to the sun she felt as if she could almost take a nap. How did London manage this? In New York benches were nailed to cement. They were uncomfortable but no one could steal them. What luxury, and what a wonderful place this must be, where nobody stole things and graffiti didn't cover every inch. She took out her knitting and worked on it for a while. Then, with the sun on her face and hands her stitches slowed and . . .

The next thing she knew, a man in an official hat was tapping her shoulder. 'I don't believe you've paid,' he said. If it wasn't for his uniform Claire would have been sure he was a madman. They certainly had enough nuts wandering through New York parks and they must have them here, too. But she was becoming wise enough to look around her and try to figure out the customs of these people she was visiting. Clearly, the chairs belonged to the park and one paid rental. Rather than being disappointed, Claire was impressed with the sensible and comfortable system. So much better than lugging the chair to the park.

'How much?' she asked

'A pound for an hour,' he said and, though she hated spending any extra money, she felt it was well worth it.

People strolled by her and she wondered about their lives. Did they work? What were they doing in this park in the middle of central London, in the middle of the day? Did they live nearby? But then, at about two o'clock, the park seemed to quickly empty out. They must all work she thought and was grateful that she didn't have to abandon her chair or the pleasant weather.

She reached into her bag, took out Toby's book and opened it in a desultory way. It was written in nineteenth-century English, a little brisker than Dickens, but a bit of a stretch nonetheless. Claire wasn't sure that she wanted to read some dead old Brit's essays, but her eye fell on a title, 'The Superannuated Man', and she began to read. She was pleased to see Lamb's style was open and there was actually some humor in his tone. After only a paragraph she felt as if he was talking to her from the page. But the sun on her face and the comfortable deck chair overcame the power of Mr Lamb's words and Claire fell asleep.

Anyone walking by her sleeping form, and several did, would have seen a young woman, just slightly heavier than she ought to be, with a face quite beautiful in repose. There was something about it reminiscent of a French Madonna carved and painted in the fourteenth century: the tilt of the head, the downcast eyes, the slightly elongated face and nose. When her eyes fluttered open, the pink that suffused her face only made the likeness greater.

Claire, of course, was embarrassed and rather flustered by her unexpected nap. The park, despite the traffic noise of the street, was fairly quiet and there was no reason why she shouldn't take a little siesta in the middle of the day. She thought of the times that she had been so tired or bored at work that she had longed to close her eyes but couldn't.

She felt grim at the thought of returning to that life. Had it only been a week since she had come to London? She counted it out on her fingers. She'd arrived on Thursday morning – just under a week ago. She had seen so much and there was so much to look forward to. She simply couldn't go back. Not in a week or even a month. She wasn't sure how she could manage it, but this wasn't going to be a two-week vacation.

Now, cheered by that momentous decision, and refreshed after putting her chair to such good use, she reached into her bag and pulled out the three postcards. Thinking of Tina, she had to decide whether her friend would bring the card into work, even if she addressed it to her at home. Knowing her, she figured she would, even if she asked her not to. Well, it was a small piece of paper and she didn't have to explain anything. It was only a postcard.

> *London is lovely. I am enjoying it so much that I*
> *couldn't come home yet. I'm seeing all the sights*
> *and making new friends.*
> *Love, Claire*

She read it over. It seemed friendly enough, but distant. She couldn't, however, explain to Tina how delicious it felt to be away from the life that Tina embraced. Claire sighed. She'd probably be back soon enough, though she knew she'd have lost her job. She shrugged and picked up the next card. She would have to address Abigail Samuels at the office, and though there was a danger that the mailroom would read it, she doubted Abigail would mention or show it to anyone. Still, she'd be discreet.

Thank you so much for the guidebook and your
help. I use the book every day and there is so
much to see that I just couldn't come back yet. I
found a little job and I may stay on longer. Once
again, thanks for everything.
    Claire

The last card was the most difficult. She wrote her home
address and then had to pause. The sun had gone behind
a cloud, and it looked as if the weather – as usual – was
about to change. Unsure of what she would say Claire
began to write.

Dear Mom,
    I had this chance from work to go to London
and I decided to take it. Sorry I didn't tell you
first, but I wasn't sure I would go until the last
minute. Don't worry about me. I'm fine. I'll write
soon. Love to Jerry.

Writing that last line was difficult but she knew she had
to add a P.S.

P.S. I used your Saks card. Don't worry. I'll pay
you back when I return.

She decided she wouldn't mention that her mother owed
her more than the card balance. After all, her disappear-
ance might come as a shock, though with her mother she
really couldn't tell. Perhaps she'd be glad that she and Jerry
had the house to themselves. She would regret the lost
income, but maybe it would finally force Jerry to go out
and get a regular job. Claire shrugged.
    She didn't want to be charged another pound for the
chair, so she rose, bought stamps and posted the cards. (She
had learned that you don't mail things in London, you post

them.) Then she wandered south through the park until she came out of it on The Mall. Turning to her right she saw the enormous stone mound that was Queen Victoria's memorial, and behind it Buckingham Palace.

When she had had a chance to take it in – the size, the gates, the guard, the gold – she opened Abigail's book. She read that it was the main home of the kings and queens since Victoria was crowned. And that when the Queen is in residence, her royal flag is flown. The flag was up and Claire approached the gates. Somewhere inside, not far from her, the Queen of England was drinking a cup of tea or reading a book or playing with one of her dogs! Claire had never been this close to royalty, and the idea that the elderly woman whose picture she had seen a thousand times actually lived right there astonished her. She read that the changing of the guard happened at eleven-thirty and decided to come back another day to see it.

She followed the fence to the right and began walking along Constitution Hill. All along the left-hand side of the road was an old brick wall, ten feet or more high with razor wire curled in gleaming coils along the top. Claire walked and walked but the wall continued. She looked on her map carefully. The wall was the one that enclosed the Queen's backyard! When she looked on her map she saw the yard – actually called Buckingham Palace Gardens – was about the same size as Green Park and had a lake with an island in it. Claire shook her head. What would it be like to have a private park in the middle of a city like this? What would it be like to live in 'Buck House' and be able to choose from a hundred rooms? It was, of course, impossible for her to imagine. But she thought, on the whole, that she preferred to sit in a deck chair in Green Park than to be walled up and alone in Buckingham Palace Gardens. She wondered if the Queen was lonely, and then for a moment, if she was. Oddly, she decided she wasn't and continued her walk with a faster pace.

She got confused at Wellington Arch: she knew it was close to Knightsbridge because she and Michael had gone past it so often. But walking was different. She took two wrong turns, and then managed to get to Park Lane where she walked past all the grand hotels on one side and Hyde Park and traffic streaming by on the other. When she finally got to the end she was on Oxford Street but she was very, very tired. She took out her map again. She simply couldn't walk all the way to Chamberley Terrace, though she'd had every intention of doing it in the morning. As it was, she had walked so much in the last week that she had noticed her slacks were fitting a little bit looser. Perhaps she was losing weight. But she couldn't walk any further. Feeling guilty she slunk down into the underground at Marble Arch.

It was four o'clock before she got back. She washed, changed, brushed her hair and teeth, ate a piece of cheese and lay down. But she couldn't nap. She took out her knitting instead. It was calming and she worked steadily at it. Her needles clicked and clicked.

It seemed no time at all before Claire finished. She spread the scarf flat on her little bed and studied it with pleasure. The piece wouldn't need blocking and it didn't have one imprecise stitch. Whenever Claire knit she had to correct every twisted yarn or reversal because if she didn't her eye moved always to the spot where the imperfection was.

She liked perfection, but it seemed achievable only in very small things. When she looked at her life and the lives of others she saw nothing but disappointment, compromise, dropped stitches and twisted yarn. She had always been wary of her mother and father's life and their marriage. Her mother's life with Jerry seemed even worse. Claire had never been envious of Tina or of Tina's marital plans with Anthony. Other people she knew – in Tottenville, the women at work, the executives at the perimeter, both male and female – all seemed to live generally dreadful lives. Either there was no challenge or too much pressure; too little or too much. Even Mr Wonderful, who seemed to have – in a phrase Tina might use – 'the world by its balls' didn't seem content.

Claire stroked the scarf flat. It really was perfect. Of course, it was only a scarf, but she had made it with her own hands, her own vision and her own intelligence. Perhaps the secret to a perfect life (or something close to it) was to keep it small and pay attention. For some reason, she felt as if here, in London, she could manage to do that. She sighed and folded the scarf to put it away in the wardrobe. It might be true that she could create a small but perfect life here, but she didn't have the means to do it. And now that she was finished, what could she knit next? Where would she find a yarn shop? Her projects always felt like friends, something she could turn to when she was bored or alone.

Of course, now she had run out of time and she fell asleep immediately. She would have been late for Mrs Patel if it weren't for the sound of Maudie's two children running up and down the corridor.

She got up refreshed, ran a comb through her hair and greeted Maudie on the way out. The woman tried to apologize for her children but Claire merely smiled and told her not to. She should have thanked her, but Maudie seemed so grateful as it was that a thank you seemed overkill. Claire ran down the stairs and out onto the street.

THIRTY

Claire hadn't been able to decide if she should be a half-hour or fifteen minutes early for Mrs Patel. She had been late the day before, and didn't want to seem erratic by coming too early today. She also wanted to make up the time and prove that she could be dedicated.

When she arrived at 7:45 dressed in her navy slacks and her hand-knit sweater she knew from Mrs Patel's approving glance she had made the right decision. 'Well,' she said, 'apparently you can be prompt.'

Claire didn't take offense at Mrs Patel's condescending tone. 'I'll never be late again,' she said. 'I really am quite dependable.'

'Well, can I depend on you to open those cartons and restock the shelves? I've been putting it off because –' she tapped her belly. 'Well, it's awkward to handle those cartons, you know.' Claire nodded.

Two customers walked into the shop and Claire turned away, found the boxes and began what she hoped was going to be her job.

Everything on the shelves was dusty, as were a lot of the new products coming straight from the supplier. Claire took the time to wipe them down carefully. While she was at it she began reorganizing. She couldn't bring herself to put the tomato soup between the soap flakes and the dog food. And she couldn't put a dust-free box right next to one that was grit covered. She also found that if she just slightly rearranged the products there was much more room, and she guessed that the new incoming items should be behind the older ones already there.

The shop was fairly busy from eight until almost nine-thirty but then it slowed down and Mrs Patel had the chance to look at Claire's work. She had unpacked all of the new stock, put it on display and had reorganized and cleaned an entire aisle of old stock as well. When Mrs Patel turned the corner she stopped and stood staring at the aisle. 'Well, you have been busy indeed,' she said. Slowly she walked up and down. Claire held her breath. Had she gone too far? Would Mrs Patel be annoyed that she hadn't asked permission to relocate the merchandise? Would she take it as a criticism that Claire had cleaned things?

Of course, Claire didn't know that Pakistanis were often victims of racial prejudice in London. Nor did she know that a good part of her charm for Mrs Patel was that the woman liked the idea of being able to give orders to an American girl. Nor did she know that Mrs Patel's husband, never very useful, had gone back to Pakistan almost five months ago and was unlikely to return. All Claire knew was that Mrs Patel walked up and down the aisle twice, raised her long dark eyebrows and then cleared her throat.

'You might do this in the other aisles as well,' she said and at the sound of the jingle of the bell, turned back to the counter.

Claire accepted that as praise. For the next half-hour it seemed to her that people lingered in that row. She told herself it was her imagination and to stop being silly. But at the end of the night she had finished another half row and the two that she had done really did seem more inviting.

Despite her desire for promptness, Mrs Patel had quite a few customers at ten o'clock and kept the store open until twenty after. Then she called Claire over. 'Well,' she said, 'it was a good night. Maybe you bring luck.' She walked to the back slowly, her hand on the bulge in her sari. She didn't say anything about the second row, half completed, but Claire saw her eye it carefully. 'This isn't so bad,' she said. 'Now, can you help me with the gate – and do you have time to sweep?'

'I'll give it a quick sweep and a mop up. Remember? We talked about that yesterday.'

'So we did,' Mrs Patel said. 'I'll just go to the back. Push the gate down all the way.'

Claire took half an hour to get the mopping done and empty out the slop bucket. It was odd, but she didn't mind doing the dirty work at all, though she tried to be careful of her clothes. There was a certain satisfaction in being able to see the results of your work. A satisfaction she never got at Crayden Smithers. She looked at the clean floors and the rows she had completed and smiled to herself. But when Mrs Patel rejoined her she merely stood and waited. It didn't seem as if she had the kind of character that enjoyed praising people.

Claire was right. There was no praise but in lieu Mrs Patel handed her a bag. 'Take what you like,' she said and moved up to the front where she began counting the money in the register.

Claire was modest in her wants. She did take some detergent and a bar of soap as well as a box of cereal that was called Weetabix and had the Queen's emblem on it. If things got desperate, Claire thought, she could give up her breakfast and eat the Queen's cereal. She didn't want to take too much or look greedy; besides she had just about everything she needed. One thing this trip had already taught her was that a person could get by happily, in fact, more happily, with less stuff to worry about. She walked to the counter, her bag only half full.

Sharp-eyed Mrs Patel took a look at the bag and once again raised her brows but didn't comment. What Claire wanted her to say was whether or not she should come back, and to her enormous relief, Mrs Patel, looking down at her figures said, 'Perhaps tomorrow you could do the window. It certainly needs doing.'

'Yes, of course.' Then Claire thought she sounded too emphatic about the window, as if she were criticizing Mrs Patel. 'What would you like me to do with it?' she asked.

Mrs Patel shrugged. 'You seem to know what to do on your own,' she said. 'Can't expect me to supervise every little thing.'

Claire nodded. She thought Mrs Patel must make a demanding mother and as if in response to that thought the girl Claire had seen before came running out of the back of the shop. 'Oh, Mum, Fala won't go to bed and she's keeping me up. She's turned on the telly and won't turn it off.'

Mrs Patel looked at the girl coolly. 'Well, it's your responsibility to get her into bed. I can't do everything, Safta.' She turned to Claire. 'This is my daughter, Safta, who has forgotten her manners,' she said.

Safta looked down. She had the longest, darkest eyelashes that Claire had ever seen. They seemed to touch her cheeks. 'Hello, Safta,' Claire said and put her hand out to her. 'My name is Claire Bilsop.'

Safta looked at her. 'You're an American, then?' she asked.

Claire nodded. Before they could continue any discussion Mrs Patel interrupted. 'Questions are not getting the telly off,' she reminded her daughter. 'And your brother?'

'I put Devi to bed, but he wouldn't brush his teeth. He said he doesn't like the taste of the toothpaste.'

'I'll tell him tomorrow that he might like the taste of soap far less. Tell Fala she must be in bed in five minutes.'

Safta gave Claire a glance, then turned around and gracefully ran to the back. 'I'll tell her,' she called.

'That takes care of that,' Mrs Patel sighed. 'I don't remember being so much trouble to my mother. We did as we were told.'

Claire nodded. 'So did I,' she said. But she thought that poor Safta had a lot on her hands. Fred certainly would have never listened to anything Claire told him to do. It wasn't the nature of brothers to listen to their sisters. It occurred to Claire that she should send Fred a postcard and she wondered if she had his address.

Meanwhile, Mrs Patel closed the till and handed a twenty-pound note to Claire. 'Here,' she said.

Claire stared at the money. Twenty pounds! That would pay for her room. If Mrs Patel would pay her twenty pounds a night, well, she could stay for months. Especially since she had the groceries as well.

As if reading her mind, Mrs Patel looked up. 'Don't expect that every night,' she said. She looked at Claire sharply. 'Are you skint?' she asked.

Claire had absolutely no idea what that was, but was too shy to say so.

'Well? Have you any money? I don't imagine you do.'

'Oh, I have some,' Claire said. 'It's just that, well, I came for a holiday and then thought I'd stay on longer.'

'Fine,' Mrs Patel said. She walked to the door and Claire followed her. 'I'll see you at the same time tomorrow and on Friday.' Claire nodded enthusiastically. 'Saturday's a busy day, though,' Mrs Patel continued, 'and the children are home. Do you think you could help out a little longer then? Could you be here by one, when I have to give them lunch?'

'No problem,' Claire told her and as she left she felt as if, for the moment at least, she had no problems in the world.

THIRTY-ONE

Since her ride from the airport Claire had wanted to see the big Victorian piles they had passed on their way to the hotel. One was the Natural History Museum, another was the Victoria and Albert Museum and there was the Brompton Something.

Now it was Saturday and, somehow, the past two days had just flown by, with work at the shop and just, well, wandering and looking. But she had her morning free until her job with Mrs Patel. What would she do with her four hours? She should use the time to read the Charles Lamb book that Toby gave her. She had so much to tell him about: her new job, how wonderful she found London, and perhaps even about Corporal Tucker. Claire could also phone the young American to arrange getting together, but she didn't feel she was ready for that visit just yet. Instead, she consulted her map, took the tube to South Kensington and set off to walk through the neighborhood, north to the museums.

On front door after front door the paintwork gleamed, and polished brass doorknockers set off the enameled colors. Somehow the bright blue or the bus-red didn't look garish the way it would in Tottenville. Maybe it was the soft color of the brickwork or the gentleness of the light. Whatever it was, Claire walked for blocks on the wet pavement until her feet were cold but her eyes were delighted with the visual feast.

She turned a corner searching for a direct route to Exhibition Road, when she saw the tiny shop. 'Knitting Kitting' it said in gold letters on the faded gray paintwork. Claire could hardly believe her eyes. She'd just finished her scarf and here was a yarn shop. In all of her walking around London she hadn't seen any place – aside from the vintage needles at Camden Lock market – that sold knitting supplies.

The door was quaintly set kitty-corner at the end of the wall where one side of the building met the other. Claire walked in. The bell jingled cheerfully and she looked around the store.

It was quite small, with bins up one side where some skeins of wool were arranged by color and yarn content. There was a table on which pattern books sat in piles and a small counter behind which an elderly woman, her white hair pulled up on top of her head, sat with her eyes downcast working on the knitting in her lap. 'Hello, my dear,' she said, looking up. 'How can I help you?'

'I'm not sure,' Claire told her. 'I need some inspiration.' Claire looked over the desk at the old woman's knitting.

'Oh,' she said, 'don't look at me. I don't have the eyes for the kind of work I used to do.' But as she shook her head she held up a circular needle and from it hung a cream colored garment.

'You're making a one-piece sweater?'

'Actually, it's a knee blanket. A very practical item when living here.'

'You're absolutely right,' Claire agreed as she reached out to feel the texture of the yarn and to examine the pattern the woman was using. 'It's so soft. It feels like lamb's wool.'

The woman smiled at Claire. 'I hate to admit this to a potential customer but I have always wanted to make a cashmere wrap and I decided that it was high time. After all, I'm in my seventies. It's working up beautifully, don't you think?'

217

'Outstanding,' Claire said. 'It looks like you used knit-one-back on the border. Is that right?'

'You know your twisted stitches,' the woman replied. 'I use it for strength and to make the interior pattern more defined.'

Claire spread the mass out along the counter to get a better look at it. 'Aran pattern.' But it was smaller and lovelier than any she had ever seen. There must have been four hundred stitches to a single row.

'I know it's done too often but I always like doing the diamond with cable combinations,' the woman said apologetically. 'And for the symbolism. I know it's because of my age, but on this one I'm using the tree of life pattern before the seed stitch edges. Let's hope I shan't die before I finish.'

Claire smiled. 'It's lovely.' If this was the kind of work the woman did now and not what she used to do – well, what could be more difficult than this? 'I think I'll just look around. I'm not sure of the colors or what I really need.'

'You'll find the cottons in the bottom four bins at your feet in front of you, the lamb's wool is in the four on the far top left, the basic worsted is by the door and the baby wool is across from that.'

'Thanks,' Claire said. She turned her back to the woman and scanned the displays of color around her. White, yellow, cream, linen, brown, black, orange, pink. This isn't the place to be inspired, she thought. She stepped closer to the bins by the door and reached up to feel the texture of the yarn. Too coarse and what a hideous green. What would anyone make out of that? She bent down to check the yarn below waist level. This was a slight improvement in color but it was only single-ply cotton – useless unless you were into delicate doilies. She noticed that there was dust on the ledges of the bins and on some of the wool as well. Well, the poor old woman's sight would explain that. She looked over at her and, for a moment, a trick of the light or Claire's own mood cast a resemblance to Claire's grandmother that was so strong Claire almost dropped the skein she was holding.

Then the old woman turned her head and the imagined resemblance faded away. 'I'm afraid there's not a wide selection,' she said. 'I've cut down on my stock. Young people don't seem to be very interested in knitting these days. I mostly do special orders.' She sighed as if she regretted it.

'Oh, don't worry,' Claire told her. 'I'll find something.' Then she thought that might sound rude. 'There's lovely stuff here in the baby wool.' And it was true.

'Yes, there are still indulgent grannies, thank goodness. But you're not one. Now, how can I help you? Not a knee blanket, I suspect. Perhaps a string bikini.'

Claire smiled. 'It's not that warm,' she said.

'Just as well. You don't really look like the string bikini type.'

Somehow, everything the woman said seemed approving, as if she already gave credit to Claire for good taste and good sense. 'I thought I would try some gloves,' Claire told her. They wouldn't take much yarn, they would take a while to do, and she could actually use them. She was safe from the London dampness most of the time because of her raincoat but her hands were often chilly.

'My, my. When I used to knit mittens for my son I didn't like doing the thumbs and gloves are five thumbs in a row.' The woman shrugged. 'Well, some people are gluttons for punishment. Mind you it's the needle ends that get in the way. I used to have short needles but I don't believe they make them anymore.'

'Oh, I'll be all right,' Claire told her. She had been looking about trying to see if there was anything in the way of wool that she might enjoy working. The old woman followed her eye.

'You know,' she said, 'I might just have the thing for

you. I have a few skeins of German wool. It's quite amazing. It looks variegated.' She held up her hand. 'I know that's usually dreadful but these are engineered so that they make figurative patterns when they're knitted up.' Claire hadn't a clue what she was talking about but she waited while the shopkeeper rummaged in a drawer. 'Here we go,' she said and took out a gray, brown and tan speckled ball. She handed it to Claire. 'I'm afraid it's rather dear but it really is quite marvelous the way it works up. I think I have a sock I did as a demonstration.'

Claire held the ball of wool while the woman scrabbled through some drawers behind the counter. 'Ah, here it is.' And she handed Claire the most beautiful sock, one with an intricate stripe that alternated with a row of tweedy dots. 'It's all in the wool, you see. Heaven knows how those Germans managed it. Sixty years of knitting and I'm sure I couldn't.'

Claire looked at the wool carefully. It was remarkable. There would be no need for color exchange bobbins or tying on a new strand. She had to have it. She nodded to the woman.

'You know, my dear, they're the last skeins I have. I may as well knock down the price, as I've had them here so long.'

'Oh, no. That's not necessary,' Claire said. She wondered if she looked indigent, but her clothes were clean and pressed. Actually, she was better put together than she had been in New York.

'I insist,' the woman told her. 'It would be a favor if you took them off my hands. Then, when you've finished knitting them up you can put them on yours.' She chuckled.

'I'll come back and show them to you,' Claire said.

'How lovely. I look forward to it.'

And when Claire left, her purchase safely tucked into her bag, she looked forward to it as well.

THIRTY-TWO

Claire was very tired after an afternoon and evening working at the grocery store. She had split her time between serving customers and keeping an eye on the children. She'd done a good job with both, though Mrs Patel seemed reluctant to admit it.

But of course Mrs Patel might, at any time, tell her not to come back. And she doubted anyone else would actually employ her. The idea gave her a chill, but then again it could be because the heat was turned off. Mrs Watson was very thrifty, and after ten o'clock there was no place warm except under the blankets in Claire's bed.

But she decided she would take a bath first. Usually the heat was enough to get her back down the hall, into bed, and snug until the following morning.

She was in her robe and walking back down the hall, exuding the last of the scent from the Berkeley's delightful bath gel, when, from behind, she was tapped on the shoulder. She gasped and turned.

But it was only Mrs Watson. She had a kerchief on her head that looked none-too-clean and was wearing a sweat-shirt over an old nylon nightie. 'You had a nice bath?' Mrs Watson asked.

'Yes, thank you.'

'And did you have a nice bath this morning?'

Claire tilted her head, feeling the warmth drain out of

her. 'Yes,' she said. 'Why? Has someone complained? I didn't think anyone was waiting.'

'I'm complaining,' Mrs Watson said. 'For eighteen pounds you don't get two hot baths a day. I can't lose money on every guest. And if you don't like it,' she added, her face looking pale green under a layer of cream, 'you can go else-where. That's my position.'

Despite her shock and embarrassment Claire felt angry. Why was it every time she felt the slightest bit comfortable somewhere something like this had to happen? If she had any courage she would tell Mrs Watson she was leaving in the morning, but instead she just stood there mutely. The cold was shooting up through the floor to the soles of her feet. Tiny waves of goose pimples radiated down from her shoulders to her wrists and began the voyage all over again. 'I'm sorry,' she told Mrs Watson. 'I should have thought.'

'Yes, you should have. Too late for that now. Twenty pounds a night. And I'd like some money in advance, please.'

Claire wondered if a tub of hot water could possibly cost two pounds. But she simply nodded, now colder than before, walked down the hall to her room, opened her purse and gave six crisp twenty-pound notes to Mrs Watson. 'Here you are,' she said as calmly as she could manage. 'And I'll be leaving after that.' Claire had had no plans to do so but her pride prevented her from even thinking about dealing with this woman. Her scarf would not allow a twisted stitch. Why should she allow one here?

She closed the door on the silenced Mrs Watson and got into bed. But Mrs Watson wasn't quiet for long. She began to yell at Maudie's children. They did make a noise, but did the woman have to be so dreadful to them? Under the blankets Claire began to shiver. This was ridiculous. At the very least she had to stay clean and warm. If she took a bath the night before would she be expected to go out with-out a morning shower? If she stood in the tub and simply washed herself, did she have to pay another two pounds, and how cold would she get?

She put her right foot against the back of her left calf hoping to warm herself. She inserted her toes into the crevice behind her knee but didn't feel much difference in temperature. Huddled under her blanket, cold and a little frightened, she began to consider her options. She had probably been too impulsive, for where would she find a decent place as cheap as this one? She didn't even know where to look.

But then the realization came to her: her life here was like a small but perfect scarf. And this dark room was far from perfect. Somehow, she didn't know yet how, she would find another place to live. It would be somewhere she could afford, somewhere prettier and somewhere more congenial. If she had done it once she could certainly do it again. Laws of statistics told her this couldn't be the only inexpensive rooming house in London. She tried to calm herself. She would be fine.

After a little while she realized she was too agitated to sleep and she had no knitting underway. She would have to see to that tomorrow. Meanwhile, she remembered Toby's book and braved the cold air to fetch it.

The fact that it wasn't a novel, which was her favorite read, had already disappointed her. But if she read it, it would give her something to talk to Toby about. She turned again to the essay she had looked at. 'The Superannuated Man' seemed to be about the author's working days – thirty-four years in 'a counting house', which appeared to be something like a CPA firm. Claire began to read and sighed. His description was harrowing, the style a little less than Dickens, although it certainly read like a Dickensian tale. She couldn't imagine why Toby – or anyone – would think that she wanted to read about a long-dead man's office struggles, but Lamb's voice, once she got used to it, was so engaging, and his ideas so heartfelt that soon Claire was deeply involved.

Poor Charles had begun working at fourteen and spent ten hours each day but Sunday virtually chained to a desk doing sums. He hated his servitude. His description of his plight was heartrending, but then, unexpectedly, he was not just freed but given enough of a pension so that he could leave and never work again. His good luck astonished him, as it astonished her. He had been feeling ill and was called into the partners' offices. She supposed that was like having to speak to Mr Crayden. He was afraid it meant he might be fired. And then, instead, they asked him how long he had worked for them and after he told them thirty-four years (thirty-four years!) the partner in charge told him they were going to retire him. (That was what superannuated meant.) And give him four hundred pounds a year.

His joy was palpable. It flooded out to her from the pages of the musty book.

If peradventure, reader, it has been thy lot to waste the golden years of thy life – the high shining youth – in the irksome confinement of an office; to have thy prison days prolonged through middle age down to decrepitude and silver hairs: without hope of release or respite; to have lived to forget that there are such things as holidays, or to remember them but as the prerogatives of childhood: then, and then only, will you be able to appreciate my deliverance.

There, in her little shabby room, Claire's eyes filled with tears. She felt as if Charles Lamb was speaking directly to her. Only a week ago she had been working at Crayden Smithers, and though she hadn't moved from youth to middle age to 'decrepitude', there were people there who had. She thought of the women at her lunch table and of the older Abigail and her unexpected approval of this adventure. Wasn't that also an unspoken warning? Yes or no, she must take warning from Charles Lamb as well, she realized. She couldn't possibly go back to that job, to that office. She thought of the windowless room where she worked. She thought of Joan, and her coworkers all breathing the same air, all more than two corridors from natural light. Things hadn't changed so very much in all the years since Lamb's time. Unlike poor Charles, Claire decided then and there not to waste thirty-four years in servitude.

But unlike Charles Lamb she would not receive a pension. She would not have any money coming in, in any regular way. How could she possibly survive? She closed the book and put it under her pillow. She switched off the light and lay down. She could feel the little volume under her head. It served as a reminder of her new promise to herself. Perhaps she could find work, work that made enough money so that . . . well, she didn't want to move too fast, but money would be necessary.

She thought of Toby and wondered if he had guessed the profound meaning the little book would have for her. She would have to go back to the Pied Piper and ask him. Or even speak to Corporal Tucker at the American Embassy. She had almost forgotten about him. He wasn't exactly the kind of personality that Claire would normally be drawn to, but Corporal Tucker must know of something, some work. Of course. Maybe even someplace to live. She would call him in the morning.

Claire pulled the blanket over her shoulders and sighed. She would have to hope that the work at Mrs Patel's would last until she could come up with another arrangement. Maybe Toby would know of something or better yet perhaps the old woman in the yarn store needed help. Claire rolled over, stuffed the pillow under her neck and fell asleep.

THIRTY-THREE

'Back in Black' was blaring so loud that Claire had to ask Adam to repeat himself. She'd never liked AC/DC very much, and here in a London restaurant she liked them even less. 'How long?' she asked.

'Almost a year,' Adam said and picked up his hamburger. He had been stationed in London that long and yet he had picked this place – he said it was his favorite – for them to meet and eat in. Claire looked around. Aside from a higher percentage of guys with military haircuts, this could be any place in New York. The menu featured steaks, burgers and buffalo chicken wings, the beers were all American, and the only tea was iced. Worst of all, it wasn't easy to have a conversation above the music and the noise at the bar.

She had called him that morning, been relieved to reach him, and jumped when he offered to meet her for lunch. She had taken a lot of trouble with her hair and her make-up, not just because he was good-looking but also because she was hoping for a favor, or at least some information. It didn't make her feel good, but she reasoned that she wasn't using him. He was free to refuse help, and who knew? They might have something in common. But looking around again at his favorite spot she began to doubt it.

Claire picked at her salad. 'Where do you live?' she asked.

She tried to sound casual but perhaps there was somewhere nearby where she could . . . The song ended and Claire was grateful to hear it replaced with a quieter (but equally American) Eagles number.

'We've got military housing near the airport. It's great over there. Good food, cheap movies and a PX that blows your mind. It's cheaper than CostCo.'

Claire nodded and tried to keep anything but a positive expression on her face. NO way was she going to live on some army base with a giant discount Post Exchange. Better to be back in Tottenville. But he didn't talk much about housing, though that was foremost in her thoughts. Instead Adam Tucker went on to tell her about the stereo, the Walkman and the laptop he'd bought at discounted prices. She tried to appear interested, but his enthusiastic simplicity made her suddenly miss Michael Wainwright. That wasn't good. Corporal Adam Tucker was nice looking, friendly, and even sexually attractive. He was big, with broad shoulders, big hands and long legs. His blond hair, though cut too short, would be lovely if it was grown in. And he seemed to like her. There must be something there, she told herself, besides Budweiser and hamburgers.

'How long are you going to stay on?' he asked her. 'Maybe I can get you into the PX.'

The PX wasn't what she needed: she had to make some money, not spend it. 'I'm not sure,' she told him. 'I've got a little job and I'm trying to make my money last as long as I can.'

'Do you have a work visa?' he asked.

'I think I'm going to get one,' she told him. If she was breaking the law, what would happen if she got caught?

'Well, if you're getting one you're lucky. Pissed-off people are coming in and out all day over them. The Brits don't want to give away jobs they can keep for themselves. How's your salad?'

If she'd been interested in it before Claire had no appetite for her meal now. But she stabbed at a hard-boiled egg with a fork. 'Really good.'

'They got great ranch dressing here. You can't get it anyplace else. Even the ranch at McDonald's tastes funny,' Adam said.

She nodded, though the last thing she would think of having here was a Happy Meal. How could she get him to talk a little more about a visa? She couldn't just come out and ask him. 'Who's in charge of work visas?' she asked.

He bit into his hamburger but answered her, his mouth half-full. 'Oh, hell, there's tons of paperwork. Best I can understand the company here writes a request that goes to the Limeys and then, if it's approved, goes up to the third floor. Oh, man, I love the Clash. Isn't this song bitchin'?'

Claire sighed. Despite the cute accent, the uniform and the good looks, Adam Tucker was as boring as the men that Tina tried to set her up with. A little different, but just as dull. And useless to her, except socially. Maybe she could date him. She told herself to try harder. 'What's your favorite place in London?' she asked.

'The PX,' he said without even a moment's hesitation.

'Does that count as really London?' she asked. 'What do you like in the city?'

'Well, the movies are good. I mean the Mel Gibson ones and *The Matrix*. And, of course, *X2*.'

'What about English movies?' Claire couldn't help asking.

'Which ones are English?' he asked. 'There was that one about servants and guests in some manor house and the guy, one of the servants, he came back to kill his daddy. But it wasn't very good.'

'*Gosford Park*?' she asked. 'I think that was made here but it was directed by Robert Altman, an American.'

'Well, whatever it was, it was real boring. Even the murder was boring.'

Claire had loved it but said nothing. In fact, there was nothing more said until Adam finished his burger. 'Want some dessert?' he asked. 'They have sundaes that kick ass. Oh, I'm sorry. They're really good.'

Claire shook her head. She was afraid to tell him she had to get to work. Perhaps he would report her. 'I have to get back. I have an appointment with a friend.'

'Is it a boy friend?'

Claire shook her head. 'An English lady. I promised I'd help her.'

'Can I take you there?'

'Oh, no. It's a long trip on the underground.'

'I don't have anything else to do,' he said and shrugged.

Though Claire didn't want to tell him about work she didn't want to hurt his feelings. She was such a chicken. That's why she never went out with people: if she did and they didn't like her she was hurt. If she did and she didn't like them, they were hurt. 'I just better go,' she told him.

He insisted on walking her to the tube and then asked if he could see her again. She nodded. Then he asked if he could kiss her goodbye. She said yes again and was surprised when she liked his hands on her shoulders and his mouth against hers. It was just a pressing of lips, but there was something about his size that made his bent head and big arms very moving. He was sweet. 'I'll call you,' she said. He smiled and waved as she walked down the stairs. When she turned her head he was still there, smiling and waving. Claire ducked into the underground station with relief and more than a little guilt.

THIRTY-FOUR

Monday afternoon Claire sat in the worn but comfortable armchair across from Toby, Lamb's book of essays on her lap, sharing space with George Eliot – the cat not the writer. 'I've read it over twice now,' Claire was saying. After the disappointment of the lack of help from Adam Tucker the day before and a long evening of work at Mrs Patel's, Claire had rewarded herself with a visit to the used bookstore. Toby had seemed happy to see her and now he seemed delighted to discuss Charles Lamb.

'His retirement was such an escape. And he was so . . .' she paused, at a loss for words.

'. . . joyful?' Toby offered.

'Yes. Shocked and joyful about it,' she paused again, too shy to say that she, too, was joyful to be liberated. 'It reminded me of the work I do . . . did back in New York and how it's possible to be so busy with paperwork that before you know it you look up from your task to find that twenty or so years have escaped you. Anyway, it has made me think.'

'Great. That's what essays are for. Stories make you feel and essays make you think.' George Eliot jumped off Claire's lap and gracefully onto Toby's. He stroked the cat and scratched her behind her ears. Claire watched his hands. He was so interesting to talk to; far more amusing and well-informed than Corporal Tucker. Claire was embarrassed to find herself almost jealous of the cat. Toby had lovely hands. She couldn't help but wonder what a kiss from Toby would feel like.

She put the idea out of her mind. She needed to ask him for help, but could not find the courage. Yet she had only four more nights at Mrs Watson's and she would hate to have to extend her stay there.

She refocused on the conversation. 'What is strange is the essay seemed as if it was meant exactly for me,' Claire said. 'As if Charles Lamb was sending me a message.'

Toby nodded. 'It's a gift I have,' he said. 'I don't know how it works and I can't seem to make a penny out of it, but I seem to divine what's wanted by the reader. Sort of like a prose consultant.'

On the one hand, Claire was flattered that Toby seemed to be on her wavelength. On the other she had to admit a certain disappointment that, as a client, his services to her were not unique.

Toby rolled George onto her back and stroked the long hairs on her belly. 'I've often thought I should put up a sign. You know, "Mystic Reading" or something of that sort. The trouble is it would bring all the wrong types in. Fools who wanted to know if their portfolio was healthy or if they were going to meet a tall, dark stranger.'

'Well, I'm not sure about them, but this was great for me.' She briefly explained about her own working life in Manhattan.

'Suited you down to the ground, eh?'

'Yes. And now I'd like one about medieval painting, please.'

Toby cocked his head. 'An expensive pursuit, I'm afraid. I have wonderful, beautiful books but all rather dear.'

'Perhaps there might be one . . .' she began, but before she could ask for the cheapest one he had smiled. She had to notice that he was very good-looking.

Toby stood, and he and George ran off into a dark aisle

of books. He was back in a flash. 'This book is a wonder, but as the cover is stained and it's missing a few pages I could give it to you. I won't ever be able to sell it and as it came in a box from an estate sale . . . well, here.'

The cover was gray leather, with a nasty ring from some hot mug that once rested on it. But when she opened it up the jewel-like colors and the actual gilding on the pages made her open her eyes wide. She looked up at Toby. 'Oh, I couldn't . . .'

'Certainly you can. Could have it rebound and sell it off, but the cost of binding – well you'd take a big loss. So take the book instead.'

'Thank you.' She put it in her bag and wondered if she might ask him if he knew how she could rent a room, or if that was too forward. What would she do if he told her he had a place she could share? The fact was that Claire felt very attracted to him. He was so different from Michael Wainwright that they could not be compared. Toby was not business-like, not manly in the way that Michael was, but he had a sharp mind and was certainly more widely read. She couldn't imagine Michael having a cat or stroking it so sweetly. From what she could see, English men seemed a lot less pushy, not nearly as macho as American men. Nothing wrong with that, she thought. Corporal Adam Tucker probably spent his free time watching football or playing it. With Toby she could talk about books forever. Of course he wouldn't, but if he offered her a place to stay with him would she accept? She pushed the thought out of her mind.

Just as she was framing a question, the little bell over the door sang out and Toby moved toward the front, lighting the center row of books. 'Hello,' he called out.

Claire heard a woman's voice answer, but both Toby and his possible client were too far away for her to see or overhear them unless she got up. Though she was curious, she sat quite still and waited. She had been shy about coming back so soon, afraid it might be too forward. She was equally afraid Toby might not remember her but he greeted her by name and had immediately invited her to sit down. Once again, she was having a very good time talking with him but reminded herself that she mustn't wear out her welcome, even if she didn't get to ask him anything about an apartment or a job.

She sat for a while uncertain about what to do, listening to the murmuring. Just as she decided it was time to go, Toby's voice was raised a bit as he said goodbye and the doorbell tinkled again. He was back, George padding beside him the way a dog might. Good. Perhaps she would get to ask him now, before another interruption.

Toby dropped his long frame into his chair. 'I sold a book,' he said. 'And I'm absolutely exhausted. I shall have to rest up. And perhaps eat a biscuit. For medicinal purposes only, of course.' He reached to a lower shelf on the stand beside his chair and took out a brightly-colored metal container. He popped off the top and offered the contents to Claire. There was a jumble of cookies inside, obviously not the ones that had originally come in the tin. Claire selected a chocolate one and Toby put the tin on his lap, eating one cookie after another.

'God, I am such a good businessman. I think I made sixty pee on that sale. Now, if we don't eat more than sixty pee in biscuits I've made a profit.' He looked down at the open container and picked up another. 'Not much chance of that though.' He smiled and passed her the canister again. Though she knew he was joking, Claire shook her head.

'So where were we? You don't want to go back to the paperwork gulag, or serve thirty-four years there the way poor Charlie did. I can certainly understand. I once actually worked for a living. I was an up-and-coming executive in an advertising agency. Couldn't bear it. Thought I would die. Then my uncle died and left me this shambles. I looked upon it as a sign.'

'Is that how you got into the book business?'

'Yes, and into the flat above as well. I don't make any money, but who knows? There might be a sudden run on Hugh Walpole. I must have almost a hundred of his books, poor sod.'

'So you live upstairs?' Claire asked. When he nodded she tried to be bold. 'I can't keep living where I am,' almost burst out of her. 'Do you know how I might find a very cheap apartment – flat – to share?'

'Well, you could end up going to Croydon for that,' he said and popped another biscuit into his mouth.

'What part of London is Croydon?'

'That's the rub, my dear. It's not in London at all. It's a dreadful place and no one wants to live there, except perhaps the good people of Croydon. No, you want something central.' He paused again, looking up at the ceiling. Was he thinking about the room overhead? 'But I shall have to think,' was all he said. He bit into another cookie and was silent, but only for a moment. 'Hang on! Have you looked at the *Evening Standard*?'

'What's that?' Claire asked, then remembered the pile of papers on Mrs Patel's counter.

'The daily London tabloid. Comes out in several editions starting at lunchtime. I think it has a whole section of flats to share, though you wouldn't know what you were getting into. Meanwhile, I'll ask among my friends. Perhaps one of them knows about something.'

'Thank you,' she said, and meant it. Silly of her to hope for another offer. It was very nice just to have him take any interest in her.

'All right, now. What are your plans for the day?'

'I thought I would walk through Hyde Park and then go to the Victoria and Albert Museum.'

'Oh, my dear. Forget the V & A,' he said. 'Dismal basement café. You won't want to take your lunch there.' He popped another cookie into his mouth and Claire had to wonder how he stayed so thin.

'Oh, I have my lunch with me. I'll just have tea out later.'

'But where will you have tea? My bit in your education is to make sure you go to the right hotels.'

Claire thought about the checkmarks Abigail had made next to Claridge's and Brown's. 'I'd like to,' she said. 'My budget is a little . . . tight, but how much could tea cost?'

'Depends on whether it's a cup of tea, a pot of tea, a cream tea, afternoon tea, or high tea. We're like the Eskimos,' he explained further, 'you know, thirty words for snow.'

Claire had to smile. It was true that tea in London was as ubiquitous as snow must be above the Arctic Circle. Of course people who descended from Shakespeare would have distinctions. But what were they? Before she had to ask, voluble Toby continued: '*A cup* of tea is just that. You get it in cheaper restaurants. All the better places give you *a pot* of tea, which doesn't cost them anything extra but costs you. *Afternoon tea* means it's accompanied by finger sandwiches – you know – those slivers of bread with the crusts cut off. A *cream tea* includes that as well as scones and Devonshire clotted cream, which you put on the scones along with strawberry preserves. No matter what they serve, insist on strawberry by the way.'

Claire's head was spinning but she laughed aloud. 'And is *high tea* even fancier than that? What do they throw in? A pizza?'

Toby plucked another biscuit from the tin in his lap and then smiled up at her. 'This is where the British fool you,' he said. '*High tea* is actually a meal that could include a sweet and a savory course. In the North it's a lower class thing – *tea* means dinner. You might call it "supper".'

'I see,' she said, though she wasn't absolutely sure she did.

Toby closed the tin of biscuits, put it back, and brushed the crumbs from his lap. 'It used to be eaten by people who are NOKD.' He grinned again. Before she could ask, he told her, 'That means Not Our Kind Dear. It was coined by Nancy Mitford. Know her?'

Claire shook her head and for the first time had doubts about Toby. Did he think she was grand, did he just assume all Americans were rich, or was there something about her that made him think that?

'Oh my dear! How lucky you are! All the pleasure of learning about the Mitford girls in front of you!' He leaned forward. 'She was from an aristocratic but what you in the States might call an extremely dysfunctional family. Nancy was a writer, her sister Deborah married a Duke, Jessica became a left-leaning journalist, and Diana married the head of the British Fascist party. Unity had an obsession with Hitler, and when Britain went to war with Germany she shot herself in the head.' Claire's own head was spinning again but she was fascinated. 'I think it was Nancy who said "Unity didn't succeed at suicide because she missed her teensy, tinsy brain."' Toby's eyes lit up. 'Have you never read *Hons and Rebels*?' Claire shook her head. 'Good heavens, my dear, every girl should read it at thirteen.' He was off like a rabbit, and his cat streaked behind him as if, indeed, he was one. He was back in a moment, a small green book in his hand. 'Forget medieval art for a few moments. You must have this,' he said. 'You will enjoy it.'

She took the little green book. She wasn't sure he was right but she certainly wasn't going to say no. Timidly, she opened the cover and saw that it was only three-pounds-fifty. She could afford it, just, but before she could say so Toby spoke up. 'I'll knock it down to two pounds. You can't ask for more – less, actually – than that. And you'll never regret it, my girl.'

He had used a completely different accent, and while she wasn't sure what kind, she realized she was beginning to notice distinctions in speech. He was imitating some-body, or perhaps a whole class of somebodies, and they were probably NOKD. Maybe, she guessed, the British equivalent of Anthony and his Staten Island pals.

Claire reached into her purse and fished around for a two-pound coin. She handed it over and Toby nodded in thanks. 'Two books sold today. I'm flush. So, back to tea. You know people argue about whether to put the milk in first.'

'No. Why?'

'Oh, I don't know. The pre-lactarians say it is to make sure that the hot tea alone doesn't crack good porcelain.'

Claire thought of the milky mug of tea that was put in front of her every morning. It could be dropped without showing a crack. 'But how do you know how much milk you need if you don't know how strong the tea is?'

'Do an approximation,' Toby told her. 'Now, you must have tea at Claridge's just to see the place. It's on Brook Street between Hanover and Grosvenor Squares. Heaven. And the Connaught, that's just below Grosvenor Square on Mount Street. And Brown's in Albemarle Street. It's a classic.'

'I'm not sure I can afford to . . .'

'A-ha, that's the trick. You see, if you go in at four o'clock they'll be serving a full tea and it will set you back twenty or twenty-five pounds.'

Claire tried not to gasp.

'Well worth the experience, my dear, if you have the money, but if you don't, then you simply show up at two-thirty or three. You ask, "Is afternoon tea being served yet?" and of course they'll tell you no because it doesn't begin until about four. And lunch service would be over as well. So you just say "Well, will somebody bring me a cup of tea?" and of course they will. And then you get to sit in a lovely room and have linen napkins and breathtaking surroundings and enjoy all of it while it only sets you back two or three pounds.'

Two or three pounds seemed like a lot of money, but

she could see what Toby was getting at; it was sort of like collecting an experience rather than consuming.

'You might also try the Lanesborough, though it's awfully overdone. It's in Knightsbridge. And while you're there, the Berkeley is absolutely perfect and the Hyde Park Hotel is a grand old Victorian pile. The trick is you get out before they begin serving a proper tea.'

The mention of the Berkeley gave her a small stab in the heart but she ignored it. 'How did you figure this out?' Claire asked.

Toby smiled, raised a brow and sighed theatrically. 'Aah. I was not always as you see me now. I live in reduced circumstances, but now and then one just must get in touch with one's inner posh.'

'Posh? Like the Spice Girl?'

He nodded. 'But before Sporty and the rest we – well, our more humble grandparents – used the term for what you might call "classy", though I could never believe that anyone who used that word could be classy.' Claire giggled. Jerry used to call her mother 'a classy lady' all the time. 'Anyway, it comes from wealthy people sailing to India. One wanted to be on the port side going and the starboard side returning to avoid the heat of the sun. Port Out Starboard Home. Hence "Posh".'

Claire thought she could listen to Toby all day. But she knew she mustn't impose. Reluctantly she stood up. 'Thank you so much for the recommendation,' she said, holding up the Mitford book. 'I'll read it, get the *Standard*, try tea, and report back.'

'Good girl,' he said, smiling at her warmly. 'You look tremendously presentable. Just tell yourself you belong in those places. And after you get your legs, I'll take you to the Ritz. But perhaps not for tea. We could have a drink.'

Claire was charmed. Toby had asked her out! She didn't know when, and she didn't know if he would actually ever get around to it, but she was thrilled. 'I'd love that,' she said. She tried to keep the wild enthusiasm out of her voice.

'Well, good luck and good flat hunting. Rubbishy paper, really, the *Standard* but it's a start.'

She nodded, thanked him and walked out of the bookshop with a new book under her arm and a lightness in her step.

THIRTY-FIVE

Claire spent the remainder of her day before work strolling
up and down the streets in the hope that, by a happy
coincidence, she would see a flat for rent. After seeing Toby,
Claire was hopeful that something could be found in the
papers. Now she just needed to find a *Standard* – as Toby
had referred to it – left at Mrs Patel's shop by the time
Claire got there.

It was hard to be alone – or lonely for that matter – at
Mrs Patel's. After only a little less than a week Claire had
become familiar with the shop regime. She'd almost finished
dusting and rearranging all the stock and had begun a list
of items that customers requested. Because she arrived a
little bit earlier each night she was now able to cover the
store while Mrs Patel ate dinner with her children. It also
helped that the shop was quiet since Claire wasn't trusted
enough to take the money, but she did sit at the counter,
help customers and call Mrs Patel only when it was time
to ring up sales.

She had a tidy mind and, to her great satisfaction, you
no longer found Fairy liquid next to Heinz Baked Beans.
Occasionally, Mrs Patel grumbled – 'I can find nothing.'
But sales seemed to have increased and so, when asked,
she would fan her hand and say, 'Move it! Move it as you
like.'

Claire was also beginning to know the regular shoppers,

though not always by name. There was Mrs Caudrey, an elderly woman who always wore a dusty raincoat and bought a sliced loaf, a pint of milk and dozens of tins of cat food. There was fat Mr Robinson, with a once-rakish mustache who each evening bought enough sweets and ice cream for an entire kindergarten. There were a few younger people who seemed to dash in almost every night for milk or juice or bread. Claire would have liked to speak with them, but they seemed busy and distracted. Unlike her, they had lives and homes waiting for them. Then there was Maudie, the woman from Mrs Watson's, who dropped by two or even three times an evening with her two fractious little boys. 'Watch her, I think she steals,' Mrs Patel said.

'No!' Claire exclaimed. 'Have you seen her?'

Mrs Patel shook her head. 'Why else would she come in so often? She doesn't have any money. If she could she'd buy milk on hire-purchase.'

But Claire knew why. Maudie had nowhere else to go except the grim room at Mrs Watson's. Dealing with the children, their noise, as well as Mrs Watson's disapproval must be murder. Far better to be out and about, as Claire herself had already discovered. Maudie might not be the most reputable of women – she had told Claire that her boys were only half-brothers, though both looked exactly like little Maudies, and that she'd been abandoned by both fathers – but she was no thief.

Claire tried to imagine what it would be like to raise two children and know that for the next fifteen or twenty years you, all alone, were responsible for them. Claire, alone and unencumbered, wasn't finding it easy to fit in or find a home. What was it like for Maudie? The poor woman wasn't shoplifting, she was just lonely and the way she started conversations with Claire every evening seemed to prove it. Claire was too new to London to realize that Maudie wasn't from London, or even from Britain. She was, like Claire, an immigrant.

After dinner that night Safta Patel stood for a long while beside the frozen foods watching Claire. At first Claire thought her mother might have told her to do it, to check to see if Claire herself was shoplifting – Mrs Patel, out of sight at the till, was far from trusting – but soon she realized that Safta's awkwardness was really shyness.

'Hello,' she said. 'Have you finished your lessons?'

'Almost,' Safta admitted guiltily. 'It's just the telly. My sister is watching it and I can't study.'

Claire thought of the hours she had spent upstairs at home, constantly distracted from her homework by Fred's blaring stereo. 'It's hard,' she said. 'What are you working on?'

'Maths,' Safta told her. 'I'm no bloody good at it.'

Claire put down her duster and shrugged. 'I think math is the same on both sides of the Atlantic,' she said. 'Very challenging.'

Safta smiled, and her narrow face lit up. Claire couldn't help but notice the girl's eyelashes, which brushed her cheeks and pushed against her glasses. They must have been the longest ones that Claire had ever seen. Claire, being fair, had always longed for dark, luxurious lashes.

But Safta must have been thinking in a similar vein. 'You have such pretty hair,' she said. 'It flutters when you move.'

Claire recognized the longing in Safta's voice. 'Yours is nicer. So straight and shiny.'

Safta shrugged off the compliment.

'So I think you'd better go back to your homework.'

Safta sighed and nodded. 'I'm studying for my GCSEs. They're very important. Did you take them?'

Before Claire could answer that she didn't know what they were, Mrs Patel called out from the front. 'What are you doing, Safta? Do you need me to tell you how to keep busy?'

'No,' Safta answered, then looked at Claire. 'I wish I could cut my hair,' she said, and as she turned and disappeared into the back her long dark braid flapped behind her. Claire would have paid cash to have hair like that.

Mrs Patel joined her. 'Those children and the telly,' she said and shook her head. 'Well, they're off to bed now and Safta can have some peace.'

As Claire had begun working longer hours, without commenting or changing the twenty pounds, Mrs Patel increased the groceries. After less than a week Claire had a stash of strange tins and jars – English things – including a dark brown spread called 'Marmite' which tasted like stove grease and was, as Toby might say, very nasty indeed. Claire had noticed they were usually dented cans, or odd things no one seemed to buy, but she had said nothing and eaten little. In fact, though she had no scale, she seemed to be losing weight. Both pairs of trousers seemed looser than they had been.

Tonight, though, when Mrs Patel gave her two bags at closing time Claire demurred. 'No thank you,' she said. 'I really have more than enough.'

Mrs Patel narrowed her eyes. 'What is it then? Do you want more money? Because I haven't got it!'

Claire shook her head. 'No,' she said. 'It's fine really. It's just more than I need.' She went to close the gate.

When she came back in Mrs Patel was on the other side of the counter, her hand on the small of her back. 'Well,' she said, 'you might come to dinner.'

'But who would watch the shop while we eat?'

'Occasionally, to be with the children, I put the "Back in thirty minutes" sign in the window. My regulars come back when I'm open or if it's an emergency they ring a buzzer on the side of the entrance. I let them in and lock up behind them. But if you come to dinner you'll miss the extra money I usually give you for the longer hours, won't you?'

Claire almost smiled but thought that the touchy Mrs

Patel might take offense so she nodded in consent. It was kind of her to offer dinner, especially when it would mean Claire got to be more involved with the children. 'I would like that very much,' Claire said. She thought, perhaps, that Mrs Patel might need a little adult company, too.

As if to dispel any idea of that Mrs Patel added, 'And you can help with the washing up as well.' Her brusqueness seemed an automatic reaction to her own hospitality.

'Fine,' Claire told her. 'May I look at a newspaper now before I go?'

But with the *Evening Standard* spread out before her she was dismayed to find that most of the furnished flats advertised were more than three hundred pounds a week, while she was paying just over a hundred. The flats to share seemed a mixed batch, and the advertisements were difficult to decipher. She circled any that asked for less than a hundred and fifty pounds, but there were few enough of those.

'What does "mod cons" mean?' she asked Mrs Patel.

'Modern conveniences.' Mrs Patel looked up from tidying behind the counter. 'You know, fridges and washing machines. Why? Are you buying a flat?'

Claire laughed out loud. 'Buying? I can't even afford to rent one.'

Mrs Patel stared searchingly at Claire. 'Don't tell me you don't have a rich family back in America.'

'My father died five years ago and I have left home.'

'Oh. I'm so sorry.' Mrs Patel actually seemed to be. For a moment her strict façade crumbled and she patted Claire's hand. 'I know what it's like to be without a family. Very bloody difficult for a woman alone.' She was silent a moment. Then she became brisk again. 'Well, I thought you were looking for something grand. If you haven't any money you won't find anything in the papers. To find a cheap flat to share you must ask around.' She paused. 'We could put up a notice. Perhaps someone here will know.' Claire was touched at the 'we'. She watched Mrs Patel's dark head as it bent over the paper. The woman looked up distastefully. 'You don't want to go knocking on doors of people you haven't even seen. Something terrible might happen to you.'

Claire was pleased to hear the concern in Mrs Patel's voice but she figured it wouldn't last long. 'I'm just going to sweep up now.'

For some reason the clean-up that night was dustier than ever and, though she had had a bath in the morning, Claire felt she couldn't get between the sheets without bathing again.

She unlocked the door to her room, gathered her toiletries, and walked down the hall with her robe over her arm. But when she got to the bathroom it was in use, steam escaping from the wide gaps of the ill-fitting door. She was torn between waiting in the hallway and creeping back to wait in her room. As she stood there, undecided, Mrs Watson came down the stairs.

She looked Claire over head to toe. 'Not planning a bath are you?'

Claire shook her head. 'Just a wash up,' she lied, but felt humiliated both by the question and her cheesy denial. Especially when she had already paid extra for the privilege of keeping clean.

'You can wash up in there,' Mrs Watson said, indicating the toilet, which also had a sink.

'Thank you,' Claire said, 'but it's a bit dirty in there.'

'Well, then you can clean it,' Mrs Watson snapped. 'Partly your dirt, isn't it?'

'No, it isn't,' Claire snapped back and walked down the hall, back to her room.

She was very upset. She was paying for this room, just like she paid for her room at home. Why didn't she feel as if either belonged to her? She never belonged anywhere, not at home, not in Tottenville, not at Crayden Smithers, nor here. Claire sat down at the edge of the bed, put her face in her hands and couldn't stop the hot tears.

She cried for a long time. Each time the sobs seemed about to diminish, she would think of Joan's insults, her mother's snubs, Tina's careless smugness, Michael's betrayal or the expression on Mrs Watson's face and they would begin again. The worst was the memory of Michael with Katherine. How wonderful it had been, those few days before when she felt he wanted her beside him. Better than his attention, than his love-making or the luxury that surrounded him was the feeling that with him she belonged: she was a member of the club of people welcomed wherever they went. Here in this nasty room she knew the truth. She was from the world of people welcomed nowhere and she probably always would be.

The crying ended and Claire, exhausted, managed to strip off her clothes. Without even washing her dusty face or hands she crawled into bed. What she needed was sleep and the dawning of a new day when everything might look brighter.

Then Claire noticed the envelope addressed to her lying on the chair beside her bed, her name and Mrs Watson's address carefully written out in Abigail Samuels's neat and beautiful handwriting. Claire picked the letter up as if it were a winning lottery ticket. Someone had thought of her, was thinking of her enough to write, and she felt, at least at that moment, closer to Abigail than to anyone else. She opened the flap carefully and took out the notepaper with Abigail's initials engraved at the top.

Dear Claire,

I was quite delighted to hear from you and so glad you phoned. Needless to say, I have arranged for your vacation days and you need not worry at all about them. Right now I have informed Human Resources that you will be gone for two weeks. If you come back before then it won't matter but do let me know if you extend your stay beyond it.

Not to worry if you do. The job will wait for you. Incidentally, I never realized quite how bullying Joan Murphy is. Since we are not lilies of the field we all must work. But is it necessary to make that so very unpleasant? I think not. Nothing worse than a tin-pot tyrant. How have you managed?

The young Mr Wainwright returned from his travels to find a bit of a mess waiting for him. Nothing to do with his apparently equally messy social life, but it would appear that some of his business judgments are being questioned. I'm sure you will trust me when I tell you that it is never pleasant to have Mr Crayden himself questioning you. The pup has been skulking about looking very hang-dog. Not that you would care, of course. Just a bit of office gossip.

And speaking of same, you are quite the subject of the day, or to be more correct, the week. Before the hush falls when I walk by the lunch table in the lounge, your name is always the main topic. One would think that with the current political situation, the new child molestation case, the recent fratricide and the dip in the Dow there would be more than that to cover. Apparently not. This seems to uphold the recent theory that humans develop speech not to exchange practical information but to gossip.

But never mind the dull happenings here. I hope you have already been received by the Queen, had a spree at Harrods and have begun a dalliance with either an MP or a notable footballer. I myself have found English men sorely lacking in passion, but that may just have been my unlucky choices. Hope you fare better.

Do be sure to enjoy yourself every legal way you

*can. After a fairly long and varied life, I find I
most regret the things I didn't do, not the things I
did. By the way, try to get yourself to Hampton
Court. It's truly lovely this time of year. Have fun
and (as they almost never say in London)*
   Cheerio.

Claire almost laughed aloud with surprise and enjoyment. Miss Samuels had written to her and advised her sexually as well as philosophically. Claire read through the letter again. It wasn't nice of her, but she took pleasure in the part about Michael being in some type of trouble, and almost as much satisfaction in thinking about Joan. It wasn't a good idea at Crayden Smithers to be disliked by Abigail Samuels. Poor Joan. That led her to wonder why she had been noticed and, clearly, liked by Abigail. It was a mystery, but Claire would save that for another day. Now however she did think about Toby and Adam Tucker. Perhaps, following Abigail's advice, she should 'have a dalliance' with one – or perhaps both. What a thought! Tina would be shocked. But Tina would never have to know, would she? Claire much preferred Toby but wondered if Abigail's critique of British lovers was accurate. After Michael she had high standards.

Now she put down the letter and realized that she was too stimulated by it to sleep. Though it made her grateful she was away from all that she had read about, she was grateful to have been told. It made her feel simultaneously connected and above the place where she had spent her days. And that, if you have never experienced it, is a very pleasant feeling.

Too excited to read, she picked up her knitting and began the first glove. The old lady in Knitting Kitting was right. She was amazed to see the way the yarn worked up. It seemed to magically make patterns without any assistance from her. It was so fascinating that Claire kept at it for a long time into the night. When she had finished the third finger of the glove, Claire set the work down on the chair by her bed, shut off the light and slid further down under the covers and fell asleep.

THIRTY-SIX

Despite the feelers she had put out and her continued search through the *Evening Standard*, Claire had found no alternative. She had ducked into a few down-and-out B & Bs but they looked as bad as, and cost more than, Mrs Watson's. She kept hoping that something would happen.

But what happened was simple: nothing. Claire telephoned a few ads and rarely got an answer. When she did get an answer she sometimes couldn't understand the accent or the diction of the people at the other end of the phone. And then sometimes, as Toby had implied, the places were so far away that she would have had to go to a train station rather than the underground to get there. The names were quaint: Headstone Lane, Barking, Isle of Dogs. But very few of them were a manageable price or an accessible location.

Despite Mrs Patel's warnings about strangers, she did go to one flat in Maida Vale but the young woman who answered the door seemed filthy, her hair matted and old make-up spread in layers on her face and neck. The place was as unclean as she, and Claire made up some excuse and scurried away. Another place in a desirable part of Putney was too good to be true. She would share the flat with a husband and wife, but unless she was reading the signs incorrectly, they expected to share not only a flat but a bed. Whatever, they gave her the creeps. One very nice room in Balham was already taken by the time she got there, and the last one she tried, in Crouch End, was a big rambling place shared among five students, male and female. They interviewed her, but it was clear they were all politically opposed to the US, and though Claire tried to explain that she neither approved of nor had voted for the President, she wasn't called back.

Meanwhile, the little sign she put up in Mrs Patel's window had produced nothing. Claire would just have to decide whether she would bathe in the morning and feel fresh or save her bath for the evening to get clean and warm. She husbanded her dwindling cash and spent the days walking, seeing sights, looking in windows for rental signs and enjoying her freedom.

Claire had also accepted the dinner invitation to the Patels'. It had been nice to help Mrs Patel out without being compensated. She was a difficult woman to understand, but underneath her hard exterior she had a soft spot for her children. When Claire herself was alone and occasionally feeling lonely, the thought of going back to her job at Crayden Smithers and her mother's house filled her with such dread that it overcame her anxiety about money.

What she realized on her walks was that while she had rarely been alone back in Staten Island she had almost always been lonely. So nothing had changed. She was simply noticing it. She told herself she was all right, but as she walked past a phone box one morning she was weak enough to call Adam Tucker because she simply needed some social contact. He seemed happy to hear from her again and his accent, though strange, was strange in a comforting way. 'Come on. Dinner,' he said.

'I can't. I work late.'

'So, your visa came through! Let's celebrate.' Claire flushed. She was a poor stupid liar. But she agreed to meet Adam at half-past ten the next evening.

* * *

'Well, it wouldn't be hard for me to find someone who wanted to share their apartment,' Adam told her over the first course of their dinner. She had suggested an Indian restaurant in Soho, not far from Covent Garden, and Adam had somewhat hesitantly agreed.

'Flat,' Claire said now. 'Not apartment. They call them flats.'

'Yeah. And they say "gay-rodge" instead of garage and "leftenant" instead of lieutenant but that doesn't mean we should.'

Claire raised her eyebrows. 'When in Rome,' she said.

'So,' Adam went on, 'where have you been?'

Just then the waiter brought their main course – chicken tikka, vegetable korma and dhal. Adam looked down at it suspiciously. 'Is there curry in any of this?' he asked. 'I don't mind chili but that curry taste makes me sick.'

Claire shook her head. 'You told me that,' she reminded him. 'The chicken is plain, just baked slowly and the korma vegetables are in a yogurt sauce.'

'Yogurt?' he asked. He made a face. Even with his nose wrinkled he was very attractive – at least as far as looks went. 'Are you one of those health nuts? No offense meant.'

Claire shook her head over more than the question. She spooned out rice, chicken and a little of the korma on his plate. Though he looked at it for a moment he did pick up his fork. 'So, have you traveled while you were here?' Claire said.

'I went down to Spain with a friend. I just did it because he was going. He said Barcelona was a real cool city. And I speak a little Spanish but it was like they didn't understand what I said and they don't eat dinner there until about midnight.'

'Was it a pretty city?'

'Oh, I don't know. I don't like cities much. I'm from a small town near Corpus Christi. I like the Gulf, and shrimp, and Tex-Mex. Not that this isn't good,' he added. 'I like the chicken just fine.' He looked across the table at her and smiled. His teeth were the whitest she had ever seen. 'You ought to come down to Texas sometime,' he said. 'You'd like it.'

Claire wasn't sure that was true. The more she saw of handsome Corporal Tucker the less she liked him. Well, she couldn't say that she didn't like him. He was pleasant and amenable. It was just she didn't like him for her. And, unfortunately, it was clear that he liked her for himself.

'Where you been in London?' he asked as he helped himself to more chicken.

'Oh, as many places as I've been able to fit in. The National Gallery, St Paul's, Claridge's. I've walked through most of Mayfair and I'm getting to know Camden and Kensington pretty well.'

'Is all of that in London?' he asked.

'Well, I'm going to try Hampton Court. That is outside of the city limits. You have to take a boat or a train there.'

'Maybe you'll show me sometime.'

Claire was touched by his eagerness, but not interested. She thought of herself being led around by Michael Wainwright. Had he thought she was so dull and ignorant? But she had had a lot of curiosity and excitement. Adam seemed to have none. Sadly, Claire realized she couldn't see him again. There was simply no point. More sadly, she wondered if that was what Mr Wonderful had felt about her when he left her for the rendezvous with Katherine Rensselaer. Claire couldn't suppress a sigh and changed the subject.

After dinner, when Adam asked if she had a phone yet, she wrote down a false number and gave it to him. She felt guilty doing it, but she didn't know how to tell him that she simply didn't want to see a person with so few inter-ests and so little desire to explore the opportunities that came his way. When she left him at the tube stop she felt twenty pounds lighter.

On impulse she bought another postcard at a late-night store – a very unflattering picture of the late Queen Mum – and addressed it to Abigail.

Thank you so much for your note. I'm taking your advice and leave of absence if you can arrange it. Don't know where I'll be living or how but I'm very glad I'm here.

She paused, smiled and continued to write.

So sorry to hear about Mr Wainwright's problems. Give my love to Joan but be sure to keep some for yourself.

She bought a stamp and dropped the card in the red 'pillar box' – the mailboxes so attractively dotting the city.

Her card was mailed. Her die was cast. The next day Claire would make one last attempt to find accommodation and then she'd have to go to Mrs Watson and apologize for her hastiness.

THIRTY-SEVEN

The next morning Claire finished the glove. Today she'd go to the knitting shop. Since neither Toby nor Adam had turned up a flat or a job, perhaps she might ask about either at Knitting Kitting. And, as a treat for herself, she'd take Abigail's advice and go to Hampton Court. As she did every morning, she took out the bag from under her bed, checked to see that she had her passport and her ticket and then counted her money. She had five hundred and fifty-five pounds. And she took fifty of them and put them in her bag.

She set out in good spirits, and her breakfast made her feel better. The waitress at the café, who Claire had found from listening during her previous visits was called Marianne, already knew her by sight if not name and cheerfully asked her if she wanted 'the usual'.

Then it was a quick tube ride to South Ken and a brisk walk to Knitting Kitting. She had asked Mrs Patel about the peculiar name and Mrs Patel had explained that 'kitting' someone out was to supply them. It took her a little while to find the right street – she hadn't marked it down as she did with most things. But after a few panicked minutes, she rounded a corner and she was there.

It was, however, only to meet with disappointment. A handwritten sign on the door announced *Shop Closed Back In A Little While*. Claire had no idea what 'a little while' might mean to a woman in her seventies. She could, of course, leave, but the money in her purse was begging to be spent and her fingers itched for a new project.

She took a walk around the corner. She could go into a café to pass the time but wasn't hungry and certainly didn't want to spend any money she didn't have to. So she walked and walked some more. Her patience paid off because when she returned the sign was down and she could enter the store. Nothing had changed and Claire got the feeling that nothing had for the last decade or two.

'Oh, hello,' the old woman behind the counter said. 'I've just been upstairs. I hope I didn't keep you waiting. I have no one to watch the shop when I need to get the phone or use the loo.' She smiled. 'You've been in before,' she said.

Claire nodded. 'We talked about your throw.'

'Of course.'

'How is it coming?' Claire asked.

'Quite well. Have you started on the gloves?'

Claire was delighted she remembered and took the finished one out of her bag. She laid it on the counter. Perhaps if the woman saw her work she might . . . well, it was possible she might give Claire a bit of a job or a lead on a room to rent. Of course the neighborhood was what Claire had learned was called 'up-market'. She doubted she could afford anything nearby, but if she got a job at the shop it was possible that she could afford . . .

'Oh, my dear! But this is quite wonderful!'

Claire shrugged. 'It was the yarn,' she said. 'I've never worked with anything like it.'

'Nor I, but it isn't just the yarn.' She picked up the glove, turning it over and examining the cuff, the thumb and the fingers. 'Well, it isn't a lost art,' she said with a smile. 'You certainly have all the knowledge in your fingers that anyone would need.' To Claire's delight, she then looked at her scarf. 'Is that your work as well?' she asked. Claire nodded again and unwound it. She put it beside the glove on the

256

counter. 'What a wonderful color! Oh, I used to stock so many different colors. It's like working in a rainbow.' She lifted the scarf and fingered it. 'Such even stitching. What do you call this pattern?'

Claire shrugged again. 'I don't know. I haven't seen it anywhere. My grandmother taught it to me.'

'Well, it's lovely. I'm quite ashamed to show you my work. And you made such a fuss about it.'

'No. No, I really meant it. May I see the throw?'

'Yes, of course.' She reached below the counter and took it out. It really was marvelous, though you had to be a good knitter to appreciate it. Claire supposed it was like anything else – only a real craftsman could truly measure the skill of another. She thought of how cold she was back at Mrs Watson's. How nice to have a throw like this to drape over her. Well, tomorrow was the last day she had paid for at Mrs Watson's. If she found another place she hoped it wouldn't be as chilly. She took a deep breath.

'You know, I wonder if you might know of a flat, one to share, that might be available. This is a nice neighborhood and I wonder . . .'

'Oh, I'm no good on things like that, dear. My son would be the one to help you with that. He's a barrister but he's been buying and selling buildings for ever so long. And he's quite friendly with the estate agents across the way. I believe he does business with them.'

Claire doubted that estate agents would be able to help her. She looked at the old lady and her courage failed. After all, Tina had hustled her into her job at Crayden Smithers and on her own she'd never gotten any work except her inconsequential job at Mrs Patel's.

'Is there anything else I can help you with?' The lady looked concerned, but also a bit flustered.

Claire forced herself to smile. It was so very hard to make a place for yourself in the world. A home, a job, friends. Wanting good ones but so often settling for poor ones, or none at all. 'No thank you. I'll wait until I finish this up. You know how it is.'

'Oh, I certainly do. I can't tell you the number of projects I've started because of the lure of a wool. And then you have to slog on and finish them, don't you?'

'I look forward to finishing the other glove,' Claire told her. 'It's so much fun to watch the pattern emerge.'

'Well, enjoy it. And do come back.'

Claire felt dismissed. The older woman sat back down and Claire put on her scarf and put the glove into her pocket. She would go. Her visit to the shop had accomplished nothing. When Claire stepped out into the crisp air she sighed deeply. She had just lost her ace in the hole and would be forced to apologize to Mrs Watson. She adjusted her scarf and decided that she'd had enough self-pity. She would manage somehow but at this moment she had to enjoy her freedom.

Claire decided to follow Abigail's advice and made her way to Paddington. The railway station was almost overwhelming. The ceiling high and glassed, people scurrying across the terrazzo floor from train platform to newsstand to coffee shop to underground in a crazy pattern. Still, it was all so much calmer and more pleasant than Grand Central Station, a phrase that people in Tottenville used to indicate chaos. Claire bought a ticket to Hampton Court, but only for one-way. In Abigail's book she had learned you could take a boat back along the Thames and she decided that, weather permitting, she would enjoy the outdoors and the views of London from the water.

The train ride was uneventful to everyone but Claire. She stared out the window at the passing back gardens and the few open parks. It seemed as if every inch of ground was gardened, groomed and planted. There was little of the New Jersey view-from-the-train ugliness she was used to. She didn't know if all of England was as pretty and cared for, but this bit was lovely.

She felt quite proud of herself, going out on this adventure, but when she got off the train she nearly lost her bright mood. At the end of the platform a uniformed man requested her ticket. She had no idea what she had done with it. The man stood calmly, his uniform looking very official, while Claire patted the pockets of her raincoat, went through her purse and emptied her knitting bag. Finally, panicked and about to give up, she found the ticket inserted in the Mitford book. Relieved, she handed it over, too ruffled to ask directions to the palace. But the signs were everywhere and even if they weren't the people from the train all seemed to be going in the same direction.

Claire had already seen Buckingham Palace and Kensington Palace from the outside. But neither one prepared her for the sight of Hampton Court. The red brick building had the crenellated top and towers that she thought of when Cinderella, Snow White and Sleeping Beauty were mentioned. It was set in a park so lush yet perfectly manicured that it took her breath away. Other people were scattered about taking photographs but Claire stared and knew she wouldn't need a picture to remind her of the beauty in front of her.

She walked up, passed the incredible gates and purchased a ticket without the slightest pang at parting with the money. The thought made her smile. Back in the sixteenth century Cardinal Wolsey had owned the palace. When Henry VIII came for a royal visit he had looked covetously around. 'It's a palace fit only for a king,' he told Wolsey, who was wise enough to give it up immediately to Henry. A higher price to pay than Claire's. Sometimes, she thought, it was good to have very little. You had less to lose and less to worry about.

In this mood, she wandered through the palace and found the gardens behind. The maze, the formal knot garden, the hothouse vines, and the indoor tennis court were impressive but, as Tina might say, 'A nice place to visit, but you wouldn't want to live there.' Just thinking of the responsibility gave Claire the willies. How many servants did Henry employ? How many gardeners? How many cooks?

The sun came out and she looked across the wide park to the river. The gray Thames sparkled in the light and she thought with pleasure of her boat ride to come. She made her way to the gate and asked directions. She found the dock easily and a boat was just departing.

Since the sunshine was intermittent, Claire turned up her collar and tucked in her scarf before making her way to the upper deck. The views were lovely, and it was worth the chill to get to see the green banks make way for the houses and then for the larger buildings of the outer city and then for London itself.

She felt an exhilarated sense of freedom and it was only when they passed the Houses of Parliament and Claire saw the terrace where she had had tea with Michael and his friend that she felt a stab of loss. For a moment the low sky seemed to recede and Claire, alone on the top of the vessel, felt as if she might be sucked up into the air, past the wheeling gulls and terns and right off the planet. Once again the thought that she was completely free had turned with frightening speed into the realization that she was completely alone. Here in this vast space there was no place for her. Shaky, Claire made her way into the cabin and was grateful when the boat docked and she could be surrounded by people again.

THIRTY-EIGHT

On Friday morning Claire realized she had been in London for just over two weeks. She had run into the lurking Mrs Watson and had to tell her she was extending her stay. It was humiliating, but her growing pleasure in the city made it tolerable. And perhaps something would turn up soon.

She had finished *Hons and Rebels* and had delighted in it. She hadn't seen Toby for a week and wanted to go back, discuss the book and buy another. The three that she had sitting beside her bed made her crave more worn, well-read volumes with the delicious smell of old paper and London dust. Perhaps she could create her own library. She definitely wanted to read another Mitford book and perhaps a biography about the mad family.

Toby's bookstore drew her like a magnet. It wasn't just Toby, although she found him handsome, charming, and amusing. It was also her need to be recognized, to be welcomed and to be snug, the way she felt in the back of the bookstore in the big, enveloping chair – never mind the books. Despite the advice from Abigail, she didn't want to throw herself at Toby or make herself a nuisance. Still, if she bought books she had a legitimate reason for being there. At least that was what she reminded herself as she walked to his shop.

When she reached the store she steeled herself to go in, and she was rewarded when she did. 'Hello,' Toby sang out a second time when he actually saw that it was she who had come in. 'Good to see you. Or anyone actually.' He gave himself a little shake, his fine hair swayed and then settled into place. 'If I sit here too long with nothing to do I start doubting I can make a go of it.'

'Haven't you already?'

'Hardly.' He looked around. 'But if I think too much about it I get the heebie-jeebies. A visit from you will drive them away.'

Claire felt herself blush with pleasure. She was afraid to take a seat in the easy chair until she was invited but Toby motioned her toward it. 'I love the book,' she said as if that justified her seat. 'I thought I might try a biography of Nancy or the family.'

'Oh, not Nancy. Far too sad. Loved one inappropriate man after the other – but haven't we all?' Claire nodded. 'There's a good book about the whole lot of them,' Toby told her. 'And then Diana Mosley wrote a strange little memoir. Oh, strike that. But you might want Nancy's letters. She wrote a lot to Waugh and they're brittle but awfully funny. Actually, *The Pursuit of Love* might be best. It's a novel, you know. But shows her family at their absolute maddest. I think I have a couple of copies.'

He wandered off down an aisle. 'At the very least,' he said, raising his voice so she could hear him, 'it will show you a bit of how jolly England was when we had a ruling class.' He returned with a pretty leather book bound in blue. 'That is, of course, if you were a member of the ruling class. Otherwise, a bit grim I'm afraid. Still, nothing about Nancy was much in touch with reality. Just enjoy it.'

Claire reached for her purse. The idea of putting this pretty little book with her others delighted her. Why had she been satisfied with nothing but paperbacks and library editions in New York? The book was marked five pounds and when Toby began to insist he could give it to her for less, she insisted he take the five-pound note she pushed at him. 'I'm paying you not just to be my bookseller but my literary advisor,' she said.

He smiled. 'Perhaps I could make more money at that.' He tucked the note into his pocket. 'But aside from your custom, for which I am very grateful, I have news and I didn't know where to get in touch with you.

'I may have found you somewhere to live,' Toby continued. 'My friend, Imogen, has a little place in South Ken. Anyway, she's looking for a few extra quid – Im is spendy. Makes almost nothing as an editor of just the worst kind of stuff. How to Decorate Your Uterine Wall in Ten Days. Clay Pots Made Simple. Absolutely lives in Harvey Nicks. Anyway, I asked if she knew anyone who might share their place and she offered her box room.'

'What's a box room?' Claire asked, not that she cared. South Kensington was a wonderful area. The knitting shop was there. Her spirits fell; it would probably be far too expensive.

'What's a box room? What does it sound like? It's a place where you store boxes, or luggage, or put the baby if you're a breeder. Anyway, it's not quite a bedroom but it does have a window and Im says that – well, I'll let you speak to her.' He lifted the phone beside his elbow and punched in a number. Then he paused and put the phone down. 'She's actually a bit of a . . . climber,' he said in an undertone. 'But after all it's the national sport. Rather like a dog enthusiast – collects people for their pedigree. Always thought Crufts was just the middle class yearning to prove their dogs were aristocrats. But there you have it. Fun to watch. Has a boyfriend. Nice enough chap. Can't think why she's marrying him except because of his connections. Don't know what she'll think of you. Either we make you a cousin to the Hilton twins or an impoverished Vanderbilt.'

If it were a small room perhaps it would be cheaper, but . . . 'Do I have to lie?'

Toby smiled. 'Well, of course the Bilsop family *is* one of

the oldest in America.' He made a little moue and lifted his eyebrows.

'Well, perhaps they are actually. My father was always going on about them but I'm not sure how much was true and how much was wishful thinking.'

Toby smiled brightly. 'Let's give him the benefit of the doubt. Assume Best in Show at Crufts.' He picked up the phone again and punched in the number.

There was a brief silence while someone spoke to Toby. 'Well, never mind all that,' he said. 'I have that lovely girl here, the one I told you about. Very quiet and neat. Perfect for a box room. But an old family. Given a land grant by George III and popped over to our colonies donkey's years ago.' He winked at Claire who had to smile. 'Anyway, she's just peachy.' Claire held her breath while Imogen must have said something. 'Oh, quite,' Toby told her. 'Would you like to speak with her?'

Apparently Imogen did, because Toby handed the phone over to Claire.

'Hello. I'm Claire Bilsop,' she said.

'I'm Imogen Faulkner. Toby says we should meet. But I don't want you to get your hopes up. The spare room is quite small and it's a bit of a tip, really. I don't know if it would do for you.'

'Oh, I'm sure it would,' Claire said.

'When would you like to come over?'

Claire thought of Mrs Patel. She really couldn't be late, and it was unlikely that Imogen would want to see her after ten. 'Could you meet me tomorrow morning?' she asked. 'I work in the evenings.'

'Morning? If it's after ten? Could you do later?'

'Sure. Eleven?'

'Brilliant,' Imogen said. 'By the way, it would be so much more convenient if you weren't around between six-ish and midnight.' Imogen lowered her voice. 'It's when I do my entertaining: I'm engaged to be married,' she giggled. 'Toby has my address and all of that. And tell him I don't want any of his bloody books. He inherited them, I didn't. He ought to keep them to himself.'

'I'll tell him,' Claire promised. 'Tomorrow, then, at eleven.'

'Brilliant,' Imogen said once more and hung up.

THIRTY-NINE

The next morning Claire took the underground to South Kensington station and walked from there to the address she had marked on her map. Kensington was a very different world from Camden. Here in Kensington, none of the terraces seemed to be broken by the unattractive modern buildings. Each row of houses curved and smiled as evenly as actors' teeth, without a gap or an ugly modern bridge anywhere.

Claire had arrived early, Mrs Patel having given her the day off. 'Not that you'll get paid,' she had cautioned. Claire smiled, remembering her fierce expression. She was beginning to realize that Mrs Patel was a softy, trying to keep her better nature under wraps as her sari protectively covered her child-to-be. Claire was beginning to think she had made a true friend.

All around her the houses were bedecked with thriving window boxes and pots of topiary. Wrought-iron fences separated the immaculate sidewalk from the equally immaculate front gardens. Claire couldn't think of a section of New York that was this charming. Perhaps they existed, but Claire had never been there.

She turned a corner and was on Imogen's street. It was only ten-thirty so she walked past number nineteen – to her delight a cream painted three-storey house with a pretty bow window – and continued to look around the neighborhood.

Just two blocks away there were a pub, a convenience store and one of the ubiquitous estate agent's shops. Claire couldn't believe how many real-estate offices there were. People must buy and sell their homes every week to keep so many agents in business. She spent a few minutes looking at the tempting pictures of interiors and marveling over the forbidding prices. She ducked into the Crown and Slipper and it seemed, though very quiet at that time of day, inviting enough. There didn't seem to be a breakfast place nearby but perhaps, if Imogen accepted her as a flatmate, she could cook her own. Even if she couldn't, she wouldn't care as long as she could take baths freely. She walked back to number nineteen, walked up the stairs to the front door and pressed the button over 'Faulkner'.

When she was buzzed in she found herself in an elegant vestibule with a black and white marble floor, a gilded mirror on the wall and two doors before her. She hadn't a clue which one to knock on and stood for a moment in the pretty little space. Both doors were painted with a faux Turkish tile design. She had stepped into *The Arabian Nights*, but didn't know which entrance she should address with 'Open sesame.' And if those weren't the magic words, she hoped she could find the ones that would make this Imogen take her in. She couldn't believe that she might be lucky enough to live in such an elegant neighborhood in such an adorable building. She paused and took a deep breath, then superstitiously crossed her fingers and knocked on the door on her right.

She had barely lowered her hand when the door was thrown open and Imogen – she guessed it was Imogen – stood revealed before her. Revealed was the right word because Imogen was in pantyhose and make-up but very little else.

'Hello,' she said in the same intonation that Toby used. The word dipped in the front and lifted at the end the way a sailboat moved through a swell.

Claire, always modest, felt her face suffuse with color, but tried to keep her eyes only on Imogen's round face and wide round blue eyes. Her hair was a honey-blond halo, and her skin was the most perfect, poreless surface that Claire had ever seen. 'You must be Claire,' Imogen said. 'Come on up. I hope you don't mind that I'm just in my smalls.' Claire shook her head but Imogen had already turned, revealing the back of her 'knickers' and the stairway in front of them. She galloped up two flights of stairs and Claire followed, wondering if panties were knickers and smalls and a dozen other words in this country.

But as she reached the top of the stairs she had to stop to take a breath. The flat opened before her, a white, sunlit space with big windows in the front as well as a skylight overhead. There was a large sofa facing a small fireplace, a lot of gray wall-to-wall carpet and not much else except piles of papers on the floor, on the counters and on the end tables. 'Would you like a drink?' Imogen asked. 'Coffee? Sherry? I'm having a sherry.'

Claire nodded and then remembered Imogen still had her back to her. 'Sherry would be nice,' she said and was relieved when Imogen returned not only with the sherries but also wrapped in a cotton robe. She couldn't imagine being interviewed by a woman in her underwear.

'Sit down,' Imogen invited Claire as she moved a stack of papers from a chair. 'I'm an editor at Sofer & Laughton. Rather fun, really, but lots of paperwork I'm afraid.' Claire sat at the other end of the sofa. 'God, I haven't seen Toby in months. Is he keeping well?' Claire wasn't sure if that was an inquiry as to Toby's health or his aging process, but she nodded. 'We were at university together. Good boy is our Toby. How do you know him?'

It was a natural enough question, but Claire hadn't prepared for it. If she told the truth would she seem a transient, undependable and unknown? If she lied, what could she possibly invent and how would she ask Toby to cover for her? 'From the bookstore,' she told Imogen.

'Oh, are you in the book trade? I always think it was awfully lucky that Toby's uncle died. Great Warwickshire family, but penniless, of course. The business suits him right down to the ground, though it's hardly a business, is it? He'd be hopeless in the City. We always knew that, couldn't imagine what he'd do, and then Sir Frederick conveniently died and there you have it. Not that Toby inherited the title, you understand. Just the shop and the flat. Can't think what he lives on, but he manages, doesn't he? Maybe good Uncle Frederick left him some money as well.'

Claire didn't know what to say. She thought the English had the reputation of being reserved but Imogen didn't seem to fit the mold. Claire surreptitiously looked around. The place was wonderful, all emptiness and light. She desperately wanted to be asked to stay on.

'Now, where are you from?' Imogen asked.

'New York, actually.' Claire heard herself imitating Imogen's intonation and told herself to stop. 'I worked on Wall Street.' Well, both of those statements were true.

'Oh, and are you in the City now? That's where Malcolm works – my boyfriend. He's from Edinburgh and a chartered accountant. Dead boring, actually, but as it's in numbers he could easily move.' Imogen leaned back and finished her sherry. She lowered her voice. 'Malcolm is actually a second cousin to the Queen. Not that it would do us any good if we got married. He does have a tea service from Sandringham, but I doubt we'd even get a wedding present.' Then she smiled. 'If we had children they'd be about three hundred and twenty-seventh in line to the succession. So I wouldn't expect to be a Queen Mum.'

Claire wasn't following everything, but she could see what Toby meant about 'climbing'. She worried about how she could present her resumé. An unemployed tourist didn't measure up to glamorous editor, not to mention a cousin by marriage to the Queen. Before Claire could get her thoughts organized, Imogen stood up. 'Would you like to see the room?' she asked. 'It isn't much, I'm afraid. If it were an annex to the bedroom I'd use it as a dressing room. But it does have windows. And as the bathroom is not *en suite*, I think we could manage.'

She walked through the living room and to a tiny kitchen with Claire trailing behind her. 'The money would come in handy, but it's just as important that someone be here. I spend some time at Malcolm's and then most weekends we're in the country. He has a place in Kent and my parents' country house is in Essex – I know, an Essex girl!'

Claire had no idea what an Essex girl was, but it must be good. So she nodded and smiled. It seemed that Toby's recommendation was all she needed – except, of course, for the money. Then they stepped into the little 'box room' and Claire was transfixed. 'I know it's quite tiny, and the mahogany washstand is absolutely hideous,' Imogen said. 'I hate Victoriana, though it is coming back. Once I'm married I'll be getting some family furniture – Georgian, you know. And then Malcolm's family has pots of stuff.'

The room was certainly small, perhaps ten by ten. But that was part of its charm. It looked as if it was something from a doll's house. There were two windows on one side looking out over the gardens in the back, the walls were a lovely light lilac and the woodwork was linen white, though quite dusty. Claire compared it to the dingy room at Mrs Watson's, the peeling wallpaper and the rug that had seen the soles of far too many feet. There, she felt like the Little Match Girl. Here she would feel like . . . well, as small but as lovely as Thumbelina. There was a small bed built into the far wall with drawers under it. 'There isn't any linen. You'll have to provide your own, but there is a washing machine.' The Victorian washstand had a white marble top and was far from hideous. To Claire, in fact, it was charming. So were the bureau and the tiny chintz-upholstered chair.

'There are no curtains, I'm afraid,' Imogen said, 'and the bed is just a single. No wardrobe, either, but you could use the hall cupboard. Does it seem as if it might do?'

Claire nodded, then forced herself to speak. She felt her heart would break if she didn't get to stay here. It was the most inviting room she had ever seen. But could she manage to pay for it? 'What would it cost?' she asked, feeling as if her heart were literally in her throat. Something was, because she could barely manage to swallow.

'Well, you know, my uncle owns the building.' Imogen laughed. 'We do seem to have a lot of uncles around, don't we? Anyway, I don't pay much. Do you think you could manage three hundred pounds a month?'

Claire quickly did 'the maths' as Safta would say. She couldn't believe it! The room was almost half the price of what she was paying now. That couldn't be right, but Claire didn't care. She'd do whatever she had to, to get to keep this adorable bower. 'I'll take it,' she said. And she left clutching a set of keys, Imogen having said she could move in right away.

Trying to get to the tube she got confused and her map didn't seem to help. What she needed was a much better one that had all the small streets named and drawn more carefully. She took a turn to the left, walked down a darling little street and then took a turn to the right. On her map it looked as if it would be a busy road but instead she was on a slightly grander lane with detached houses, lovely gardens and old trees.

When she got to the end of the lane she saw that it led into the busy street she was looking for. But that wasn't the surprise. On her right side she saw the kitty corner door she knew. Surely there weren't two like that.

She crossed the lane and found herself in front of Knitting Kitting. Claire blinked once or twice. Here she was, just a few blocks away from her new home and beside her favorite

– well, not counting Toby's or Mrs Patel's – shop in London. She had almost finished her second glove but realized that she couldn't go in for more wool. A polite sign said, SORRY. WE ARE CLOSED. PLEASE COME AGAIN. And the hours of the shop were posted below it. Claire realized the place was only open on weekdays and Saturday mornings nine to twelve. Rather silly when you thought about it, since most women would shop after work or on the weekends. Still, Claire took the proximity as a very good omen. And perhaps she could get a job if she offered to extend the hours. It was worth a try and after all the success she had had, she was beginning to believe the adage 'nothing ventured, nothing gained'.

FORTY

'But why do they call it prime?' Safta asked.

As the oldest, Safta seemed to take everything quite seriously, from supervising her two younger siblings to achieving the best possible grades in school. Her eyebrows were such exact copies of her mother's, that if anyone had doubted Mendel's theory of genetics they would have only to look at Mrs Patel and Safta to see the power of DNA.

One could also see the power of environment. Instead of arching her brow in the gesture of questioning contempt that her mother routinely used, Safta made a little pucker just at the bottom of her forehead, slightly to the right of her nose. The pucker in her brow indicated worry, confusion, dissatisfaction and all the other negative emotions that Safta the elegant perfectionist was forced to live with.

Claire smiled at her and looked down at the textbook. 'They're prime numbers because they can't be evenly divided by any other number.'

'Well, what's so prime about that? It makes them irregular or unevenly divisible, or annoying. I don't see why it makes them prime.'

'That's one way to look at it,' Claire agreed. 'But the official definition is a whole number that has itself and unity as its only factor. It isn't like other numbers that aren't prime, and it also isn't like other prime numbers. Because they have their own unity.'

Safta looked down at the textbook and then up at Claire. 'I'm so stupid,' she said. It wasn't true, but Claire had already noticed that Safta didn't feel good about herself. She hated her glasses, her school uniform, the practical shoes her mother bought her, the traditional way she was forced to wear her hair, living in the back of a grocery store, and the foolish programs her sister liked to watch on the telly. She was a serious girl who had already confided to Claire that she never wanted 'to marry and have all those bloody babies', but wanted instead to be a botanist. 'So prime numbers have one quality that they share, but that is their uniqueness,' she said.

Claire nodded.

'That's rather like me,' Safta said. 'I have uniqueness and unity.'

Claire sat back from the table and glanced over at Mrs Patel who was busy at the stove stirring something, while she held Devi on one hip and scolded Fala. Aside from dining regularly with the Patels, Claire had begun tutoring Safta, a job that she was enjoying very much. In addition, she was learning about real Indian – or Pakistani – cuisine, very different from the birianis and kormas Claire had had before in restaurants. 'Garbage,' Mrs Patel had sniffed. 'They don't bother to do anything right.' Claire had to admit that tonight's dinner was more extravagant than the previous meals she had eaten at the Patels'. The beautifully spiced vegetables, the lamb and chicken served in small pieces amidst healthy greens, and the dressings of dhal and homemade relishes were not only healthful and fresh but they also seemed to help her effortlessly continue to slim down. She had actually had to borrow sewing things from Mrs Patel and, with her help, had taken in the waist and the back seam of her two pairs of slacks as well as her skirt. How odd, she thought, that she was losing weight now without trying when she had failed to in New York, trying so hard.

Claire looked back at Safta and nodded. Safta was one of those children with gifts that did not help them to 'fit in'. She was too intelligent and mature in school, she was too fastidious at home and, unlike Claire, she didn't escape from her reality with novels but, rather, observed everything with a scientific detachment and the slightly puckered brow. Claire might have felt sorry for her if she wasn't so very formidable.

'Is the table clear?' Mrs Patel called out. 'Safta, get Devi his feeder.' That turned out to be a bib, and Claire helped fasten it around Devi's neck. All of the pots were steaming, Devi had stopped fussing and Fala was carrying a tin cup to the table.

'We'd better put these books away,' Claire said and in a moment Safta had jumped up, neatly replaced the books on her shelf, wiped down the plastic tablecloth and put out strange round trays that held smaller metal cups and bowls. There were no china dishes, knives or forks. The children took their places and Mrs Patel began spooning out fragrant vari-colored messes into all of the bowls on each tray.

'These are lentils,' she said. 'They are mixed with a kind of onion. And this is sahg. Spinach, you know. We mix it with cheese.' Claire's face must have shown some of her dubiousness because Mrs Patel continued. 'I know if you just look at it, it might be enough to put you off your feed. But try some.'

Claire tried not to show any more dismay at the idea of spinach and cheese. It certainly didn't look like either one. 'And this is korma which has yogurt and almonds and raisins.'

'Korma! Hooray!' said Devi. 'And rice. And peas. And . . .'

All the little bowls were filled. Devi, Mrs Patel and Fala ate with their hands, delicately mixing the various dishes with the rice. Safta fetched two teaspoons, handed one to Claire and began eating with the other. Tentatively at first, then with greater pleasure Claire tasted dish after dish and found they were all very good.

'Dish up some dhal for Claire,' Mrs Patel chided Safta. 'You put it on your rice, Claire.'

Claire did, and it was delicious. So were the sweet chutney and even the spinach and cheese. The stainless steel plates and the cups from which they drank water seemed strange, but as the family ate and talked and teased one another it all began to seem not only natural but sensible. As she continued eating, Claire felt the back of her tongue and the top of her throat react to the flavors. It wasn't just spicy. It was subtle and most things had an aftertaste and mixed with whatever new flavor she spooned into her mouth. 'Do you often eat like this?' Claire asked.

'No,' Safta said disapprovingly. 'Sometimes we eat in front of the telly.'

'Not if I am here,' Mrs Patel said. 'Devi, put the bowl down. You'll spill.' But Claire noticed that, even if some of the contents spilled, they were caught by the metal tray the bowls sat on.

'What I meant was, do you eat this way, and I mean all this food, often?'

'Oh, yes. This isn't much. If I had time I would have baked roti and made some mutton. When my sister comes to visit we have big meals.'

'Auntie! Auntie! I want Auntie!' Devi yelled.

'I want you to sit down and to be a good boy or there will be no Auntie,' Mrs Patel told him. He did as he was told.

Claire looked across the table as Mrs Patel supervised Fala eating and then wiped Devi's hands. She refilled the water cups and managed to finish her own dinner as well. Claire wondered at it all. Her mother had sometimes only managed bologna sandwiches, and complained about that. Mrs Patel was raising three children, bearing a fourth, stocking, staffing and managing a shop, keeping house, and seemed to think that none of it was too much. Her slim arms moved over the table, her wedding bracelets flashing and tinkling, adding to the clatter as she collected the empty dinner plates.

'Safta, you do the washing up, Fala, help your sister.' She looked at her youngest. 'Devi, you keep out of the Fairy liquid.' She gave his hair a loving pat then, as if to make up for it, she added, 'Sometimes you're enough to make me go spare.' Mrs Patel turned to Claire. 'I'm going back to reopen the shop,' she said. 'Thank you for joining us for dinner.'

'Thank *you*,' Claire said. 'It was delicious.'

'Mummy, can I show Claire my room?' Safta asked.

'Mummy, can I show Claire my room?' Fala echoed.

'Yes,' Mrs Patel said. 'Safta, put on the kettle and bring me some tea. Claire, would you like a cup as well?' Claire nodded. She couldn't get over how many cups of tea everybody drank at all times. Even the children had milk and tea morning and night.

Claire helped Safta clear the table, put the dishes in a pan of hot water to soak and then watched as she filled a kettle which, like Toby's, instead of putting on the cooker you plugged into an outlet. Claire thought what a convenience it would be to have one like it for herself but before she got any further with the thought Safta turned and pointed down the little hallway.

'Would you like to see my room?' she asked shyly. Claire nodded.

With Devi and Fala on their heels they made their way down the dark narrow hall and into the overcrowded room the two sisters shared. There, Claire was met by another surprise. Along the windowsill, on a shelf, arranged on the desk and even under the bed Safta had grouped small pots of plants. African violets, sansevieria, Irish moss, and a host of other plants that were unfamiliar to Claire were arranged on trays of pebbles or in open plastic boxes. There was also a terrarium filled with ferns and mosses. On Safta's desk a notebook lay open with a drawing of a plant. But it wasn't a sentimental little flower, it was a botanically accurate rendering of a carnation. Complete with leaves, flower and roots.

'Safta! This is wonderful! Did you do this yourself?' Safta nodded. 'It's a perfect carnation,' Claire told her.

'I have to keep moving plants,' Safta explained. 'There's only the one window and they don't get enough light. I have a rotation system.'

Claire looked at the windowsill and beyond to the desolate little plot behind the shop. A thought began to form but just then the kettle began to whistle.

'I better make the tea,' Safta said.

'Biscuit! Biscuit!' Devi cried.

'And I better bring some to your mom,' Claire said. But the two of them exchanged a look of understanding.

But the friendship with Mrs Patel was about to be damaged. 'I've had a stroke of luck,' Claire told Mrs Patel. 'I found a new place.'

Mrs Patel smiled. 'That must be a pleasure. If you're living in the same spot as that Maudie it must be tatty. Did someone see the note we posted?'

Claire shook her head. 'It was another friend. He helped me get a room. It's really lovely. Small, but clean and sunny and I only have to share the bathroom with the woman who lives in the flat.'

'How close is it?' Mrs Patel asked as she sipped her tea, her hand on her belly.

'Oh. Quite far away from here.'

'That's too bad. I hope it isn't inconvenient.'

'Oh, I can manage the underground,' Claire said airily. 'I'm hoping to move right in.'

'Move right out, more likely,' Mrs Patel murmured, but Claire didn't hear her.

FORTY-ONE

Claire didn't have much to pack and certainly wouldn't mind telling Mrs Watson that she was leaving. Her only problems were her lack of money and the question of traveling from Kensington to Mrs Patel's. If she did, it would eat up more than four pounds of her 'salary' each day. If she didn't she was without any income at all.

Sitting on the bed the next morning, she counted out her cash. She would have to give Imogen three hundred pounds in advance, and although that was a lot of money she counted herself lucky. It was a cheap rent, a lovely room, a chance to make a new friend and apparently she didn't have to give a month's security.

She'd also have to buy curtains, blankets, sheets and towels. Though it was an extra expense, the idea actually thrilled her. She'd never done it before. She didn't suppose they had Bed, Bath and Beyond in London. She wondered where she would go and she decided that she'd also buy herself an electric kettle, a teapot and cups to match. Of course, all this wouldn't leave much of her fund. She wondered if there was someplace else she could get work and it occurred to her again that the old woman at the knitting store might need part-time help, even just to dust, though she wouldn't make much at that either. She sighed. Writing to her mother and asking for money would be useless at any time and especially so now when she had actually charged things on her mother's card. Claire sat for a while, trying to think of what else she could do. Just then there was a tiny noise at the door. Claire turned in time to see the edges of two envelopes being pushed through. She got up and almost ran to them.

Both had the return address of Crayden Smithers. She recognized Tina's handwriting immediately, but the address was typed on the other. She tore Tina's open.

Claire. I don't know who you think you are. Ever since Michael Wainwright asked you out you've been acting snootier than usual. What's the matter? Couldn't you come back and face me once he dumped you? Who do you know in London? Like you might know somebody.

Everybody is asking me where you are. And I tell them I'm not your mother. Marie Two said she thought you were pregnant, but I know you weren't when you left. Ha, ha.

I think it takes a lot of nerve to take other people's money and just disappear like you were the Who Deanie or something. You couldn't even afford to go to Atlantic City.

For your information, Mr Wonderful is back to his old tricks. Now he's not just going out with Ms Rensselaer but he started up with some new one who owns a fancy art gallery. I'm making reservations for them all over town. Are you dating anyone yet? Yeah, right.

Your mother called me twice. She says you wrote her too. Fine. Like she's your best friend too. Anthony says I shouldn't care because you're just selfish but I guess I have too much heart to be like that. Too bad you don't.

Your ex-friend Tina

Claire stood with the letter in her hand. She had to read it through a second time before she began to understand what she was looking at. For a little while she couldn't understand it – not at all. What had she done to make Tina so angry? Had there been any slight before she left? Had Michael said something to Tina? She tried to think, but she knew she had left on good terms and couldn't think of a single thing that Michael might say that would affect Tina in any way. That was when she had realized what she had done wrong: she'd done something adventurous.

She read the letter again and became more sure with every line she went through. People in families, and even in friendships, played certain roles. Her role with Tina was that of a sidekick; someone played by Joan Cusack in a movie. Tina played the lead, of course. Tina had a flamboyant family, an active social life, a fiancé, and marriage plans. Claire had to listen. She couldn't remember any movie where, halfway through, the second banana runs off to Europe. Tina was outraged. Claire had deviated from the script. It left Tina with no part. So, if she couldn't be the sidekick, so Tina could stay the heroine, she would have to be a victim. The fact was that Tina loved movies about victims – beaten wives, abused children, raped teenagers, all of it played well. Claire couldn't bear to read the letter again. She folded it, put it back in the envelope and hid it in her pocket.

She looked at the other envelope with misgivings. Had Joan gotten her address and decided to send her an insulting note that fired her? Whatever. Claire shrugged and tore the envelope open.

Dear Claire,

Thank you for your card. I've needed a photo of the Queen Mother for some time. How exciting! You are having what sounds like the beginning of a lovely adventure. How I envy you.

*Good for you. My suggestion (not advice, I
never give advice) would be to resign and stay on
as long as you can. I took the liberty of checking
in with personnel and found that you are owed
quite a lot of overtime. Over eleven hundred
dollars' worth, it appears. I thought it might come
in handy, and I enclose it. If you have any trouble
cashing this check, please call collect. All banks
should honor it, and if they don't Mr Crayden will
want to know why.*

*As they say in London, 'Jobs are thick on the
ground.' You are resourceful and can always pick
one up if you have to. And we are moving ahead
with some plans to open a branch in London. Who
knows? Perhaps there's a job for both of us there.
With hopes I don't see you too soon,*

Abigail Samuels

As Claire picked the note up in disbelief, a check fluttered out onto the floor. She picked it up and found it was
very close to twelve hundred dollars. Claire was certain
that she'd been paid for any overtime she'd ever done. She
didn't know what Abigail had done and didn't really want
to think about it in detail. She just looked at the Crayden
Smithers check in front of her and hoped that Abigail
hadn't embezzled the money, though she supposed that
embezzlers didn't bother with such small amounts – small
amounts, that is, to people like Michael Wainwright. Claire
stared at the check and saw her own future in it: a lovely
room, soft sheets, fluffy towels and new friends.

FORTY-TWO

By late morning Claire had said goodbye to Maudie, who promised to bring any mail that came in to Mrs Watson to her at Mrs Patel's, and had been to thank Toby for introducing her to Imogen. Her reward, aside from the visit itself, was his promise to visit her as soon as she was settled. She consulted her list. The next items were cashing her check and shopping for the sheets and towels. Toby had advised her to stay out of Harrods and Selfridges and to go to 'Marks and Sparks' or BHS.

Claire walked up Regent Street and took the time to wonder at Liberty's lovely Tudor-style building. When she got to Oxford Street she turned left at the busy intersection and enjoyed the sophisticated feeling of not being a tourist and instead being a shopper for her 'flat in South Ken'. First she cashed the check at a branch of Barclays Bank, then turned back to cross Regent Street again.

When she got to Marks and Spencer she was at first overwhelmed. She found the linen department and spent a long time looking. In the end she decided on a lilac and gray pattern of flowers set on a white ground. It would, she thought, go with the room as well as with the rug and there were matching curtains! She bought two fitted sheets, two top sheets and four pillowcases – quite a splurge when she saw the cost of them. Then, of course, she realized she would need pillows and bought two of the cheapest she could find. She also bought a white cotton blanket and then went for a late lunch in the café. That was when she remembered about the kettle.

A shop assistant directed her to John Lewis where she saw one that, compared to some of the others, looked like a miniature. It was white with a pattern of green vines in a celery color. Small lavender flowers were dotted among the vines. Thrilled, she knew it was meant for her.

At the very last, she went to John Lewis's china department. She looked and looked, falling in love with a pattern and switching her affection to another. But her bags were already bulky and tedious to carry, and when she realized that all of the cups, saucers and teapots that she liked were not inexpensive she looked at all her purchases and began to be concerned about the amount of money she had spent. So, instead of buying china she allowed herself a final splurge on a taxi.

She gave her destination to the driver. 'A Yank are you?' he asked in a friendly way. She nodded. 'Where are you from then?' When she told him New York he became very chatty indeed. 'Love the place,' he said. 'Went with me wife two years ago. Couldn't believe the pace. It wasn't like Orlando.'

'Have you been to Florida?' she asked.

'Oh, sure. Made that trip twice with the kids. So, what are you doing in Camden? The market isn't really at its best today, you know. And it looks like you've done plenty of shopping already.' He laughed.

'It's not for shopping,' she said. 'I live there, but I'm moving.' She said it proudly, and he seemed to accept it as if it was the most natural thing in the world.

'So, where are you moving to?'

'South Kensington,' she told him and named the street.

'Hey, moving up in the world,' he said. 'Will you need help to move your things then? I can give you my mobile number.'

It was a good idea. She hadn't thought about how she was going to get her luggage and her new purchases over to the new flat. 'That would be great,' she told him. And when they arrived at Mrs Watson's she paused before she paid him. Why not do it now she thought? It wasn't as if she owed Mrs Watson money – the woman wouldn't allow that to happen – and she certainly didn't have to bid her goodbye. Though she never would have considered leaving anything in a New York taxi, she looked at the driver's friendly face and decided to chance it. 'Could you wait for me?' she said. 'I'll be right back. I'm leaving my shopping. I only have a few more things to get.'

He shrugged. 'Why not?' he asked.

She left her purchases in the backseat and ran up the stairs. In less than five minutes she was back, a bit breathless but with all of her worldly goods. She was delighted with her stealth, and hoped that Mrs Watson would at least wonder where she had gone off to, though the woman would probably only think about who might provide her next eighteen or twenty pounds, depending on how many baths they required.

The ride to Imogen's took a while, but Claire told herself this wasn't the time to look at the meter. Instead she looked out the window and tried to mentally follow the route without opening her map. She watched the people walking their dogs and waiting for buses. She felt very regal in the taxi and realized it wouldn't take her long to get used to a luxury like this one. Oh well. She reminded herself there wouldn't be any need for taxis in the near future.

She was almost disappointed when they got to Imogen's, but then the excitement hit her again. Giving up another of her twenty-pound notes, she over-tipped madly, and carefully maneuvered herself and all her purchases up the stairs to her new home.

She didn't have time to unpack. She had to go right back to Camden for her job, but despite all the shopping she wasn't the slightest bit tired. She left a note with the three hundred pounds on Imogen's sideboard and ran out the door humming. As she made her way to the tube station it seemed to her that she must be the happiest person in all of London.

But walking by the knitting shop she decided she had enough time to go in. There was something she wanted to ask. Also, having finished the second glove, she had no knitting project and she needed more wool so she opened the door to the shop without a tremble. The room was empty of customers but the woman looked up at the sound of the bell. 'Oh. Hello, my dear. Finished with the gloves, are you?'

Claire smiled. She made her way to the counter. 'Yes.' She held up her hands warmly encased in them, then took them off and laid them on the counter for the woman's inspection.

'Oh. Lovely.'

'I thought I'd try a lap robe next.'

'Really?'

Claire thought of the little chintz-covered chair in the lavender room. An afghan made of lavender and celery baby wool would be beautiful as well as practical. For a moment she imagined exactly how it would feel to sit in the chair and work the wool between her fingers. 'You have inspired me,' she said. She took down some beautiful merino wool and counted the skeins. There were six skeins of lavender but only five of the celery. She decided she would do stripes, with a lavender border. For the lavender she'd use a size two needle; for the celery she'd use a four. The work would be intricate, but she would enjoy it and the throw would be beautiful and subtly textured when she was finished. And she wouldn't have to buy yarn again for quite a while.

Claire explained her project as the elderly woman nodded her approval, then began to write up the sale. She did it by hand, in a little receipt book with a carbon. Claire hadn't seen one like it in years, not even in the old stores in Tottenville.

'Very ambitious of you, my dear. You must promise to show it to me if you finish it while you're in London.'

'Oh, I'll finish it here,' Claire said with assurance. 'I just live around the corner now.'

'So we are neighbors. How delightful.' The old woman held out her hand. 'I'm Caroline Venables,' she said. 'And it's very nice to see you again.'

'Nice to see you. I'm Claire Bilsop.'

Mrs Venables looked at Claire's gloves. 'Well, I can see that somebody taught you how to knit properly. You can't imagine how much slipshod work I see here. It's actually quite distressing. I've sometimes offered to take up dropped stitches and people have told me they haven't the time.' She shook her head.

Though she didn't want to be late for Mrs Patel, Claire knew she had to ask her question now. 'You know,' she said, 'I wondered if you might . . . well, if you needed . . .' she paused. 'Would you be interested in someone to help out here at the shop?'

Mrs Venables laughed, but in a gentle, almost embarrassed way. 'Ah,' she said. 'If only. The truth is, my dear, I barely have enough custom to keep the doors open. My son owns the shop, you see, and charges me almost nothing to rent it. He's always quite eager for me to shut it down. I suppose he's humoring me.'

Claire tried not to let her disappointment show. Normally this would be enough to truly daunt her but she'd had such a delightful day that, for once, she had courage to continue in the face of adversity. 'It's a pity about the business,' she said. 'But I noticed you do only half a day on Saturday and you close early in the week. With most women working during the day . . .'

'Ah, but I couldn't do more. I'm not really young, you

know.' Mrs Venables smiled. 'I need a nap at noon and I close at four.'

'That's when I could help out,' Claire said, trying to sound relaxed rather than desperate.

'But I couldn't pay you.'

'Oh, that wouldn't matter. Not at first.'

'Or at last, I'm afraid. I simply don't do enough business, you see.'

'You know,' Claire said, 'I think there's a way to attract quite a few more customers. Have you advertised?'

Mrs Venables laughed again. 'Oh, my dear. You are hardly talking to a businesswoman. I wouldn't know where to begin. And I wouldn't even like to consider the costs. And knitting seems to have gone out of favor. You know, young women today all go out to work. They have no time for homey practices.' Claire considered this. 'Anyway, my dear, I would love the company and the help but you see it simply isn't practical.'

Claire nodded. Before she had a chance to be disappointed she remembered the time. 'Well, I must go. I do have a job.'

'Very well, but do drop in again. I'm longing to see how the throw progresses.'

Claire nodded. She wanted to prove to Mrs Venables that young women – anyone for that matter – could take the time to participate in 'homey practices'.

FORTY-THREE

Claire woke Wednesday in her new room for the first time. The sun was pouring in. She hadn't returned home last night until very late – she had tutored Safta and then, on the way home, had made the wrong connection and gone north instead of south at her transfers. But this morning she was up early and would have the whole day to organize her new home.

There was a knock on the door and Imogen popped her head in. 'Oh, good,' she said. 'You're here. Like a cup of tea? I'm just making one.'

'That would be lovely,' Claire told her. 'I mean if it's no trouble. You don't have to wait on me.'

Imogen laughed. 'Wait on you? Don't worry, not likely. I'm such a slut I'll probably leave you with the washing up.' She returned in a couple of minutes and gave a steaming mug to Claire. 'I'm off,' she said. 'I'm going to see my parents tonight and I'll stay over. You know where everything is?' Claire nodded. 'See you, then,' she said and disappeared.

Lying in bed, Claire regarded her shopping bags through the steam of the tea. They seemed like presents waiting for her on Christmas morning. Of course, she knew what was inside them but the lack of surprise was more than made up for by the tremendous pleasure she had knowing that she was actually going to like the contents. In Christmases past, she had been almost certain not to.

The day was, with the exception of her time with Mr Wonderful, the most pleasant she had ever known. Before she did anything else she unpacked the cleaning things she had brought from Mrs Patel's. She shampooed the rug, wiped down the woodwork, opened the windows and carefully wiped the inside of the drawers, then lined them with scented lavender paper. When she was done she was delighted with the neat sparkling room that she could hardly believe was hers. She made herself another cup of tea and sat for a few minutes admiring her handiwork, before moving on to scrub the shared bathroom.

She went out shopping, bought a sandwich, needles and thread, scissors, and some 'loo paper' and a couple of candles. She also bought a bunch of lilies which she arranged in a borrowed jug on the bureau. Only then did she unpack. She hung up a set of towels in the bathroom and put the spares in one drawer under the bed and the extra sheets in the other. Her shoes and hanging clothes she put neatly in the hall closet. Her sweaters, nightgown and underwear went into the drawer. She even had a drawer left over for her knitting supplies and the extra skeins of wool.

She took out the precious little box Michael had given her and put it on the stand. *When this you see, remember me.* She sighed. She never thought she would have such a pretty little antique nor did she ever think she would be putting it in a room like this one – a room that was now hers. She slid her fingers across the top and could feel the slightly raised surface where the inscription lay.

She wondered how many people before her had been given the box and whether any of them had received it from men who loved them. Once again, she thought of Michael and the golden hours she had spent with him. Then she looked at the pretty stand and the reflection of the box in the mirror. What would be nice, she thought, would be a little pink or blue vase beside it with some flowers. She knew she couldn't afford the kind of antiques that she and

Michael had seen. But surely somewhere she could find an inexpensive but pretty little vase.

She ate the sandwich she had purchased and spent the afternoon altering the curtains for the windows. It took quite a while but the results were worth it. Her room seemed a perfect little haven.

Looking out the back window onto the garden she felt a flood of happiness so exquisite that it was hard to contain. Everything was so pretty and so restful. She could hardly believe that it was hers and that she had wound up not just comfortable but luxuriously so. She had never enjoyed her old bedroom in this way.

Sitting there in her reverie she almost forgot to leave enough time to get to Mrs Patel's. She had to run both to the underground in Kensington and then from Camden station. But she got there in time and was so excited by her day that she had to tell it all to Mrs Patel.

'Kensington. That's a very good area indeed.'

'Oh, it's lovely. There are flowers everywhere and gardens at the back. In fact, my room overlooks a garden.'

'Well, I have a garden at the back as well.'

Claire thought of the space behind the building and almost smiled until she looked over from the carton she was unpacking and saw the expression on Mrs Patel's face. 'Yes, you do,' she said. 'But the people in Kensington seem to do so much with their gardens. Of course, they've got plenty of time and money.'

'If I had the time I could do quite a bit more,' Mrs Patel said defensively. That gave Claire the opening she had hoped for.

'Would you like me to make you a bit of a garden? I used to help my dad with ours when I was growing up so I know something about it.' She looked nervously at Mrs Patel and continued. 'I wouldn't want to get paid,' Claire hurried to explain. 'I would really enjoy it.' She thought she saw a flicker of the old distrust in Mrs Patel's dark eyes.

'I wouldn't mind,' Mrs Patel told her. 'It's not something I need, but it might be nice for the children. Still, it would be bound to cost money.'

'Not too much and the children could help. It will be good for them, the outdoors. And it's nice exercise.'

'How much would it cost?' 'Mrs Patel asked. 'I mean for the plants and such.'

'I don't know,' Claire told her truthfully. 'Why don't I do a little research and see if I can find out.'

'Well, I'm not just handing over a packet of money,' Mrs Patel said.

'Of course not,' Claire agreed. If it wasn't for Mrs Patel she would have left for the States a long time ago. But sometimes the woman seemed unnecessarily difficult.

A customer came in and Mrs Patel went off to deal with business. While Claire swept up she had the time to reflect that, after all, she was happier telling Mrs Patel all about the flat than she would have been telling Tina.

As they closed up that night Claire could feel Mrs Patel looking over at her. Each time she turned around Mrs Patel's dark head turned away but that didn't fool Claire. Mrs Patel had something other than gardening on her mind. But she said nothing. A little after ten, when Claire was ready to leave, Mrs Patel handed her not only her twenty-pound note but another bill. It was ten pounds.

'For plants?' Claire asked.

Mrs Patel shook her head and looked away. 'For you,' she said. 'Safta has done quite well in maths. I hope you have the time to continue helping her.'

'Oh, Mrs Patel. I love to be with Safta. You don't have to pay me extra for that.'

'I certainly don't,' Mrs Patel said. 'It is only for the extra time you work here.' Then she briskly turned back to the till. 'Business is picking up a bit,' she said. 'And –' she patted her stomach – 'it isn't getting any easier for me.'

'Of course not. Is there anything else I can do?'

'You can go home to Kensington,' Mrs Patel sniffed.

Claire smiled but was careful not to let Mrs Patel see it. Though she didn't let it show, she felt jubilant, triumphant. It wasn't just that she could now pay for her commute back to Camden, and have five pounds left over. It was that Mrs Patel valued her whether she was willing to admit it or not.

There was now only one thing on her list that remained to be done. Before she left Mrs Patel that night she asked for an envelope and a sheet of paper. She also bought a stamp. When she got off the train back at her new neighborhood she walked slowly, composing carefully in her mind the letter she was about to write. She also felt ridiculously superstitious and so, instead of waiting until she got home, she stopped in one of the cafés that lined the avenue. She bought a decaf cappuccino and then, feeling that she had 'rented' the table with the price of the coffee, she began to write.

> Dear Tina,
>   Thank you for your letter. It was nice to get news of you and I'm glad all is well in New York.
>   I have managed to find a part-time job and that is going to allow me to stay on in London for at least a little while longer. I am sending in my resignation to Crayden Smithers and I wanted you to be the first to know. I am grateful that you helped me get the job and for all your help before and after.
>   I also wanted to return the money that you and the girls were so kind to collect. I'm sure that you'll see that everybody gets theirs along with my thanks for their generosity. I'm doing fine and I won't need any more help.

Here Claire paused and read over what she had already written. It seemed formal and overly polite, but it was the best she could do and, in some ways, she thought it was just as harsh as any insult because it was cold. And she didn't want to be out-and-out mean – she was grateful to Tina and didn't know what she would have done at times if Tina had not helped her. For one thing, she never would have met Mr Wonderful and for another she wouldn't be in London right now. For that alone she felt as if she couldn't be anywhere as mean in her note as Tina had been to her.

She drank the rest of her coffee and thought about what had to come next.

I'm very sorry if I have made you angry. Our friendship like all friendships had its down side but I am really grieved to find that you are so angry with me. I promise you that anything I did that hurt or upset you was quite accidental. I hope you believe this.

I have decided to stay on as long as I can here in London. I have been lucky and found a room-mate with a very nice apartment. I'm not sure when I'll be back. Best of luck to you and Anthony.

Once again, she hesitated. Tina's pissy tone almost demanded an equally nasty response but she wasn't going to do it. She couldn't however sign the note 'love'. Instead she simply told the truth.

I am not sure what my new postal code (that's what they call zip codes here) will be so it's useless to send on my address. There are so many streets with the same name that unless you have a map and know what neighborhood you're going to it is hard to find anything. I'll write when I get more organized.

The last line was a lie. Claire knew she wouldn't write to Tina again and though it made her sad, it made her sad in a rather distant way. Somehow, right or wrong, it seemed as if she and Tina had never been friends, not true friends. They had instead some sort of agreement to stick together. Claire had to admit that, on her part, she probably did it because she had no other choice. She wasn't as sure about Tina's motivation. Perhaps it was because Tina really did like her. But it might have been because Tina could feel superior to Claire. Claire decided it was best not to think too much about it and smiled as she thought, instead, about Mrs Patel, Toby, and Imogen. All of them might turn out to be good friends and, if they did, what a wealth of different experiences her friends would represent. Very different from a shared Tottenville childhood and dead-end jobs which seemed in retrospect to be all that she shared with Tina.

Before she gathered up her things she jotted a quick note to Abigail Samuels so that at least there was someone who could share her enthusiasm for what she was doing. Claire slid her things into her bag and walked out the door. As she walked by Knitting Kitting she felt no sense of failure. Her mood was too good and she was heartened by the fact that she had just made another new friend in Mrs Venables. At the next corner she dropped the letter into the red pillar box. Then, fishing for her keys in her purse, she turned the corner and walked home.

FORTY-FOUR

The next morning Claire drank her tea, tidied up her things and decided to clean the kitchen. While Imogen was away might be a diplomatic time. She had learned from Mrs Patel that 'slut' was actually closer to what Americans would call a slob. And Toby was certainly right to use it in Imogen's case. Claire washed down the refrigerator, scoured the 'cooker', washed the dishes and dusted. She noticed that Imogen barely had two plates of the same pattern – her cupboard was a hodge-podge of patterns and colors that looked like the remnants of a yard sale. After two hours of steady work there was still more to do, but Claire did not want to appear too interfering nor play the role of a galley slave.

As she tidied the rest of the flat she left all of the manu-scripts exactly as they were. She couldn't figure out how Imogen could do her work; most of the books she edited seemed to be 'how-to's' and she had them mixed up all around the flat. Sections on building a stone wall sat next to pages on cookery, interleaved with what looked like parts of a sex manual. Claire giggled at the thought of the result if bits of the three were accidentally combined at the printer's. Still, she left it all as it was since Im seemed to have some kind of order to it that worked for her, and sat down to some tea and toast – a smaller breakfast than she was used to.

The morning passed slowly but luxuriously. She felt so lucky; there were so many things to look forward to. There was a possible visit from Toby; getting back to the museum and medieval art; the Nancy Mitford book; watching the gardens outside her window begin to bloom; finishing her throw.

She had tried very hard to keep thoughts of Toby to a minimum, and to spread her visits to him out. She knew only too well – especially since her adventure with Mr Wonderful – that it was unlikely that a man with looks, charm and wit would be interested in her except in the most casual way. She was teaching herself to accept that, and using Toby as an object lesson. He was, she reminded herself over and over again, just a casual friend, someone she could drop in on, discuss books with, and expect very little more from. And, after all, wasn't that enough? She wasn't the kind of girl that men like Toby got involved with. She knew that, but she couldn't help the fact that her mind, when left to its own devices, frequently reverted to Toby and whatever he had said the last time she'd seen him. Other thoughts that crept into her head right before she went to sleep were too embarrassing to even admit to herself.

Perhaps even better than all the things she had to look forward to was that there was nothing to dread. No more long commutes, no jammed elevators, no grinding job, no Joan, no gossip from Tina, no need to avoid Jerry. Freedom was bliss.

As she sat in the beautiful apartment, surrounded by music, Claire realized that she had never really had a nice space of her own. Most people would consider her 'home-loving' but that was a difficult thing to be if you didn't have a lovely home. Her parents' house had been filled with old junk, them and her brother. After Fred left and Jerry moved in there still hadn't been much room for Claire. Here, in the quiet and the sunshine from the skylights, she began to feel not only as if she was starting a new life but also that she was becoming a new person. She was, of course, still Claire Bilsop, but it seemed as if she knew – and was willing to admit – what she liked and disliked. More importantly, she was willing to act on those preferences and do the things she enjoyed no matter what she had to give up. She looked around her. It was magical.

After a while she showered, dressed and went to her room where she took out her knitting. The pattern was indeed complicated and she had to pay a great deal of attention to it, but she enjoyed the concentration. She sat, her legs crossed, in the small armchair and every now and then rested her eyes by looking out onto the back garden or glancing around her small, pretty room. Then, after a satisfied sigh she would go back to the lap robe that was starting to grow, just as her life here was.

Her only true disappointment was that Mrs Venables couldn't use her help. It was a pity that the shop wasn't thriving. A person with Mrs Venables's skills shouldn't be wasted. Claire could never understand why more people didn't knit. It was relaxing and soothing, yet productive. When knitting, one could watch television or converse, or supervise children. It filled up the interstices in life – waiting for planes, riding in buses, sitting in waiting rooms. It allowed for a pleasant meditative state while keeping one's hands busy and one's conscience clear. When you knit you could enjoy being, simply being, though you were actually doing something.

It was odd how Imogen and Tina and other people thought knitting was boring. For Claire it was a way to create with her hands and eyes while her mind was often free to wander, sometimes thinking of the past, occasionally planning the future or simply daydreaming. When she looked at the sweater she had finished before she left for London she remembered the hope she had knit into it. Her scarf reminded her of the way she had come out of the misery of Michael's betrayal. Her gloves (which Im, always fashion-conscious, coveted) were her first project from London. And now, her lap robe would remind her of how she worked with pleasure in her new home and planned an ambitious new idea.

As she changed bobbins a thought occurred to Claire: more women would probably knit if they only knew how. There just weren't any in-house grandmothers like Mrs Venables or Claire's dear Nana to teach anyone. In America grandmothers lived in Florida, or senior housing or gated communities. She wasn't sure where they lived in London, but it didn't seem as if they were thick on the ground. Yet knitting was simple to learn if someone taught you, though almost impossible to learn from a book. If, somehow, she could teach people to knit, then Mrs Venables . . .

Claire put down her needles and sat up very straight. She had an idea, but it was very daring. Her mind raced. Did she have the courage to try? She'd have to be – well, if not pushy then pretty assertive. She thought it over. Embarrassing if she failed, but other than that, what had she to lose? And there was so much to gain.

The whole thing formed more fully. As it did, words and phrases fell into place. Excited, she got up, searched the kitchen until she found paper and a pen (extremely difficult to find despite the piles of manuscript everywhere) and began jotting her ideas down. In less than five minutes she had a draft prepared.

LEARN TO KNIT
FREE Introductory Knitting Lesson.
Get the Basics in Only Two Hours
With no Charge
You will master:
Casting on
Knit stitch
Purl stitch

Selection and use of needles
How to read a simple pattern
Gauging your work
AND MORE
Bring your own supplies or purchase them at the class.
Individual instruction available.
Mistake correction service provided.

Claire paused. When should the class – if it ever took place – be offered? Saturday morning might be a bad time since many women had errands and family responsibilities to catch up with. Saturday afternoon was for the children and Saturday night was certainly impossible. Claire shrugged. It might not work at all, so perhaps the time was irrelevant for now. And, of course, there had to be a place. But that would come next. She took another piece of paper, rewrote the text neatly and drew a little sketch of needles and a ball of yarn. When she was done she looked up and found that it was almost four-thirty. She'd have to wait until tomorrow to show Mrs Venables, but, in her excitement, the person she most wanted to tell her new idea to was Toby.

FORTY-FIVE

Claire took the throw with her the next day. With the work in her knitting bag she set off to Mrs Venables's shop, her flyer tucked beside the project.

She stepped into the store, hoping she wasn't going to be received as a nuisance. But Mrs Venables greeted her with a smile. 'Take a look,' Claire said and placed the uncompleted piece on the counter.

The woman picked it up carefully. Claire had done the bottom border and almost half of the rows of stripes. Bobbins hung off willy-nilly but the old woman was not only careful, but very exacting in her examination. 'Why, my dear, this is extraordinary.' She looked up at her. 'Quite ambitious!' Claire felt herself color. 'And very well done.'

'May I show you something else?' she asked.

'Another project?'

'Not exactly. Well, sort of.' Claire took out a flyer and handed it across the counter. She held her breath as the old woman looked at it. 'What an original idea!' Mrs Venables held the paper out as if to get the full effect. 'An advert. I would never have thought of it.' She paused, tilted her head to the side and looked at Claire. 'Do you think it might work?'

Claire shrugged. 'I don't know,' she said truthfully. 'I've never tried anything like this. But if you don't mind teaching there's really nothing to lose.'

'Oh, but I love to teach. Of course it might be difficult to teach a large group, especially here.'

Claire laughed. 'Don't worry,' she said. 'I doubt we would get a large group.' She paused, flustered because she had said 'we' and must not presume. She was also taking in the fact that Mrs Venables had actually assumed the classes would take place at her shop. 'Anyway, I could help if it comes to that.'

'Of course you should, my dear.' Mrs Venables paused and looked at the flyer again. 'But if we offer the classes for free how would you be paid?'

Claire smiled. 'Well, the classes are free, but you know how we knitters are,' – she looked around at the goods lying on the shelves – 'people will want needles and yarn and knitting bags . . .'

Mrs Venables laughed. 'Of course. They'll want to be kitted out.'

'And you know how enthusiastic we get. I'm only half through with my throw and I'm already thinking about a cotton sweater for summer.'

Mrs Venables's watery blue eyes surveyed her again. 'You are a really clever girl, Claire.' She looked down at the flyer again. 'Why don't we tie them up with colored yarn?' she asked. 'So much more original than Sellotape. And a kind of promise of things to come, isn't it?'

Did that mean she would do it? It must! 'What a good idea!' Claire exclaimed.

Mrs Venables picked up some scissors and selected a cherry red four-ply yarn. 'How many flyers do you have?'

'Only the one, but I'll make photocopies.' Her heart was beating so hard she was afraid Mrs Venables might hear it. 'Do you think I should make fifty?'

'As many as that?' Mrs Venables asked. 'Where would you put them all?'

'Oh, I'll find places,' Claire promised. 'Corner lamp posts, church railings, next to post boxes.'

'What a good idea!' Mrs Venables exclaimed. 'Here, help me cut the yarn.'

It was half-past three that day when Claire walked into Toby's shop. As she emerged from the dark stacks, Toby looked up and smiled. 'Hello,' he said and Claire smiled with relief. She was afraid of the day that he wouldn't seem glad to see her. Today, luckily, was not that day. 'Have you finished with Uncle Matthew and Co?'

'Oh, yes! I loved the whole family,' Claire said, referring to the Mitford book. 'Time to move on, though. Something more . . .'

'Oh, don't tell me. It's time for Barbara Pym.' As usual he walked back to the stacks and rooted around. George Eliot, hearing the activity, jumped down from the desk and followed him, just the way Claire would have liked to. When Toby returned he had a book with a green and gray jacket. Claire took it.

'You'll love it,' he said. 'Vicars and jumble sales and lots of warm, milky drinks. Just what the doctor ordered.'

Claire took out a little wrapped box and put it on the table beside Toby's chair. 'What's all this, then?' Toby asked, assuming another of his funny accents.

'Just a little gift for you,' she said. 'I wanted to thank you for setting me up with Imogen.'

'Oh. The flat? So it's working?'

'It's wonderful. It's really the best place I've ever lived.' Claire began to describe it and went on and on until she realized that she was gushing and that Toby was staring at her with an odd expression. 'I'm sorry,' she said. 'I'm boring you.'

'On the contrary. Your enthusiasm is charming – I haven't been that excited since I was sent down from Oxford. Well, I'm glad it's working out. And this –' he picked up the box – 'this wasn't necessary. But it's very welcome.' He opened the gift. 'Chocolates! Perfect,' he said. 'Let's eat them all.'

He popped one in his mouth and handed the box to her. She laughed. 'So, what else are you up to?' he asked.

'I do have a . . . a project that I'm trying to get off the ground.'

'Really?' He stood up, plugged in his kettle and shooed George Eliot off the tabletop where she had settled. 'You can tell me all about it over tea and chocolates. Much more satisfying than sympathy.'

Claire withheld a sigh. It wasn't that she didn't like tea, but she could go for more than a quarter of an hour without a cup of it at her elbow. Still, she took the cup he gave her.

She began to tell Toby about the knitting class and showed him the flyer. 'Well done,' he said. 'Perhaps I could offer classes to teach people to read, just to drum up a bit of trade.' They both laughed. 'Where will you put the flyers?'

'I thought I would try Imogen's neighborhood. After all, people won't want to travel too far on a Saturday morning. And besides,' Claire paused to contain her enthusiasm, 'I may have found a possible location in a small shop near there.'

'Outstanding! And you're probably right about the traveling,' he agreed. 'And they have more money to spend in Kensington. Good business sense you've got.' He looked wistfully around the store. 'Wish I had a bit.'

Claire had wondered how he stayed in business, but Imogen's assurance that he had an inheritance comforted her. 'Where could I get photocopies made?' she said.

Toby took another look at the flyer. 'Hmm. You don't want this to go off like a damp squib. You know,' he continued, 'I have a friend on Shaftesbury Avenue. He's quite artistic and runs a typesetting and paste-up shop. Why don't you take it around to him? He'll do it, although he'll act as if it's nothing but agro. He might just do something with the text as well – you know, improve on your handwriting a bit. Then he could print them from his computer.'

'I'd love that,' Claire said, 'but I really can't pay for . . .'

'Oh, he won't charge you. He's . . . an old friend. I'll call him now. And speaking of calling, you ought to have a phone number on this. People might want to ask questions, you know.'

Claire shrugged. He was right, but 'I don't have a phone. I'm not sure Imogen would like me to use her number, and the knitting shop doesn't seem to have a phone although there is a number over the door.'

'Ridiculous! I'm a Luddite, but even *I* have a landline and a mobile. Though there have been times when, according to British Telecom, I ceased to exist.' She raised her brows. 'I know it sounds rather existential but it's actually financial,' Toby went on. 'It's what they say when they cut your service. We had a little dust-up over the bill. But things are fine now. I'll tell you what, you can put in my shop's number and if anyone calls I'll take the message for you.'

Before she could thank him he had scrawled some figures across the bottom of the sheet, lifted his own phone and punched in a number. 'Hello, Thomas, dear? I'm sending a friend over. No, not that kind. Her name is Claire and she needs a few moments of your time. Yes, yes, I know. Like I've never helped you. By the way, can you make it?'

Claire was watching from the corner of her eye, and she thought she saw Toby's usually cheerful face close up. Perhaps he was asking too much of his friend. She hated him to call in a favor on her account.

He didn't seem to like Thomas's answer. 'Fine. No trouble. No, I have someone else lined up, anyway.' He cleared his throat. 'So, I'll send Claire over. Right.' He hung up the receiver, put a smile on his face and tilted his head. 'That's all fixed up, then. He's on Shaftesbury Avenue – Piccadilly Circus tube.'

'Toby, I don't know how to thank you,' Claire said. 'You've done so much for me. I'd like somehow to . . .'

'Then you'll go to the opera with me tomorrow. *Lucia*. One of my favorites. What do you say?'

Claire had never been to the opera, she had to work in the evenings, and she had no idea who Lucia was, but she said yes, of course. And when she did she felt another flash of joy, as strong as the one she had had in the morning. Toby was asking her out! And even if she found she didn't like opera, and she knew that nothing would come of it anyway, she couldn't stop the hope that sprang up. Because she was almost speechless at the unexpected pleasure, all she could manage to say was, 'What time?'

'Curtain's up at eight. Why don't you meet me here at six? I know that's ungallant of me, but I do need to close up shop and then we could tube to Covent Garden together.'

She agreed of course, paid for the Pym book and then wanted to linger, to ask him a little about the opera and even perhaps to get a book about it. But she realized that if she was to go to Thomas's and get to work, she simply didn't have the time. 'Well, thank you,' she told him. 'Thanks so much for everything. I'd better be off.'

Toby nodded. He stood up and scribbled an address on a piece of scrap paper. 'Thomas is on the third floor,' he said. 'At times he's a total bitch but tell him I'll smack him if he isn't nice to you.'

She giggled, took the address and ran.

FORTY-SIX

On the Saturday of her date with Toby, Claire spent the morning and early afternoon working at Mrs Patel's and tutoring Safta so that she could have the evening off. She didn't notice the troubled expression on Mrs Patel's face when she asked for the change in schedule.

As well as helping both of the Patel girls with their homework, she started clearing some of the rubbish from the back garden, before she left to take the tube home. Though she was tired, she took the time to put up more of her signs. Thomas, not quite bitchy, not quite cooperative, and without looking at her much either, had done a beautiful job and had printed out fifty copies on a variety of colored papers. As Claire tied them with the contrasting yarn to lamp posts, fence palings and tree trunks she was impressed with the bright spot of color each one made. She covered several blocks in the neighborhood and, when she had gotten half of them up, she stopped, feeling she had done more than enough for one day. She couldn't resist, however, leaving a few on her own street. When she got to the front door of the flat she turned around and had to smile. She had been a modern day Hansel and Gretel, but instead of bread crumbs she had left a trail of papers and bows. She wasn't sure if they would get a single inquiry, or if anyone would actually show up, but she decided that, even if they didn't, she was glad she had tried.

She turned her key in the lock and ran lightly up the staircase to the little haven at the top of the house. As she shrugged out of her coat, Im's voice floated out from the bedroom. 'Hello, hello. What have you been up to?'

Claire was too shy, too afraid of failure to mention the flyers. 'I'm going to the opera with Toby,' she said as she went to the hall closet to pull out her clothes for the evening.

'Oh, really?' Im said, both her voice and her eyebrows raised. She watched Claire, who wanted to be rested for her visit to Covent Garden. But Im kept her chatter up and Claire listened to her talk about Malcolm and their plans. It wasn't that different from listening to Tina's constant monologue but the accent was far more pleasant.

She made herself a cup of tea, ran water for her bath and wondered why she didn't feel quite the same sort of anticipation about going out with Toby as she had with Michael. She told herself not to be foolish. She was going out to the opera – something she had never done – with a man she liked and admired. If she didn't feel that total suffusion of love that she had with Michael, it was because it would be inappropriate. She didn't really know Toby, she'd never kissed him, and she had no idea how he felt about her.

Of course, she thought, as she soaked in the hot water, she had known that Michael didn't share her passion, yet she had felt for him. Love didn't seem to be something you could control. It was or it wasn't. She had done her best to forget her feelings for Michael but now, because of this new opportunity with a man she supposed, they had come flooding back, reminding her how dangerous they could be. Well, she wasn't confused about Toby. He was no ladies' man, and he was charming and intelligent and generous. He may have simply asked her out because he had a spare ticket. This time she would take things very slowly and expect very little.

* * *

She arrived at the bookstore in plenty of time. She wore her navy-blue dress and her pearls. It wasn't an exciting ensemble but Toby seemed to eye her approvingly. 'Ah, here you are.' He turned back to two older women who were both holding carrier bags and watching him intently. 'I'm afraid I can't take them off your hands,' he said. 'I'm really having trouble selling the stock I've got.'

Claire watched as the women's shoulders drooped. They began to repack books into their bags. She felt sorry for them – they were obviously desperate to make a few pounds – and apparently so did Toby.

'Wait a minute. Here we go,' he said, picking a volume up. 'I've got a customer for this one.' The two women brightened immediately. 'Would you take ten pounds for it?' Toby asked. They chimed their assent together and the business was quickly completed. Once they were out of the shop, Toby sighed. 'I'm too soft by half. I should be under-written by the local council,' he said, confirming Claire's suspicion that he had absolutely no one willing to buy the book he'd just purchased. 'Well, do unto others,' he said. 'Now if only someone would do this to me I could afford better seats at the opera.' He smiled at her. 'Actually,' he said, 'I inherited the box from my uncle. Quite good location. Dress circle. But it rather puts a burden on me. Can't give it up, can't afford to keep it.'

'Oh, perhaps I should pay . . .'

'Don't be daft,' Toby said, took her arm and escorted her from the shop.

Lucia di Lammermoor was going crazy. Her brother Enrico – worse than Fred – had tricked her into confiding her love for Edgardo. Then he'd married her to Arturo. She had just discovered the horrible ruse and now, drenched in blood, she had not only murdered Arturo in reaction, but she was mourning the loss of Edgardo, and the love she could have had for a lifetime.

Unlikely as the plot might be, Claire leaned forward breathless and watched Lucia go mad. Her voice was the most beautiful sound Claire had ever heard, and though she couldn't understand the Italian she knew all of the feelings that Lucia expressed. Her voice dipped and soared and Claire felt herself begin to sob at the tragedy of what poor, innocent Lucia had been robbed of. It was the third act, and though Claire didn't know that it had been a famous classic almost from the time it was written, she felt its power grip her. She clutched the balustrade and wept unselfconsciously until Toby handed her a clean folded handkerchief. Only then was she recalled to herself. Lucia wasn't singing to her, nor had she lost Edgardo. *Her* Edgardo, Mr Wonderful, had never loved her, and she wasn't important enough to be tricked into marrying someone else. Embarrassed at her reaction, she mopped up her face and tried to calm herself before they left the theater.

'I didn't know you were such an opera buff,' Toby commented when she had managed to quiet herself. 'Elizabeth Futral was wonderful. Did you ever hear her in the States?' Claire just shook her head. She didn't feel like explaining that she had never seen an opera, that she'd never even heard of Elizabeth Futral, and that she had confused some of Lucia's feelings with her own. She looked down at Toby's handkerchief and realized she couldn't return it to him in its present condition. She stuffed it into her purse and gave him a watery smile. He smiled back. 'I actually prefer the stalls to the dress circle.' He looked away, letting her gather herself. 'The drop-scene was good, don't you think? Back in my student days I used to sit in the gods but since Uncle dropped off the hooks I've moved down in the world.' He took her arm. 'Here, you can have this, too,' he said as he handed her the program for the opera.

'Oh, no. You can keep it.'

'I have enough of them already. Consider this your first

of many. Now, come, my little chicken,' he said, 'I know a delightful *boite* where I can ply you with wine and a savory until you feel yourself.'

Claire recovered long before they reached the restaurant. Toby put his arm through hers and patted her hand. Oh, she was beginning to like him so very much. He must like her. Once at the '*boite*', Toby talked about his student days at Oxford before he had been 'sent down' – which seemed to be English for expelled. 'So. Now on the gossip. What do you think of Our Im?'

'I like her.'

'As do we. Did she hit you with the second cousin to the Queen bit?' Claire nodded. Toby laughed. 'We all make bets on how long it will take her in any conversation before she mentions it. Six minutes has been her record. Can't think what they have in common. Im's dad can be a bit toffee-nosed but he's not such a climber. And her mother's pretty down to earth – in fact he seems to get tired of the old bird. They're certainly no Antony and Cleopatra.' Toby shook his head. 'The only thing the two of them seem dead keen on are loose covers, loose-boxes and loose water-proofs.' Before Claire could ask what any of those were, Toby continued. 'Have you met Malcolm?' Claire shook her head. 'He's a bit wet, but I suppose rattle-brained Im could do worse.'

Claire wondered if she would ever meet Malcolm – Im only seemed to have him over when Claire was at work. But what did it matter to Claire? She was grateful to be living there – Im wasn't obliged to introduce her to her friends. 'She's lovely,' Claire said, loyal to her generous roommate.

'Yes, but what does it all mean? She'll just marry and breed and her children will marry and breed and so on and so on.'

Claire shrugged. 'Well, isn't that what everyone does?' she asked. Didn't Toby ever plan to 'marry and breed', as he put it.

Toby looked over the top of his glasses at her. 'Not quite everyone, my dear,' he said. 'Let's share a pudding, shall we? Afters is always the best part of the meal.' Claire knew by now that pudding was the generic for dessert. She supposed 'afters' meant the same. 'Shall we be naughty and have sticky toffee pudding?' Toby proposed.

Claire admitted she'd never tried it. 'Pure ambrosia,' Toby assured her. 'Of course, I always like the opportunity to ask for spotted dick but I don't really enjoy it.' The waiter appeared, Toby asked for the toffee pudding and ordered a dessert wine. 'Simply because you need to keep up your strength,' he told her with a grin.

The 'afters' was the best thing she had ever had and Claire tried not to eat more than her share. They were just finishing and Toby was paying the bill when he turned to her, his glasses slightly askew and his hair tousled. 'I completely forgot. My charity in the bookstore and your reaction to Lucia put it out of my mind. But I've had a call about your classes.'

For a moment Claire didn't know what he was talking about. She was a little fuzzy from the opera, her feelings for Toby, and the drink. But she thought she had heard good news. 'A call?'

'Yes. Some woman wanted to register. I had no idea what to do so I faked it. I told her she didn't need to do anything but give me her name. Was that right? Shall I take you home?' he continued, not realizing the importance of the news he had just given her.

FORTY-SEVEN

When Claire walked into Knitting Kitting on Monday morning, to her surprise, there was a customer. At least she thought at first that he was a customer, though an unlikely one. For one thing he was a man. For another, he was very well dressed in a business suit and actually rather good-looking – what Imogen might call 'dishy'. He was very fair with eyelashes, eyebrows and hair almost the same light color as his skin. That made the blue of his eyes even more startling when he turned them on her.

Claire had a smile ready but didn't have a chance to greet him. 'Ah. Here she is. I think I need to speak to you,' he said. Claire smiled at him inquiringly. To her surprise he didn't smile back. Actually, his lips compressed into a narrow white line. 'Are you the one who's done this?' he asked and held out one of her flyers. Claire nodded. Perhaps he wanted to enroll his wife in a class. 'What do you think you're doing? Don't you know people don't like trash tied to their private property? And that you don't advertise a business the way you do a church fête?'

'Now Nigel,' Mrs Venables began.

'Don't "now Nigel" me. This is irresponsible behavior. And it's illegal. Full stop.'

Claire had put signs up all over but didn't know it was illegal or wrong. Could he be from the police department? Certainly not in that suit. More likely an angry neighbor.

But she had been careful to space out the notices. Could somebody be annoyed over one page of paper tied to a lamp post? 'I don't think . . .' she began.

'You certainly don't. And do you read? You posted all over the "No Hoardings" signs.' Claire had seen signs saying that. She'd thought they were about some law against saving up food or something. She had tied up flyers right over them.

'I'm sorry . . .' she began, but he gave her no time for apologies.

'And whose idea was this? Who asked you to interfere?'

Claire was completely chagrined, then relieved when Mrs Venables came out from behind the counter. 'Nigel, stop that right now. You may be a barrister but Claire is not on trial. She asked me if she could do it and I agreed.'

Clearly this pale and angry man wasn't threatening to Mrs Venables. The old woman put her arm around Claire's shoulder. 'She was helping me. I asked her to. You have no right to blame her. And I certainly don't approve of your tone of voice.' Claire felt Mrs Venables's arm tighten. 'I'm sorry, my dear. Permit me to introduce you to my son. Claire Bilsop, this is my son Nigel. He's a good boy but sometimes he's overprotective. Please excuse him.'

'Mother, I . . .'

'Nigel, don't raise your voice.'

To her surprise, Claire felt tears rising, blurring her sight. How humiliating. She didn't want to wipe at her eyes but she certainly didn't want this arrogant man to see her cry.

'I didn't raise my voice. I was simply taken off-guard. I had to respond to half a dozen phone calls.'

'Were they complaints?' Mrs Venables asked.

Nigel Venables turned his head, walked to the window and looked out onto the street. 'No. Not exactly. But you must understand that homeowners don't want commercial establishments to post notices . . .'

Claire, so excited about her list of possible class attendees, now felt ashamed of them. And why had people called Mrs Venables's son? His number wasn't listed.

'Were they inquiries about the class, Nigel?'

He looked back at them. 'I suppose so. And I felt a proper fool knowing nothing about it. The point is, Mother, this idea is ridiculous. It's going to come a cropper.'

Claire hated to appear pathetic, but even worse was to appear ridiculous. Her idea, which had sounded so practical and effective, something she'd been so proud of, was ridiculous? But people had called, not only Toby but this detestable Nigel. Her heart lifted a little. And some were people who wanted to register? How had they gotten Nigel Venables's number? Why hadn't they called Toby's?

Nigel crumpled one of the flyers and tossed it onto the window seat. 'Since I bought this property the neighborhood has been watching to see if I plan to develop it. I don't need any extra attention.' He looked back at Claire. 'You can't treat people's private properties as if they were billboards. This isn't the United States, you know. Next you'll be handing out freebie subs at tube stations.'

'Nigel, that will be quite enough.' Mrs Venables turned to Claire. 'I'm sorry, he's not at his best right now.' She took a deep breath. 'Claire's idea is a good one. Shake hands with her, Nigel, and behave properly.'

Reluctantly, Nigel extended his hand which was long, very pale and surprisingly warm. But he made the handshake brief and hardly looked at her. Then he sighed, letting both of his hands drop helplessly to his side. 'You're quite impossible,' he told his mother. 'If you need help, why didn't you tell me? You know how I feel. This place is altogether too much for you to manage.'

'I know, dear. I should stay home and dust the Staffordshire. But you see, I don't like to dust.' She turned to Claire. 'Come and sit over here at the pattern table. I'll make you both a cup of tea.'

'Oh, fine! Let us make you extra work. Why not cook us dinner?'

'I'd be delighted to,' said Mrs Venables, already filling a kettle. 'Perhaps you'd like to come to dinner sometime next week, Claire?'

'Mother, you're getting into one of your moods and . . .'

'I? In one of my moods? I can't imagine what would ruffle my normal calm, except perhaps for an over protective son descending like an enraged headmistress and scolding his mother as well as an innocent stranger.' Mrs Venables turned off the tap. 'Do you want a biscuit as well? I have your favorite macaroons.'

Nigel put a long hand over his eyes and Claire almost felt sorry for him. He seemed calmer now, resigned almost, and not nearly as frightening. He leaned against the counter, took a deep breath and made quite a production of exhaling. 'Can we discuss this whole idea? I take it it was Miss Bilsop's?'

'Well, don't be so sure. You underestimate your mother,' Mrs Venables said.

'It was my idea,' Claire admitted. 'But I asked permission. I just thought it might increase business . . .'

'Just what my mother doesn't need, increased business! Which means increased work. Which means increased blood pressure. Don't you know . . .'

'Nigel, I don't want to have to be sharp with you but I am going to insist you drop this subject and change your tone of voice,' his mother interjected. 'Claire isn't interested in my medical reports. Is this what they teach you at the Inns of Court? Now, tell us how many phone calls you have had about the class.'

'Well, about five,' he admitted, 'but there's probably another three on the ansaphone.'

'And they all objected to a bit of paper tied with wool to a lamp post?'

Nigel sat on the corner of the pattern table. 'No. Some

did, but some inquired about the class. They said they didn't get an answer at that phone number. So they rang my number on the shop sign.'

Claire wondered if Toby had taken the phone off the hook. Had she imposed on him too much?

Mrs Venables filled the teapot and brought it to the table. Then she took out a tin of homemade cookies – they looked far too moist and good for Claire to think of them as biscuits – and put them on a plate. 'Claire, my dear, how many signs did you hang?'

'Almost fifty.'

'Fifty!' Nigel repeated.

'Well, then. Two or three complaints over fifty signs. That's one in twenty-five. My goodness, with the number of cranks in London I would think that's a low percentage.' She poured out the three cups of tea. 'Claire did it with my permission and didn't mean any harm. A couple of complaints aren't going to ruin your property empire. Now, apologize to Claire nicely and we can move on.'

Nigel cleared his throat, but before he said anything Claire spoke up. 'I'm sure it's all my fault. I didn't realize what the signs meant or that the fence posts were private property. I won't do it again.'

'I'm glad to hear it,' Nigel said. 'My mother doesn't need to advertise the shop as if it were a side show. And she certainly doesn't need the income. Let's just forget about it, shall we? No harm done.'

'Exactly what I was trying to say,' Mrs Venables told him serenely. She handed the plate of macaroons to Claire, who took one but felt that the lump in her throat would make it impossible for her to choke it down. Nigel felt no such difficulty and took three, making short work of them. 'He's loved them since he was a little boy,' Mrs Venables confided. 'I used to send them to him at school.'

Nigel bit into yet another macaroon. He turned to Claire. 'Bilsop?' he asked. 'Where are your people from?'

It reminded her of Im. Did everyone in this country want to place you in some hierarchy? She wasn't second-cousins to the Queen. 'I don't have any people,' Claire said. She stood up. 'I'm afraid I have to go,' she told Mrs Venables. 'I'm going to be late for work.' That, of course, wasn't true.

'I understand,' Mrs Venables said, and it looked as if she did.

Claire left the shop and trudged the two streets home. Things had been going so well. She should have known that meant too well. Being cornered and scolded as if she were a child or an opportunist was deeply disturbing. But she hadn't pushed Mrs Venables into anything, she told herself. It was just that detestable Nigel who made her feel so guilty. Now, she would be too embarrassed ever to go back to the shop again. Claire felt tears spring to her eyes once more, but this time she didn't have to hold them back.

FORTY-EIGHT

After an hour or two in the haven of her new home, Claire felt in better spirits and decided to do something positive. She had found a garden center in Chelsea and thought she'd ask permission to take the Patel girls to it. When she left for work – even earlier than usual – the sun was breaking through the flat silver clouds. There was a smell of soot mixed with earth, and that indefinable odor of new growth that heralded the spring. Of course, early flowers were already blooming, but this scent marked the season as truly begun. It would be lovely to make a garden.

She had just reached the corner when she recognized the man approaching her as Nigel Venables.

'Miss Bilsop.'

Claire waited, carefully keeping her expression neutral – he was the last person she wanted to see but, in her new, positive mood, she was determined not to let him upset her again.

'I must apologize for my outburst,' Nigel said. 'Can I take you for a cup of coffee?'

Caught completely off guard and temporarily robbed of the powers of speech, Claire just found herself nodding.

'There's a decent café just up the road; it's very kind of you to come.'

'Well,' Claire said, recovering. 'I haven't much time.'

'We won't take long.'

Claire tried to match her strides to Nigel's long ones but couldn't, and had to take an undignified skip every three or four steps, just to keep up. When she was beside him she snuck a glance at his face, pointed resolutely toward the café. This confirmed her first impression; that he was nice-looking, having Mrs Venables's aristocratic features which, Claire had to admit, looked better on a man.

She was expecting peace-making but, once in the café, he was just as arrogant as he had been earlier. He seated her and fetched them coffees and then he began to question her. 'What brought you to London?' he asked.

A man, Claire was tempted to say. That would shock him. Instead she told him she had decided to come on a whim.

'Doesn't your family worry about you?'

Claire sensed that he was trying to 'place her' the way Imogen did. What was it with these English and their odd strata of class distinctions? 'My father died about five years ago and my mother . . .' Claire paused, '. . . is about to re-marry.' That was pushing the truth, but Claire certainly didn't feel like explaining the sordid Jerry.

'I'm sorry. My father died when I was a boy,' Nigel said, softening just a little. 'Were you and your father close?'

'Yes. I miss him very much.'

'What did he do?'

There it was again, that need to place her. 'About what?' she asked. She looked at her watch. 'I really have to go,' she said. 'Thank you for the coffee.' Which she hadn't touched. Before he could say anything more, she turned and walked out the door. He hadn't wanted to apologize. He wanted to pump her; to make sure she wasn't some wandering grifter or con artist! He wanted to make sure she was 'the right sort', and Claire was sick of it.

On Friday afternoon, when the Patel girls were out of school, and with their mother's permission, Claire took them to the garden center where they selected dozens of flowering plants, some ground cover, and ten square feet of sod, which Claire learned they called 'turf'. She arranged to have it all delivered and spent the rest of the afternoon working with the girls on the ground behind the shop. She'd purchased a hoe with her own money, but said nothing about it to Mrs Patel who looked on, expressionless.

Once all the rubble had been cleared away, the space was not as bad as it had, at first, appeared. There was a concrete walk (or 'path' as the girls called it) that made a U-shape across the back and two sides of the area but the center was clear. The delivery arrived and, first of all, Claire added some peat moss and topsoil which she and the girls worked into the cindery soil. After that it didn't take long to put in borders of plants, with the little piece of grass in the center. The girls were good helpers, and though they couldn't manage to dig deep they did take the plants carefully out of their plastic containers and sink them into the prepared earth. 'This is just like *Ground Force*!' Safta exclaimed, and told Claire all about the 'telly' program. In less than four hours the little space had been transformed and, though there was no outdoor spigot or hose, Claire and the girls managed to water everything using buckets and pitchers.

When Mrs Patel took a break the girls, so excited that they had to hold their hands over their mouths to keep from shouting, pushed her into the garden from behind. Claire was left to cover the counter and waited to hear exclamations of pleasure.

But there were none. Five, and then ten minutes went by, and still nothing was heard from the back of the shop. Maudie came in with her boys, had a chat and Claire was finishing up her few purchases, carefully placing them in a sack when Mrs Patel, her head lowered, came walking toward the front of the shop. She didn't approach the counter until Maudie had left. Claire had Maudie's money ready. But it was only when Mrs Patel raised her head and looked straight at Claire that she knew this was very important. Mrs Patel's dark eyes were wet with tears. 'How did you do that?' she asked. 'How did you manage it? It is quite marvelous.'

Claire was as surprised and touched as Mrs Patel. 'It wasn't very hard,' Claire said. 'Really. They delivered the heavy stuff and the girls helped.'

'But it's beautiful. It's a real English garden. It will be so lovely for the girls. And I can sit there in the evenings. No smell of cat. It smells of flowers.' She paused, took a napkin from the counter and patted her eyes. 'I didn't think I could have such a thing,' she said.

'I'm so glad you like it,' Claire said.

'I must make a confession to you,' Mrs Patel said. 'I thought that when you moved, we had seen the last of you. I was sure that you would get tired of slumming.'

'But Mrs Patel . . . I never felt that I was . . .'

The woman held up her hand. 'No, no, you must hear me out. I was unjust. I underestimated you and I was afraid, not just for the children but for myself. I have come to count on your help.'

It was the first time Mrs Patel had acted as if she were doing anything but a favor for Claire. 'It's my pleasure,' Claire said. 'Safta is terrific, and the little ones . . .'

'No, please. I have distrusted you. I haven't let you go near the till. I've paid you very little. I apologize for all of it.'

Claire had to stop her before the two of them were crying.

Mrs Patel took a deep breath. 'You know, it is more difficult to accept a kindness than a cruelty,' she said, 'when you're used to cruelty.' She looked away from Claire and into the empty streets. 'Sometimes they call us "Pakis". And we are from Pakistan originally. But I have lived here my whole life and I am British. And so are my children. But you see we do not fit in with the British. And we do not fit in among the Pakistanis because my family is not Moslem, but Hindu.' She looked at Claire. 'My father was a very holy man, but when he died my mother asked my uncle to send for a husband for me from Pakistan. When Lak came he was handsome and it turned my head. What could I do anyway? Perhaps my father would have stopped it but he was gone. It was not a good match.' She looked away again and Claire took a deep breath. She had wondered where Mr Patel was, but wouldn't, of course, ask. 'He took money. He hit me. Not once, but many times. Though I was giving him a citizenship and children he was angry, always angry. You see my father had bought the shop for me. Lak was angry that I owned the business, that I spoke English, that I had opinions.' She sighed but there was an angry glint in her eye. 'Perhaps there was another woman he had to leave behind. Perhaps it would have been as bad, and he as difficult, no matter what.' She looked at Claire.

'But they forced you to marry a stranger,' Claire said. She tried to imagine what that would be like and failed completely.

Mrs Patel shrugged. 'You see, though I am very modern I don't believe that an arranged marriage is a bad thing. You almost never know the person you marry until you have had years of being together. Love can grow just as it can die.'

'Didn't you try to get help, from your mother or the police?'

Mrs Patel gave her a look that told her she understood very little. 'I told my mother and then my aunt but never the police. You don't involve them in your family problems.'

'But what did your mother say? Couldn't she stop him? Didn't she tell you to leave him?'

Mrs Patel shrugged again. 'My mother is very traditional. Without my father to guide her she turned to my aunt and uncle. But my uncle's family had been the ones who made the match. I was told to be quiet, that my complaining was causing the problem.' She made a clicking sound.

'What happened?' Claire finally had the courage to ask.

'It went too far. He began to hit the children. He thought he could do whatever he wished, with me, with them, with the money. I did call the police. I put him out. Five months ago. He went back to Pakistan. And then I went to a solicitor for divorcing him.'

'Good,' Claire said. 'Well, that was the right thing.'

'Not to my family. So we don't see them – haven't seen them for yonks. They don't speak to me. The children don't meet their cousins. My uncle came to me and said "If you do this shameful thing then all of us will turn our backs on you." You see, it caused all kinds of financial difficulties. There was a dowry that had been paid to Lak's family in Pakistan. Now that money is lost forever. Everyone was very, very angry. They said I was a whore, that Lak had put up with me as best he could but that he wasn't even sure the children were his.' This time a tear rolled down her face but she angrily wiped it away. 'It made my children pariahs. How cruel of a father. And all over false pride and money.' She looked down, straightened her clothes and put her hand protectively across her belly. 'Let me check on the children,' she said. But Claire thought she wanted to gather her feelings. 'Flog the bread off,' Mrs Patel said as she waddled to the back. 'It's about to go off.'

To Claire's relief no customers came in to push the day-old bread on. Mrs Patel returned, more composed. 'My children have had a difficult time and have suffered, but since you have begun to help Safta she is much happier and perhaps now, with this garden, she will invite a friend over. If not, she can read and study there. It is very English and very fine indeed. Thank you, Claire.'

'Oh, it really isn't a big deal,' Claire said. But she knew now that it was. 'We all had fun working together.'

Mrs Patel gave one of her rare smiles. 'Yes, fun is very good.'

'And I can teach the girls how to dead-head and snip the grass.'

'Dead-head? Is this some American thing or is it English?' Mrs Patel asked, one brow raised again. 'I know precious little about gardening.'

Claire smiled. 'It means picking off the dead flowers so new ones can come in. The girls will be good at it.'

'I can be good at it as well,' Mrs Patel declared. 'I can keep this garden.' She patted her belly. 'And the baby can enjoy it, too.' She smiled at Claire. 'How can I thank you?' she asked and took Claire's hand.

Claire shrugged. 'You already have. You gave me a job. Because of that I've been able to stay here in London.' She paused. 'You know, I am something of an outcast too,' she said.

Mrs Patel nodded. 'I thought as much,' she said.

FORTY-NINE

Claire woke up at seven on Saturday morning filled with excitement at the prospect of the first knitting class in just two hours. She didn't think that Imogen was an early riser on the weekends, but she wasn't sure because every weekend but this one Imogen had been away. Claire tried to be as quiet as she could as she tip-toed to the bathroom, took her bath, washed her hair and then, wrapped only in a towel, headed to her hall closet to pick out what she would wear for the class. But as she passed the door to Imogen's bedroom it opened and a man – totally naked and very well-built – appeared. He gaped as much as Claire did. 'Sorry,' she managed to gasp as she turned and scuttled back to her room.

Once there she closed the door behind her with a bang so loud that everybody in Kensington would hear it. Oh, god, she thought. The very last thing she needed was for Imogen's boyfriend to complain about her presence in the flat. She hadn't met him before, and this wasn't exactly the way she'd envisioned their first meeting. This must have been the first time since Claire had moved in that he had stayed over. Claire couldn't get over her bad luck, or the fact that she hadn't had a chance to get her clothes. She was stuck in her room.

She looked at one of the flyers sitting on her bureau. The class was scheduled for nine and now, looking at her watch, she realized she had only an hour and ten minutes to find a way to her closet, avoid Imogen and her fiancé, get something for breakfast and hope that she still had a place to stay by the end of the day.

She needed to calm herself and hope that this wasn't a bad omen for the rest of this very important day. Then she remembered her electric kettle. Luckily it had water in it and she merely had to plug it in and wait. She had her mug from the previous night and some tea bags in the top drawer of the bureau. A hot cup of tea and a little calm reflection while looking out the window soon helped her put things in perspective.

If they couldn't laugh about it, at least she doubted that they would evict her. Surely that would be an overreaction. At eight-thirty, hearing nothing outside her door, she gathered up her nerve and went out into the kitchen wearing her clothes from the day before. They were dirty, but the last thing she wanted to look was provocative. She knew how quick Tina had always been to think that women might be flirting with Anthony.

Although Claire expected to meet no one, Imogen was there in a robe, making a pot of tea. Claire winced but Imogen simply said, 'Good morning. Would you like a cup?'

Claire shook her head. 'I don't have time. I have to get dressed properly: I'm going to give a class this morning.' But, as she made her way to the closet, Imogen stopped her.

'A class in what?' she asked. 'Are you teaching American English?'

Claire tried to laugh. 'Actually, I'm teaching knitting – at least I think I am, if people show up.'

'Knitting! How absolutely brilliant! God, everyone is knitting. In my office half of the girls are working on something or other. They all swear by it.'

At that moment Imogen's fiancé came out of the

bedroom. His hair was tousled and his eyes were the darkest brown Claire had ever seen. His arms were too long for the robe he was wearing and his skinny legs were exposed to the thigh. 'Hello,' he said.

'Claire, this is Malcolm. I gather you already met.'

Claire blushed. Malcolm smiled and asked Imogen for tea. It seemed that he was not offended at all.

Incredibly relieved, Claire went back to her room and dressed quickly. She was about to leave when Imogen stopped her at the door.

'Do you think I could come to your class?' Imogen asked.

'I'd love it,' Claire said.

'What time are you teaching?'

'Actually, it begins in just a few minutes. Nine o'clock.'

'Oh, my goodness,' Imogen said. 'Nobody would make it to that. You should have made it eleven or maybe noon.'

Claire's chest tightened again but it was too late. She would, as Tina frequently said, have to like it or lump it. Well, if she didn't get everyone, she hoped she'd get at least some of the dozen people who had left messages with Toby or Nigel. And if some came late, she could just start them while the others moved along. 'You don't have to come to a class,' Claire said to Imogen. 'I'd be happy to teach you anytime you want.'

'Oh! How absolutely fabulous. You are just too good. You do all the work here and then you offer that as well. You'd make a perfect wife. Malcolm,' she called, 'you'll have to introduce Claire to some really nice men from work.'

'There are no nice men where I work,' Malcolm drawled from the kitchen.

Imogen laughed. 'Well, perhaps I'll make it to the class. Do you mind if I come later?'

'No. Of course not,' Claire said and thrust a flyer into Imogen's hand. 'It's just around the corner,' she said. 'But I'm going to be late. I really have to go.'

Claire raced down the stairs and out onto the street. It was just a few minutes past nine and she almost ran to the corner but, as she turned, she stopped and stood stock-still. In front of the shop seven women stood about, obviously waiting for it to open.

Well, it wasn't a dozen people but it was a start. Claire put on her brightest smile and went up to the door. Mrs Venables had entrusted her with a key and she proudly took it out and opened up. 'Please come in,' she said to the women. 'Are you here for the class?'

They assented and filed past her into the shop where a circle of chairs was already laid out round a table. Three of the women were middle-aged and dressed very well, three were about Claire's own age or perhaps a little younger, and the last one was a very slight teenage girl in a lot of black eye make-up. 'Why don't you take a look around,' Claire said. 'We'll be ready in just a little while.'

She began to arrange needles, scrap-yarn and a sign-up sheet with spaces for their names, addresses and phone numbers. The shop bell rang and Claire looked up to see another woman enter. She had well-cut blond hair and though her face was long and a bit mannish she was quite attractive. She turned to hold open the door and a much older woman, obviously her mother, came in as well. That made nine.

Just then Claire heard Mrs Venables making her way downstairs and the two of them smiled at one another. Mrs Venables looked at the group who were now all finding seats and nodded at Claire in a most approving way. When she got to the shop floor, Claire figured they were ready to go.

She cleared her throat. The women looked up. 'My name is Claire. This is Mrs Venables. We'll be helping you today.' She took a deep breath. She had never been a teacher before. 'We'll start by passing out materials for you to practice on, and there's a list here for you to add your names to.'

There was a bit of bustle as everyone sorted themselves out. Claire asked Mrs Venables to start a few women off at one end of the horseshoe of chairs and she did the same at the other end.

'I'm Leonora Atkins,' a dark-haired woman Claire's age told her when Claire got to her. 'Do you know that half of the women at my office knit and the other half want to?'

'Really?' Claire asked as she looped wool onto Leonora's needle.

'Well, when Gwyneth Paltrow, Winona Ryder and Julia Roberts are doing it, everyone wants to.'

'I didn't know they all knit.'

'That's the least of it. David Arquette and Russell Crowe are at it. I'm just waiting for David Beckham to pick up needles.'

'Heavens, is that true?' It was the mother of the attractive blond woman who had spoken. 'Of course the Queen knits. I don't know why I never learned, but if she can make the time I shall, too.' She laughed, as if she were making some kind of joke. Claire recognized her accent as being similar to the Queen's, though she wore an old, pilled, machine-made cardigan. The daughter, however, was elegantly dressed in casual but well-cut trousers, with a silk scarf knotted stylishly around her throat. She looked up when Claire asked them their names as she helped them.

'I'm Ann Fenwick,' she said. 'This is my mother.'

Claire got them both started then stood to address the group. 'I see that you all have needles and you are beginning to get the idea of how to cast on.'

'No,' said a middle-aged woman with a high voice and an equally high bridge to her nose. 'We're just making these damn knots, sweetie. I think I've got it all bollixed up.' Some of the others laughed.

'Actually, it *is* a knot that you've made, but that's the first step to casting on,' Claire explained. All the faces looked at her expectantly. 'Does everybody have their slipknots on?' she continued. Most of the women nodded. 'I'll come along and check and then I'll show you the next step which is to knit within that slipknot and then knit within each stitch made after that. Then you've cast on and that's the basis for your garment.'

'But I so hate this color,' said the teenager. She was stuck with a small ball of sickly green worsted that clashed horribly with the long violet dress she wore.

'Yes, that is pretty dreadful,' Mrs Venables agreed. 'But this isn't for your garment. It's to learn on and for your gauge.'

'What's a gauge?' the girl asked.

'It's the tension that you knit with,' Claire answered.

A jolly-looking woman in a red silk blouse and smart trousers with pointy shoes laughed. Claire thought her name was Emma Edgers or Hedges. She checked the register. Hedges. Though she looked about Claire's age, her manner made her seem older. 'I'm so tense I need either this, a massage or a Harley Street psychiatrist,' she sighed and a few of the other women giggled.

'Well, it's one of the reasons I knit,' Claire admitted. 'It's very relaxing. But I didn't mean tension in that sense. It's how loose or tight you make your stitches. We need to measure so that we can predict the size of the garment you make in the end. Some people will have five stitches to the inch, others will have ten. And we need to measure the inches vertically as well as horizontally. But let's not get ahead of ourselves. Let me check your slipknots and then we'll begin knitting.'

Now Claire smiled at Mrs Venables over the heads of the students.

'It's important to keep the pull on the slipknot and the pull on your wool as you knit it about the same. Otherwise you'll have an uneven, sloppy look,' Mrs Venables explained.

There were a few, notably Emma Hedges, who had done

their slipknots perfectly, but almost everyone else needed some correction. One of the more elderly women – her name was Mrs Willis – had pulled the wool so tightly Claire was afraid she might break the needle in half when she knit her first row.

When she and Mrs Venables had got them all started, Claire had them take their second needle and demonstrated the next step over their heads. 'Pick up your right needle in your right hand,' she said. 'Now we're going to begin to knit. We are going to start with stockinette or stocking stitch, which is the most basic one. It isn't the knit, purl, knit, purl that you find in the rib. It's one side knit, the other purl.'

Mrs Venables smiled. 'This way you can't make a mistake and forget which side you are on.'

All of the women picked up their second needle, some awkwardly and some as if they were going to eat a Chinese meal. Claire showed them the two needles in her own hands. 'Hold the needles like this. Take the right needle and push the point to the back of the first loop on your left needle.' Out of the corner of her eye she noticed Julie Watts, the woman with the high-bridged nose, push the needle through almost to the capped end. She restrained herself from laughing or jumping up and stopping her. 'You only put the tip of the needle, between a half inch to an inch, into the loop,' she told them.

'Whatever's comfortable for you,' Mrs Venables added, going to Julie and gently helping her. 'Now take the wool and, holding it lightly between your index finger and your thumb, wrap it around the needle at the back, then draw the wrapped wool through the hole of the slipknot and off onto your left needle.'

'Wait. Wait!' several women cried.

'Let us show you,' Mrs Venables suggested.

Claire helped Ann Fenwick's mother and the teen, whose name was Charlotte. In a few minutes the women were all busy. Claire looked around the room at the faces with their expressions of concentration. She thought, to her delight and relief, that she and Mrs Venables were pulling this off. 'Okay,' she said. 'You've completed your first knit stitch. It's the start of the entire row. We'll come around while you each do it again and again until you all have fifteen stitches on your left needle.'

She moved from woman to woman. Two – one of them Leonora – dropped their needles and had to begin all over, but Claire helped them. Virtually everyone but Emma Hedges dropped stitches, and their yarn and the tension was all over the place, but all of them completed their first row of stitches and Claire had them start on the second.

'What is this?' one of the younger women asked, picking something off the shelf.

'It's a bobbin,' Mrs Venables answered. 'You use it for alternating colors.'

'Funny-looking,' Julie commented. 'Looks like a piece from a children's game.'

Charlotte picked up an item Claire had placed on the table earlier. 'This looks like a weird protractor.'

'It's a gauge,' Claire explained. 'It actually has many uses.' She took the item from Charlotte and held it up.

'It's an essential piece of equipment,' Mrs Venables said. 'And we're not simply trying to sell them,' she added with a smile. 'See the different sized holes along the top?' The women looked at the gauge with interest. 'Those are for checking the size of your needles. Sometimes the numbers on the needle heads wear off – especially on the plastic ones – or sometimes you're dealing with double-pointed needles which don't have numbers on them. So all you have to do is slide the needle into the holes until you get the perfect fit.' She picked up a needle from the table and demonstrated.

'Now, as for the cut out area of the gauge . . .' She showed it to the group. 'When you look at it more closely, you'll see there is a small ruler along the bottom. This allows you to measure the length of the garment. Then you can turn the gauge in this direction.'

'What's that for?' Ann Fenwick asked.

'From that you can easily count up the number of rows that equal the height you are trying to achieve,' Mrs Venables said.

Claire handed the gauge back to Charlotte. The class was drawing to an end now, and as the women finished off their knitting they one by one began to rise and look for their own gauges, then at the yarns and the knitting bags. Soon Mrs Venables was busy with questions about various products and wools, while Claire tidied up.

She looked round at the group with satisfaction. Ka-ching! Mrs Venables's till would be busy. Claire smiled. Screw Nigel. Despite his pessimism the class was definitely a success.

FIFTY

'Do you know who she is?' Imogen asked excitedly.

It was Sunday morning and Claire was telling Imogen about the women in the class. Im, who hadn't apologized for not coming, listened absently until Claire mentioned Ann Fenwick.

'*Lady* Ann Fenwick? Her mother is the Countess of Kensington, you know.'

'Really? She was there too.' Claire thought of the cheap old cardigan. It wasn't quite what she expected a countess to wear, but she supposed they didn't walk around with crowns on their heads. 'Are they royalty?' she asked.

Imogen laughed. 'No, no. Just higher aristocracy. They were created in the sixteenth century.' Claire raised her brows. For once she was going to ask what the hell Imogen was talking about. And she did.

'It means,' Imogen said, 'the time they were raised to the nobility. New creations aren't anything like as important as the old ones. I mean if you received a title from Edward VII it isn't like one from Elizabeth I.'

For a moment Claire thought of her father calling the Bilsops 'an old family'. Somehow she didn't think the term meant the same thing in Tottenville as it did in London. 'Well,' she said, 'she's not very good at knitting and neither is Ann.'

'Lady Ann,' Imogen corrected gently. 'When someone

has a title before their name you need to use it even in casual conversation. It's not like my Honorable. That's only for formal use.'

'If you say so,' Claire responded. 'Anyway, it all went very well. I hope they all come back.'

'Well, I shall certainly come,' Imogen said. 'I meant to be there yesterday.'

Claire doubted it. She felt Imogen's enthusiasm had more to do with Ann Fenwick than with an interest in perfecting her ribbing. But it didn't matter. Claire began to straighten up the kitchen, while Imogen asked her about the other attendees. No one else seemed to make the grade in Imogen's eyes, though. As she put a mug in the sink Claire noticed an envelope on the counter beside it. It was addressed to her.

Claire lifted it and turned. 'When did this come?' she asked. What she meant was how long had it been sitting there amongst the clutter. But Im, on her way into the bathroom, just nodded.

'I meant to tell you,' she said, as she closed the bathroom door. 'Must dash – I don't want to be late for Malcolm.'

Claire took the letter back to her room and sat down on the chintz chair. She carefully opened the envelope.

Dear Claire,

Thank you for the new address. I hope you don't mind that I gave your last one to your friend Tina. I was surprised she didn't have it, but perhaps I shouldn't have been, nor should I have given it to her. Sorry if I have made a mistake. I won't give out your new address again unless you tell me.

I was very pleased to hear that you seemed to have landed on your feet. If I have one regret in life – and believe me I have more than one – not

*traveling as much as I would have liked is almost
the biggest. I'm so glad you're getting the
opportunity to. Be sure to visit Syon House. It's
right outside of London on the way to Heathrow.
(As I remember that's the A4, but I could be
wrong.) Anyway, it's the first Palladian house in
England and it changed British architecture forever.
There's nothing in it, but it doesn't matter. Promise
me you'll see it. I passed it for years before I ever
found the time to stop. Things at home are fine,
though my dog, Brady, seems to need an operation
on his hip. It's very upsetting, but he's in pain and
the veterinary surgeon has promised me he'll come
through just fine. Funny how attached we get to
our pets.*

*There's lots going on in the office. It seems that
Junior has gotten into some kind of trouble via the
project of young Wainwright's that soured. We're
not sure if it was simply an unwise recommendation
to a mutual fund manager or something worse. Mr
Crayden is very upset about it. In his later years he
has come to regard the Security Exchange
Commission as a kind of mafia with a whole series
of hits planned. He lives in fear that his name will
somehow get on the list. I've tried to reassure him,
but this doesn't look good. Anyway, it seems the
stock that Junior recommended was one of
Michael's offerings. Did either of them know it was
about to tank? Don't know, but it certainly has
made some people very tense. Just as well you're
not here.*

*Enjoy every moment.
Abigail*

Claire folded the letter and put it back into its envelope.
She was sorry that Abigail was worried about her dog, and

she would write back to her immediately. But she was more fascinated by the news about Michael. Had Mr Wonderful made a really big mistake? Somehow, she couldn't imagine him winding up in any trouble. Anyway, she told herself firmly, it was none of her business and she wouldn't allow herself to think about it. And she'd be sure to visit Syon House. She'd look it up and see if there was a bus or two that she could take to get there. It would be a perfect way to spend her Sunday.

FIFTY-ONE

Claire spent the next week wandering around London, working on the garden at Mrs Patel's, helping out in the grocery and – in spare moments – helping Mrs Venables go through her paltry inventory and the catalogs she might order stock from. It was a full week, and a pleasant one.

She also went to visit Toby during this time and helped him arrange some of his books. Although he preferred to spend most of the time telling her what the story was about as he picked up each volume. She couldn't explain what she was feeling about him. It wasn't as sexual as the attraction she had felt for Michael, but she was drawn to Toby and she liked being around him.

Claire had been in London for just over a month, now. But she felt quite settled in. She had begun to keep a sort of daybook that recorded the places she'd been, her reactions and conversations she'd overheard. She also kept a growing list of terms in the back of the book – words she'd never heard of or ones that meant something else than they did in the States. The intention was to prepare herself for any conversation.

But she wasn't prepared for the next Saturday's class. She arrived early this time, but was shocked to see a crowd of at least twenty women milling around outside Knitting Kitting. Claire could hardly believe it. Had Toby or Nigel had more calls? The women seemed to be of various ages and dress-styles. A few of the younger, more fashionable ones were in either very long or very short skirts. Claire saw Charlotte, laughing with two young black girls, and Emma Hedges, who also had someone new with her. Claire rushed up to the group. It was only then that she saw something even more astonishing. Clearly, Mrs Venables had gotten downstairs early and had opened the doors because the shop, too, was filled with women. Claire recognized Mrs Willis and Ann and some of the others from last week, but the rest were new. She tried to push her way into the store but found her way blocked.

'I'm afraid you'll have to wait your turn like everyone else,' one of the more matronly women scolded. She turned to a friend. 'This seems to be very badly-run indeed.'

'It isn't,' Claire said. 'Well, I mean, it won't be. I'm the teacher. Just give me a few minutes.'

The women moved back and Claire had a chance to enter the shop, though that meant the door pressed against several of the women who were already fingering the yarns. One or two more protested as she tried to push past them. Outside, the group had only been murmuring, but inside there was a great deal of talking and some higher-pitched complaining.

'I don't see how they're going to do it,' a plummy voice commented. 'They aren't set up for a class this big.'

'And I'm all thumbs,' another voice said. 'I must be the only woman in England who can't arrange two roses in a vase, so I'm sure I'll need individual attention. Then it will probably all come to nothing.'

'Oh, this isn't hard,' Claire assured her. 'You'll be doing it in no time.' She got over to Mrs Venables who was clearly flustered.

'I can't tell you how relieved I am to see you,' she said to Claire. 'My goodness; I was down here at eight-thirty and there were already three people at the door. Whatever shall we do?'

'One thing we'll do is sell a lot of yarn,' Claire said and managed a grin. It was going to be up to her to organize this. Her delight was mixed with a little fear that the whole thing could become a fiasco. She couldn't let that happen. This meant too much to her. She would deal with the fifteen or so women in the shop first, then talk to the others outside.

She gave some quick instructions to Mrs Venables, then climbed onto one of the chairs. 'Excuse me,' she announced. 'May I have your attention please? Sorry for the over-crowding, but some of you must not have booked.' She heard a murmur go through the room. If they thought they were supposed to have a reservation, they might not complain if they were made to wait.

'I did try to phone but the line had ceased to exist,' someone said.

Claire just looked at the woman and continued, not want-ing to waste any more time on language translations. 'Don't worry,' she said. 'We'll have plenty of time for everybody. If you'll just –' she bent and scrabbled behind her, taking a pad and a pen from Mrs Venables's counter – 'if you'll just line up over here please, and write your name and phone number on this sheet. And those of you from last week –' she nodded to Ann and Julie – 'please take seats.' Before Claire continued she went over to Ann who had chosen a place at the end of the table. 'Will your mother be joining you today?' she asked.

'I'm afraid not. She's not feeling very well. But she is just loving her knitting and she was hoping that you'd be willing to come over in a couple of days to make up for missing this lesson.'

'It would be my pleasure,' Claire said.

'Great. How about Monday – late afternoon?'

Claire thought about her schedule. 'That would work beautifully.'

'See you then,' Ann smiled.

Claire had to get back to the rest of the women. She

climbed back onto the chair and started in with the organization of the newcomers. 'Now, as for the rest of you, the class is free and we'll give you some yarn just to get started. Meanwhile you can take a look around and see what yarn you might want to use for your first project.' There was a murmur of assent and Claire took a deep breath. 'As soon as everyone has put their name and number on the list, we'll begin.' She stepped off the chair.

'How in the world will we do that?' Mrs Venables asked her, *sotto voce*.

'Do you have any chairs upstairs?' Claire asked.

'Well, yes. But I don't think you or I could get most of them down here.' Mrs Venables paused. 'Claire, why don't we have some of the women up in my flat and some of them down here?' She looked around. 'I don't know what we'll do with the others. The ones outside.'

'I'll take care of them,' Claire said, greatly relieved. 'Though the ones from last week must come in.'

Women were eagerly signing their names and those who had signed seemed equally eager to finger the bright wools. So far, so good. Taking another deep breath Claire opened the door and stepped into the crowd outside. She took a pad of paper with her. 'How many of you are confirmed for the nine o'clock class?' she asked. 'Would you please raise your hands?'

The group had grown. No one raised their hand but that gave Claire time. 'Well, you are,' she said to Charlotte and nodded at her friends as well. 'And you,' she said to Emma, who smiled, superior to the hoi polloi. There was a little murmuring here and there but, by and large, the group seemed to accept her ploy. That was one thing she had learned about the English. In New York some wiseass like Tina would shout out, 'What reservations? What friggin' nine o'clock class?' But Claire decided not to push her luck. 'I'm afraid that the popularity of the class and the fact that there's no charge has created a problem. You see,

I'm afraid we underestimated the demand for classes. So I'm going to have to ask the rest of you to come back at eleven. If that isn't convenient then we will run the class again at two. Let me just get your names and numbers and you can put yourself in either group.'

'I simply can't do it later today,' a woman in a severely-cut black pantsuit said. She walked away, and a young blond girl went with her. But the rest seemed to be willing enough to pick one of the other times.

'I'm so sorry,' Claire called to the black pantsuit. 'You can drop in anytime during the week for a private session with Mrs Venables. Our apologies.' Then she went through the rest of the crowd and quickly signed them up for eleven or two. It was already twenty-five after nine and it wouldn't give her much time to deal with the group inside. But she'd do the best she could.

Mrs Venables, however, had already done surprisingly well. The women from last week, with a few additions, were seated in the shop downstairs, the new ones already kitted out with needles and wool to practice on. Helped by the more experienced students, they were attempting slipknots. Then Claire ran up the stairs to find Mrs Venables had just seated the rest of the group in her lounge and was calmly handing out wool. Her cheeks were flushed and her eyes were very bright against her white hair. It gave her a charming grandmother-in-a-fairytale look. 'I can hardly believe it,' she whispered. 'What in the world did you do with all the people outside?'

'I think they're coming back,' Claire said.

'Coming back?' Mrs Venables looked around. 'But there's no room. That woman in blue is sitting on my shower chair.'

'No, no. They're not coming back now. They're coming back for the eleven and the two o'clock classes.'

'Eleven and two? My goodness. I'm not sure we'll have enough needles,' Mrs Venables said.

'I'll go home and get some of mine,' Claire promised. 'We'll do what we have to do.'

Mrs Venables smiled. 'It's just like the war. We muddled through.'

Claire ran downstairs again. She had less than an hour before the next class began – if any of the women who had signed up came back. She moved from woman to woman, checking their work and helping them correct problems. She was amazed at how many had twisted their yarn, dropped a stitch or simply knotted them here and there, and most had begun 'loosey and goosey' as her grandmother used to say, then gotten tighter and tighter. As she helped each woman correct her work she casually mentioned the problems.

Then it was time for Claire to race back up to the flat to check on what was happening with Mrs Venables. The group there seemed calm and getting along well. Mrs Venables had had them do ribbing – one knit, one purl – instead of stockinette, but there were only eight of them, and a formidable woman called Mrs Lyons-Hatchington was assisting whomever she could get at, though not always usefully. 'I've got them doing stockinette downstairs,' Claire told Mrs Venables. 'But we're both going to have to stop soon. We have to get ready for the next class.'

Mrs Venables looked up at the clock on her wall. 'We have almost a quarter of an hour, my dear,' she remarked, mildly.

Claire smiled at her. 'Yes, but we have to give them time to buy things. Yarn, knitting bags, needles. The whole kit, right? And they might even want to take a look at the simple pattern books.'

Mrs Venables laughed. 'Of course. I completely forgot that bit. Nigel is right: I'm hopeless as a businesswoman.' She smiled at Claire. 'But you, my dear, well you're just . . .'

Before she could hear the praise she craved Claire had to interrupt. 'I've got to get back downstairs,' she said.

'Why don't you check their gauges, I'll do the same and then we'll give them the yarn to finish as homework. They don't have to buy anything, and if they choose not to continue and leave the needles behind, well then, it won't cost them a thing.'

'Very good, indeed.'

Claire rejoined her class, took out a small ruler and gauged their work. Leonora was doing fine, having finished several dozen rows since the week before. A new young woman in the shortest of lilac skirts and a very thin older woman in a gray tweed outfit had already done a pretty good and even job. But the youngsters – Charlotte and her friends – were all over the place. Still, Claire encouraged them and showed them where they had gone wrong.

'All right. For new class members, your homework is to finish your little ball of yarn. When you're done with that, we can pick a simple pattern or you can just make a scarf or a shawl.'

'I'm dying to do a little white bonnet for my grand-daughter,' said Mrs Willis.

'I'd like to do a woolly,' said the mini-mini skirt, whose name was Jane. 'Have you any cashmere?'

'Well, let's take it a bit more slowly,' Claire told her gently, wondering if a woolly was tights or a sweater or – for all she knew – smalls. 'Why don't we put this away and before you plan knitting a Union Jack you can take a look at the wool we have. If you want anything else we can order it and have it by next week.'

Some of them said that they wanted to come back before next week and Claire encouraged them to stop by any time the shop was open. Only one woman gave up and left her needles on the counter. The rest were joined by the class from upstairs. They all trooped around the shop, looking and touching and commenting on everything.

Then, in a moment of inspiration, Claire took out her throw, laid it on the table and put Mrs Venables's cashmere

345

Aran-stitch beside it. 'Don't expect to get here right away,' she said as the women 'oohed' and 'aahed' over them. 'But I did knit this sweater,' she said, pointing to the one she wore, 'and that's something you could aim at.' After all, she might as well motivate them. Good teachers did. But the women hardly needed that to spur them on to make purchases. By the time the eleven o'clock class arrived, the stock had been greatly diminished.

Mrs Venables looked tired and Claire insisted she go upstairs for a lie down. Claire kept the eleven o'clock class until one, had a quick lunch, and then ran over to her room and brought back all of her needles. She hated to have to give up her vintage ones, but most of the people signed up for eleven had shown up. If the same was true for the afternoon, she couldn't disappoint the last group.

In fact, more people showed up for the two o'clock class than had signed on. There were a couple who had not appeared at eleven, and three women had brought other friends who had been interested but couldn't make the early-morning time. Then, at a quarter after two Imogen waltzed in the door. She displayed no self-consciousness as everyone turned to look at her. In fact she greeted Claire as if the two of them were alone. 'Are you still at it? I had no idea that knitting was so difficult. I'm thick as a plank and I'll probably be worse than everyone.'

'Impossible,' said a young woman called Sarah. 'I have that distinction. But I must persevere because I've been dragooned to help with a layette. Of course my sister's only just married, but it doesn't stop Mother from hoping for an heir and a spare.'

A few of the other women laughed. But Imogen raised her brows, smiled coolly and, instead of taking the available place on the window seat, sat down at the edge of the table itself. 'Can I catch up?' she asked Claire.

By four o'clock Claire was exhausted, but pleased to see the class had changed from a silent group of individuals to happy, chattering clusters. Imogen stepped over to her again. 'What are you doing later?' she asked. 'You're probably knackered, but would you like to join Malcolm and me for a drink? We could go to a terribly nice wine bar I know near Sloane Square.'

Claire was touched by this gesture of friendship, but she had to get to Mrs Patel's before six. 'I'd have liked that,' she told Imogen, 'but I have another engagement.'

'How mysterious,' Imogen said. 'Well, I'll see you tonight then. Or perhaps not until tomorrow morning.' She raised her brows in a suggestive way.

Claire ushered Imogen and the others out of the shop. Though she knew it would take her almost an hour to get up to Camden, she sat down for a celebratory cup of tea with Mrs Venables. Then the two of them counted out the day's take.

'It's just astonishing,' Mrs Venables said. They had sold close to three hundred pounds' worth of yarns, taken special orders for more, and sold out all the needles as well as a significant number of knitting bags and patterns. 'I've never made this much in a month. It's astonishing,' she repeated. 'You're a wonder.'

Claire almost laughed with pleasure. 'As long as we're not arrested for putting up illegal signs,' she said.

Mrs Venables smiled ruefully. 'Nigel's not said anything more about that.' Then she counted out fifty pounds and handed it to Claire. 'However, if it comes to that, this will help pay for a barrister, though I don't suggest Nigel.'

'Oh, no,' Claire protested. 'It's too much. After all, it was your wool and the rest of the stock was yours and . . .'

Mrs Venables folded the money into Claire's hand. 'You're a very foolish girl,' she said. 'Now take this and do be quiet. You've given me a great deal of satisfaction today and all I've given you is some filthy lucre. I think you ought to come back when I'm not so tired, and we can discuss your new job.'

'You mean here? With you?'

Mrs Venables nodded. 'Clearly, we have enough business to support it. I couldn't handle a crowd like this one on my own and I imagine everyone will be back next weekend and perhaps even bring more of their friends.'

Claire was so happy she couldn't even thank the older woman properly. Her fatigue seemed to disappear. She would be able to get up to Mrs Patel's, do whatever was necessary, and come back with energy to spare. 'Oh, thank you,' was all she could say.

'No. Thank *you*.' Mrs Venables smiled. 'I'll just have a word with Nigel.' She patted Claire's knee. 'Oh dear, I expect he'll worry that I'm getting too tired.'

FIFTY-TWO

On the first half of the underground trip to Mrs Patel's, Claire felt nothing but joy. She looked from one passenger to another and knew that she was the luckiest person in the car. She had found a lovely home with Imogen who might actually become a friend. Then there was Toby, who was someone she hoped might become more than a friend. Mrs Patel and her children were almost a family to her, and now she had Mrs Venables and a new and wonderful job that she had created herself. She put her hand in her pocket and touched the two twenty-pound notes and the ten-pound note folded over it. She couldn't believe it. All of the women, many of whom looked successful and well-to-do, had turned to her as an authority. No one had questioned her ability and each one had asked for help as if it was the most natural thing in the world. Best of all, Mrs Venables had been not just pleased but, well . . . tickled by their success. Claire couldn't remember ever feeling this excited, optimistic or proud of herself, not ever.

She was so filled with her pleasant thoughts that when the train pulled into Leicester Square station she continued daydreaming until the doors almost rolled shut. She scampered out onto the platform and followed the signs to the Northern Line.

It was while she waited for a train to Camden that the difficulties of her situation began to nibble at her fragile joy. What would she do about Mrs Patel, the children, her work in the shop, and her tutoring? She hadn't discussed a salary with Mrs Venables, but she couldn't imagine a way that she would be able to help in Knitting Kitting, commute to Camden, work in the evening and have any time left for herself. If she had to make a choice, she certainly preferred the work with Mrs Venables but how could she desert the first friends she had made in London?

She had come to love Mrs Patel, with her delicately arched eyebrows, her protective suspicions, and her warm and loving heart. And once the baby came Mrs Patel would need even more help. She also enjoyed the children, particularly Safta, though the antics of Fala and Devi almost always made her laugh. She hadn't had any young children in her life back in Tottenville and she was surprised and delighted by how good she was with them and how good they made her feel. Lastly, there was the garden. Creating it had been a real work of love, and Safta's excitement over it was a pleasure to watch. But it would need care and careful tending. Mrs Patel certainly wouldn't find the time to dead-head or to pick the slugs off the delectable leaves, nor water daily. If the garden withered and died, Claire was afraid that Safta's new confidence and optimism would as well.

The Northern Line train lumbered into the station and as Claire boarded it she felt her shoulders and head droop with dejection. Most important of all, she had proved something to Mrs Patel about trust, and friendship. She had given Mrs Patel as much as she had gotten from her, and she didn't want to disappoint her now. Quitting the work at the shop was possible but quitting the tutoring or the work in the garden was just not an option. As she got closer and closer to Camden she felt more and more apprehensive.

The train rolled into the station, the doors rolled open and she made her way slowly to the shop. As she opened the door she was greeted by all three children. 'Oh, Claire, oh Claire! Come out and see,' Safta said. Devi took her hand and pulled her in the direction of the back of the shop. 'Come see. Some of the pansies are opening. And the wallflowers are out as well.'

'And we have two difficult cartons to open. I tried to do it myself but one is washing powder and it's very heavy indeed,' Mrs Patel put in.

'I'll be right with you,' Claire said. She allowed herself to be pushed and pulled by the children out the back door and into the transformed space behind the house. The border of green looked lovely and Claire thought how very pretty the addition of a trellis and some climbing roses would be. She wondered if Mrs Patel would consider the expense. And whitewashing the other brick wall might also be a good idea to set off the little square of grass in the center.

'Devi was naughty and picked some flowers,' Fala said. Devi picked up a bit of gravel and flung it at her, luckily going wide of the mark.

'No, Devi, you don't throw stones.' Claire turned to Fala. 'And you don't snitch, either.'

'What's "snitch"?' Safta asked.

Before she could explain, Mrs Patel spoke from the doorway. 'It's so very pretty, Claire,' she said. 'It's like the telly show. You know, the one where they come and fix up a back garden in one weekend.' Claire didn't have a telly but Safta had told her all about the show, so she nodded.

'I'm glad you like it.'

'I sit out here early in the morning. There's sun in the corner and I have my tea there.' She smiled at the three children. 'We must all thank Claire for making it so very, very nice.'

'Thank you, Claire,' the children chorused, though Devi's lisp came a bit after the other two.

Claire smiled, but instead of feeling the happiness she ought to she was swept by a feeling of discomfort. How could she possibly tell them that she could no longer work here?

'See the clematis? It's got two new buds and over here, look how much this has grown,' Safta said.

'It's lovely,' Claire said. 'You've been doing a very good job.' She turned and smiled at Mrs Patel. 'Maybe later we can get a climbing rose,' she said. 'It would look lovely on that wall.' She stopped and had a thought. 'It would be my present to you,' she added.

'A rose. Climbing rose tree?' Safta asked.

'I want red,' Fala said.

'No, I want red.' Devi put in his two-pence.

But it was Safta whose eyes glistened. 'White,' she said. 'Like moonlight.'

'White it shall be,' Mrs Patel said. 'Now, all three of you leave Claire alone. I need her help.'

They went back to the front of the shop. 'I am sorry,' Mrs Patel told Claire. 'These boxes are becoming more and more difficult.' She looked down at her belly.

'Well, you shouldn't be doing heavy work. Surely the doctor told you that.' Claire began to open the top of the first carton.

'Oh, I haven't been to a doctor,' Mrs Patel said. 'This is my fourth. I don't need someone jabbing at me.'

Claire was shocked, but refrained from speaking. 'When is the baby due?' she asked. She had never been brave enough to refer to the pregnancy before.

'I think I must be seven months,' Mrs Patel told her. She shook her head. 'I'll have to do this one alone,' she said.

Claire looked at Mrs Patel's face and for the first time she saw something that looked like fear. 'I can help,' she said.

Mrs Patel looked up. 'I believe you will,' she said and smiled.

A customer came in and Claire got back to unpacking the cartons. When she was done she put the washing powder neatly on the shelves. She looked around. The shop had really changed. Not only was it more orderly but there was more stock and more variety. Mrs Patel was buying three brands of dishwasher detergent, several different kinds of baked beans – standard, pork, and low salt and sugar. There were more and different jellies and jams, a real selection of salad dressings, and a host of other products that Claire didn't remember from her first visit.

The evening got busy with the usual quick-what's-for-dinner crowd. Maudie came in, pushing the rickety stroller. Mrs Patel greeted her with a smile and the children shyly waved to Claire. They spoke for a little while until Claire thought she should get back to work. 'Give my love to Mrs Watson,' she said as a joke.

'Oh, Lord! I almost forgot,' Maudie said. 'You got another letter. If I hadn't seen it first I'm sure the old witch would have torn it to bits. I have it here somewhere.' She went through her pockets, then the pockets at the back of the stroller, then began scrabbling inside the canvas sack she used as a purse. Meanwhile, Claire tried to think of who a letter could be from. Probably Tina she thought and hoped it wasn't going to be unkind.

But when Maudie took out the envelope, now rather soiled and wrinkled, Claire recognized her mother's handwriting. For a moment she felt guilty. She should have written again, given her new address and told her mother something of her plans. But she really didn't have any plans; not permanent ones. And somehow writing back to her mother, Tottenville, Jerry, and knowing that any news would be spread among the disapproving neighbors and to angry Tina had stopped her. She took the letter and stuffed it into her pocket. 'Thanks, Maudie,' she said. Maudie made her usual rounds, talking to the children and herself, then returned to the counter with her usual purchases. When she left both Claire and Mrs Patel waved her off.

'A nice woman,' Mrs Patel said, 'a little strange, but very sweet with her children. They need a bath, though.'

Claire remembered Mrs Watson and the bath water. 'What they could use is a decent place to live,' Claire told her. 'My old landlady watches every liter of water and begrudges toilet paper.'

Mrs Patel shook her head. 'You know, my father came to this country with nothing. My uncle was here and he helped my father find work. Then after many years my father was able to buy this shop for me. If that hadn't happened . . . well, we've been very lucky.'

Claire wondered how a single mother with three children and one on the way, a woman who lived on a rough street in tiny rooms, could consider herself lucky. Mrs Patel looked up at Claire. 'And it was lucky that you came along,' she said. 'Safta just got her school report and she's doing very, very well.' Mrs Patel looked around the shop. 'Each week we have more customers. And each week I buy a little more. It keeps selling.' She smiled at Claire. 'Thank you,' she said. Instead of going to the till and taking out the twenty pounds in the usual way, Mrs Patel held up an envelope. She put it in a bag that she had under the counter. 'It's a little present for you,' she said and handed the bulgy bag to Claire.

She peered into it, but it wasn't the usual mixture of groceries and cleaning products. Instead there was something wrapped with tape and newspaper and plastic bubble wrap. 'Don't you open it until you get home,' Mrs Patel said. 'I don't want you to break it or scratch it.'

Claire took a deep breath. There was no way she could tell Mrs Patel the news tonight.

FIFTY-THREE

Claire slept late on Sunday morning. The day before had been so filled with anticipation, excitement, achievement and guilt that she'd exhausted herself, and she'd been too tired the previous evening to open Mrs Patel's gift. However, when she opened her eyes she felt well rested. The clean and cheerful little room was filled with watery sunlight, her knitting was spread across the little armchair, and the stand held not only the Battersea box from Michael but also the program from *Lucia*, Toby had given her.

The thought of him made her smile. She so enjoyed his company, and she had to thank him once again for so many things and report on the success of her classes. She was free all morning and afternoon and decided that she would buy him a present; not just chocolates like before, but something more substantial, to show her appreciation. It couldn't be too personal, partly because she didn't know him well enough and partly because she didn't want to seem, well, as interested in him as she was. But if it was too impersonal it would hardly be worth giving.

Thinking of the gift for Toby, she remembered the bulging bag from Mrs Patel. That reminded her of the letter from her mother which Maudie had given her and which Claire had completely forgotten. She jumped out of bed, put on her robe, filled the kettle and then went out to wash her face, getting back into her bedroom without disturbing

Imogen or Malcolm. If they were there. It was a shame she couldn't have gone for a drink with them. Perhaps she could make dinner for the three of them sometime.

Thinking about these pleasant plans, she took out the envelope and the crudely-wrapped package. She had to go back out to the kitchen for a knife because the tape and the layers of plastic and paper proved difficult to remove. But when she finally got the top of the paper unwrapped the rest of it slipped off easily.

Claire caught her breath. Revealed before her was the most perfect little vase. It was made of some kind of metal, but the tiniest pieces of mosaic had been laid into it in a delicate pattern of vines, flowers and birds. Claire picked the vase up and slowly turned it in her hands. The light picked up the pink of the mounded petal pieces and gave the lapis blue more depth. Perhaps the mosaic pieces were ceramic but they might have been semi-precious stones, Claire couldn't tell. She just looked at the fine tracery of the leaves and the incredible detail of the birds that perched on tiny branches and wondered at it. Where had it come from? Was it something from Mrs Patel's family? How old was it? And how marvelous of Mrs Patel to give it to Claire.

Claire turned the vase over and over in her hands, each time seeing a new detail, a new bit of workmanship. She thought about how lovely it would look filled with flowers. It was smooth and cool in her hands as she put it up against her cheek. If one was ill, surely the touch of this on the forehead would end a headache, stop a migraine. When she could bear to stop touching it she placed it on the bureau and had the pleasure of looking at it from a distance, the back of the vase reflected in the mirror behind it. Oh, how could Claire keep such a valuable gift at a time when she had to stop working for Mrs Patel, but how could she consider giving it back?

Next she opened the envelope. It contained a page obviously ripped from Safta's exercise book and taped into an untidy pouch. *For you because of help and the garden. Safta, Devi, Fala. And for the store.* Mrs Patel hadn't even signed her name. Carefully Claire tore at the tape and, to her complete surprise, a bundle of grubby five-pound notes fell into her lap. Claire looked at them astounded. A hundred pounds! And then there was the fifty pounds that she had from Mrs Venables. Half a month's rent! Or enough to take Toby out for a very nice dinner and have plenty to spare. Or perhaps money to buy her own teapot and cups and saucers. Or . . .

She took the money and put it in her bureau drawer. She picked up the wrapping paper and envelope, thrusting them into the plastic bag, but Mrs Patel's homely note had to be saved and she placed it, tape and all, inside the cover of *Hons and Rebels*. She poured herself a cup of tea, sat down near the window and took up her mother's letter.

She sipped the tea and looked out the window at the soft sunshine and the gardens below. A cat crept along the top of a fence, and a laburnum tree waved its fronds, so that the cat lifted its paw and batted at one. Claire felt pure happiness. It was odd that in less than two months she had created a little home for herself here in this strange city she loved, a home that was far more comfortable, far prettier, and far more 'her' than Staten Island had been. She had certainly been astonishingly lucky with this flat, but part of the charm of her new life was that she had so little, but that each thing she had was necessary or beautiful or both. From her kettle to her raincoat she liked and used each one of her belongings. The thought of her bedroom in Tottenville with the old knick-knacks, the dreary prints on the wall, the unwearable clothes in the closet, was utterly distasteful.

But Tottenville waited for her. She sighed, finished her tea and then opened her mother's letter.

Occasionally life juxtaposes events so diametrically opposed, in such a short space of time, that it seems as if there must be some cosmic intelligence – not necessarily a pleasant one – at work.

Dear Claire,

    I don't know what you are thinking. You just picked up and left. Tina says you are having an affair with some guy at the office. Is that true? Jerry says he was probably married. I don't want to believe that. Why haven't you come home? Tina says you quit work. Are you pregnant?

    I went to church and lit a candle for you. Father Frank told me I should pray for your well-being but I said you sounded well enough in your card. Taking in the sights and living the life of Riley. Other people have to work.

    Frankly, Claire, I'm surprised at you. You've always been quiet but you've never been sneaky. When I go to church I can't even look at the other women. Just don't come back with a baby.

    I got the bill from Saks and Jerry nearly hit the roof. We were talking about a timeshare in Sugarbush, Vermont. We can forget that now. Thanks a lot. Jerry says we should turn your room and Fred's into an apartment the way the O'Connors across the street did. I haven't heard from Fred lately so I don't know when he comes back from Germany, but I sure know we can use the money. Especially with that Saks bill. I don't know what you were thinking of. Two hundred and ten dollars for shoes? If you want to buy jewelry and shoes, why don't you let your married boyfriend pay for them?

    So I don't know what we're going to do upstairs. Property taxes are probably going up – school taxes surely are. I'd like to hear from you and know if you're coming back soon and when

you plan to pay the bill. Right now I'm just paying
the interest but Jerry says it's a lot of money to
throw away every month. Father Frank said he
might be able to get us a tenant, but I'm not sure
if I like the idea.

Claire crushed the letter in her hand and, on impulse, opened the window and tossed the paper ball as far as she could. She couldn't sit back down so she paced up and down the small room. What was the matter with people? Perhaps she should have told her mother she was going to London, but would it have changed anything or produced a softer response when she told her she was staying on? Why in the world would her mother think she would become involved with a married man? Or that she was pregnant? Surely Tina wouldn't tell her that. They might no longer be friends, but Tina was never a snitch.

She went to her bureau, took out all of the cash she had, including the money from Mrs Patel and Mrs Venables, and counted it. It was nowhere near enough to pay her mother back, and if Claire did give it to her, it would be more difficult, maybe even impossible, for her to stay on.

And the moment after she had that thought, she knew she was staying on. She was never going to return to Tottenville, her mother, Tina, Jerry, Crayden Smithers or any of her previous life. She had no idea how unhappy she had been until she had experienced the happiness she felt here almost daily.

And then the thought of her father and his early death came to her. He'd spent so much time talking about the things he was going to do, but he never got a chance to do them. And – if she was honest with herself – she would admit that he might never have done them, no matter how long he lived. She decided to try and live every day as if it was her last.

FIFTY-FOUR

The next morning Claire had an important errand and though she was nervous about undertaking it she was also very determined. She had spent a lot of time – it felt like hours and hours – awake in the middle of the night thinking about her mother's letter, her life at home, her new life in London and her future. Her daring plan – to cash in the return ticket, pay her mother back and live in London permanently – gave Claire the determination she needed to make a bold move and, as she opened the door to the airline office in Regent Street she told herself to be brave.

The long queue moved slowly. Claire tried to counteract the butterflies in her stomach by looking at the posters on the wall and imagining herself in Crete, Amsterdam, Lucerne, or Milan. Perhaps she'd manage to visit these other places someday. The most attractive poster was for Nice, and the price seemed very cheap – it was a four-day 'excursion' which included the flight, hotels, transfers and 'two Continental dinners' (whatever those were). The picture of the water and the hills behind it seemed, Claire thought, the perfect combination of beach and town. She wondered if Fred had ever taken vacations away from his base in Germany. He was far more adventurous than she was and had probably been all over.

The line had cleared and she was next. An older woman nodded to her and Claire smiled as she walked up to the counter. Perhaps a smile would help. She laid down the ticket and her passport. 'I'd like to return this ticket please,' she said. Her heart seemed to thump almost audibly.

The woman, who wore a name tag that identified her as 'Sara Brackett' picked up the ticket and looked at it. Then she looked at Claire. 'Oh. You didn't have to wait,' she said. Claire felt her face pale and hoped her heart wouldn't stop beating. She clutched the counter with her right hand. 'This is a first class ticket. You could have been served over there.'

Confused, Claire looked in the direction Mrs Brackett was indicating. Another agent sat at a low desk with two comfortable chairs in front of it. A discreet sign indicated the area was for first class tickets only. Relief flooded her. 'Should I go . . .'

'Oh, I can take care of it,' Mrs Brackett said. She examined the ticket more closely. 'Do you want to change the date and reschedule?'

Claire shook her head. 'Just a refund, please.'

Once again Mrs Brackett examined the ticket. 'Well, you see, this was bought through your travel agency in New York. So normally the refund would go through them.'

'But I'm not returning to New York,' Claire said. 'You see, that's the point. I came here for company business but . . . I stayed on. And I've had this ticket since then. And I . . .' She could feel tears tremble on her lower lids. Oh, how could she explain what she'd done and how she'd changed since she first got into the limo on her way to JFK airport?

Mrs Brackett looked over her reading glasses and then back at the ticket. 'You know,' she said, 'what we could do is exchange this for a much cheaper flight elsewhere and refund the rest to you now.' She looked back at Claire. 'Is there another destination you want to book in the near future?'

Claire saw the opportunity and she took it. 'Yes,' she said. 'I'd like to inquire about that excursion to Nice.'

'Oh, that's very well-priced. It's not for first class, though. I'm afraid a first class round trip would be much dearer.'

'I don't need first class,' Claire said. 'I'd like to go to Nice . . .' She tried to quickly compute something slightly believable. 'When does the offer end?'

'Just let me check for a moment,' Mrs Brackett said. She looked down at her computer console and then walked over to the agent at the first class ticket desk. Claire held her breath, then reminded herself that she had to keep breathing. She watched the two women chat casually about her future. She actually crossed her fingers.

Mrs Brackett walked briskly back to her station. 'I'm afraid there'll be a surcharge for exchanging a single,' she said. 'It will be an extra fifty pounds.'

Claire thought about the huge amount the ticket had cost and the small percentage that this would deduct from the balance. 'That's fine,' she said, and felt as if she was a con-artist cashing a forged check. But, after all, the ticket was hers, wasn't it? It had her name on it. And neither Michael Wainwright nor Abigail Samuels nor anyone else from Crayden Smithers had contacted her. Obviously, the ticket hadn't been cancelled and Claire was sure they could have done so if they wanted to. Of course, Tina might have been told to and forgotten, but whether or not that was true, Claire was going to simply be grateful.

Mrs Brackett lowered her voice. 'A bit of advice to you. If you're going to Nice this time of year look out your woolies. We lower the price because it can be cold in the south of France.' Claire thanked her and waited while they issued the new ticket.

In less than ten minutes Claire was back on Regent Street with a round-trip ticket to Nice and a check for more than three thousand pounds in her pocket. She didn't have a bank account, but she was sure she could ask Toby, Mrs

Patel or even Mrs Venables to pay it into theirs and cash it for her. It wasn't as if she needed the money immediately – she just had to send two thousand dollars to her mother to be free of that debt forever.

As she got into the underground and took her seat she nervously checked again that the blue slip of paper and the gaily-colored folder with her new tickets were still in her purse. She was lucky. At that time of day there were many empty seats and she got the one she preferred; facing forward and against the window. It was silly, since there was nothing to see out the windows but she felt happiest and most secure there. She stared out at the gray murk of the underground tunnel streaming by. She would be able to pay off her mother and she would have some money left over – at least three months' rent and maybe more. More importantly, she would owe nothing to anyone.

Claire had never felt as if she were a proud person; if she were, she certainly wouldn't have let Tina treat her as a lackey or allowed her mother to displace her the way she had. But perhaps she had always been proud and perhaps their behavior had always rankled – she simply hadn't had an option back then or hadn't had the courage to find one. As she looked out at the tunnel whizzing by, interrupted only by bright posters at the stations, she thought how she had let her life – up to now – whiz by as gray as the tunnels were. When they stopped at a station in front of an enormous ad for BT, she thought of the smaller poster of Nice. She was not only going to pay back her mother, but she was going to have another adventure! The fact that she spoke no French and knew no one there made her slightly nervous (after all, she had been brought to London and shown around by Michael) but surely she could do this on her own. And, it was only four days. She decided she would ask Toby for any novels he had, set in Nice, and perhaps buy a travel guide as well. She was proud of all she had accomplished that day; having the nerve to return the ticket,

363

the 'exchange' she had created, the spontaneous trip to Nice, and the check in her purse.

When she got off the train she passed a flower stand and paused. She would buy a bouquet for Mrs Venables and a smaller one to put in her darling vase from Mrs Patel. In fact, she would buy flowers for Imogen as well.

Laden down with lilies, roses, statice, fragrant stock and lilac, she went home. She filled two vases, wrote a thank-you note to Imogen for coming to her class, admired her room with its exquisite vase filled with pretty pink roses and ferns and headed back out to Knitting Kitting.

When she got to the door of the shop she was pleased to see three women customers inside. She entered and every-one, including Mrs Venables, looked over at her.

'What absolutely lovely flowers,' a woman whom Claire did not recognize said.

'Oh, I adore early syringa,' a bossy-sounding woman she identified as Mrs Lyons-Hatchington said and smiled at Claire as if she liked her. 'While you're here,' she added, 'can I use this cotton instead of the wool yarn? Does it make a difference?'

'Well, it depends on what you're making,' Claire said. 'Cotton is lovely and very flexible, but it tends to split more easily when you push the needle into it instead of around it.'

'Well, I was thinking of a summer jumper but I . . .' Claire gently led Mrs Lyons-Hatchington to a decision then she walked over to Mrs Venables at the counter. The third woman was standing beside it and Mrs Venables was wrap-ping up what looked like a large order. When she raised her head her blue eyes opened wide at the bouquet Claire held.

'Oh, my dear!' she said. 'Those are quite astonishing. Aren't you lucky.'

Claire nodded. 'But not because of these,' she said. 'These are for you.'

'My word,' Mrs Venables said. She stood for a moment staring at the blooms. Before her customer could get impatient, Claire handed the wrapped flowers over and quickly packaged up the purchase. She thought she recognized the middle-aged blond woman from Mrs Venables's class but couldn't be sure and simply smiled.

'Enjoy your wool,' she said.

'Oh, I will. I also want to thank you for starting these classes. I love getting out and meeting people and the two of you work so well together. I never expected knitting to be so relaxing and fulfilling but to take a ball of wool and turn it into something useful is – well, it's like spinning straw into gold.'

'That's lovely that you feel that way and thank you for the compliment,' Mrs Venables said.

Claire, not knowing how to react to the praise, turned to Mrs Venables. 'Shall I go upstairs and get a vase?' she asked.

'No, dear, I can do it.' Mrs Venables looked at the flowers. 'These are quite magnificent. You really shouldn't have, you know.' She pursed her mouth and puckered her eyes in a mask of mock sternness. 'You don't want to go spending all the profits, especially before we've made them.' Then she laughed. 'I do sound like Nigel, don't I?'

Then, as if his name had conjured him up, Nigel Venables walked into the shop, holding open the door for the last customer to leave. Claire looked away from the door and over to his mother. '*Shall* I get you a vase?' she asked. 'It will save you a trip.'

'Certainly.' Then Mrs Venables turned to her son. 'Well, Nigel, what a very pleasant surprise. Are you here for a visit or are you thinking about buying some knitting goods? I'm afraid stock is pretty low and we don't have a great deal ready to hand but I could always do a special order.'

As she turned to go up the stairs Claire hid her smile but not as well as Mrs Venables had. She didn't want to linger in the lovely apartment. She was quite sure Mrs Venables trusted her, and almost equally sure that Nigel did not. She saw a ceramic jar on a table and picking it up, filled it with tepid water as quickly as she could. She wiped it carefully with a dishtowel and carried it before her, being sure not to spill even a drop on the Persian rugs or polished wood floors. As she came down the stairs she heard Nigel's voice. She stopped.

'Because I simply don't. She comes from nowhere. Starts this up, bribes you with flowers –'

'Nigel, there's no bribery going on. And keep your voice down. She's done a very clever thing and she's a very clever girl and –'

'Mother, you must be careful! You're much too trusting and we really don't know anything about her, do we?'

Claire flushed. Perhaps she shouldn't have been so cold to him when he had begun to 'interview' her over coffee. But she wasn't used to people being suspicious of her. She meant no harm. Why should he think she did? She cleared her throat and took the next step with more noise to be sure she could be heard.

When she got down to the shop floor another woman rushed in, ending for the moment Nigel's lecture. It was Leonora Atkins. With a sigh of relief Claire watched Nigel leave the store, but not before he turned and gave her what Tina would have called 'the once over'.

'I hope I didn't interrupt anything important,' Leonora said to Mrs Venables.

'No, no. It's only my son, Nigel. Nothing that couldn't wait till later,' she reassured her.

Claire approached the two women and set the vase on the counter. 'Nice of you to stop by, Leonora.' She arranged the flowers and put them to the side. 'How have you been?'

'A little frustrated. I think my stitches are twisted and I was hoping to get some help. I have thirty minutes left of my lunch break. Can one of you take a look?' Leonora took out her needles and laid them on the counter.

'You can handle this, dear,' Mrs Venables said to Claire. 'I have to take care of some papers.'

'Certainly,' Claire replied as she picked up the jumbled piece of wool. 'Let's see what we have here.' She studied the rows and started to explain what Leonora had done wrong. She could see the look of confusion on the other woman's face. 'Do you think you can manage this on your own?'

'Actually, I really have to get to work. Do you have any time tomorrow around lunchtime? That way I can pay closer attention to what you're explaining and try to work up a few rows with you right there?'

Claire mentally ran through her schedule. 'Mrs Venables, can you spare me tomorrow for about an hour?' she asked in a raised voice so Mrs Venables was sure to hear her.

Her employer looked up from her papers. 'That would be fine. Take as much time as you need, dear.'

Claire nodded and turned back to Leonora. 'Sure. Just write down the address for me and I'll meet you then.'

'Great.' Leonora searched her bag for a paper and pen and left the information with Claire. 'This is perfect. Thanks for this,' she said and packed up her needles and wool. 'See you later, Mrs Venables.' She waved and left the shop.

'My, my,' Mrs Venables said to Claire. 'You're a popular girl, aren't you? Don't you have a meeting with the Countess too?'

'Yes, I do. I hope you don't mind that I'm helping the ladies when it's not a scheduled lesson. If you'd prefer me not to, I'd understand. We're supposed to be in this venture together.'

'Claire, my dear, I don't mind at all.' Mrs Venables walked over to Claire at the counter. 'In fact I think it's absolutely wonderful that you're getting out more and meeting different people. It's good for you.' She smiled and took Claire's hand in hers. 'You're a very special girl, Claire,' she said, and gave her hand a gentle squeeze.

Claire left the shop feeling another surge of pride in herself. She was working two jobs, she was making friends with some of the women from the knitting classes, and now she was on her way to see the Countess of Kensington and perhaps Lady Ann Fenwick.

When she arrived at the Countess's house she was impressed with how calm she felt. If Tina had been with her she'd have been all jittery and talking a mile a minute about meeting someone of such stature. Claire had to smile at the thought. She pressed the buzzer and, before her finger was completely off the button, the door opened.

'Miss Bilsop, please come in,' said the formally dressed gentleman. He helped Claire out of her coat and hung it in the closet. 'The Countess is waiting for you in the drawing room.' He led the way to a large carved door with shiny brass doorknobs. The door was opened and Claire was escorted into the room. 'Countess, Miss Bilsop.'

The Countess, looking frail, was sitting on the couch with a blanket wrapped around her. 'Claire, thank you so much for coming. That will be all, William.' The gentleman bent slightly and quietly exited the room. 'I'm sorry Ann couldn't be here but she had a business meeting she couldn't get out of.'

'That's understandable,' Claire answered. 'I'm sorry you missed Saturday's class. Are you feeling any better?'

'Yes, I'm coming round. I expect to be out and about soon. How is Mrs Venables faring?'

'Just beautifully. She's a lovely lady and she just adores teaching the classes.'

'It's a wonderful thing, this knitting.' The Countess reached down to the floor and produced a small bag. 'I've been busy as a bee on this. How does it look? Come and sit next to me and tell me what you think.'

Claire sat and carefully examined the piece of knitting. 'You've done a good job for the most part. I see a couple of twisted stitches and, based on the shape of the edges, it looks like you have a habit of knitting two together and then gaining a stitch a couple of rows later. That gives the edges a wavy look.'

'Oh, dear me. Do I have to take it all out?'

'I won't worry too much since this is just a practice piece. But if you were doing something major, then yes, you'd have to I'm afraid. It's important for you to notice when you've made a mistake.'

Claire spent quite a bit of time pointing out the errors that the Countess had made, showed her what she had missed in last week's class and took the time to instruct her in a few other stitches, just in case she didn't make the next class.

Claire had assumed that having a title would mean that one's lifestyle would be extravagant and glamorous. But she felt as if she were with any elderly woman that she knew in Tottenville. When she finished up with the Countess, Claire left regards to Lady Ann and hoped that the two of them would be able to go to the class this Saturday.

'We wouldn't miss it for the world,' the Countess reassured her.

FIFTY-FIVE

'I can't believe that you went to visit the Countess and didn't let me know,' Imogen called in to Claire.

Claire was finishing up in front of the bathroom mirror, preparing for lunch with Leonora. April had come to London, Easter had passed, and the weather had warmed up, but then the rain had descended. Im had caught a bad head-cold and was spreading her usual manuscripts and also lots of wet tissues around the flat. She was also spreading some ill-will; her cold was making her cranky.

'And now a lunch,' Im said. 'Is there a new man in your life?'

Claire was almost afraid to mention Leonora Atkins. She had no idea whether or not Leonora had a place in Im's social landscape or what that place would be. 'It's just a girl I know,' Claire said.

'Oh. An American?' Im asked, her interest obviously waning.

Claire emerged from the bathroom, gathered her bag and her raincoat and shook her head. But Im's own head was bent over her work so, with a cheery bye-bye, Claire escaped into the rain.

She was drenched by the time she reached the restaurant on Brompton Road. Leonora was already there, wearing a gray suit and a white T-shirt. For a moment Claire thought of Katherine Rensselaer, but the moment

Leonora smiled and took out her knitting, the unpleasant image dissolved.

'So, tell me what I've done wrong,' Leonora said, and showed her work-in-progress to Claire.

Claire picked up the beige muffler and looked at it. 'You're out of sequence.' She pointed out the spot. 'It started here,' she said. 'You should have purled only once and you purled twice. It threw off the rest of the row.'

'Is the only solution to rip out the rest?'

'Yep,' Claire said. 'All the way back to the mistake.'

'I was afraid so,' Leonora said. Looking at Leonora's clothes, her purse, her designer leather knitting bag and her perfect haircut, Claire knew this was not a woman who would leave a mistake in her work. 'Oh, well,' Leonora said and stowed the knitting away. She picked up the menu. 'I recommend the steak au poivre, but you might be vegetarian.' Claire assured her she was not and they both ordered the steak.

Then came the usual questions: Where are you from, what brings you here, what did you do before? Claire was relieved, though, that Leonora didn't ask where her 'people' came from.

'What did you do on Wall Street?' Leonora asked as they cut into their steaks.

'Nothing important.'

'Well, I work in the City. I specialize in retail – I mean I follow the stocks on things like The Body Shop and Benneton. Anyway, it occurred to me that knitting is hot. I Googled it on the Internet and it seems as if everyone's interested. Did you ever think of opening a shop of your own?'

Claire shook her head.

'It might make a good business and expand into a chain – I mean, it wouldn't become Sainsbury's, but I could see some fast growth.'

Claire put down her knife and looked at Leonora. 'I

wouldn't know anything about it,' Claire said. 'I've never run a store and I have no money to start one.' She wasn't sure if Leonora was offering to help in that department, but she was certain it wasn't the right thing to do, anyway. 'I work with Mrs Venables. I want to carry on working there.'

'Loyalty is good,' Leonora said. 'But thinking big might be better.'

Claire looked at her very directly. 'I've been thinking small,' she smiled. 'Small seems to suit me.'

Leonora shrugged. 'It was just an idea,' she said lightly. 'Probably not a very good one,' she added. 'How do you like your lunch?'

They talked pleasantly after that and Leonora proved to be very interested in gardening. Claire told her about the garden at the Patels' and how well it was going. Leonora told her all about the Chelsea Flower Show and promised to get her a ticket for opening day.

The lunch turned out to be quite enjoyable and Leonora insisted on paying. 'After all, you consulted on my scarf. I'll bring you what I've done on Saturday.'

They parted on the Brompton Road. It was still raining, but Claire decided to walk to the knitting shop anyway.

People were coming in and out of the shop for most of the afternoon and Mrs Venables decided to stay open late. Quite a few customers were from the class, but some were not and it seemed as many of them wanted to talk as to make purchases. Claire and Mrs Venables were kept busy listening to stories about troublesome daughters-in-law, delightful grandchildren, remembered cardigans knitted by grandmothers decades dead. Claire decided she liked many of the women but, of the ones her age, Leonora Atkins seemed the most friendly.

Suddenly it was almost four o'clock and Claire was beginning to worry about getting to the Patels', but when Mrs Venables offered her tea she couldn't say no. Somehow, in this short time, she seemed to have got as addicted to it as everyone else was. As there was a lull, Mrs Venables suggested they go upstairs. 'It's so much more comfortable and we can hear the shop bell from there.' Claire agreed and the two of them settled down on the couch with the teapot, biscuits and sponge cake between them.

'I'm completely amazed, Claire,' Mrs Venables told her. 'You really are a genius. I never thought we would have a response like this no matter what you tried.'

Claire thought of Nigel and his suspicious attitude but she forgot it when she looked into Mrs Venables's very sincere and very blue eyes. It seemed as if every part of the woman had aged except for the lovely sky-colored irises. They chatted for a while about the orders that they would make for stock and gossiped more than a little about a few of the women who had amused them. The time flew and Claire realized that it was already a quarter past five.

'I must go,' she said.

'Oh. I'm sorry to have kept you so long. But we really must talk about your salary, or however we're going to arrange the . . . well the money.'

'Oh, don't worry about it,' Claire said. 'I'm sure you can work it out.'

Just then the shop bell rang. 'I'll run down and see who it is,' Claire said. 'I'm sure you want to clear these dishes. Then I'm off.'

She ran down the stairs but stopped short when she saw Nigel Venables striding through the shop. He looked up at her with surprise and obvious disapproval. Well, she disapproved of him too. 'What are you doing upstairs?' he asked. 'Is my mother all right?'

'She's just fine,' Claire told him. 'We had tea.' She came downstairs and began to walk toward the door. 'She'll be down in a minute to close up the shop,' she said and had her hand on the knob before his voice stopped her.

'I'd like a moment of your time, Miss Bilsop,' he said coldly.

'I'm afraid I'm late,' Claire answered just as coldly.

'That won't do,' he said and actually put his hand on hers. 'I want to know what you're about.'

'I'm about to leave,' she said.

'You never seem to have time for anyone except my mother,' Nigel almost hissed. 'I don't know what game you're playing nor who you think you are. You come in here, give my mother ideas, overwork her, and maybe threaten her health. Why? What's your game?'

Claire was furious but could barely speak. She felt the blood rush to her cheeks. But she tried hard to keep her voice steady. 'I'm not playing any games,' she hissed back. 'I think it's you who have some other motive. Your mother loves this store. It gives her something to do. And she's enjoyed talking to and teaching new customers. What's wrong with that? Should she be upstairs polishing the silver?'

'So you've had a bit of a nose around, have you? And saw the silver.'

Claire drew in her breath sharply. Did he think she was some kind of common thief trying to rob an old woman? But before she could say a word Mrs Venables spoke from the staircase. 'Nigel, it's my eyesight not my hearing that is going. Stop cross-examining Claire this minute.'

He didn't even turn to look at his mother. 'I will not. None of this is good. None of this is normal. Some stranger just drops in and transforms this place. This isn't a fairy tale.' He turned back to Claire. 'What are you looking for?' he asked. 'Money? A percentage of the shop? Are you planning to find a place in my mother's will?'

Mrs Venables had crossed the room and now she took Nigel by the arm. 'I'm very, very sorry,' she said to Claire. 'I must apologize for my son, again. It's clear that I have brought him up badly.' She turned to Nigel and her voice changed into something so cold and imperious that Claire was startled. 'Nigel, go upstairs. We'll discuss this in a moment.'

'Mother, I . . .'

'Nigel!' There was no ignoring or arguing with that command and Nigel did leave them. Mrs Venables took Claire's hand. 'You must pay no attention to what he said,' she began.

'But he thinks . . . you know I have no . . .'

'Of course you don't. He's overprotective and he's under a lot of financial pressure. I think he counted on selling this building. And good business in the shop wasn't part of his plan.'

Claire felt a tear roll down her cheek and touch her nose. She wiped it away with her hand.

'Here, dear. Take this,' Mrs Venables said and handed her a handkerchief that she had withdrawn from her pocket. 'Nigel will apologize and you must try to forgive him. He's not always in such a strop. I can't remember the last time I had as much fun as we have this week.' She raised her voice so Nigel would certainly hear. 'The fact is, I jointly own this property and even if I close the shop I have no intention of moving from my flat. He shall have to wait until I go before he gets the house.' Then she lowered her voice. 'I also think he fancies you,' she said. 'That always makes him more prickly.'

Claire looked at the old woman. She must be mad. Nigel disliked her, possibly hated her and Claire wouldn't call his behavior to her 'prickly'. It was hostile and she felt almost obliged to respond in kind. But she wanted Mrs Venables to know 'I didn't mean to cause any trouble. If you want me to . . .'

Then Mrs Venables patted Claire on the shoulder. 'I want you to forget about this as best you can and come back tomorrow and help me go through the catalogs. Then I want you to help me prepare for the weekend class. Would you do that, my dear?' Claire nodded. And Mrs Venables looked down at her wrist. 'I'm afraid you will be late for your appointment,' she said. 'I feel quite responsible.'

Remembering Mrs Patel, Claire shook her head. 'I do have to go, though,' she said and ran off down the street.

When she arrived at Mrs Patel's, the shop was busy with customers. Claire used this time to straighten up and get her thoughts together: how was she going to deliver the news to Mrs Patel that she had a new job?

When Claire saw the last shopper leave, she made her way to the front counter where Mrs Patel was sitting on a stool.

'Hello there, did you see the new cartons that need to be put away down in aisle four?' Mrs Patel asked.

'I did but I wanted to consult with you about where you wanted the products placed.'

'Since when? Usually you do it on your own. Why question yourself now?' Mrs Patel looked curiously at Claire. 'What is it?'

'I don't know how to . . . I . . .'

'Out with it, girl.'

'Thank you for the lovely vase. You didn't have to give me anything. I enjoyed working in the garden, tutoring Safta, and working with you. I actually don't feel that I can keep it.'

'That's nonsense. You deserve to be rewarded for a job well done. I don't want to take it back,' Mrs Patel said firmly.

'But you don't understand. I . . . I've been . . . offered a job closer to where I live.' Claire was relieved to finally get the words out.

Mrs Patel smiled and patted Claire's shoulder. 'I think, perhaps, you have found something else you may prefer to do. This knitting you told me about. It makes you money, ah? And the ride from Kensington can't be pleasant.'

'Oh, but how could I leave you now?' Claire looked at Mrs Patel's belly. 'You need the help.'

'I'll find someone else to fill in for you,' Mrs Patel assured her. At that moment the door opened and Maudie came in with her two kids in tow. 'In fact, I thought I might hire her.' She pointed to Maudie who, hearing what Mrs Patel had said, wore a surprised look on her face that matched Claire's.

'You want me to work for you? What will I do with the boys?'

'We'll simply have to arrange it so that you can work while the girls are at school, and then you can bring the boys here. I'm sure Devi would love the company. Then, if Claire can manage it, perhaps she could still work a few hours to cover us until we get the schedule organized.' Mrs Patel looked over at Claire. 'It will be good for all of us, yes?'

'Yes,' Claire replied with a relieved smile.

FIFTY-SIX

'Please say yes,' Im begged. 'It'll be fun.'

Claire never thought she'd see Imogen Faulkner pleading with her for anything. 'It sounds lovely, Im, but I've had a tiring week and after today's knitting classes I'd really like to take a hot bath, relax and read my book,' she said.

'How dreadful. I want you to meet my parents and it's a special occasion, Claire. Please. For me?' Claire leaned against her bedroom door and sighed. 'Toby will be there,' Im continued. 'He'd be sorry to miss you.'

Claire looked down at the floor. She hadn't seen Toby since she had helped him in the bookstore, and she had so much to share with him about everything that had been happening lately. She looked up and grinned sheepishly. 'Okay, I'll go with you. Thank you.'

Im ran over to her and hugged her. 'Great! Now go in and get ready. We can't be late.'

At Imogen's parents' London house, dinner was a very different affair from the ones with Mrs Patel. Claire had dressed carefully for it: she wore a new black dress she had recently bought from Marks & Spencer and, with her pearls and her slimmer hips, she thought she looked quite smart. She hadn't really seen Imogen dressed formally before – mostly she slobbed around the flat in her robe – and she hadn't noticed in the taxi but, once Claire was shown into the opulent drawing room, she could easily see that Imogen and her friend Georgina, as well as Mrs Faulkner, wore clothes that were on a whole other level. It wasn't the way Tina dressed when she was celebrating – no shiny textiles, no bright colors or flashy jewelry – but there was something about the fabrics and the cut of the women's clothes that told Claire that they most likely weren't from Marks & Spencer. She was glad to see that Toby was his usual rumpled self, but slightly dismayed by the tailored appearance of Malcolm, and the other two male guests. One, Thomas, who looked vaguely familiar, was almost overdressed in cravat and cummerbund and the other, Edward, who had come straight from work, wore a well-cut suit and one of those distinctly English shirts where the cuffs and collars were white but the shirt itself was striped.

Edward was nice looking, with dark hair and light brown eyes. During drinks he spoke to her a bit about his job in the City, before Toby and Thomas joined the conversation.

Mrs Faulkner approached them. 'Do you know the geography of the house?' she asked. Claire shook her head. 'Well you might want to powder your nose.' This, Claire had learned, meant 'wash up' so she nodded and Mrs Faulkner took her to the loo that seemed to be the only geography on offer.

On her way back, Im was waiting for her. 'Do you like Edward?' she asked. And Claire nodded, though she didn't think she did like him particularly. 'His father is a baronet,' Im continued. 'Close friends of the Mountbattens. They know everyone. And Edward is a nice sort.' She took Claire's arm and led her back to the group. Then, as Claire realized the import of what Imogen had told her, the talk became general. It turned to Imogen's nuptials, Claire's classes, her forthcoming trip to Nice and the opera.

As they spoke, Claire realized that Thomas seemed to be eyeing her in a hostile way. The idea that she knew him and simply couldn't remember where from, gnawed at her. Then they were called into dinner, and she was seated between Toby and Edward. The dining room was as impressive as the drawing room had been, with high ceilings, silver candelabra and a mahogany dining table that – to her surprise – wasn't covered by a cloth but instead had the delicate porcelain service and the softly glowing silver laid directly on the wood. She recoiled at the thought of spilling so much as a grain of rice on the lovely, patinated surface.

Mr Faulkner, who was dressed almost exactly like Edward and was only a little larger and beefier, started talking about the Euro and the upcoming Wimbledon tournament and Toby took the chance to nudge Claire when their host became a bit long-winded. But, once the main course was served, it was Edward who took her attention. He asked about her home in 'the States', what she worked at, how she liked living with Imogen and told her about his days at Oxford with both Imogen and Toby. When he asked her what brought her to London, Claire was rather unprepared and she shrugged. 'A man,' she said. 'In an airplane.'

Edward laughed. Before he could get any further, Claire was grateful for the interruption of plates being removed and the pudding being served. She turned to Toby and hoped he might either talk about books or make another date but he had Georgina on his other side, and the two of them seemed engrossed in some gossip that Claire couldn't follow.

As they were finishing dessert and the accompanying sweet wine Mr Faulkner tapped his glass. 'We're so pleased you could all be here,' he began. 'My wife and I want to make an announcement.'

Claire looked across the table at Imogen who was looking like the cat who had got the cream. She wondered what it would be like to grow up in a house like this, wear clothes like that, and go to a school like Oxford University. It clearly wasn't enough, because Imogen was obviously working toward something higher. Claire didn't feel envious, but she did feel very different.

'We are delighted,' Mr Faulkner went on, 'to welcome Malcolm into our family. It seems he has the courage to want to marry Imogen.'

'George,' Mrs Faulkner chided gently. 'I believe Malcolm is to be congratulated.'

'Indeed,' said Mr Faulkner. 'Here, here,' he began and murmurs of it ran around the table. Everyone lifted their glass so Claire followed. Selfishly she thought of herself, instead of the happy couple. Now Im's engagement was official, Claire realized that the actual marriage meant she would be homeless again. She could only hope it was going to be a long engagement because she couldn't face going back to Mrs Watson's. Claire pushed the thought out of her mind when Toby said something witty, and Imogen and Malcolm kissed chastely. And Claire looked at Toby. She hoped that he would exchange a look with her, just to give her the slightest encouragement, but he kept his eyes on the happy couple and Claire had to be satisfied with that.

When it was time to leave, Mr Faulkner called a mini cab for Claire. Imogen and Malcolm were spending the night with the Faulkners, and though she knew the ride back to Kensington would be expensive, Claire thought the splurge was worth it. She kissed Toby goodbye, shook hands with Thomas, and then was quite surprised when Edward offered her a ride. 'Is it out of your way?' she asked.

'Not a bit. I have to go west anyway. It would be my pleasure,' he insisted and called to cancel the mini cab.

It was only as they were leaving that Claire, seeing Thomas in profile as he walked away beside Toby, remembered who he was. He had done the layout for her flyer. The computer graphics specialist that Toby had sent her to. She remembered that he hadn't liked her then, and he seemed not to now. But before she had time to think about it, Edward began talking about his flat on the river, his spaniel, and a pub that he knew right on the Thames that got half-submerged in a very high tide. 'I'll take you sometime. Give me a shout.' He jotted down his number and gave it to Claire. Though Claire wasn't much interested in him she smiled, nodded and took the paper. At least he wasn't asking her where her 'people' came from.

They were silent for the rest of the trip back, but Claire looked out at the city and thought about the evening. The dinner had been delicious, the rooms beautiful, the guests (with the exception of Thomas) welcoming, and she told herself how lucky she was. She had a lovely place to live, some good friends, delightful work, and quite enough money. Even if her dress hadn't been quite up to the standard, it was a size ten. And while Toby had not asked her out, he had smiled at her often. The dinner had been a success Claire decided, and so was her life in London.

FIFTY-SEVEN

Claire found that she had a talent for stocking Mrs Venables's store, as well as waiting on customers. She was really interested in their projects, delighted to help them with pattern selection or knotty – sometimes literally – knitting problems. And when the shop was empty of customers she never tired of chatting with Mrs Venables. They told each other stories from their past, and while Claire found Mrs Venables's traditional English upbringing in the country the most charming of fairy tales, Mrs Venables in turn found Claire's stories of Tottenville, Manhattan, and of Tina and her friends absolutely riveting. To her it all seemed exotic. In fact, something that the women shared was the mutual attraction they had to the exotic in one another, as well as the deep similarities. Both of them were self-effacing, both loved to read, both had a sly, unexpected sense of humor, and of course there was their passion for knitting. In very short order Claire finished her lap robe and Mrs Venables declared it a 'treasure'. In the following Saturday's nine o'clock class Mrs Venables insisted on displaying it across the table to the astonishment, praise and envy of the attendees.

While there were some dropouts, most women turned up without fail, and Claire regularly taught three classes on Saturdays. She believed the students enjoyed the chance to relax and gossip with one another as much as they had the desire to learn new stitches. Over time she became quite friendly with some of them and when Leonora invited some of the nine o'clock class to a meal at her flat one evening, Claire went and had a good time. And Leonora was as good as her word about the tickets for the flower show.

Claire continued to visit the Countess to help her when she was too unwell to make the class. Her daughter Ann, who actually became quite good and quite devoted to knitting, ran her own PR agency and, as a way of saying thank you for helping with her mother, often slipped Claire invitations to receptions and parties that her celebrity clients threw. Claire didn't even think of attending them until she showed a few of them to Toby, who absolutely insisted they go.

Imogen was almost equally enthusiastic and sometimes went along as Claire's guest. Just as frequently, Claire gave her the invitation and Imogen went with Malcolm. 'The only parties I get to attend are dreary book launches,' Im complained. 'At the last one my author was useless. He works like a dog, then drinks like a fish and gets sick as a parrot.'

'My god, he's a one-man menagerie.'

Im laughed. 'Yes. And he's not the worst. Then I have all those dreary goodbye parties. There's always someone leaving one house to go to another. But heavens, Lady Ann knows how to publicize anything. She certainly brings out a crowd. I wish I could get her behind a few of my books.' She sighed. 'No budget for that, I'm afraid. Well, it's nice to see the fashionistas – and there's the free booze. You know I love my drink.'

One of the pleasant developments in Claire's life was that she had clearly moved up in status with Imogen. She was never to know that it was partly because Toby had sworn Im to silence over the fact that Claire's family were the Staten Island Bilsops and the Murrays of Newport, that they owned acres of ocean-front real estate and were, like all old money, incredibly discreet about it.

Even without knowing that, Claire had to admit to herself that Im, whom she enjoyed and had come to truly like, was more than a bit of a snob and Claire's friendships with Ann (Claire was amused that 'Lady' Ann rarely used her title) and some of the other more prominent women raised her to an appropriate social level in her roommate's eyes. She was no longer the caretaker living in the box room, but an equal although she did continue to do most of the cleaning in the flat. Since the successful visit to Im's parents at which she had apparently aroused Edward's interest, she'd gotten even more invitations, some of which she accepted, though it sometimes meant missing an evening at the Patels'.

One Saturday, after a long day of classes, Imogen wanted her to double with Malcolm and Edward. When Claire refused because of exhaustion, Imogen wouldn't stop pressing her. 'Oh come on. Don't be so wet. It'll be fun.'

'Please. All I want is a bath and a bed,' Claire said. 'I'm completely knackered.' She loved to use English words like knackered and brilliant and knickers. Calling a sweater a jumper and an undershirt a vest gave her a silly little thrill of pleasure as if she were somehow in costume.

'But Claire,' Imogen protested, 'Edward is a real catch. And I've told you he fancies you.'

Claire thought of the stolid Edward. He had been very attentive when she had dined with Imogen's parents, and it had been nice of him to drive her home, but she hadn't thought of him once since then. Comparing his qualities to the excitement and physical grace of Michael Wainwright or the wit and education of Toby Stanton only made Edward even less attractive to her.

'I'd better not raise his hopes then,' Claire said. 'You see I don't fancy him.'

'Oh, Claire, how do you know? It took me years to

notice Malcolm.' Claire could easily believe that but refrained from saying so. 'The fact is, Claire, you live like a nun. No men here, working with women, seeing those Camden people.' She paused. 'You're not gay, are you?'

Claire actually blushed. 'No. The truth is I . . .' she paused. Imogen had become a friend, but she loved gossip and interfering in people's lives, especially their love lives. Still, in the face of the speculation on her sexuality, and Imogen's enthusiasm for Edward, Claire felt she should say something. 'The fact is I really like Toby.'

'Of course you do. As do I. Everyone likes Toby. He's a bit of a disappointment professionally, and he's always been lazy, but he has all that charm.'

Claire paused. She and Toby hadn't only seen each other at his bookshop, but at various PR parties and at a few dinners before or after them. Though he had never kissed her or made a sexual advance, Claire wrote it off to shyness. In fact, he didn't seem to be a very physical person. Claire put the thought of the wild sex she had had with Michael Wainwright out of her mind and thought of the pleasantness of being with Toby. He was certainly smarter and far more well-read than Michael. And he made her laugh instead of cry, which, she had learned to her cost, was important.

'Oh, take your bath,' Imogen said. 'It will give you more energy and if you do something with your hair you'll be quite presentable for dinner.'

'Absolutely not,' Claire said. 'I'm too tired, I'm not hungry, and I certainly don't want to lead Edward on when I prefer Toby.'

'Prefer Toby?' Imogen paused, sat down on the sofa, and then began to laugh. 'You don't mean . . .' She kept laughing and Claire felt a wave of anger mixed with dread.

If Toby were a romantic compromise she certainly didn't want Imogen to tell her he was out of her league. She may have not gone to university while he had gone to Oxford, but she knew he liked her. 'Toby really cares for me,' she said, feeling her cheeks redden.

'Of course he does. Of course he does, but not that way. Claire, he's *gay*. And he's with Thomas. Always did like rough trade.'

Claire stood with her robe clutched around her. For a moment she felt disappointment and then was flooded with embarrassment. Of course Toby was gay. Hadn't she always known that? There was nothing effeminate or flamboyant about him, but the lack of any sexual energy toward her should have, almost had . . .

'That's a corker! But didn't you know?' Imogen looked up from the sofa and saw Claire's face. She got up and went to her, putting her arm around her. 'Oh, but you didn't.'

'It's just that, well, here in the UK all the men seem, well, different.'

'Do they all seem gay?'

'No, no. It's just that I can't place anybody. Toby or Lady Ann . . .'

Imogen gave her a brief hug. 'Well, no harm done. I mean, you haven't made an ass of yourself, have you? You haven't thrown yourself at him?'

'No. Of course not,' Claire said. All she wanted to do was get to her room and lie down with the blanket pulled up over her head and cry. Only now was her disappointment beginning to overtake her surprise.

'Why don't you join us for dinner? We'll all get pissed and, who knows, you might end up snogging Edward and finding you like it.'

Claire stiffened. 'I really can't,' she said. 'I have a pounding headache. I'm just going to take some aspirin and lie down.'

Imogen sighed. 'All right. I better call Malcolm.' She let Claire go back to her room for which Claire was grateful. She closed the door and the few steps from it to her bed seemed to take half a lifetime.

She curled up on her little bed. Why was she so stupid with men? Toby had seemed so very friendly – no, *was* so very friendly – but she had completely misread the signs. It was embarrassing. She was ridiculous. Just as she'd been ridiculous in front of Michael Wainwright, Katherine Rensselaer and the security guard that night when she'd nurtured the foolish hope of dining with Michael. Other men would be Toby's romantic focus, just as other women would be Michael's.

Claire tried carefully to remember what she had said to Toby and if there was any way in which she had exposed her feelings for him. It must be clear that she liked him, but had it been clear that she liked him in an inappropriate way? She flushed, and her temples started to pound. The aspirin was having no effect and tears sprang to her eyes, partly from the pain and partly from her feelings. She was hopeless. How could she bear to face Toby? Wouldn't he look at her with slightly amused pity?

There was a knock on the door and Imogen put her head in. 'A letter for you,' she said and brought it to Claire. 'Oh, you don't look well. Do you think it's flu?'

Claire would have shaken her head if it wouldn't have had a catastrophic effect. 'No,' she told Im, her voice weak. 'Just one of my headaches.'

'Would you like a whisky? Sometimes that helps.'

The thought made Claire sick to her stomach but she just declined and took the letter that Imogen was holding. When she looked at it, Tina's handwriting didn't make her feel any better. What fresh hell was this?

'Well, call if you need anything,' Im said. 'I'm working on the DIY garden pond book until Malcolm gets here.'

Claire waited till she left then opened the letter.

I thought you might want to know that Mike is getting engaged to Katherine Rensselaer. I'm going to be very busy planning not just my wedding but

*helping with theirs, too. Anthony gave me an
eighteen-karat gold cross for my birthday with two
diamonds in it. I wear it all the time. It looks like
the one Madonna wore on her second album cover.
Guess you didn't remember my birthday, but I'm
sure you're way too busy. Abigail Samuels told me
you wrote to her. I guess now that you are living
in London you've forgotten your other friends.*

*Well, I just thought you might want to hear the
news.*

As she pulled the blankets over her head, Claire wondered
why, no matter whom she desired, she was bound to be
disappointed. It couldn't be genetic. Her grandmother had
been married for almost fifty years, and her mother had no
trouble attracting men – even if they were low-lifes like Jerry.
Only she was a complete failure.

FIFTY-EIGHT

Claire got through the next day by taking a long walk through Regent's Park. She walked for hours, and though she got lost several times the fatigue did her good. The revelation about Toby made her feel stupid, but that was so often the case that she couldn't be surprised. She was grateful she had never revealed herself to him, or been more aggressive pursuing him. The meek might not inherit the earth but at least they didn't embarrass the hell out of themselves.

She was grateful, too, that the flat was empty when she got home and just as grateful that she had work and Mrs Venables the next morning. She tried to test her feelings, to work out how deep her disappointment over Toby was. She sat in the small armchair, looking out at the garden and comforted by the lap robe she wrapped herself in. Toby could still be a good friend she reminded herself. This didn't mean that she couldn't continue to see him. But she was not going to be one of those pathetic women who pursued hopeless relationships. If I walked away from Mr Wonderful I can walk away from any man she thought.

A light in the garden to the south threw the shadows of dancing branches onto the ceiling. Perhaps she'd have a cup of tea she thought and had to smile at herself. Perhaps someday she'd also speak the way the English did. Only the other day she had told Devi he was being 'very, very naughty indeed', which would not have gone down well in Tottenville. She sighed. How could she have imagined that someone like Toby could be central to her life here? No, like Mrs Patel, Nigel and Imogen, he must see her as an outsider, someone to be amused by but not to take into your life.

Claire sighed again and stood up leaving her throw on the chair. She prepared for bed and slipped into it. She would keep her dignity in front of Imogen and put her disappointment away. For the first time she reflected on Tottenville and how, despite living there her whole life, she had always felt like an outsider. Here, where everything seemed so comfortable, so right to her, she actually *was* an outsider. She had better not forget it.

But the next morning, after a long night's sleep, she woke up in a more positive frame of mind. After all, she loved the routine of her days. Getting up relatively late, having time for tea and breakfast, the short walk around the corner to the shop, and her morning greeting to Mrs Venables was all such a dramatic difference from her old two-hour commute, and the work was so much more pleasant. She loved working with the colors and textures of the yarns, she was delighted that Mrs Venables allowed her to select the stock, she enjoyed opening the boxes, handling the new goods and arranging them attractively on the shelves. It was interesting to talk with each new customer, and delightful to add more money to the till. The shop seemed to do more business every day. Now, as well as the three classes on Saturday, they had begun planning a Wednesday evening session to accommodate people who couldn't make the weekend ones. As Claire finished brushing her hair she reminded herself of how lucky she was. Perhaps the Toby fiasco wasn't as embarrassing as she thought. She'd just avoid seeing him for a while and then go on with their friendly relations. And what did Michael's engagement mean to her? Nothing at all. She had a life here.

* * *

This morning, when she got to the shop the door was locked. She jiggled it and then tried to pry it, but it definitely hadn't been opened and Mrs Venables was nowhere to be seen. Claire walked to the estate agent's shop across the way and asked to use the phone. She called Mrs Venables's flat but there was no answer.

Claire felt a rising sense of dismay. Surely Mrs Venables wouldn't have taken a day off without telling her. 'I'm worried about her,' she said to Mr Jackson, the estate agency manager. 'She hasn't opened the shop or answered her phone.'

'Well, I have the key. You know, the building has been listed with us for some time.' Claire didn't know that but her concern for Mrs Venables didn't leave much room to be surprised. Mr Jackson was fishing through a drawer of keys. He lifted one up. 'Here it is,' he said. 'I'm sure Nigel won't mind. Just bring it back later.'

With relief, Claire promised she would and ran across the road to the shop. Once inside it took her only a moment to know Mrs Venables was not behind the counter or getting something from the little cupboard under the stairs. Claire ran up to the flat. Mrs Venables was not in the sitting room or the kitchen. But as Claire called her name and tentatively started down the hall to the bedroom she thought she heard, well, something.

The door to the bedroom was partially open. Claire knocked. 'Mrs Venables? Are you . . . are you . . .' The door swung open from the slight pressure of her knuckles, and Claire could see a long bare foot lying on the carpet. She gasped and ran into the room.

Mrs Venables was lying face down on the floor. For a terrible moment Claire thought she might be dead but then she heard the noise again, the half whimper half groan she had heard in the hallway. She crouched beside Mrs Venables and, afraid to move her, put her head down to the old woman's face. Had she fallen and broken her hip? That happened with old people. Or had she had a heart attack? Perhaps it had just been a dizzy spell or even a fall out of bed. 'Mrs Venables?'

Claire put her cheek to the carpet so that she was inches away from the old woman's face. 'Are you ill?'

Mrs Venables made a noise in her throat. It wasn't speech, but it was an answer to what Claire considered her most stupid question. Claire didn't know if she should try and pick her up or leave her where she lay until help came. Then she realized she didn't know how to call for help. What did you dial in London instead of 9-1-1? She felt a fine sweat break out all over her body. She shivered but she took Mrs Venables's hand in hers. The old woman made another sound and weakly tried to squeeze Claire's hand. Claire couldn't bear to look at her, face down on the rug like a corpse. 'It's all right,' she said, though she felt it was all wrong. 'I'm here now. It's all right.' The old woman's hand was icy cold. Claire reached for the bare foot and it was colder still. Slowly, gently, she began to turn the old woman over, waiting for the slightest sound of pain.

But there was none. Once Mrs Venables was face up Claire grabbed the pillow and coverlet from the bed and tried to make her more comfortable. One of Mrs Venables's eyes stayed focused on her as she moved, but the other rolled independently, as randomly as a blue marble in a tumbling box. It must have been a stroke, Claire thought, and became even more frightened. 'Don't try to speak,' she said. 'We'll have a doctor in just a few minutes.'

She wasn't sure that was true, but she went to the phone on the bedside table and dialed the operator. It all took almost more time than she could bear, but at last she was able to give the address to a dispatcher. Then she went back to Mrs Venables's side. She took her hand and though its grip wasn't any stronger, it did feel a bit warmer. Claire chafed it gently between her own two hands. 'You're going to be fine,' she said. 'I'll call Nigel. He'll come here or meet us at the hospital.' Mrs Venables made a noise, this time a kind of gurgle that frightened Claire even more than the first look at her had done. 'We have to go to the hospital,' she said. 'And Nigel will come and you'll feel much better. They'll fix this.' She paused. 'I'll put some socks on you,' she added. She went through a few drawers in the bureau until she found some very old knit socks. 'These ought to do.'

Praying for the arrival of the ambulance, Claire rubbed the woman's feet and put the sock on each one as gently as she could. It seemed as if she had been there for ages, but it was only a little before ten on the bedroom clock. 'I'm going to call Nigel,' she said.

Claire opened the little drawer beneath the phone. 'I'm looking for your phone book,' she said. But the top drawer only held a small pack of paper tissues, a pen, a box of lozenges and some hairpins. Claire said a little prayer. 'I'm going to look in the second drawer,' and her prayer was answered because as soon as she pulled it open, a little red leather book with gold embossing lay in front of her. It said 'addresses' and Claire snatched it up. How would an English mother list her son's phone number? Under 'V' for Venables? Or 'S' for son? Or 'N' for Nigel? She was about to rifle through the pages when she noticed that the first page had not only Mrs Venables's name and address but also Nigel's. Several of his phone numbers had been crossed out and replaced. Claire prayed again, this time that one of the numbers was current. There were three. The first got no response, not even a machine. The second produced the fax buzz. 'I'm calling him,' Claire said. 'Just one more minute.' She dialed the third number which she remembered was the one on the shop sign. After three rings it was picked up.

'This is Nigel Venables,' his voice said coolly. 'I am not able to take your call. If you leave your number I will call you back.'

Claire waited for the beep. 'I'm here with your mother. She's ill. I've called for an ambulance. They should be here any moment – at least I hope so. I don't know where we'll take her but I will go to the hospital and call you again from there. If you get this message please call your mother's number right away.' She glanced at the clock. 'It's now ten oh nine in the morning,' she added. Not knowing what else to do she put the phone back on its cradle and sat down on the floor beside Mrs Venables. Once again she picked up her hand. 'Everything's going to be all right,' she said. 'We're taking you to the hospital and Nigel will be there in just a little while.'

FIFTY-NINE

But Nigel wasn't there, nor was he at home to answer his calls. When the ambulance arrived Claire ran across to tell Mr Jackson where they were going. Mrs Venables was taken to the Chelsea and Westminster and Claire stayed beside her every moment except when she was physically examined.

The nurses were kinder, it seemed, than the ones in the States and the doctors a bit more formal. Dr Winters, the first physician to examine Mrs Venables, took Claire aside almost immediately. 'I can't say for certain without a few neurological tests, but it would appear to be a stroke. And a rather serious one. Were you with her when she was taken ill?' Claire shook her head. She explained that she had arrived and found Mrs Venables on the floor.

'A shame, really,' the doctor said. 'It's hard to know how long ago it happened and with a stroke recovery is based very much on timing – how quickly we can begin to treat the patient. She lives alone, then?'

'Yes. I work for her.'

'A paid companion?'

'No. No, in her shop. I work for her in the store that she owns.'

'So, until you found her today she was quite active? No indication of neurological impairment?'

Claire wasn't sure what an indication would be and

certainly Mrs Venables had seemed normal in every way except for her arthritic knees. 'I think she was normal; I mean normal for a woman her age.'

'No confusion? No weakness in her hands? No dragging of one foot or the other?'

Claire shook her head. 'She was fine,' she said with more conviction. 'Certainly her hands were fine. She knits. She runs a knitting store.'

'Well, her hands aren't fine now. At least her left one isn't.'

'But is this only temporary?' Claire asked anxiously. There was a bustle down the hall and several nurses and a doctor pulled aside a screen. Claire hoped she wouldn't see that happening at Mrs Venables's bedside.

'Hard to say. Let's wait for the test results and an examination by the neurologist. Has she any relatives?'

'Yes. Her son.' Claire felt herself flush with annoyance. 'I haven't been able to reach him yet.'

'Well, when you do, let him know that he should come straight away.' The doctor turned and walked down the hall, leaving Claire to return to Mrs Venables's side. She sat there, holding her hand and talking to her for most of the day. She left her position only when the doctors came in or orderlies wheeled the old woman away for tests. Then Claire grabbed a sandwich and a cup of tea, also purchasing a phone card that she used over and over to try to reach Nigel.

By five o'clock that evening both Mrs Venables and Claire were exhausted. Mrs Venables closed both of her eyes – to Claire's relief since she no longer had to be distracted by the floating eye. Claire wished that she could lie down as well, but where? There was a lounge for visitors and perhaps she could lie down there on the battered sofa, but she hated the idea of Mrs Venables waking up in a strange room alone.

It was only when she was at the phone, trying Nigel yet

again that she thought of Toby. She felt embarrassed at the thoughts she had had about him until she was rudely awakened by Imogen's announcement of his sexual preference. But she couldn't take the time now to worry about that. Claire needed some help and she knew she could depend on him.

'You're all alone,' he said after she explained the situation. 'Well, where's that bloody son of hers?' She had told Toby on a previous occasion about her difficulties with Nigel.

'For all I know he's on holiday in China,' she said and thought briefly of her own ticket to Nice booked for this Saturday. She had organized the time off with Mrs Venables, but of course she couldn't think of going now. 'I just don't know where he is or how to contact him. He usually carries his mobile with him.'

'Well, you've been brilliantly resourceful and loyal,' Toby said. 'I'll ring up Imogen, have her give me a change of clothes for you and come right over. Have you eaten?'

'I had a sandwich,' Claire told him.

'Well, it must have been vile hospital food. When Thomas was in hospital I catered. Shall I bring you some smoked salmon? I will,' he told her, without waiting for her reply.

'Thank you. But don't make any special trips.' She looked around at the people bustling by. 'I better get back to her room,' she said. She gave Toby the ward's number and quickly climbed the stairs and made her way back to the sleeping Mrs Venables. She sat there for more than an hour and several times she fell into a doze, but woke up with a start each time, straining to be sure that Mrs Venables was still breathing.

It was a little easier when Toby arrived. He brought flowers, a few sandwiches, hot tea in a thermos and, of course, several books as well as a change of clothes. 'You poor dear,' he said and gave her a warm look. 'Don't thank me for the flowers. Imogen insisted. She said she'd come in tomorrow.'

Claire washed, changed into a fresh pair of slacks and a sweater, then took up her vigil again. 'Look what else I brought you,' Toby said and triumphantly pulled out a bag that held her knitting. Claire took a deep breath and felt tremendous relief. She could bear to sit beside Mrs Venables, listening to her labored breathing, if she had something like this to do.

'Toby, I'll never be able to thank you.' She was so glad that their friendship seemed to be the same and felt a strong rush of affection for him. Perhaps it wasn't going to be so difficult for her to adjust to her new knowledge of him.

'Don't be silly,' he said as he poured her out a cup of tea. 'You already have.'

A little later, a nurse offered to sit with Mrs Venables so Claire could rest. Claire kissed Toby goodbye and lay down on the scruffy sofa.

It seemed as if she had been sleeping for only a moment when the nurse shook her awake. 'He's here,' she said. 'Mrs Venables's son.'

Nigel was at his mother's bedside, her limp hand between his two, his face almost as pale as hers. He looked up at Claire and she thought his eyes were glassy with tears. He was wearing a white dress shirt, the sleeves rolled up; his beautifully tailored jacket was thrown carelessly on the windowsill. 'They think your mother has had a stroke,' she said as calmly as she could manage. 'I found her on the floor early this morning. I don't know how long she was lying there or when she got sick.'

'I only just got the message. I left my mobile in a taxi this morning . . . on the way to Bristol . . . Jackson got me. I was in court in Bristol,' he said, managing to sound both defensive and accusatory. 'Why didn't you call my office? I could have been here hours and hours ago.'

Claire moved closer to the bed. She lowered her voice, but couldn't hide the pent-up frustration. 'Because I didn't have your office number. Neither does your mother, or if she does, she didn't write it down with your other numbers. Believe me I tried to get you. I know all of your numbers by heart. You have a dozen messages on the one line that takes them, and I must have called your other phone thirty times today.' Claire looked at him. 'Do you think I was comfortable with this kind of responsibility? Don't you think I was frantic to reach you?' Nigel's concern for his mother was clearly clouded by his suspicion of Claire – and perhaps his guilt. She felt he was telling her that she had done something wrong. 'I'm sorry if you don't approve of how I handled this but I am really not practiced in dealing with severe medical emergencies either in New York or London. I've been with your mother since ten o'clock this morning. That makes it fourteen hours. And I made sure she had tests and saw the doctor, and I didn't let go of her hand, unless someone else was beside her when I went to the toilet or took a nap. She was never left alone.'

'I'm sorry, I'm sorry.' Nigel shook his head and rubbed his eyes, which were red with tiredness and grief. 'It's just I hardly know you and . . .'

'I'm Claire Bilsop from Tottenville New York,' she interrupted. 'Now I live in London, work for your mother, and I may be the person who saved her life.' She picked up her bag and turned. 'The neurologist still hasn't come by with her test results. They think she had a severe stroke and I guess he'll confirm that. You should know that she doesn't seem to be able to speak and she can't focus her left eye. Now I'm going home.' She sighed and, seeing how upset he seemed, took a piece of paper from her purse and scribbled Imogen's number on it. She said more gently, 'I don't have a cell phone but I'm giving you my roommate's number in case you want to call. I'll come back tomorrow if you don't mind.' She dropped the paper on the bed, turned and walked out the door.

SIXTY

Exhausted as she was, Claire had trouble sleeping that night. The vision of Mrs Venables prone on the carpet kept flashing each time she closed her eyes and began to drift into sleep. Lying there, on her narrow bed in the dark, she began to think of her own future. When she was old, who would be there for her? Certainly no one from her family. Her mother had Jerry, Tina had Anthony, Imogen had Malcolm, Toby had Thomas and, it seemed, Michael Wainwright would have Katherine Rensselaer. They also had sisters and brothers and children and aunts and uncles and god knows how many cousins. After an hour or two in the dark, Claire didn't know if she felt more sorry for poor Mrs Venables or for herself.

But in time, as she thought about it, she realized that marriage and children didn't keep you safe from being left alone, unconscious on the floor. Mrs Venables's husband had died two decades ago and Nigel, her only child, was obviously not infallible. But what son was? Fred was somewhere in Germany and after his hitch in the Army, who knew? Fred going back and living near their mother in Tottenville seemed unlikely.

By four in the morning, the hour of the wolf, Claire's thoughts had become almost unbearable. All of the fun, laughter, wisdom and humanity of Mrs Venables might have been wiped out forever in the cloudy moments before her fall. She might never hear another word from Mrs Venables's mouth. And what would Claire do now? Without being selfish – at least she hoped she wasn't being selfish – she realized that she might have no job and, aside from the money left from her first class ticket, no financial resources. How would she get another job? And if she did, how could she manage to be paid when she wasn't even supposed to be working in England without the correct visa? Even if Mrs Patel offered to take her back, she couldn't make enough to live on and, anyway, she wouldn't take the job away from Maudie.

The birds in the garden had begun to twitter and the window was just beginning to lighten before Claire fell asleep. When she woke it was nearly ten and she heard Imogen moving about in the living room, chatting on the phone in an even cheerier than usual voice. Claire rubbed her eyes, went to the bureau and looked at her face. She was very pale, except for her bloodshot and puffy eyes. Looking away from the mirror she saw the beautiful vase and the wonderful box that sat next to it. In the light of day, things – except for her – didn't look as bad. She had already begun to collect adventures and friends. A small pile of books, the places she'd been to, the people she'd met, these gifts all represented the more authentic life that she had lived in the last few months than she had been living for the previous decade.

Perhaps it was the case for her as for Mrs Venables and Toby and Mrs Patel; one collected experiences – both good and bad. As long as they were real, as long as your heart was involved, you used your life in a way that enriched you and meant you were never truly alone. You were filled with the experiences and the love you had collected and exchanged over the years. Claire used that thought to comfort herself when she pictured poor Mrs Venables, stuck in hospital almost unconscious. Perhaps when she was lying there she could remember all of the wonderful things she had done with her husband, all of the places she had seen, all of the little bits of china, and the paintings and the furniture that they had lovingly collected. Perhaps she remembered raising Nigel, the fun she had had with him as a toddler and a young schoolboy, and the pride she must have felt in him as he grew.

Claire shrugged herself into her dressing gown, wiped at her eyes and emerged from her room into the kitchen. Imogen was just putting the phone down. 'Hello,' she said in that distinctive intonation that she, Toby and all their friends used. 'So, you finally learned to sleep in?' Claire nodded and decided not to begin with a long recitation of yesterday's trouble. Imogen, no doubt, was getting ready for work and already late. 'Have you heard the news?' Imogen asked.

Claire nodded, confused. Of course she had heard the news. She'd asked Toby to call Imogen with it.

'Coffee?' Imogen asked and waved toward the pot. Claire shook her head. She'd actually come to prefer tea. 'Toby told you, huh? I should have known he couldn't keep his cakehole shut. He loves a wedding, that boy.'

'A wedding?' Claire asked, and then realized they had been talking at cross purposes. Imogen must – as usual – be talking about herself and that meant that she and Malcolm had finally . . . 'Have you and Malcolm set a date?'

'We're getting married in two months. Can you believe it? He's been transferred to Hong Kong – just for a year, but still – and, well you can imagine. My mother is in complete raptures, but hasn't any idea how she'll get the wedding breakfast pulled together in time. Malcolm's mother, of course, is disappointed.' Imogen sniffed, then smiled again. 'But of course his father adores me. And she'll come around in time, especially once I give her a grandchild.'

Claire filled the kettle and plugged it in. She knew she should feel delighted for Imogen, though the good news seemed completely separate and boxed away from Mrs

Venables's illness. 'Well, congratulations,' Claire said and gave Imogen a hug. 'Malcolm adores you and I know you'll be absolutely beautiful as a bride.'

Imogen hugged her back. 'You will be a bridesmaid, won't you?'

Claire was truly touched. She knew that she was not really a part of Imogen's world, but this gesture was unexpected and very, very kind. 'I'd love to,' Claire told her. 'I'll have to start knitting you something extraordinary as a wedding gift.'

'Oh, would you?' Imogen asked. 'Once I have my color schemes worked out could I tell you what I've decided?' Claire nodded and smiled. That was Imogen. She had probably planned on a bedspread before she even told Claire her news. 'Of course, we're going to move. Malcolm's father owns a few houses in St John's Wood. Two have been divided into flats but one is still untouched and, as luck would have it, their tenants' lease will run out next year. Malcolm pointed out to his father it would make a perfect new home and we'd pay for the refurbishment.'

Claire looked around the flat. 'So you'll be leaving,' she said, realizing the implication this had for her all at once.

'Well, of course I'll go with Malcolm to Hong Kong after the wedding. We'll probably honeymoon in Bali first. And then, after I come back, we'll do up the house.' She stopped. A tiny line appeared between her brows but it disappeared almost as quickly as it came. 'Don't worry,' she assured Claire. 'You can stay here. I'll put a word in with my uncle.'

The kettle began to boil and Claire took down her cup and saucer. They rattled as she carried them to the kettle – she was so upset, her hands were actually shaking. There was no way she could afford the rent on the entire flat, even though Imogen had told her she had a good deal. It must be a thousand pounds a month – way beyond anything Claire could afford. And anyone who could pay that much wouldn't want a roommate. Claire, her back to Imogen, tried to fill her cup but spilled the boiling water on the saucer and counter. She put the kettle down, much harder than she had meant to and got control of her face if not her feelings. She turned back to Imogen. 'Thank you,' she said. 'It's a very kind offer. And I'm very happy for you. It all sounds so exciting.'

Imogen nodded then looked at the time. 'Oh my god. I'm going to be dreadfully late. I'll have to give notice at work, too. Do you mind if I use the bathroom first?'

Claire shook her head. Of course she didn't mind. It was Imogen's flat. It always had been and now that it wasn't, it would not be Claire's either. While Imogen bathed, Claire managed to mop up her saucer and get her cup of tea into her room. Well, it wouldn't be her room for long. The news about Toby had been a blow, Mrs Venables's illness had been far worse, but, added to those, the news about losing this room, this little home, seemed insupportable. She felt tears rising in her already-painful eyes.

Her vision blurred, but the airline ticket taped to her mirror somehow stayed in focus. Nice. She was supposed to leave on Saturday. The last thing she wanted to do was take a holiday and she certainly couldn't leave Mrs Venables now. It would be such a waste though, to have to go back to Tottenville without ever seeing France.

For it seemed she would have to go back. Otherwise she'd have to start again from scratch and she wasn't sure she had the heart to do it. Some people were lucky, and each step they took made their lives richer and more stable. But it seemed that, for her, life was like climbing on shale, and at any point the hill beneath her feet would slide and she'd be left back at the bottom where she began.

Imogen shouted her goodbyes and Claire, finishing her tea, showered and dressed. She had to return the keys to Mr Jackson at the estate agent's and she'd better check the store, empty the till and put up a notice in the window before she locked up. Once again, Claire felt tears rise. She would do all of that and then go back to the hospital.

Even if Nigel were there, it wouldn't deter her from visiting Mrs Venables. She took some extra money from her drawer to buy flowers and was on her way out when she noticed an envelope taped to the outside of her door. For a moment she thought it might be Imogen's wedding invitation, but surely she hadn't been that quick to get them in the mail. Once her eyes cleared she saw that it was mailed from the US and that it was her mother's handwriting. Oh, no. Not again.

Claire carefully removed the white square. She tore open the envelope and took out two pages that were bent in quarters inside.

> *Dear Claire,*
> *I hope everything is well and that you're having a swinging time in London. Things back here are not quite so swinging. Jerry and I have broken up. I never met a man who was so selfish. I did everything for him. And even when we went out I usually paid for drinks and dinner. Can you believe that when I asked him to help out with the bills he told me he 'couldn't manage it'. When I think of all the presents that I gave him, and the meals that I cooked for him. Do you know that I did his laundry? I went to confession with Father Frank and was able to take communion for the first time since Jerry moved in. It's a real comfort.*

The letter went on for a few more paragraphs with a long list of complaints. But it was the last part of the second page that Claire reread wincing.

> *So, anyway, I told him to forget about it. But I didn't think that he would just pack up and leave.*

I thought he'd stop being so goddamned cheap.
Instead, he moved in with that blond slut who
works down at Tiny's Tavern. Like I care? She
might be twenty years younger, but she's at least
thirty pounds heavier. And we'll see how long it
takes before she gets tired of paying his expenses
out of her tip money.

Anyway, I miss my daughter. I wrote to Fred
and he sent me a check, but I'd love to have you
back home. It could be like a dormitory, or a
sorority house. You know, Jerry wanted to turn
your and Fred's rooms into an apartment but I
would never let him. After all, the two of you are
my children and you always have a home with me.

So, if you're ready to stop swinging, I hope
you'll come back soon. I ran into Tina, and she
says there's a woman at Crayden Smithers who's
some kind of big shot and really likes you. You
could probably get your old job back. So write me
back real soon and let me know when you're
coming home. It's been a real long vacation, and I
hope it's been nice for you. But everyone here in
Tottenville misses you.

Love,
Your mother

Claire uttered a silent prayer that she wouldn't have to
return to the home that was 'always there for her'. She
hoped that, even without the benefit of Father Frank, her
prayer would be heard. It was hard for Claire to accept
that just five days ago everything was looking up for her.
She had gone full circle – all she had to do now was go
back to New York.

SIXTY-ONE

Claire went to the hospital every day trying to be cheerful for Mrs Venables while suffering with her own worries about dealing with her gloomy future. She sat with Mrs Venables, often holding her hand. Sometimes she read to her. Other times she knitted and talked to her about her life in Tottenville, her grandmother, her father and his harping on the past glories of the Bilsop family. She fed her lunch and dinner because she thought that Mrs Venables might be embarrassed at being spoon-fed by a stranger.

After the first two days, Mrs Venables started trying to talk, but the noises she made were not clear. Yet Claire thought she was speaking. She tried to listen as carefully as she could and after a few more days she could distinguish some words – drink, cold, Nigel, doctor, and her own name.

When Nigel appeared, usually after five, Claire left. One night she had dinner with Toby and Thomas, who seemed a little less hostile to her. Another night she went to dinner with Imogen, Malcolm and Edward who apparently hadn't been deterred by her complete lack of interest in him. The thought did cross her mind that Edward was pleasant enough, far from poor, and would probably make a devoted husband. She could live in England and perhaps even open a knitting shop or buy Mrs Venables's business. But each time she looked at his flushed pink face she knew she couldn't possibly.

One afternoon, instead of just greeting her with a stiff nod of his head, and a brief exchange of factual information, Nigel asked her to stay and talk in the lounge. 'I think I shall have to find an invalid home or sheltered housing for my mother,' he told her. 'She is improving but the doctor says that she might not regain much use of her left side. She certainly can't live alone.'

Claire felt upset, but she tried to keep her voice calm. 'Nigel, she would hate that. Surely you can find someone to stay with her in her flat.'

'Fine. And I imagine that "somebody" ought to be you. Is that what you're planning? And how would she manage the stairs? And the bathroom?'

This time Claire's face went as pale as his usually was. She actually felt dizzy. 'You are insulting,' she said. 'And surely the flat can be adapted.' She knew he had a point there. 'Have you found a buyer for the building? Is that it?'

'Certainly not,' Nigel said. 'This is only about my mother's well-being.'

'Well, if that's true, then find her some nurses and put in a stair lift. I'm not equipped to take care of her. In fact, I – I might be returning to the States.' She walked past him and down the hall to Mrs Venables's ward. Somehow, telling her 'plans' aloud to Nigel had made them into plans. She supposed she'd have to begin to pack up and use whatever funds she had left for a one-way economy ticket home.

She went in and sat at Mrs Venables's bedside. As soon as she did, the older woman opened her eyes. Claire had noticed that the left one had stopped its wild wandering and tonight Mrs Venables seemed to focus both of them on her. 'Hello, Claire, dear,' Mrs Venables said. And while her voice was a little blurry, it was clear enough for not only Claire herself to understand, but also Nigel, who was now standing in the doorway.

'Mother,' he said, his eyes lighting up.

Her eyes turned to him. 'Nigel.' She had trouble with the 'j' sound in the middle of his name but it was plain enough for him to acknowledge. 'Being naughty?' she asked, and while the first word was slurred the second was clear enough.

Now it was Nigel's turn to blush, but not with anger. He moved a chair to the other side of the bed and took his mother's good hand. But Mrs Venables, with her weakened left hand, gave a squeeze to Claire that she could definitely feel.

'She's getting much better,' Claire said over the bed. Then she turned to Mrs Venables. 'Aren't you?' she asked. And the old woman gave her hand another squeeze and seemed to nod her head.

'We're arranging for physio- and speech therapy for you,' Nigel said. 'As soon as you're strong enough.' Mrs Venables nodded again though Nigel may not have seen it as a nod. But she again squeezed Claire's hand and Claire noticed that Nigel looked down at his own. To her complete surprise she saw his eyes get wet and then a tear trembled at the corner of one lower lid.

'I'll leave you two alone,' Claire said and wasn't sure if she saw just a tremor or a nod of permission. She forced herself to continue. 'Pretty soon I hope you're ready to knit. And maybe you'll bake me a sponge cake.' She was sure she saw a smile flicker not only on the right side of Mrs Venables's mouth but also on the slack left side.

In the hallway she was surprised to see Leonora Atkins and the Countess. Both looked very uncertain, and it wasn't until they saw Claire that they seemed to feel they were properly placed. 'How is she?' the Countess asked. 'Leonora heard from the estate agent across the way that Mrs Venables was ill. And I called my daughter . . .'

'What's the matter with her?' Leonora asked. 'I rang your number but there was no answer, and none at the shop.' She looked at Claire's drawn face. 'It doesn't look good and neither do you,' Leonora said. 'Everyone is anxious to know how she is.'

Claire was touched by their concern. Clearly, it wasn't only she who realized how special Mrs Venables was. 'She's had a stroke,' Claire said and briefly explained the situation as best she could.

'And you're about to leave for France, aren't you?' Leonora asked.

Claire shook her head. 'I can't go now,' she said.

'Of course not,' the Countess agreed and patted her hand. 'I've brought some very soft sponge cake, and I could bring some soup – either for her or for you. There's nothing like beef consommé for strengthening the blood.'

'Actually, for a stroke I think the blood has to be thinned, but that's neither here nor there,' Leonora said. 'You look ghastly, Claire. Come and have a cup of tea with us. We won't disturb her today. I see her son's here.'

Claire nodded and joined them in the little lounge where there was a vending machine with vile tea and packets of even more vile biscuits. There they talked, all three trying to be as cheerful as possible. When they left, the Countess pressed the bag of sponge cake into Claire's hands. 'I'll call some of the other knitters,' she promised, though Claire doubted Mrs Venables was in good enough health to receive them. The two left, Claire gathered herself and her belongings and was all the way down the hall and to the lifts when Nigel caught up with her. 'Are you really going back to the States?'

Claire nodded. 'Probably. I don't know what else to do.'

'It will upset my mother dreadfully, especially now.' The lift arrived and the doors opened. 'May I accompany you?' he asked.

Claire nodded again. He was oddly formal, and for the first time it occurred to Claire that what she had always seen as arrogance might just be social awkwardness. She herself knew plenty about that. When they got out of the lift Nigel looked around. There was nowhere to sit except the uncomfortable benches in the waiting lounge. 'Do you mind?' he asked. And she shook her head. What was he going to say? she wondered. Accuse her of stealing his mother's watch or rifling her purse?

But instead he sat down across from her, his hands hanging limply from his knees and his head bowed. He started to say something but, instead of his usual incisive tone, he was mumbling. Claire didn't catch what he said and had to interrupt him.

He looked across the empty space between them. His eyes were very, very blue like his mother's. 'I said that I may have been guilty of wronging you. I can't help but blame my mother's condition on overwork, but I don't think you meant her any harm. She's very fond of you and . . . and . . . I believe you're very fond of her. I'm so grateful for the way you've looked after her.' He looked away. 'I've been very busy, quite distracted with my financial affairs and this combined with my worry for her might have led me to overreact.' He looked back at her. 'Anyway, I mean to do my best for her, but that doesn't alter the fact that she is very, very fond of you. Do you really have to go away? I mean, just now, when she's ill?'

With his feelings so obvious, Claire saw him more clearly than ever before. Perhaps she hadn't been quite fair to him either. He had only been a bit too protective. She didn't like him, but she had to admit there was something about his pale intensity that was moving. Still, she didn't believe for one moment that he liked her. He simply needed her.

'I won't be leaving for New York for a few weeks yet. I'll spend as much time as I can with your mother. Not because you asked, but because I like her so very, very much.' Without waiting for his response, Claire rose and left the hospital.

* * *

When Claire got back to her room she was exhausted by the day's events. She was sitting on the edge of the bed to take her shoes off when she saw two envelopes held in place by the bedside lamp. She was relieved to see one was from Abigail, but was filled with apprehension at the sight of Tina's. She decided to save the worst for last.

Thank you for your concern. Brady is just fine, though he truly resents the Elizabethan ruff that he has to wear around his neck. It seems his hip is fine, but he might tear out the stitches if he can get at them and the cone stops that. I feel very sorry for him but very relieved that he's going to be quite well again. The weather here has been astonishingly wet. Isn't it London that's supposed to get all the rain? I look at the Herald Tribune *every day and see that you're getting better conditions than we are. Enjoy them while they last. We haven't had any spring at all.*

I've been busy because of April 15th. I'm not sure if you remember that our fiscal year closes then, though most firms consider that out of date. Anyway, bonuses are about to be distributed and I'm afraid there will be some unpleasant surprises. Young Wainwright's envelope will be very thin, but I hope he has enough brains to be grateful that he has kept a job here at all. The dodgy stock recommendation has luckily blown over but not without a lot of blowing by Mr Crayden and our General Council. A lot of favors were called in.

Claire read the rest quickly. It seemed as if Mr Wonderful did have some imperfections. She couldn't help feeling a stab of pity for him, though however thin his bonus might be, it was certainly more than she had made in her life.

Still, as a golden boy, it would be hard for him to have his reputation or performance criticized in any way.

It was only at the end of the note that Claire focused again.

By the way, the chastened Mr Wainwright was asking about you. He had heard that I might have your address and wanted to know where you were living. I told him that if he had anything to tell you he could give me the envelope and that set him scurrying away. Just wanted you to know I'm not the only one thinking of you.

As if in proof of that, Claire had the letter from Tina right in front of her. She put the thought of Michael Wainwright out of her mind. How or why he had inquired after her was none of her business and irrelevant. It had taken her almost two months to stop thinking of him. Quite an achievement when he had been her obsession for longer than a year. She was grateful Abigail hadn't given him her address. It might have begun a dangerous yearn, an ongoing expectation that she might get a letter from him and then disappointment that she didn't. And what would the point of all that be? They really had nothing to communicate to one another.

Tina, on the other hand, seemed to have quite a bit to tell her.

You were right about Michael Wainwright. He is a total asshole. He broke off his engagement, but he also screwed up here so bad that my bonus was two hundred fifty dollars. Is he fuckin' kiddin' me or what? Me and Marie — Marie Two — are both bat shit. Mike and Junior got into some kind of problem and the firm is really busting their nuts. But why should that affect me? Anthony says I

should tell them to stick it and quit. But I don't
want to work with my mother, even though I have
my cosmetology license. So I hope you're doing
well. Abigail says you're living in an apartment in
some fancy part of London. Maybe me and Tony
could come visit you for our honeymoon! By the
way, did you hear that your mother broke up with
that scumbag, Jerry? He was banging Jessica
O'Connell, the one who was two years ahead of us
in high school. Can you picture that?

The rest of the letter was brief and dull, but the revela-
tions she'd already read were enough to make Claire put
it down and want more than tea to drink. Michael
Wainwright and Katherine Rensselaer had also split?
Somehow the uncouplings made it seem as if her world
back in New York had changed dramatically.

But it really hadn't, Claire told herself. Neither one had
to do with her. Couples came and couples went but she,
solitary, would go on. Even if it was back in New York.

SIXTY-TWO

Despite the uncertainty of her situation, Claire's schedule was busier than it had ever been. It seemed that she spent every moment she could at the hospital and the rest helping Maudie at the Patels'. Mrs Patel's pregnancy was so advanced that she found it difficult to stoop or even stand for long. Claire found herself doing all of the unpacking and shelf stocking, as well as carrying and breaking down the cardboard boxes that arrived, it seemed, by the dozen every day. It was clear that business had picked up, but Mrs Patel hadn't offered any more money, nor did Claire expect any. The problem was that without anything coming in from her knitting work, the cash that Claire had left was quickly dwindling. It was too bad she hadn't been able to get a refund on the Nice trip. It was clearer every day that her plan to stay on in London had been foolish and it was only a matter of time before she had to return to New York.

On Mrs Venables's eleventh day in hospital, Claire came home a little early from her visit to her, as she was so tired. There was a phone message waiting for her – apparently in the short time since Claire had left, Mrs Venables had been showing sudden signs of great improvement. Claire made her way to the bedroom, barely noticing the boxes and disarray in the rest of the apartment. She sank into bed and it was only the next morning, when she emerged from her room that the significance of the confusion in the living room made an impact. Imogen had begun packing up! The tears that Claire had been holding in check for over a week finally couldn't be restrained and she cried, loudly and very messily.

After she'd mopped up her face, bathed, dressed and forced herself to swallow some tea and toast she felt better. Then she noticed the envelope on the table. It was beside two cartons, half obscured by newspaper and tissue paper. She felt irritation. Couldn't Im leave her mail in her own room? Claire wondered. It wouldn't be too much to ask. But, she supposed it would. Living with a roommate, it seemed, was only slightly better than living with her mother and Jerry. Maybe someday she would have a place of her own.

She could see the letter was from Abigail, whose handwriting had already become familiar.

At last we've gotten some good weather and my flower boxes are thriving. I don't know why everybody here doesn't have flower boxes. They certainly do in London and they must be magnificent. Such a civilized feature.

I must tell you that Michael Wainwright, who has really been through a rough few months, is quite persistent about your address. I have had to be curt with him. But I thought you should know that I have, reluctantly, given it to him. I think he's feeling very sorry for himself right now, but I wouldn't have a thing to do with him until he learns how to feel compassion for others. In his case I'm afraid that might take a few more decades, but I, of course, am pessimistic. Brady continues to recover. When I take him to the park he runs around like a puppy. The surgery has been quite miraculous. If only he were a puppy again. I

cringe when I realize he's twelve years old and that
in the next few years . . . well, the problem with
loving anything is how it eventually dies or leaves
you. Best to be a Buddhist, don't you think?

Claire couldn't believe that Michael ever even thought of her. She wondered if Abigail was exaggerating. Perhaps he wanted her little box back. She picked it up and ran her fingers over the smooth enamel. *When this you see, remember me.* She put it down and decided not to take advice from a box.

She glanced in the mirror, ignoring her pretty knick-knacks and just ran a brush through her hair. She would take the bus to the hospital, see how Mrs Venables was and then come back to straighten out this mess as best she could.

She opened the top drawer of her bureau and took out the envelope of five-pound notes she had stashed there. She counted them carefully, and then she counted them again. Claire shouldn't have paid her mother back because now she couldn't believe how little there was left. If a single ticket to New York was two hundred pounds she had only . . . Claire shuddered. The reality was becoming more and more clear. She would have to pack up, go back to Tottenville and figure out what kind of life – if any – she could build on that Tottering Foundation. Of course, now that Jerry was gone, her mother would welcome her, but it would be only because she was lonely and needed mortgage money. Claire was not foolish enough to believe otherwise and if, by some astonishing chance, another man appeared on Mrs Bilsop's horizon, Claire knew she'd be lucky to keep her room. Perhaps, in time, she could save up and get her own apartment.

Putting thoughts of her future out of her mind, Claire set off for the hospital. As she approached the entrance she found her step quickening. What if Mrs Venables had worsened? What if Imogen – never very attentive to other people's lives – had gotten the message wrong? When she stepped out of the lift she found herself almost running down the hall.

As she came to the corner leading to the neurology ward someone came round it from the opposite direction and they literally bumped one another. Claire dropped her purse, he scrabbled on the floor to pick it up, and as they turned to one another, both of their faces expressed the same surprise. It was Nigel and though Claire still felt coldly toward him, she felt relief flood her.

'Your mother . . .'

'Claire!'

They both stopped speaking. Claire rubbed her shoulder where she had collided with him and watched, with a nasty secret satisfaction, the red spot on his cheek where she had bumped him begin to swell. Nigel handed her purse back to her. 'I've very glad to see you,' he said. And to her astonishment he took her hand. 'Mother has been talking about you without stopping since you left yesterday.'

'Your mother is talking?' Claire asked.

'I can't stop her. The nurses are gob-smacked. Even the neurologist says he hasn't seen progress like this before, at least not in a woman her age. And yesterday evening she wanted knitting needles. Can you believe it?'

Claire nodded. With no one but Nigel to talk to, she would want to distract herself with knitting too. But the news was too wonderful to continue being small-minded. 'Is she awake?' Claire asked.

'The day sister just took her down to physiotherapy. I was going to nip down for a cup of coffee. Care to join me?'

Actually, in her current frame of mind she couldn't think of anything she'd like to do less, but she supposed that, since Nigel was offering an olive branch, she should drink a cup of oil with him.

And the coffee was oily. Though she'd fallen for everything British, Claire had to admit hospital cafés were as bad in London as they were in New York. Nigel had brought a 'white coffee' for her, a black one for himself, and rustled up a plate of biscuits so hard that they could probably be used to scratch their initials on the dusty window beside them. Once he took a chair opposite her at the little corner table an embarrassed silence set in. The main thing they had in common so far was, after all, Mrs Venables.

The silence was getting prolonged and more than simply awkward. 'Do you take sugar? I'm so sorry. I forgot to ask. Shall I get you some?'

Nigel's exaggerated politeness reminded Claire of her theory that he was socially awkward. Of course, as she was too, she found it a most annoying trait.

'Mother can't go back home after discharge,' Nigel announced.

'Found a purchaser for your building?' Claire asked with an insincere smile, then felt guilty when she saw Nigel's face fall. He wasn't really so bad. In fact, he was probably a better son than most. She wondered why he was unmarried; perhaps he too was a homosexual. She had learned to her discomfort that it was something she couldn't judge here.

'As a matter of fact, no. Besides, I can't sell it without Mother's approval. So I think what is going to have to happen is that she goes into special housing, and perhaps a nursing home first for rehabilitation.'

'I can't imagine your mother taking orders from someone else, never mind having to live someplace other than her own flat. She loves it there,' Claire said in Mrs Venables's defense.

'She'll have to accept the change. There's no other choice.' Nigel took a sip of his coffee.

As the gray light that filtered through the grimy window fell on him, he looked aristocratic and, as Claire had noticed before, rather handsome. His fine forehead and pale hair emphasized his eyes, which were as blue as his mother's, and though his lips were thin, he did have an attractive smile – when he chose to smile.

He was trying to smile now. 'She'll adjust to the situation in time.' But as Claire stared at him without a response he gave up. 'Look, I don't expect you to like me; well, perhaps I do but that's just bloody arrogance. I know I've been beastly, and I'm very much ashamed of myself. May I offer a sincere apology?' He looked at her again and now his pale face flushed with what she thought might be embarrassment. The pink set off his eyes. God, she thought, I'm a truly desperate woman when I start to think that Nigel Venables is sexy.

She reached across the table and patted his hand, then withdrew her own. 'Apology accepted,' she said. 'Don't worry about it. You were just being protective.'

'No. I was being an ass. I still don't know much about you but you've been marvelous.'

Claire was more than surprised – she was stunned by Nigel's admission. Her life might not be good, but at least it was interesting, she thought. Far more interesting than it had ever been. Oh, she would hate to give up all of this for a commute on the subway.

'I wanted to thank you for all that you've done for my mother,' Nigel continued. 'She really can't stop talking about you. And she's even eager to get back to the shop. I'm still not sure she'll be able to manage it, but well, is there anything I can . . . do for you?'

Claire looked down at the plate in front of her and then nodded. 'You can find some biscuits that are edible,' she said.

'My dear!' Mrs Venables said from a bed that was surrounded by cards and so many arrangements of flowers that she looked like a mannequin in one of the store window displays in Knightsbridge. She certainly still slurred her words, but she would be understandable to anyone, now, not just Claire. The improvement was overwhelming and Claire went to the old woman's bedside and took her weakened hand in both of her own. 'You look wonderful,' she said. 'Someone's done your hair.'

Mrs Venables nodded. Her blue eyes were bright with mischief, and both of them focused on Claire. 'I tried to do it myself but couldn't manage the hairpins . . . yet. So Nigel helped me.' Claire saw her mouth tremble, but she thought it was with a suppressed laugh rather than a neurological tremor. 'He was quite good. Here is my news. The doctor has told me I can be discharged soon.'

'That's wonderful,' both Claire and Nigel said.

'Yes. I've been lucky. He's going to talk to Nigel. I shall have to have a visiting nurse at first, and more speech and physiotherapy, but I can do quite a lot of it at home. And I'll make Nigel drop his silly idea that I can't manage in the flat.'

'Great. That's great. So why don't you rest now?'

'I will,' she agreed. 'But perhaps you can check the shop. Just to see if there are any inquiries.' The old woman closed her eyes and Claire thought, with a pang, of closing the shop. But of course it would have to be done. As Claire watched Mrs Venables's face go slack with exhaustion she felt her own fatigue overtake her.

'Let me take you home,' Nigel said. 'You live near here, don't you?'

Claire let him take her arm, lead her to the lift and to the taxi rank. He helped her into the cab and she closed her eyes. She must have actually fallen asleep because when she opened her eyes the taxi was turning off the Brompton Road close to the shop. 'I'm two streets down and just to the left,' she said, slightly embarrassed. Nigel was discreetly looking away.

'Oh, good,' he said and tapped the plastic screen between

them and the driver. He gave the direction and they pulled up in front of Imogen's building.

'Thank you very much for the ride,' Claire told him.

He reached across her and opened the door. 'You're very welcome. You mind if I take the taxi on to my office?'

'Of course not,' she said.

'I'll be going back to see my mother this evening. Would you like me to pick you up?'

Claire shook her head. 'I'm just going to run a few errands and then I'll go back this afternoon.'

'Perhaps I'll see you then.'

She smiled and nodded and stepped out of the cab. She waved him off then turned back to the house. It was only then that she noticed a man was standing on the doorstep. His broad back was toward her. For a moment she thought it must be Malcolm, but this man was much taller and his suit fit. Then he turned around. To her utter surprise, it was Michael Wainwright.

SIXTY-THREE

Claire didn't know what to think. She was almost speechless, and rooted to the sidewalk. For a moment she doubted that it could be Michael Wainwright, but as he approached her she knew there was no mistake. There had been a few times when she had thought she had seen him but now it was truly him and he was standing on her doorstep! How did he possibly find her? And what in the world was he doing here? As he got closer she felt panic setting in. Try to act casual, she told herself, though it was the most ridiculous approach.

'Hello, Claire,' he said and took her hand. She had forgotten just how handsome he was.

'Hello, Michael,' she responded. 'What are you doing here? Need something photocopied?' The moment she said it she could have bitten her tongue but it was too late. She saw him recoil.

'I guess that's fair,' he said.

Claire took as deep a breath as she could manage. 'Would you like to come in?' she said.

He looked around. 'Maybe I could take you out,' he suggested. 'For a drink perhaps?'

Claire nodded. 'There's a place around the corner,' she said. It was a posh wine bar and, though it was across from Mrs Venables's shop and just next to the estate agent's, Claire had actually never been in there. She walked a little bit ahead of him so she did not have to look at his face or let him see hers. How had this happened? And what did he want? She tried to gather her wits but found it impossible. Out of the corner of her eye she looked up at him. After all the dreaming, after all the imagined conversations, now that he was here actually beside her, looking better than she remembered, she hadn't a clue what to say.

He opened the door for her and they entered the place. It was early, so there were virtually no customers except a middle-aged man sitting alone at a window table. She and Michael moved to the back without even consulting one another. They sat down and he looked over at her, or perhaps he looked her over. It was hard to tell. 'You don't know how difficult it was to find you,' he said.

'Why were you looking?'

'Well,' he paused and took a deep breath. 'I know you probably won't believe this, and I'm sure you'll blow me off after I say it. Which you'll have every right to do. But the fact is I haven't been able to stop thinking of you since you walked out of the hotel.'

Claire actually laughed out loud. In all the different conversations she'd imagined with Michael, this had never crossed her mind. Not once. 'And am I supposed to believe in Santa Claus?' she said.

A waiter arrived at their table. Without even asking her Michael ordered. 'Two Chablis,' he said.

She interrupted before the waiter could leave. 'As it happens, I don't like Chablis. The house Beaujolais, please,' she said. She was very proud that her voice didn't quaver. She remembered a phrase that Tina used to use when someone back in Tottenville was very full of himself: thinks who the fuck he is. And that was Michael. If he wanted her, of course he could find her. And if he found her he was capable of saying anything. Watch it Claire, she told herself sharply because she felt, despite her cockiness, the old attraction.

Once the waiter had left, Michael looked at her. It seemed he had the grace at least to act ashamed, but she remembered how he had acted when he told her about his 'business dinner' and she couldn't repress a tiny shiver at the memory of the shame of that moment. 'Are you cold?' he asked.

And she remembered, too, how attentive he could be. 'I'm fine,' she told him and tried to say it with enough conviction so that he knew she wasn't only talking about her body temperature. Of course, the trouble was that two weeks ago she was fine. It was only now, after all her recent problems and with her complete uncertainty about her future, that telling him that she was fine was not strictly true.

'Claire, I know I don't even deserve a chance at this conversation,' he said. 'But I hope you'll hear me out.'

The waiter arrived with their wine and she made a noncommittal gesture. Her heart had stopped its crazy pace and she took a swig of wine to try to ensure that she would keep calm. But only a little wine she reminded herself. Too much would be as bad as any other overreaction.

'Okay,' he said. 'To begin with I know I behaved very badly.' He paused. She didn't make a move. 'You saw me with Katherine, didn't you?' She gave as small a nod as she could manage. 'I'm sorry,' he said. 'That was really stupid and wrong.' She shrugged.

'Perhaps,' she said. 'But you were free to do whatever you wanted to do. We had no arrangement. You didn't break your word.' She knew when she said it that she sounded stiff and angry but there was nothing she could do. She was stiff. She was angry.

'Look,' he said. 'I don't expect you to listen to me but I want you to listen anyway. Now, if you tell me to get up and go away, I will, right this minute. But if you don't then I'd just like you to give me three minutes without saying a word.' He took off his watch and placed it on the table. 'Just three minutes,' he repeated. 'What do ya say?'

Claire nodded silently. What could she say? Of course she was far too curious to simply tell him to leave; though she had certainly imagined running into him and turning on her heel herself.

'Let me just tell you what's been happening,' he said. For another moment she thought he was going to launch into a description of business at Crayden Smithers. But thank goodness he didn't. 'When I asked you to come with me to London I was, well, in a bad place. I'd been going out with a few different women and one, well Katherine, was serious. I didn't know what to do, so I behaved like a louse to her and to you. Of course, I didn't know you, so behaving badly was easy.' He looked away from her for a moment. Claire reminded herself that his job at Crayden Smithers was to pitch and he was doing a great pitch right now. And that, she told herself, was all it was.

'The thing is I lost her and I lost you.' Michael raised his hand, showing her his palm. 'Before you say I never had you, I just want you to know that I know that. I was really –' he paused – 'I was really into myself. I mean, everybody on The Street encourages that. And you know I'd had a couple of good years.' She nodded. 'Anyway, I made a couple of mistakes at Crayden Smithers and haven't had a really good follow-up. But that doesn't bother me. What does is that I had time to think and I realized I didn't like what I was thinking. The truth is I backed off on the relationship with Katherine because she didn't really mean very much to me. The window dressing was there – the degree from Harvard Business School and her job and her looks and – well, you know her social background.'

Claire tried not to wince. It was, perhaps, the most difficult conversation she had ever had and that, she realized, was without her doing any of the talking. Dozens of thoughts had come to her mind and words to her lips, but she bit them back.

'But the thing is, I didn't really like her, and I didn't

have a good time when I was with her.' He reached his hand across the table. 'I had a good time with you, Claire.'

She pulled her hand back before he could touch her. Yes, she thought, and I am marrying Prince Harry. She picked her purse up with one hand and lifted his watch with the other. 'Time's up,' she said.

'Give me one more minute,' Michael asked and extended his hand for the watch. His hand brushed hers as she allowed him to take it.

'I don't understand why you're telling me this,' she told him.

'It's because I can't get you out of my mind,' he said. 'I never knew anyone who simply got up and walked out of their life and into a new one. I couldn't stop thinking about that. It was an act of tremendous courage.'

'Or sheer idiocy,' Claire told him.

'I think not,' he said. 'But even if it doesn't work out perfectly, you did something that was completely unprogrammed. I've never done that in my life.' He turned and looked out the window toward the street. Claire could hardly believe it was the same street she had spent so much time observing from its other side. She thought of the hours she'd spent with Mrs Venables, knitting companionably and looking out at the road. It was so symbolic that she couldn't repress an ironic smile. Yes, that was the difference between her and Michael: even when they looked at the same things they looked at them from opposite sides.

'I went to prep school, I played the right sports, I applied to the right universities. I moved on to Wharton, I dated the right girls, I graduated and joined the right firm. I live in the right neighborhood, I go to the right restaurants and I should get engaged to the right girl and move to the right house in Connecticut. Then I'll just procreate and my children will do it all again.'

'Sounds all right to me,' Claire told him.

He turned back to her and Claire was shocked to see

tears in his eyes. 'I know that a white Anglo-Saxon Protestant male with a lot of entitlement doesn't have any right to whine,' he told her. 'And one who's behaved the way I have to you certainly shouldn't be doing it to you. It's just that, well, sleeping with you was . . . different. I knew it then but I ignored it. And being with you was different, too. You were, you are so . . . present. Do you know what I mean?'

She shook her head. If she was Maudie she would ask what rubbish he was going on about, but his unshed tears had made her pay attention. He might have been lying, but if he was, he was doing a mighty good job.

He looked as deeply into her eyes as she would permit before she turned away. 'I have no right to ask you and I'll understand if you say no, but I'm here for a week and I'd really like to see you again. Just see you, that's all.'

She started to shake her head when he stretched out his hand again. 'Just think about it,' he said. He handed her his card, a London phone number scrawled across it. 'I'm at the Berkeley.' He had the good grace to blush. 'Will you think about it?' he asked. 'Please think about it.'

She nodded, though she knew she shouldn't. The waiter came over. 'A refill?' he asked. Claire shook her head.

'I have to go,' she said and managed to stand up. She turned her back on Michael and walked out.

The sunlight and passing traffic caught her unprepared. It felt as if she'd been in the wine bar for hours and it certainly should be nightfall. It was like coming out of the movie theater in the middle of the day, unsettling to leave one world abruptly and enter another.

She walked past the estate agency, paused at the corner and made sure that she was very careful to look both ways before she crossed the road. She was so rattled, she wasn't sure she was seeing straight. What a very bad time for Michael Wainwright to show up. Now, when she had no job, almost no money, no place to live, and no future in

London or New York was not a time she could be rational. If only, she thought, things hadn't gone so badly for Mrs Venables and the shop.

But then, as she looked up, she saw that Knitting Kitting was decked with pieces of taped-up paper. It looked as if the store had been toilet papered. But as she got to the shop window she saw that each of the papers fluttering against the glass was a note. *'No one was here for my class.'* *'Are you accepting new students?'* *'Has the time of operation changed?'* *'I need help with blocking . . .'*

Claire carefully took each one down and folded them together. It was incredible. She and Mrs Venables, they had been missed. More than that, some of the notes were angry. They were needed! And, she reminded herself, these were only the notes from the people who had been motivated enough to leave one. Others might have dropped by to shop, gossip or knit. Her hand trembled as she got out the key. To her stupefaction, when she opened the door there were another dozen more notes stuffed under it. She gathered them up, closed the door behind her and put the lights on. After careful consideration Claire put a large sign in the window of Knitting Kitting that said 'CLASS TOMORROW AS SCHEDULED'.

She didn't notice Michael Wainwright, across the street, in front of the wine bar, watching her.

SIXTY-FOUR

The following morning Claire went to the shop for seven. She had not consulted with or asked permission of either Mrs Venables or Nigel to do so but felt that some response to the loyal following they had created was necessary. She would explain to those who didn't know about Mrs Venables's illness, teach what she could and leave her number for women who required more help. For she could help them, at least until she left. Exactly when that would be she wasn't sure since, although she had set a date for the wedding, Imogen had not yet announced (or probably even determined) the day she would move out. So there could be one more farewell class.

Nigel had called to tell her that Mrs Venables would be released from the hospital on Monday. It had taken a few extra days to complete her assessment, since she had begun to progress so rapidly. Apparently, though she would need assistance at first, the medical staff expected she would be able to become self-sufficient once more, or at least close enough to it so that she would require only a little bit of help – even that might not be for long. Claire was relieved not only for Mrs Venables but also for herself. Although the doctor had reassured her that the classes had not caused Mrs Venables's illness, she had still felt guilty. But in the end, the damage was minimal.

Claire unlocked the doors early but was unprepared just

the same. The first wave of women were in before nine. She helped several women increase the jumpers they were working on, helped Mrs Willis set in a shoulder, taught Charlotte and her friends to cast off and pick up for button holes, turned heels on two pairs of socks for Julie Watts and was exhausted by eleven – when the second wave hit big time. Claire carried on: picking up stitches, deciphering patterns, advising on yarns, and continued with many of the morning class's problems straight into the afternoon, when the third wave hit, and continued past three o'clock. Then what with people picking up special orders, boxes of stock needing to be unpacked, and new purchases of both wool and needles, Claire had no time for even a tea break, much less a minute to think about Michael Wainwright.

In addition to helping with the difficulties and technical questions the women brought to her, Claire had to make apologies for the missed classes, explain about Mrs Venables's illness, accept sympathy and break the news that the shop would close.

This was greeted in several different ways. Some women were sad and made their sadness obvious. Others seemed to maintain their English cool. But, to her surprise, more than a handful of women became angry and outraged. 'Ridiculous,' snapped Mrs Lyons-Hatchington. 'Where will I come to knit? This is an excellent location. There's no reason for Mrs Venables to shut down. She has you to manage things.' And her friend, Mrs Cruikshank, dropped not just a stitch but the entire jumper she was working on when she heard the news. 'I can't believe it,' she said. 'This has been such a satisfying endeavor. I shall not allow it.'

Claire smiled. Some of these women were so imperious, either because of their husbands' positions or their own business or social success. They were used to getting what they wanted. Their reactions were difficult to deal with but she had handled them and, in this, Claire found two kinds of satisfaction: She herself was wanted, a useful and appreciated commodity; and, in a contrary way, she enjoyed being able to give them 'no' for an answer. No, Mrs Venables would not continue. No, nor would she. No, the shop would not stay open. No, she wouldn't give lessons elsewhere – as if they would come *en masse* to Camden and take tea in Mrs Patel's back room! For without a place to live, it was foolish for her to even consider continuing. Then she smiled some more, assisted everyone, expressed regrets, answered questions, wrapped packages, and at the end of the day closed the shop up.

As she put the keys in her purse, Leonora Atkins hurried up. She hadn't been to class and Claire assumed she needed some help or some merchandise. 'Oh. I'm sorry. I've just closed up,' Claire said. 'But if you need something I can . . .'

'I need to talk to you,' Leonora told her. 'Why don't I just walk along with you? You live nearby don't you?' Claire nodded.

'I know that when we talked about another knitting shop you weren't interested. But I've done some research since, and I've come up with a good place to get some capital from. I just thought that with Mrs Venables's situation you might be reconsidering . . .'

Claire shook her head. It wouldn't be fair to Mrs Venables – it would feel like cashing in on her misfortune. And she didn't have the emotional resources for this kind of enterprise now, anyway.

Claire must have shown some of her feelings because Leonora smiled and shook her head. 'Of course, I didn't really mean for you to think about it now. I know how . . . involved you are. But I'd hate to see someone else take advantage of a market niche. This would be so right for you. And lucrative.' When Claire said nothing Leonora shrugged. 'Just a thought,' she added. 'As a friend.' They had come to a corner. 'I have to go north here,' she said as if she felt that her deal had gone south. Claire shrugged.

'See you soon,' Claire said and turned away.

It was only then that she had time to think about Michael Wainwright, but not much. She had to talk to Mrs Patel. Without even stopping at home to wash or change she walked to the tube to go to Mrs Patel's. Only when she was seated on the Piccadilly Line for the long run, did she have a chance to consider Michael's offer. It seemed like weeks since their encounter, but it was only yesterday. She had only four or five days before he left. While she had nothing to lose by seeing him again, she also had nothing to gain. A few dinners, a night or two at the Berkeley? His flirting and attention would be more than pleasant, but where would it leave her in the end? Claire wasn't just concerned about her dignity. She remembered the long and painful process of recovering from his behavior and the emptiness it had left – an emptiness that still resonated. She certainly didn't need that kind of pain again. But as she changed trains she remembered how his body had felt next to her own.

Only the thought of Mrs Patel soothed her. She wasn't going there to work or fulfill an obligation today, but because she felt Mrs Patel would understand and speak to her condition in a way that no one else could. After all, she'd stood up to a man and made a life for herself.

The moment she walked into the shop she knew her instincts were right. Mrs Patel took one look at Claire's face, finished giving change, ushered the customer out and locked the door behind Claire. 'What is it? Has she died? But she was doing so well.'

'No, no. Mrs Venables leaves hospital on Monday afternoon.'

'Then what is it? You must sit down. You don't look well.'

'You're the one who ought to sit down,' Claire said, looking at Mrs Patel's swollen ankles.

'Oh, I've been sitting down all day. Maudie did everything. Never you mind. What's up?' Claire hesitated, but

Mrs Patel was clearly going to be implacable. 'Come on now, you'll have to blow the gaff.'

Claire looked at her curiously.

'Spill the peas or whatever they say,' Mrs Patel encouraged.

Claire sat on a box and put her head in her hands. She managed to tell Mrs Patel the whole long story of Michael, ending with the conversation at the wine bar.

'That takes the biscuit. So he's the reason you came to London?' Claire nodded. 'And once you walked out you never saw him or heard from him?' Claire nodded again. For some reason her throat had closed up. She felt ready to cry. But she was over him. She knew she was. 'And now he's back?' Mrs Patel narrowed her eyes. 'Oh, he's a clever dick. Very, very sly. It took him this long to see your virtues? Thick as a plank, isn't he?'

Claire almost laughed, despite her tight throat. 'You don't understand. In New York I'm nothing. I was a clerk in an office. I really . . .'

'You really underestimate the effect you have on people,' Mrs Patel said. 'You are not just anyone, you know.' Claire blinked. In fact she felt that she *was* just anyone, but perhaps a little duller. Mrs Patel sniffed. 'Why do you think he came back to you? For the same reason Lak kept coming back to me: because we are so good, so sure of what we do, that it's irresistible and irritating to them because they are neither. Do you know why Lak hit me? Really?' Claire, fascinated but horrified, shook her head. 'He was envious. Yes, it sounds mad, but it's true. I could do so many things that he couldn't. He tried to convince me that I was stupid.' Mrs Patel laughed, but it wasn't because it was funny. 'At first I believed him, but I came to see it was only that he was stupid. Well, not stupid perhaps, but slow. There were many things I didn't know, but I could learn them. How could he learn when he couldn't admit that he didn't know everything? He had always been treated like a prince in his family. Then he came here, to London and to me. It was hard to learn that he was not so excellent, really not very important at all. I was faster, I was stronger, and I was braver. It's a woman's burden.'

Claire thought of Michael Wainwright. There was a certain logic to Mrs Patel's world-view. Hadn't Michael found out he wasn't so special, so excellent at everything he did? And hadn't Michael told her he admired her courage, or something like that? Claire shook her head as if it would help her to wake up.

'Don't you disagree with me,' Mrs Patel said, misunderstanding Claire's gesture. 'I've been married to a lunatic. I know what I know.' She raised her hand and waggled her finger at Claire the way she sometimes did at Devi. 'Don't you go on pretending you don't know how special you are. It isn't attractive.' She paused, putting her hands on her belly. 'So what will you do about this ridiculous man?'

'I don't know,' Claire admitted. 'I think it's probably best if I don't call him. But I am tempted to. Anyway, I thought I'd talk to you.'

Mrs Patel folded her arms with satisfaction. 'Very good idea,' she said. 'But why not call him?'

Claire paused. Had Mrs Patel been listening to her whole story? 'Because he hurt me,' Claire admitted. 'And because I don't trust him.'

'Well, in that you are wise. There is no reason to trust him. But remember, he did not really know you and everyone – especially men – makes mistakes. I don't think it was wrong of me to give Lak another chance. But so many chances, that was dim. Of course, he was the father of my children and that is quite a different thing.' Mrs Patel narrowed her eyes again. 'I think here you can take the chance to be hurt, especially if you are on your guard. And there is a great deal to benefit from, if he is telling the truth.' She sat down. 'Now here's something I'll tell you. You don't pretend his behavior didn't happen. After Lak begged to come home the first time we both pretended. This man has hurt you, perhaps as much as Lak hurt me. So you tell him what you suspect he is. And add that if you see him he must provide assurances. He must give you tokens of good faith in behavior and goods.'

For a moment Claire thought she might have been transported to a souk in Pakistan. Good faith in behavior and goods? She pictured Michael rolling out a silk rug with a flourish and almost laughed aloud. 'What do you mean?'

'What I mean is you must ask him his intentions. Of course, it will be better if a male in the family would do it for you but you can do it yourself. You must ask him: does he mean to take care of you and protect you? If he does, how will he show it? You have a right to know before you make any decision.'

The logic and audacity of this made Claire's eyes open wide. 'Just ask him?' she said.

'Why not? That's the first step. You know, for thousands of years marriages were arranged by families.'

'But we're not talking about . . .'

'Of course you are. You aren't talking about a brief affair are you? Or even a long one, wasting your time. You must find out his intentions. But then you must see if his behavior indicates they are sincere. He must make up for the wrong he has done you. Is he proposing marriage? He had better be.'

'But he barely knows me,' Claire protested.

'He knows you well enough to travel all across the ocean to see you. And what good does knowing somebody do? You think you know somebody for twenty years and find out they're not trustworthy. But if they tell you they will be trustworthy and they give you assurances in behavior and goods, then you can begin to trust.'

There was a mad logic to it all that fascinated Claire. 'What goods?' she asked.

'Perhaps a ring, for a start. Or a place to live.'

'Are you crazy? I should ask him for a place to live?'

'Don't you need one?'

Mrs Patel had gone too far. 'But we only spent four days together,' Claire reminded her.

'Four hours, four days, four years, four decades. You gave yourself to him. Does this count for nothing? I don't know that he will be able to keep his word. Choices like this are always a gamble. So, to help make your decision you must know what assurances he can provide. They cannot be easy ones. If he is rich, and you say he is, then he must give you very rich gifts. And if his family is substantial he must certainly take you to them.'

Claire shook her head. 'He wouldn't. Ours is a different culture,' she said.

'Oh, don't pretend we are discussing yogurt,' Mrs Patel said. 'With men and women it is always the same. All stories are the same story. Love and honor or betrayal and disgrace. What else is there to consider?'

There was a knocking on the door. One of the regular customers stood outside pointing to his wrist.

'Ah. It's Mr Jepson. He must have his eggs.' Mrs Patel sighed. She got up to open the door and patted Claire on the shoulder. 'You think about this, missy.'

They got busy then, and there was dinner with Devi, Safta and Fala. Claire helped close up, but she did think about it all the way home.

SIXTY-FIVE

On Monday afternoon, Claire made sure she was at the hospital long before Mrs Venables was to be discharged. In fact, she was there before Nigel was. Mrs Venables was already up and dressed but her things still had to be packed up. Claire busied herself with that while the physiotherapist came to make a brief report. 'We've made a great deal of progress,' she said. Claire winced at the 'we' but was grateful for the news. 'Here's the report and her prescriptive advice. The address of the clinic is right here, but if it's difficult for her to get there . . .'

'It won't be,' Mrs Venables said clearly, though with some effort – too much talking still exhausted her.

Not recognizing a put-down when she heard it, the woman turned and smiled. 'See how well we're doing,' she exclaimed. Claire couldn't tell if Mrs Venables shook her head in a gesture of disapproval or if she had a tremor. Either way, Claire was relieved when the therapist left, trailing 'we-we's behind her.

'You're all packed,' Claire told her friend. 'Shall we sit by the window until Nigel arrives?'

Mrs Venables looked at her. 'Do you like him better now?' she asked. This time Claire was surprised by the question as well as the enunciation. Before she could answer Nigel walked in. He kissed his mother who, Claire noticed, raised her cheek to receive his greeting. She really had improved very quickly and for that Claire was deeply grateful. Even though she would, most likely, have to leave London, she didn't want to have to think of Mrs Venables alone and unwell. Then she realized that, of course, Mrs Venables wouldn't be alone – she had Nigel. He was tucking his mother's throw around her, ready to push the wheelchair. Suddenly, Claire felt unnecessary. After all, they'd been friends for only a couple of months. It was her son, her own flesh and blood that she depended on. When the doctor arrived with release forms he spoke only to Nigel. Claire, to look busy, did a once-over, checking the drawers and under the bed. Then they were ready.

'I have a car waiting,' Nigel assured them.

Claire walked beside Nigel, holding the two small bags she had packed. She helped him get Mrs Venables into the passenger side of the back seat, and watched as he stowed things in the boot. 'Shall I sit beside my mother?' he asked.

Claire thought of his long legs and the discomfort of sitting in the middle where there was so little room but perhaps it would be pushy of her to suggest that she sit beside Mrs Venables, so she let him in first and got in beside him.

'This must be very tiring for you,' Claire said to the older woman. 'You'll be back to your flat in no time.'

Mrs Venables simply nodded and leaned deeper into the seat. Nigel took her hand. 'You've both been a great comfort to me,' Mrs Venables murmured and closed her eyes.

Then, to Claire's complete surprise, Nigel moved his other hand and put it on her own. Claire froze; it was such an unlikely gesture that she did not know how to respond. So she sat there, her face still turned to the window, her hand limply in his. When the car swerved at a roundabout the movement gave her a diplomatic opportunity to pull away. She snuck a sidelong look at Nigel and thought that he looked as relieved as she felt.

When they arrived at the shop it wasn't terribly difficult

to get Mrs Venables out of the car but once she was on her feet she objected to going in through the separate door to the flat and instead insisted on entering through the shop. She walked through the shop, lurching a little, Nigel at her elbow. She touched a skein of wool here and patted the table there. It was clear that she was delighted to be back. But the stairs weren't easy. In the end, Nigel simply scooped his mother up and, despite her weak protests, carried her up to her flat above. Claire, surprised yet again, followed close behind them, holding tight to the banister in case he should falter. But he didn't.

Once upstairs, Nigel introduced them to Mrs Britten, the home nurse that he had engaged. She quickly took over, settled Mrs Venables into bed and then joined them. 'She'll need a bit of a sleep now. She's quite exhausted,' Mrs Britten told them. Claire was exhausted herself. 'I'll sit beside her in case she needs anything,' Mrs Britten continued. Then, to Claire's delight, she took a knitting bag from her things beside the door. Claire felt it was a sign that all would be well.

Nigel, in the meantime, had disappeared into the kitchen, emerging with a pot of tea. Were there no limits to the surprises today? Claire wondered. 'Would you like a cup?' he asked. Claire nodded and the two sat awkwardly side by side on the sofa.

'She has good color,' Claire said.

'Yes, I thought so too.'

'And she spoke to me very fluently this morning.'

Nigel put down his cup. 'Oh, really? What did she say?'

Claire thought of Mrs Venables's odd question and colored. She couldn't repeat it. 'That she was feeling perfectly well. And she put the smarmy therapist in her place.'

'Well, that's good news. Her spirit hasn't been impaired.' He turned to face Claire. 'I know we have already taken up a great deal of your time, but I wonder if you'd be free for dinner this evening?'

Claire stared, then caught herself. 'I'm sorry,' she said. 'I have a dinner engagement.' She was invited to Toby's loft.

'Of course you do.' Nigel rose, though they had hardly sipped the tea. She felt dismissed, but remembered her theory that he was, perhaps, as extremely bad at social niceties as she was. And he did, indeed, recover himself. 'Well, how about tomorrow?'

Claire didn't have the courage to say no again, though it meant missing the Patels. 'Yes. I'll be back here tomorrow afternoon to see your mother,' she said. 'And afterwards, well, that would be fine.' She looked at the clock and realized she'd be late for Toby if she didn't leave immediately. 'I do have to go,' she said.

'Of course,' he said. He reached into his pocket. For one horrible moment she thought he might offer her money as Michael Wainwright once had. But he took out a set of keys and handed it to her. 'Here. To the flat. For whenever you need them.'

Dinner at Toby's was very interesting. She had avoided him more than a little since it had become clear that his interest in her was platonic at best. But she had never been to the flat before, and she was curious. Once there, she was taken aback by how very different it was from the bookstore below. Toby had renovated the two upper floors and turned them into an airy loft-like space with a sleeping gallery on top and a kitchen tucked away below it. The rest was open and two stories high, modern and white and neat as a pin. When she arrived Thomas was helping Toby prepare the salad. Six places had been set and champagne was chilling. 'I haven't really celebrated Imogen's upcoming nuptials,' Toby explained. 'This ought to do it.'

Claire nodded but looked with apprehension at the sixth place setting. As she feared, Edward arrived. Lord, for a young woman with so few social options, she seemed to be awash with unwanted men. Edward, Michael, Nigel. It almost made her feel nostalgic for her solitary bread and cheese in Mrs Watson's dingy digs.

After Edward greeted them all Claire turned to Toby and, behind Edward's back, rolled her eyes. Toby shrugged, while Thomas gave her a wicked grin. She couldn't blame this on him, though. It was clearly Imogen's and Toby's handiwork.

Malcolm and Im joined the group. 'Ah! Harry Champers,' Imogen said, eyeing the iced champagne. Toby poured some out and after general conversation everyone inquired about Mrs Venables's health. After a quick report from Claire they went on to the business of drinking, chatting and eating.

Claire kept a covert eye on Toby. She couldn't get over the fact that she had completely missed the indicators that he was gay. This was the first time she had seen him since she found out, apart from when he came to the hospital, and she had been too exhausted and anxious then to give much thought to the subject. Of course, to her all English men with the possible exception of lorry drivers and soccer hooligans seemed a bit . . . sensitive compared to Americans. But here, in his own setting – and perhaps with the influence of Thomas beside him – Toby's sexual preference was unmistakable. Looking down at her plate, Claire blushed.

And as if that wasn't enough, Edward's awkward attentions brought up unwanted memories of Michael Wainwright's grace and charm. Mrs Patel's words came back to her. 'Tokens of good faith in behavior and goods.' Claire looked around the table and wondered at the reactions of each of the diners should she tell them about Michael, and Mrs Patel's suggested strategy. Thomas, no doubt, would hoot. Imogen would tell her to ignore the louche American and focus on Edward – the good catch. Edward would be downcast, but probably no more than he would be if his old school rugby team lost to Harrow. Malcolm would grin and elbow her. Only Toby might come up with something useful, perhaps from some novel. She would talk to him alone, she decided, if Thomas gave her the opportunity.

But the opportunity didn't present itself and, to her dismay, Claire found herself, despite her best efforts, once again seated beside Edward in his car. 'Shall I drop you in South Ken, or shall we go for a bit of a ride?' he asked.

'Well, I can't drive,' Im said. 'I've had one over the eight, I think. Another and I'll shoot the cat.'

Shoot the cat? She supposed it meant throw up. Though it was a funny phrase, the thought of vomiting made Claire a little queasy. She'd drunk her share of champagne but the prospect of yet more time with Edward was enough to sober her. 'Oh, I can't,' she said. 'I have to be up early to visit Mrs Venables.'

'Ah, of course. You are an angel. Well, I'll just drop you home.'

That night as she tried to sleep, Edward's comment came back to her again and again. It echoed Michael's calling her that, his voice so full of tenderness it was still hard to disbelieve its sincerity. She could almost hear him. After an hour of tossing she got up, went to the phone and dialed the Berkeley.

SIXTY-SIX

When Claire came out of her room on Tuesday morning Imogen was up and lounging in her pajamas. 'No work?' Claire asked.

'All work and no shopping makes Imogen a hostile girl,' Im announced. 'Anyway, I have to put together something roughly like a trousseau before Mother takes me shopping next weekend – you know what a fiasco *that* will be.' Claire had to nod. Shopping with her own mother created fiasco after fiasco, though she was sure that, unlike her own mother, Mrs Faulkner would never try to press a Wonderbra on Imogen. 'I've made a pot of tea,' Imogen told her. 'Oh, do sit down. Tell me what Edward said to you? He's quite besotted. Do you really not like him? Malcolm tells me he's got absolutely tons of cash stashed away in Jersey and the Caymans.'

Claire laughed and shook her head. She poured herself a cup of tea and sat down beside her friend. 'Immy,' she said, using the diminutive that Malcolm and her family used but Claire had never yet dared. 'I'm going to have to go back to New York. I'm afraid I won't be able to take the flat.'

'Oh, that's a shame. Is everything all right at home?'

For a moment Claire longed to tell her that everything at home was all wrong. But what was the point? 'Nobody's ill. It isn't like that. I just . . . well, I don't have a real job anymore and I really can't get one without papers. I won't be able to get those, which means I can't afford the flat, even though I love it.' Claire felt her lips tremble, but she'd cover it. 'I'll just have to go back,' she said.

Her effort was wasted. Imogen, of course, didn't notice how upset she was and instead thought of the impact the news had on her. 'But I wanted you to come to my wedding,' she said. 'And are you sure there isn't, well, someone back home you miss? Some man.'

Claire shook her head. Recovered her composure and smiled. 'Actually,' she said, 'the man I rather fancy is here in London. I'm having dinner with him tonight.'

'Oh! Aren't you sly? I knew there had to be someone. So? When do I get to meet him? Are you going back to the States with him?'

'I don't know,' she told Imogen and then, because she simply couldn't help it, her whole history with Michael Wainwright poured out. By the time she finished telling about the meeting in the wine bar, Imogen was completely entranced.

'I'd be cheesed off, I can tell you. But it does sound so romantic,' she said. 'I could sell it as a novel in a minute. So, what are you going to do?'

'That's just it,' Claire admitted. 'I have no idea.'

'Well,' Imogen said, 'I certainly do. You're obviously mad about him and he's come all this way because he's mad about you.'

Claire shook her head. 'I'm not so sure,' she said. 'He might just be here on business and have decided to look me up. He plays well with others but he's no good on his own. And he's just dumped his fiancée – or she dumped him. He might only be rebounding.'

'Somehow I doubt that.' Imogen launched into the story of how she 'pulled' Malcolm, and a few of the blokes she had gone out with before. 'It's rather a game, Claire,' she summed up. 'It's too bad, but you have to play it. Once you make them think that you have better things to do, they come back and just want to sit on your lap and purr. Look at Edward. A dozen women have tried for him. You show no interest and you could reel him in.'

Claire shook her head again but Im continued. 'If you want this Michael it's your best chance. You know how it is with a cat: they only come to you when you're reading the paper and then they lie all over it, begging for your attention. It seems you've read the paper long enough and now he's begging for your attention.'

'Oh, I don't want anyone on those terms,' Claire protested. 'Anyway, once I do pay attention he's likely to . . .' she thought of the English term. 'He's likely to just piss off and, well, I'll be . . .'

'You're not going to let that happen. Not if you want him. All you have to do is play hard to get. For god's sake, meet him in the bar but be there with another man. Tell you what, I'll let you borrow Malcolm. That'll fox him good and proper. And then you introduce them and excuse yourself.'

So that's exactly what she did.

'The lady would like the sole and I'll have the prawns,' Michael told the waiter. He looked across the table at Claire. 'Are you sure you don't want a starter?' Claire shook her head and smoothed the lap of her dress. She and Imogen had gone to Harvey Nichols and spent the entire morning shopping for something for Claire to wear to dinner. They had decided, at last, on a simple Anna Sui, in a shocking cerise with a pattern of leaves. Then she bought heels – very high ones – in the same insane color. And Imogen had bought her a pair of earrings that were far too sparkly but, Claire had to admit, were perfect for Vong's.

She had visited Mrs Venables after she got back from her shopping with Im and then raced home to put on her new finery.

The restaurant was just around the corner from the hotel and very busy. Claire, surprised to find she was now a perfect size ten, almost felt at home in her new clothes but wasn't the slightest bit interested in the menu or the food. She simply wanted to look at Michael and to watch him drink her in.

When they had met in the Berkeley's bar she had watched him react, both to her looks and to Malcolm, who seemed to enjoy playing his role. After Claire had kissed Malcolm goodbye and sent him off to have dinner with Imogen, Michael had taken her arm almost possessively. And she knew she must look good because when they got to Vong's she had been fussed over by the maître d' as if she was somebody. Clothes might not make the man, but they certainly help a woman, she thought. The unfairness of life had never been lost on her but today, with a new lipstick, a lot of mascara and the perfect outfit, she felt as if the score might be evened up a bit.

'What would you like to drink?' Michael asked. 'I won't be an ass and assume that I know. It seems that there are a lot of things I assumed about you, all of them wrong.' His eyes flicked over her.

Claire merely smiled. 'Would you mind a Chardonnay?' she asked. 'We're both having fish.' It was the only white wine she knew but it sounded knowledgeable and Michael seemed only too happy to comply.

There was an awkward pause while they waited for service. Claire, thinking of the advice from both Mrs Patel and Imogen, tried hard not to break the silence or make it easy for Michael. After all, why should she? He certainly hadn't made it easy for her.

'Well, what have you been doing?' Michael asked. She dared to look at him. Handsome devil. But he did seem somehow, just a little less . . . smooth? Secure? 'Are you working over here? And who was that Malcolm?'

Claire looked down to hide her smile of pleasure and

the cerise of her lap gave her confidence. 'I've actually found work I really like.' She told him a little bit about the shop, the classes, and Mrs Venables. 'The nicest part is how much I enjoy it. It doesn't really feel like work. I like the teaching, selecting the stock, putting out the wools. It's all fun.' She made it a point *not* to tell him that the shop was going to close. She talked for a little while about some of the more interesting customers and how she had started the classes.

'Ingenious,' Michael said. 'I'm always reading about young socialites going to hen parties where they crochet or something. Knitting seems to be the "it" thing, the book circles of the new millennium. You hopped on a hot trend.'

Claire shrugged. 'I've been knitting since I was a kid,' she said. She couldn't help looking at him again. His skin had a wonderful color – darker than pale but lighter than one of those permanent suntans. Despite any setback in love or business, he seemed to have a healthy glow, and his hair had the shine of a well-cared-for pet. He actually looked more handsome than ever with that slightly anxious look in his eyes. Sternly, she told herself not to appreciate these things, though she couldn't deny to herself that they moved her. She looked down at his hand – near hers on the table. She remembered how it had felt on her body. Then she thought of Mrs Patel's advice.

While they ate dinner she asked him about Crayden Smithers. He filled her in very generally. No mention of the problems that Abigail had written of. She managed to finish her fish before she asked, in a voice as neutral as she could manage, 'And how is Katherine Rensselaer?'

He had the good grace to flush a bit. 'I told you,' he said. 'We don't see each other now.'

They ordered dessert, though Claire was feeling a little bit sick to her stomach. It wasn't until the profiteroles arrived that Michael addressed the real reason they were there.

He leaned forward and tried to take her hand, but she gently pulled it back. 'Look, Claire. I'm sure you despise me. But even if you never speak to me again I want to thank you for giving me this chance to talk with you. I've already told you that I know I made a mistake and that I can't get you out of my mind. You're so . . . individualistic. You're not like anyone else I know.'

Claire shrugged. 'I'm sure you haven't met anyone like me,' she said. 'I don't think you move in Staten Island circles.'

'Come on, Claire. That isn't fair. I know Tina and I've met plenty of her friends. I'm not saying anything against her, but I am saying that you're nothing like her and my guess is you're not much like any of the other girls you grew up with. The fact is, Claire, you are a very special person.'

Claire thought of the conversation she had had with Mrs Patel. Could she be right? She reminded herself that Michael might say this to every one of the women he went out with. After all, every woman wanted to be special, and being special in Michael Wainwright's eyes would make you very special indeed. But, 'Thank you, Michael,' she said. And she meant it. Even if she was just another girl that Michael pursued, she still felt somewhat honored, if only to be a notch on his belt. As long as she didn't let him get under her skin, she told herself, she would be just fine.

And then Claire asked the question that all women want an answer to, an answer most men are so inadequate at giving. 'What is it about me that's so . . . well, that makes you think I'm special?'

Michael didn't even pause. 'Your courage. You gave yourself to me. I know that now, and you didn't hold back. Then you walked away to start a new life without any safety net. And look at the work and the people you've already found. I've been back and forth to London for two decades but in two months you seem to have made more friends and done more authentic things than I . . .' he paused. 'You're generous, Claire. You're not like most of the people I know, always selfish, always playing the angles.'

He looked down at his untouched pudding. 'I want to tell you something else,' he said. 'I spoke with Abigail Samuels.'

Claire blinked. She tried to remember exactly what she'd written to Abigail about her feelings for Michael and for a moment she panicked. But Abigail was her friend, she reminded herself. Surprised to hear this new development she was also interested. 'About what?' Claire asked.

'About you. When I asked for your address, well, it wasn't altogether pleasant.' Claire allowed herself to smile. She imagined that a conversation with Abigail could be very unpleasant indeed. 'Anyway,' Michael said and flashed her a bit of his old grin, 'she read me the riot act. She told me what kind of idiot I am and she had it pretty accurate.'

His grin dissolved and he looked away. For a moment Claire felt sorry for him. Abigail would not have minced words. 'Anyway, she wouldn't give me your address until I promised her that I was serious about you. And even then I could tell she wasn't crazy about doing it.' He shrugged and looked back at Claire. 'I know I haven't behaved well, and I've been spoiled all my life. But the fact is, Claire, I've had a lot of time to think. This tough financial climate and my . . . well, my poor performance, made me feel for the first time as if I was . . . vulnerable. No one can keep a winning streak running forever. I don't want to go Buddhist on you, but even if you're young and healthy and success-ful, in the end you're going to lose everything. Death evens things out. And I don't want to go through life or face my death without somebody beside me that I can trust and love. I know I haven't been worthy of trust, but I swear that I can be trusted now. You know how well I focus on work when I want to. Well, now I'd like to focus on some-thing else. At least part of the time. I'd like to focus on being with you.' He took a deep breath. 'Would you consider going back to New York with me?'

The offer wasn't something Claire was prepared for. She expected he would, perhaps, apologize some more and then . . . well, maybe want her to sleep with him. Maybe even ask her away for a weekend – one of his favorite strategies. But not that he would want her to go back to New York with him. What did that mean?

'I know you've been making a life here,' he said. 'I saw you in the shop. Of course, I didn't know that you were working there but, well, despite your friends, that Malcolm or whoever you're seeing, do you think that you might want to come back?'

Claire thought of the reality she was facing. In a way it was completely unfair to let Michael think she'd been successful. But she wasn't exactly lying, she told herself. Imogen would definitely approve. He was assuming things and she simply wasn't correcting him. It was time, she decided, for her to speak.

'Michael, I don't want you to believe that I haven't thought about you. I've thought about you very often. But I knew, even before I saw you in the bar with Katherine, that you didn't take me seriously and you never would.'

He began to speak but she put up a hand and he stopped himself. 'You don't owe me anything,' she said. 'In fact, I owe you a great deal. I never would have gotten here to London if not for you. And this trip has meant a tremendous amount to me. I have changed my life. You're right about that. But you were the catalyst and I'll always be grateful.'

She looked at him and trembled. If he simply bent forward now and kissed her, could she go on in this calm way? Or would she stand up like a mesmerized rabbit and follow him to his room – or any other place else he wanted to take her? He was so handsome, so perfect, that even with him sitting just across from her telling her how he cared so much for her, Claire found it impossible to really believe. Was that because it wasn't true or because she couldn't accept the idea?

Once again, she thought of Mrs Patel. It was insane, but the only way she could begin to judge him was using Mrs Patel's method. Imogen's strategies only went so far. 'Michael, I'm a surprisingly serious person. I'm not really good at dating or social events or office politics. I used to think it was a flaw of mine but now that I've found another way to live, I just accept it. It's the way I am.' She shrugged. 'If we ever were together I'd be useless to you in your career. I'm not good at parties.'

'That's not what I'm looking for,' Michael said.

'So, what exactly are you looking for?'

'You. Just you.'

If she was the butter in the little pot on the table she'd have melted, but she steeled herself. 'I'm afraid that's not enough information. I really can't afford to get involved with you unless . . .' she took a deep breath. 'The fact is, unlike you, I have no family to watch out for me. My dad is dead. My mom isn't really . . . well, she isn't really very involved. So I've had to make my way alone and . . .' she knew she was stammering. Mrs Patel would expect her to be stronger than this. But she felt even more awkward than she had imagined she would. Before she could begin again Michael interrupted.

'I know about our social backgrounds and the differences there, but I don't care.'

She bridled. 'That's not the point,' she said. 'The point is I have to ask you what your intentions are.' She blushed. This certainly wasn't following Imogen's rules.

'My intentions?' Michael repeated then paused. 'My intentions are to ask you to come back to New York and to live with me. Isn't that clear? I didn't come all the way to London or wait all this time in my hotel room just to ask you out for dinner.'

Claire literally dropped her fork. Michael was inviting her to live with him? As far as she knew he had never done that with any of the women he had dated. Still, she didn't think it measured up to Mrs Patel's tokens of good faith. She didn't know what 'behavior and goods' she should expect or ask for but she would have to come up with something. Or, better yet, let him come up with something. 'I'm afraid that's not good enough,' she said. 'To take the chance of leaving here, moving in with you, and not knowing when you'd change your mind or how it would end . . . Well, I know that's standard for relationships today, but we both agreed that I'm not like a lot of other girls.' Right now she felt as if she were a silly, useless combination of Mrs Patel's stern straightforwardness and Imogen's strategizing, neither of which were her style. She sighed. She wasn't really being herself, and she wasn't good at pretending to be anyone she wasn't. But the advice of both women had merit and she had never, in her limited experience, had any real success with men. If she were as brave, as spontaneous as Michael seemed to think she was, what would she do? It was an interesting thought. Claire had so rarely acted spontaneously, especially with men, that she had no history to draw upon. But, she thought, what would she really like to do?

Then she got an idea.

She leaned forward and she took his hand. 'I'd like you to come up with some way, in your behavior and . . . well, and some tangible things to show you're ready for a real commitment. And in the meantime, I'd really like you to invite me up to your suite.'

Michael opened his eyes wide. 'You mean to . . .'

With perfect confidence, Claire smiled. 'I like you very much that way,' Claire said. 'Making love with you was, well, it was unforgettable.'

'So you'll . . . you'll come back to New York with me?'

Claire looked at him as calmly as she could. 'No matter

what happens I don't see why we shouldn't at least . . .' she paused. 'Repeat history.' She smiled seductively. 'I know this great hotel that has a giant bathtub, a soft bed and silky linens. What do you say?'

SIXTY-SEVEN

Claire left the hotel the next morning feeling exhilarated. The sex with Michael had been wonderful – if anything better than she remembered. Perhaps it had been better than before. After all, now that Michael was a supplicant he had to prove himself to her. When Mrs Patel had talked about 'tokens of behavior' Claire didn't think she meant *that* sort of behavior. But it really was part of the picture. Claire would not let herself be seduced by sex alone, but it was an important part of any relationship and Michael's passion was mixed with what seemed like enormous tenderness and gratitude.

As she got on the underground Claire realized there had been two more reasons to sleep with Michael: because she hadn't slept with anyone in a long time, and because it would further remind Michael of exactly what was at stake. As she took a seat in the train she smiled again. The sex had been so very, very satisfying and this time as she walked down the hotel hall she felt that it would be impossible for Michael to put her out of his mind.

The problem was that it began to seem equally impossible for her to put him out of *her* mind. Of course, she had taken that into consideration as the risk of sleeping with him. But somehow she hadn't thought her longing to be loved would kick in quite so strongly. Life is dangerous if one takes risks. It is meaningless if one doesn't.

In front of her was the painful process of leaving London, one way or another. Back at the flat she began, with a sigh, to pack up her belongings. Imogen had decided she would be leaving at the end of the month and Claire wanted to be sure she was out long before it was necessary. As she folded some of her clothes Michael's face, his brow furrowed with longing, his voice insistent and hungry, came back to her. She closed her eyes and savored the feeling. Being truly wanted was so novel that it had a special thrill. Of course Edward wanted her, but that had seemed such a detached feeling with no passion at all, that she could hardly count it. The novelty of being wanted by somebody that she wanted back was something very special and it was the first time in her life Claire had experienced it.

She stopped her packing and looked out the window at the gardens. She would regret losing the view. How could she live without the civilizing influence of flower boxes, blooming parks, potted topiaries and front and back gardens everywhere? New York – even Michael's luxurious apartment – could not compare.

But one thing she determined: she would not go with Michael because her other choices were unpleasant ones. She wouldn't take the easy way out. It wouldn't be easy because in the past months she had somehow gained a lot more pride than she once had. Even if she had failed to find a permanent home here, she had made a good effort and with only slightly better luck might have succeeded. If she had to return to New York – and it looked certain that she would have to – regardless of what happened with Michael she would not live with her mother. She might have to temporarily, of course, but she would make it only temporarily. And she wouldn't keep living in Tottenville either. If she had found a place and a roommate in London she could find one in New York. And she would do it. If it couldn't be in Manhattan, it would be somewhere else.

But it would be her own place and it would be somewhere she felt comfortable and at peace.

She looked around her pretty room. Of course she couldn't expect it to be this lovely. Claire felt a stab – a real physical pain – in her chest at the thought of leaving. In New York, somehow, she'd just felt like a lonely person in an indistinguishable crowd. Here she felt as if each person – though unknown to her – was separate and unique, that if she only spoke to them she would find a potential friend, an interesting story, or an eccentric passion. She knew she was probably wrong, that her prejudice was only that. New York would no doubt be full of as many stories, friends, and eccentrics if she'd only try. But London had been so very good to her – and for her – that having to leave was a reality too painful to contemplate at the moment.

She thought of the first evening she had expected to have dinner with Michael and the hundred dollars he had given her instead. And given to her in front of witnesses. The vast change in her position since then made her smile, but it was a rueful one. The humiliation and disappointment were still there. And always would be, though this reversal was especially pleasant to contemplate. Claire wasn't spiteful and did not want to inflict any pain on Michael or anyone else but she was human. And there was . . .

Nigel! There was Nigel. She had forgotten all about her dinner date with him. She couldn't believe it. Her hands actually began to shake. Mrs Venables had been such a good friend to her and, even if Nigel had been rude and even hostile at first, their relations had become so cordial that the thought of standing him up, blowing him off without even a phone call, upset her deeply. Only those who had been forgotten can understand the deep pain of it and she had forgotten Nigel altogether.

She dropped the sheet she had been folding and ran to the phone. Then she had to run back to her bedroom and search for his numbers. She only got his machine at the office, another at his flat, and no answer on his mobile. Perhaps he was looking at her number and refusing, out of pride, to answer it. She called the other two numbers and left long apologies, explaining how exhausted she was and how she had fallen asleep. She only felt a little bit guilty about the lie, since telling him the truth would have been impossibly hurtful. She also left an invitation to dinner, her treat as a token of apology.

She didn't want to think about any pain she'd caused Nigel but she couldn't stop thinking about pain she might feel in dealing with Michael. Thinking that her future was in his hands and that she would have to make the difficult judgment about whether or not he was trustworthy just upset her. Instead she kept returning to the feeling she had had when his arms were around her and how his voice in her ear had been almost unbearably thrilling. Claire shook her head as if she could shake out unwanted thoughts. Sleeping with Michael, she realized, had probably been a mistake. But how could she make a rational decision if she didn't? And how could she be rational now that she had? All of her confidence from the morning seemed to leak away, leaving her, once again, insecure and more than a little frightened. Michael had had so many women that there was no reason for her to think that sex with her would make her more special in his eyes. Probably it had done the opposite. And though it had been wonderful, wasn't giving it up – if she did – going to leave her feeling hungry and unsatisfied? Yet if she made her decision because of the passion she'd felt wouldn't she regret . . . oh, it was all so confusing and disturbing.

Claire shook her head again. She would have to keep herself busy or she would go crazy. These thoughts were not going to help her. Right now she had to wait and see what 'tokens in behavior and goods' Michael came up with. Of course, there was always the possibility that he would come up with nothing; that she would never hear from him again. Perhaps, once again, she'd been a quick conquest, a diversion. The thought of that was too much to contemplate and, with a determination she did not feel, Claire gathered her purse and sweater, took an umbrella and left to do her tasks of the day.

She had promised to see Lady Ann. And after missing her appointment with Nigel she wasn't going to miss any more. On her way to the meeting she tried to think what might be the reason for the invitation. She couldn't imagine that Lady Ann wanted her to look at her knitting. Perhaps her mother had a difficulty. At any rate, she took the tube to Bond Street and walked along South Molton Street until she found the right address. It was an office, not a flat, and she took the lift to the third floor as Lady Ann had directed her to. When she arrived the office was bustling. And Lady Ann seemed to be the person in charge of all of the activity. It was her name on the door and in bold letters over the back of the reception desk.

After a few moments Ann Fenwick appeared and greeted her warmly. 'Why don't we go into my office,' she asked. 'Would you like a cup of tea? Or perhaps coffee?' Claire declined both. They walked down a long hall, also filled with busy workers, to Lady Ann's office. Claire was surprised to find it was decorated with chintz and floral wallpaper – very homey. She took a seat on the sofa and Lady Ann sat in a well-worn chair to her right. 'Awfully bad news about Mrs Venables,' she said. 'My mother was very upset; you know, they're about the same age. She hates to think of herself incapacitated.'

'Actually, it isn't as bad as they first thought,' Claire said. 'Tell your mother Mrs Venables is already home and talking. With a little more therapy she'll probably be able to live on her own.'

'But that's wonderful!' Lady Ann said. 'So she will keep the shop open.'

'I don't know yet.' Claire explained about Mrs Venables's

weakness, Nigel's concerns and the fact that the building was up for sale.

'Well,' Lady Ann continued. 'Would you go on and work in another knitting shop? Because, you see, my mother has got very fond not only of the classes but also of being there with other women. Before you started them she barely went out. Now she looks forward to them.'

'I'm sorry, I'm going back to the States soon. But in the meantime I could certainly go over to your mother's again. Quite a few of the women wanted more help. Since she's just a few doors away, we might be able to arrange a little party. Let everyone get together at least once more. That is if you don't think it would be too much for your mother to manage.'

'I think it's brilliant! Mummy would love it. She hasn't entertained in so long. I'll call her and set it up. Will you come? Will you bring a few of the younger women too? Mummy does like to see them.'

Claire agreed and gave Ann Imogen's number. 'Though I'll be moving soon,' Claire warned.

'You know, it's very silly that we can't continue this. So many women are interested. And all ages and back-grounds. I looked it up on the Internet and there are dozens of sites. It's the thing in the States right now. Do you know there's a café in Los Angeles where movie stars gather to compare their stocking stitch? You know, most trends move from your west coast to the east coast and then on to us.'

Claire didn't know and she didn't particularly like the idea. Second-hand American trends didn't seem right for London. But she had to agree that knitting was popular here. However, Ann seemed to be looking at her curiously, as though assessing her, so she decided it would be wise to say nothing.

Claire left and stopped in at Toby's. She had to tell him about her plans to return to New York, though she didn't want to. 'Hard cheese!' he said after she'd explained. 'Dreadful! You simply can't leave just because the old woman fell ill. And Imogen, self-involved as she is, would never forgive herself if she found out that putting you out on the street had sent you back to Hooterville, or whatever it is.'

'Tottenville,' Claire corrected.

'Right.' Toby paused. 'Do you know, Claire, I was reading a history of New York. And your name – it's spelled B-i-l-s-o-p?' Claire nodded. 'Your name was very prominent.'

'What do you mean?'

'Well, apparently the Bilsops are a very old family. They received a royal land grant. They were – well, *you* were – among the first British settlers. Your ancestor was given a good part of the island.'

Claire was what the English called 'gobsmacked'. But what did it really matter? Her dad had been a failure and if some of his stories about 'the Bilsop name' had a basis in truth, there certainly wasn't any money or visible 'breeding'. Oh, these English and their pedigrees. 'My father used to talk about the family,' she said. 'But we never paid much attention. I thought it was a way of making his past sound better than his present.'

'That may be so,' Toby told her. 'But I think he was accurate about your past. Here.' He went to the lowboy and pulled out a green volume. 'Let me give you this. I've marked the place. Take a look at it.'

'Thank you,' she said. She thought of her small but precious collection of books. Well, perhaps she could add to them in New York but it would never be the same. 'You've been so very kind,' she told him.

He smiled at her. 'And so have you,' he said. 'Now, can you stay for tea?'

Claire was very tempted but, 'I must go,' she told him. 'I promised I'd look in on Mrs Venables.'

'Aah. Well, do give my regards to that dishy son of hers.'

'Dishy? Do you really think so?' She told Toby about the ride back from the hospital, the handholding and the (forgotten) invitation to dinner.

'Ah. You see? He fancies you.'

'Nigel? You're mad.' But all at once she remembered Mrs Venables saying much the same thing. Silly. Totally silly. 'He'll be only too happy to take me to the airport and see me off.'

'I think not.' But Claire wasn't listening. Talking of the airport made the idea of leaving hit her hard. She tried not to let Toby see her react. Instead, she turned to go.

'I must be off,' she said.

'Don't forget your book,' Toby reminded her. He walked her to the door and kissed her on either cheek. She left, fighting the tears in her eyes. Toby watched her from his window and murmured to himself, 'If he doesn't fancy you, he's a fool.'

Claire got off the tube in South Kensington and wished that she could go home, just lie down and pull the covers over her head. Between the trains and the sharing of her news with Toby, she was exhausted. Somehow, telling her news made it a reality.

Well, if she couldn't nap perhaps she could drink. She decided she would stop in the wine bar before she went to Mrs Venables, just to revive herself. After all, what did the cost of a three-pound glass of wine matter when she was going back? She told herself she deserved a little splurge, entered and took a seat near the window.

But it was a mistake. From where she sat she could see on one side the shop – soon to be empty – and on the other side the empty table where she and Michael had been together. Thoughts of him again flooded her mind and heated her body. This was the very thing her busy schedule had prevented her from doing. If she hadn't already ordered a glass of Pommard, she would have jumped up and crossed the street. But the wine came and she drank

463

it, lingering over the memory of her dinner with Michael, his declaration, the things he had told her and, of course, their night at the Berkeley. She couldn't help but indulge herself a little. He was a dream. Truly Mr Wonderful. But did he love her? Could she trust him? And did she love him as he was?

Claire finished her wine, trying to think as deeply as she could to answer those questions. She had just emptied her glass when she saw Nigel Venables walking into his mother's shop. She sighed. She had indulged herself too long and her punishment was that she would have to see Nigel now, after she'd stood him up. She only hoped Toby's surmise was dead wrong. It was odd: she had avoided him at first because he disliked her. Now she wanted to avoid him because she was afraid he didn't.

Claire paid up, left an overly generous tip then dodged the traffic to get to Knitting Kitting. To her surprise the shop door wasn't locked. Very careless since neither Mrs Venables nor Nigel was about. She was about to call up the stairs when she heard their voices.

'Mother, you really don't have a choice. You can't possibly keep the shop open.'

'Not for long, without Claire's help I . . .'

'But Claire is leaving, Mother.'

'Let me talk to her and maybe she can be persuaded. There are people who want to learn. Customers who still need service. People have placed orders that have come in . . .'

'Damn them. Mother, they're only playing with some colored string. We're not talking about national security. If they have paid you we can simply return the money.'

Claire winced. She shouldn't be eavesdropping on this, but didn't know quite what to do. Perhaps if she went back to the door she could ring the bell again and they would hear her. But before she could move she heard Mrs Venables speaking in a voice that she could barely recognize. She sounded tougher and more imperious than any of the imperious women in their classes.

'How dare you speak to me, your mother, that way? We are not talking about "a bit of colored string". We are talking about an ancient craft that turns your piece of string into, at the very least, a useful article. And occasionally into a work of art. I wonder how many centuries women have been knitting pullovers for their fisherman husbands or socks for their farming family only to be told that they were only playing with bits of string.'

'Mother, I didn't mean to . . .'

'I don't care what you meant! Though I think I know perfectly well what you did mean. But let me tell you what I mean. Women come here as an outlet for their creativity. Knitting relaxes them and gives them a sense of purpose. And it challenges them. The magic of their hands transforms nothing into something. Lately there have been some customers who badly need to turn nothing into something.' She paused and her voice dropped so Claire could barely hear it. 'Maybe we all do,' she said.

'Mother, I meant no disrespect . . .'

'You may not have meant it but you certainly showed it.'

'I'm very sorry. Getting upset isn't good for you. Just relax. I'll go and . . . well, I'll call in later.'

Claire heard Nigel's footsteps and jumped. If she were caught here he would know that she had overheard his mother reading him the Riot Act. She skipped across the shop, opened the door and closed it then walked, as loudly as she could, across the floor and called up the stairs. She heard Nigel coming down the stairs as Mrs Venables called out. 'Is that you, Claire? Please come up.'

So, pretending she'd heard nothing, Claire began to climb the stairs. Nigel was on the landing. 'Hello,' she said as he attempted to pass her.

'Hello,' he mumbled and seemed to be about to continue past her.

'Did you get my messages?' she asked. He shook his head. 'I called your office and your house. I couldn't get you on your mobile.' She gave him her lame excuse about their missed dinner date and his face seemed to soften.

'Oh. I . . . I've been so busy I haven't had a moment to get my messages.'

'Well, I asked you to dinner instead. Do you think you could make time? I'd like to take you out to make up for my rudeness.' She thought of what she had overheard and decided to ignore it. 'Would you please?' she asked. He nodded. 'How about tonight?' She hoped Michael – if he did call – wouldn't ask her out for this evening, but she'd have to take that risk.

'That would be just fine,' Nigel said, his face lighting up. 'Why don't I pick you up around eight?'

She agreed. 'And now I'll just go up for a quick visit,' she told him.

'See you later then,' Nigel told her and was off.

'Hello, my dear,' Mrs Venables said when Claire reached the upstairs flat. Her color looked good, and though the left side of her face still had some slightly visible slackness she stood up to greet Claire. 'How nice to see you,' she said. 'I'm afraid Nigel and I were having a dust-up, so please accept my apologies on his behalf.'

'That's all right,' Claire said. Somehow, overhearing Mrs Venables in such a temper assured Claire that the older woman would make a complete recovery. She smiled at her friend. 'Would you like me to make some tea?' she asked. 'I have some things I need to discuss with you. Most important is the fact I have to go back to the States.'

SIXTY-EIGHT

To Claire's great relief, that afternoon Michael called her and asked her out for dinner that evening. 'I'm sorry,' she told him. 'I'm booked.'

'But I must see you,' Michael said. 'Tonight. I'm leaving London soon.'

Claire knew she couldn't – wouldn't cancel on Nigel again. 'I must go out but maybe after . . .'

'How long will your dinner last?'

'Not past ten,' she said, wondering what she and Nigel could possibly talk about for two hours.

'Well, could I meet you for a drink then?'

Claire blushed and was grateful Michael couldn't see it. Was he simply hoping for another sleep-over? Not that she didn't long for his body, but she certainly didn't want to be used, or appear easy.

'Please don't make me beg,' Michael said. 'This is important to both of us.'

Of course Claire agreed. But she found that dressing for dinner with Nigel and drinks with Michael presented more than a little problem. She couldn't wear her wild cerise outfit again, so she put on the navy-blue bridesmaid dress. But she hadn't worn it since Michael left and it was now far too big for her. She took the belt off the cerise dress, buckled it around her waist, then pulled the blue dress up so that it was quite short and the top bloused over the belt.

She thought it didn't look too bad with her new shoes. Anyway, it would have to do.

She was almost ready to leave when Imogen walked in. 'Going out?' Imogen asked.

Claire explained she was going to meet Nigel, then Michael.

'In that?' Imogen asked. 'Are you mad? You've got to look swish tonight.'

Claire shrugged. 'I don't have anything else.'

'Well, I do. Come on.' Imogen went into her bedroom, dropped her purse on the bed and threw open her closet doors. 'Looks a bit like a jumble sale in here. Let's see. You're not as tall as I am so we'll need something kind of short.' Claire stood in the middle of the room, grateful but embarrassed. In Imogen's full-length mirror she saw that even 'improved' the dress wouldn't do at all.

'Oh. Just the thing,' Imogen said and emerged from her closet with a black skirt. 'Have you got a sexy blouse?' she asked. 'Something that shows a little cleavage?'

'I only have a little cleavage,' Claire said and smiled her thanks.

'Hold on,' Imogen said. 'I may have just the thing.' She pulled out a blue shirt with deep V-neckline. 'It doesn't suit me at all and it cost the earth. But keep it if it looks good on you.'

Claire went back to her room and changed. Then – at Imogen's insistence – came back into her room. 'Yes, that's just right. And I have some blue earrings I must have been mad to buy.' Im took out two chunky objects that looked like blue and pink pearls glued together in mounds, with twinkling rhinestones stuck into the corners between the pearls.

'Oh no,' Claire protested.

'Just try them on.'

Reluctantly Claire did and, to her surprise, they looked good.

'Rather marvelous, eh?' Imogen asked. 'Now, do you have a pink lipstick?' Claire shook her head. When had Imogen become such a soul of generosity?

The possible reason came out as Im rummaged in her purse. 'I spoke to Toby today. He said you might be going back to New York. And he mentioned your family's land grant. Fancy the king giving you an island. I'd rather like that. Perhaps Mustique.' She pulled out a lipstick tube. 'Try this.' Claire smiled at Im's new generosity but put the lipstick on and had to admit that with the earrings and the blouse, the lipstick was the perfect touch. 'Now that's a get-up that will make a man regret he's ever been caddish to you. How's it going?'

'I'm not sure,' Claire admitted.

'But you are being cagey?'

'Well, I think I'd call it stand-offish.' Then she thought of the night at the hotel and wasn't sure if she'd told the truth.

'Great!' Imogen said. 'Nothing like a little coolness to heat things up.'

Claire almost laughed. Heating things up was the last thing she needed. But, she reminded herself, the ball was in Michael's court and she had very little to do but to see what was on offer.

'Well, good luck,' Imogen said and hugged her.

Nigel picked her up five minutes early but Claire was ready. He took her to a small, elegant restaurant just south of Cadogan Square. Though it was *luxe* and chic Claire was so involved with her thoughts about Michael that she found it difficult to appreciate. It was almost impossible to focus on Nigel, sitting, somewhat stiffly, across from her. They ordered and Claire waited, but Nigel, seemingly, had nothing to say. So Claire told him about her visit with his mother. 'Her progress has been amazing, hasn't it?'

'She's a game old bird,' Nigel agreed and smiled. Using

slang like that to describe his mother was clearly a joke, though a mild one. In the soft lights of the restaurant he looked his best. If he wasn't such a stick, so awkward and intense, he would be an attractive man. Claire wondered for the first time if there was a woman in his life. Or perhaps it was a Toby situation.

'What do you do when you're not in court?' Claire asked just to see where the conversation would go.

'I read a lot when I travel. I love to walk around the parks when I have time off and I like to go to places for fun and not for business.'

Claire started talking about all the books she had read and Nigel chimed in when she mentioned something he liked. Even when he didn't like a book that she did they had an in-depth talk about their opinions.

Before Claire knew it, they were being served dinner. She kept up the discussion until they were almost ready to order dessert. When Nigel asked her impressions of London, she became even more passionate and forthcoming.

Claire began to tell him about how she found every aspect of London fascinating, endearing, odd or strangely comfortable. She talked about the antique markets, the long wooden escalators in the tubes, the dozens and dozens of strange sweets and candy bars, the food department in Marks and Spencer, the plaques on so many buildings commemorating forgotten composers or world-famous writers. 'I don't believe in reincarnation,' she said, 'but if I did I would tell you that I'd lived here before – or that I was meant to.'

Nigel smiled. 'You know,' he said, 'there are parts of London that aren't so congenial.'

Claire smiled at him. 'I'm sure you're right,' she said. 'Perhaps I just haven't been there. Or like a woman in love, I refuse to see the negative side of my beloved.'

'Lucky man to be loved by you,' he said and Claire blinked. Since taking her hand in the car, Nigel hadn't displayed any particular warmth toward her, not even in his invitation to dinner. Perhaps he was merely being polite, thanking her for her care of his mother. But she remembered what Toby had said. Was it possible that Nigel fancied her?

She was struck dumb by the possibility. Then she pulled herself together and asked him a few questions about growing up. When he talked about his childhood she found that he was actually more engaging than he had ever been. His stories about school, the Welsh cottage that the family summered at, his youthful escapades and his father's death would have been rather interesting if she wasn't so distracted by time passing and her date with Michael getting ever-nearer.

'Would you care for dessert?' the waiter asked after their plates were cleared.

Claire surreptitiously looked at her watch and shook her head. It was almost nine-thirty. Nigel had picked her up in his car. She wondered if he would insist on taking her home or if she could get him to drop her at the Berkeley – only five or six blocks away. If he did, what could her excuse be?

'Why are you going back to the States?' Nigel asked her suddenly. 'For a visit? Is there a problem?'

Claire shook her head. 'No,' she said. 'The problem is I can't stay on.' She didn't want to bring up the shop or her employment. She didn't want to make him feel guilty. 'I just haven't managed to settle in,' she said. 'And I have a real job waiting in New York. In fact, I'm going to see one of my co-workers after dinner. He's in London and I may return to his firm.'

It was all a bit of a lie but Claire couldn't see her way clear to saying anything closer to the truth than that. And, after all, she owed Nigel nothing. In fact, despite the expensive meal, the conversation about books, London and his growing up, the only thing they really had in common was their mutual concern for his mother. There wasn't any more to it than that.

'Ah. I see,' Nigel said. 'Well, perhaps we had better get

going then.' He signaled to the waiter to bring the check. 'It's really been most pleasant.'

Claire nodded with relief and had the novel experience of being driven by one man to meet another.

'I've been thinking about everything you said,' Michael told Claire as he leaned across the table toward her. They were, somewhat ironically, seated back in the Berkeley bar. From their corner table Claire could see over Michael's shoulder to the stools where he and Katherine Rensselaer had sat snogging the evening she had come in from her walk. 'You know, Claire, you're not like anyone else,' Michael said. 'I can't predict what you'll do or say.' He smiled. 'That's a good thing. I hate boredom.'

Claire knew it wasn't true. 'Only because we're in a special circumstance,' Claire said. 'When I'm settled I'm actually a creature of habit.'

'Just what I need. Stability. But you're unsettling from time to time. The best of both worlds.'

If he really knew her, wouldn't he be bored in a New York minute? The bar wasn't crowded, at least not yet, but there was still a lot of noise and cigarette smoke. No one in the UK seemed to have heard that smoking was bad for your health. Claire was uncomfortable not only with the situation but the surroundings as well. 'Michael, would you mind if we took a walk?'

'Of course not,' he said.

As she walked down the steps of the hotel, Michael at her right, she was wished good evening by the doorman. She remembered her previous stay. On that occasion she never could have imagined this one.

They walked for a little while, Michael holding her elbow. At Eaton Square they found a bench and sat down. The evening was mild with a real promise of summer around the corner. Michael took Claire's hand. 'You do know that I love you, don't you?'

Claire shook her head. She didn't know what she knew. She tried to think of Mrs Patel and her strict advice to demand tokens in behavior and goods. She remembered her father telling her 'Words aren't deeds.' But those particular words, coming from Michael's lips, gave her the inclination to melt in his arms. Luckily, he sat up straight, not giving her the chance. Then he put his hand into his jacket pocket and pulled out a small box.

'For you,' he said. Claire took the velvet case. Was this an example of Mrs Patel's 'goods'? 'There's no reason for you to trust me,' Michael admitted. 'Inviting you back to New York was arrogance. I realize that now. And after our night together, well . . . Claire, I lost you once because I was an idiot. I don't want to lose you again. Will you marry me?'

Claire almost let her jaw drop. She never expected this. 'Are you going to open it?' he asked. She did, and the street light made the sapphire and diamond ring flash deep blue and white, like fireworks in a box.

'Michael, it's beautiful.' She looked from the ring to his equally deep blue eyes.

'May I put it on your finger?' he asked.

'I . . . I don't know,' she said. She felt as if she were in a waking dream, as if she had perhaps imagined a scene like this so often that it was coming true.

But she had never imagined it. She didn't have the self-confidence or nerve to do it. 'Do you really want to get married?' she asked him. 'We hardly know each other.'

He put his arm around her. 'I don't think that's true,' he said. 'I know you enough to know how much I want you.' He kissed her again, and again she couldn't help but kiss him back. She did want him or she wanted him to want her. Oh, there was so much wanting in her life that she'd probably never catch up. But her mind raced. She couldn't sit still. She asked if they could walk a little more. 'Of course,' Michael told her. 'We can do whatever you want.' He took her hand and they walked to Sloane Square, then along the King's Road. She didn't talk much. Certainly the ring and the proposal would fulfill Mrs Patel's requirements. But did it fulfill hers? Why wasn't she thrilled? Was she too shocked?

Michael calmly described his apartment, and how they would probably want to move on from it. He asked her when her birthday was and told her his own. 'Would you want a big wedding? I think my mother would. Eldest son, and all.'

Claire tried to imagine her mother paying for more than a cake. 'I don't know,' she said. 'I really never thought about it.'

Michael smiled. 'You see? Another way you're different. Haven't Tina and the other women been planning their weddings from the time they were sixteen?'

Claire shook her head. 'Tina's been planning hers since she was eleven. Long before she met Anthony.'

Michael laughed. 'Have you gotten your invitation yet?' he asked. 'I just got mine.'

Claire felt a surprising stab of pain. After all these years, Tina had set the date, was finally going to do it and she hadn't even told Claire. Well, things and people change. 'I suppose you could take me,' Claire said. Wouldn't that give the Maries something to talk about!

They turned and began to walk back. Michael stopped, encircled Claire in his arms and kissed her yet again. 'Will you come back to the hotel?' he asked. 'Will you marry me?'

'I think I need to go home,' Claire told him and she wasn't playing at Imogen's game. 'I'm very, very tired and, well, I need to think.'

'Of course you do,' Michael said. He kissed her again, then easily flagged down a cab and insisted on taking her home. He remembered her address and held her hand tightly all the way to South Ken. When they arrived he asked the cab to wait while he walked her to the door. 'Just try the ring on,' he said. 'Sleep with it tonight.'

Somehow he made it sound very sexy, but Claire – to her own surprise – found that she didn't know what she should do or even say. Then she wondered if it could possibly be the same ring he had given to Katherine Rensselaer. 'Thank you, Michael,' she said. 'Let's wait. Let me think. I'll call you first thing tomorrow.'

SIXTY-NINE

It was still dark when the phone rang. Claire looked at the clock. It was 5:32 in the morning. Was Michael calling her already? She rose and tried to make it to the telephone in the kitchen before it rang again and woke Imogen, but she was too late. 'It's for you,' Imogen called from behind her bedroom door.

Claire picked up the phone to hear Safta's voice. 'I think it's time to go to hospital, Claire,' Safta said. 'Mummy's having contractions. And her waters have broken. It's time, isn't it?'

Claire tried to clear her head. 'Yes. Do you have the number for a mini cab?' she asked. There would be no black taxis tooling around Camden at this time of the morning. 'Do you have some money?'

The always-prepared Safta told her she did. 'Call the mini cab right now. I'll meet you at the Royal Free Hospital,' Claire said – she had checked, some weeks back, which maternity unit was nearest to the Patels' home.

By the time Claire threw on some clothes and arrived at the hospital, Mrs Patel had already been taken into the labor room. The children, all three of them, were huddled in the visitors' lounge. 'I wanted to leave them to sleep, but Maudie doesn't have a phone and I couldn't leave them or Mum to go get her,' Safta explained.

'You did the right thing,' Claire told her. She patted Safta on the arm and chuffed Devi under the chin. She tried to do the math and figure out how long Mrs Patel had been pregnant. Was it eight months? She wasn't sure. 'They took Mummy on the wagon,' Devi said.

'It wasn't a wagon. It was a bed with wheels,' Fala corrected. All three, graced with large expressive eyes to begin with, now had them open so wide that enough white showed to make them look like brown spotted eggs. Claire crouched down beside the little ones.

'There's nothing to worry about,' she said. 'Mummy is going to be fine. Making a baby isn't easy but your mummy has done it three times before.' She looked at Devi. 'The last time it was you.' Devi shook his head, his silky hair flying.

'I was the first time,' he said.

Claire smiled, reached into her pocket and took out five pounds. 'Here,' she said, handing it to Safta. 'Take them to the café, get some breakfast and then come back. Do you think you can manage that?' Safta nodded. 'I'll go and check on your mother.'

Claire wasn't so sure she would be allowed to, but a maternity nurse nodded and took her into the labor room. Claire, of course, had never been in one. She vaguely remembered Fred being brought home from the hospital, but there were no babies in her life at home. Mrs Patel was lying there, her hair unplaited, sweat beading her entire face. A nurse was busy at the side of the room but Mrs Patel had her eyes closed and seemed very alone.

As Claire approached the bed Mrs Patel was taken by a contraction. She balled her hands into fists, her eyes flew open and she let out a deep frightening groan. The noise scared Claire. This, after all, was Mrs Patel, always strong and self-contained. Of course, she also contained a new life which was pushing to become its own self. Claire approached the bed. She wasn't sure if Mrs Patel, whose eyes were turned upward, could see her. As gently as she

477

could she put her hand on her friend's shoulder. For a moment, while she felt the body under her hand tense and hard as mahogany, there was no other reaction. But after the contraction ended Mrs Patel turned her head.

Her wet face glistened, and the top of her gown was open. Sweat pooled between her breasts. 'Claire?' she asked. Her fists unclenched and she reached for Claire's hand. 'What are you doing here?'

'Safta called. I came over as soon as I could. Is it time for the baby? I mean, have you gone full term?'

'It's just a few weeks early,' Mrs Patel said. 'A doctor looked and she says there's no problem.' Then she was racked by another pain. Her hand clenched around Claire's and Claire could feel her knuckles pressed against each other until she too felt like crying out. Mrs Patel began to pant and moaned again. It was the moaning that scared Claire. The nurse, busy all this time in the corner of the room, turned around.

'There, there, Mum. It's not so bad.'

'It is!' Mrs Patel gasped. 'And I'm not your mum.'

The nurse paid no attention and approached the bed. She felt Mrs Patel's stomach and looked below. 'About two centimeters,' she said. 'You have a long way to go.'

Claire felt like smacking her but turned back to Mrs Patel who had loosened her hold on Claire's hand.

'I always forget how hard it is. But I always did this alone,' Mrs Patel said. 'It's nice you're here.'

'But didn't your husband come in? Wasn't he . . .'

'He was useless. And he didn't want to see. And now he's gone, and won't ever see the face of his child.' Once again her hand tightened around Claire's but this time it wasn't because of the pain. 'Where are the children?' she asked. 'Are they very frightened? I had no time to fetch Maudie. Are the children outside?'

'They're getting something to eat and they're behaving well and they're waiting for their new little sister or brother,'

Claire assured her. 'By the way, Devi says he was your first baby.'

Mrs Patel smiled, and despite the sweat, the circles under her eyes, and the rat's nest her hair had become, she did look lovely. 'He would. No fear. Safta will set him straight.' The smile left her face and her eyes softened. 'Thank you, Claire,' she said. 'I don't know how to thank you. Doing this without family, without anyone to help . . . it's very hard.' To Claire's complete surprise tears welled in Mrs Patel's eyes. Claire knew it had been hard for her to break from her family and to put her husband out, but she didn't know, she couldn't know, how very frightening it must be, even for a woman as strong as Mrs Patel. She paused and licked her lips. 'Believe me, you must make sure of this man before you go further. You don't want to be in a room here as I am unless you trust him and love him very much.' Claire put one hand on Mrs Patel's shoulder and squeezed it. Her other was in her pocket, where the little box with the big ring waited. She thought of taking it out and showing it to Mrs Patel, then thought better of it. 'Promise me you'll do that,' Mrs Patel asked.

'I promise,' Claire told her.

'Good. Now go to the children. Tell them not to eat too many sweets or I shall be very cross with them. And remind Devi not to be naughty. And ask them to think of a name for their new brother or sister.'

Claire nodded. 'Fala suggested "Beckham".'

'I think not,' Mrs Patel said and laughed – until another contraction hit. Claire took back her hand.

'I'll stay with them for a little and then I'll come right back,' she promised.

Mrs Patel, gripped with pain, managed to nod. Claire didn't like to leave her, but she certainly didn't like to witness it either. Another nurse came in, moved to the side of the bed and Claire took her leave.

The better part of the next three hours had Claire

shuttling back and forth between Mrs Patel and the kids. Devi fell asleep on her lap, while Fala drew and colored pictures with the crayons and paper a nurse's aide supplied. Only Safta stayed focused on her mother and the baby. 'It will be all right?' she asked Claire several times. Claire assured her it would be.

And in the end it was.

Claire was allowed into the delivery room though she stood back and was more than a little frightened. But though she had seen births on television, the birth of Mrs Patel's third daughter seemed so miraculous that Claire found herself crying.

When the baby, cleaned and wrapped in toweling, was given to Mrs Patel her face was transformed. All the pain and fatigue seemed to disappear. The baby, though small, was beautifully formed and already had eyelashes long enough to touch her cheeks. 'She's a beautiful little girl,' the doctor said and smiled. 'Have you named her?'

Mrs Patel nodded. 'Claire,' she said. 'Her name will be Claire.'

After the children saw their mother and new sister, Claire took them home and settled them in with the help of Maudie – who she had Safta call from the hospital.

On the way back to Camden, through the cab window, Claire had watched the morning sun as it changed the colors of the horizon and the clouds. She tried to imagine what it would be like to have Michael's baby and was repelled by the thought. He was, even now, essentially a selfish person. Though he wanted her, it was once again because he had decided on it. Would she be a different acquisition from the ones he made at Crayden Smithers? Would she be more important to him than the BMW convertible he traded in every year or so? Even if she was, how could she live the life he did?

What she had witnessed – the reality of a woman birthing a child fathered by a man who wasn't there – was the essence of a question between men and women. Michael Wainwright might have been what she once wished for, but he wasn't what she wished for now. Then with equal certainty she knew she couldn't return to New York. Somehow, she had been lucky enough to find her place and she couldn't give it up. London was where she felt real, most alive and truly at home. It was if she was born to live here, amidst the low buildings, the clean tube, the books and the people she had met. Perhaps the gamble she had made by wishing upon a star had paid off in the end!

It was late afternoon before Claire had a chance to call Michael. She knew he was leaving that night and though she was exhausted and bedraggled, when he begged her to meet him she agreed. She took a taxi to Harvey Nichols and tried to use the cab time to comb her hair, put on some lipstick and brush enough mascara on her lashes to at least look as if she had made an effort. Then, walking past the makeup counters on the ground floor she let a cosmetician apply some blush and eye shadow to her face. She took the elevator up to the roof and moved through the aisles of specialty foods, espresso cups and glossy cookbooks to the restaurant. It was big and noisy, but Michael – of course – had secured a table beside the large windows that looked out onto a small terrace, roofs and chimney pots. Claire made her way to the table and took the seat opposite him.

He stood up, kissed her, and took her hand. 'Would you like some tea?' he asked. 'Or an early dinner?' He took the seat beside her, facing away from the window.

'I'm not hungry. Maybe some coffee.' She actually felt light-headed. Going from the focused intensity of the delivery room to the frivolous bustle of the restaurant seemed too wide a gap to breach. Though she hadn't had a cup of coffee in weeks, somehow it seemed not just good but necessary right now.

They ordered – staff always hovered ready to serve Michael with alacrity – and he took her other hand, this time her left. 'Do I get to put a ring on that finger?' he asked.

Claire looked down, bit her lip then tried to look Michael in the face. The light was behind him and it was difficult to see his features. That was just as well, Claire decided. She put her hand into her pocket, took out the box, and placed it on the table between them. He reached for it. 'Let me put it on you,' he said, his voice assured. Claire realized he was certain of her answer. He probably always had been.

But she shook her head. 'I can't say yes, Michael,' she told him.

She heard him actually take in a breath as if he'd been punched. 'But why not?'

'We aren't right for one another,' she told him, though it was such a cliché.

'Of course we are,' he said. He gently squeezed the hand that Mrs Patel had bruised just hours before.

'Claire, I love you,' he said. 'And I think you love me. If you want to move, for us to get a new place together, I'll do it. If you want to elope, that's fine. If you want a big wedding, I can pay for it. We can have a wonderful life. I've learned things about myself. That success at any price is too expensive, that you need someone truly loyal at your back. Claire, won't you become Mrs Michael Wainwright? I know my parents will love you.'

Claire doubted it, but it didn't seem to warrant a response. She knew she couldn't possibly marry him. 'Michael,' she began, 'I just can't. You . . . you lead a big life. You deal with big business. You like big restaurants and big hotels. You want the most expensive car and the best clothes.'

'But you can have those things,' he said, interrupting. 'Let me give them to you.'

Claire shook her head. 'Michael, I don't want them.'

'What?' he said, and for the first time Claire saw Michael Wainwright truly confused. 'What do you mean?'

'Michael, I like small businesses. Little shops and small groceries. I like the local pub, not a posh hotel bar. I don't like to go out at night. I like to read. And knit. Michael, I like to knit.'

He blinked. 'Well, knitting is okay, Claire.'

'But I like to knit my own clothes. And I don't like to have too many. And I don't feel good when I'm all dressed up. I didn't like that cerise dress I wore, the one that you loved. I bought it for you, but it wasn't me. And the clothes I had on yesterday, the blouse with the low neck, that was borrowed. They weren't even my clothes, Michael.'

'That's okay, Claire. I mean, I don't care how you dress. We can buy you a little shop. It will all work out if you love me.'

Claire shook her head. There was no pay-back here, no pleasure in hurting him. 'I don't think I do,' she said. Though she steeled herself to say it, it was still hard to get the words out of her mouth. She felt sick. It wasn't easy to be rejected, but she didn't find it any easier to reject. 'I'm very sorry, Michael,' she told him.

He picked up the ring box and without a word pocketed it. 'You have nothing to be sorry about. I'm the one who's sorry.' He moved and the light from the window fell on his profile. She could see his face and it did have a look of pain. She turned her eyes away. This was not what she had wanted, but she didn't have another choice.

'I guess there's nothing else to say.' He stood and threw some notes on the table. 'Goodbye, Claire.'

But she didn't have time to say goodbye to him. Before she could utter the word he was halfway across the restaurant and on his way to the elevator.

SEVENTY

Claire was putting the last of her possessions in a cardboard carton while Imogen fluttered around from the living room to the bedroom to the doorway of Claire's box room moaning about the difficulty of packing. 'There is just too much to put together,' she said. 'You're so lucky, Claire, to not have to worry about lots of stuff.' Claire tried to smile and nod. She wasn't sure that Imogen would feel lucky if she had as little as Claire did, but she had no need to point that out. Claire looked at the boxes surrounding her. She was going to Mrs Patel's for the short-term. She'd help with the shop and, to a lesser extent, help with the baby. It would be a good temporary arrangement for both of them, but only temporary, because Claire knew she could not and would not permanently move in. She needed her own place, and though the idea of going back to Mrs Watson's or some place like that made her blood run cold, she would do it if she had to.

As Claire reached down to pick up a box, she noticed an envelope addressed to her resting on the corner of another carton. It was from her mother. Claire lowered herself onto her bed, slowly opened the letter and began to read.

Dear Claire,
    I miss you very much. The empty house is
lonely. I go up to your room and it's very weird to
be there without you. Remember all the fun we

*used to have? I hope you're thinking about coming
home. Anyway, I got this letter for you. I hope you
don't think I opened it. It came in the mail like
that, with the flap torn. I certainly hope it's good
news, and that you'll share it (the news) with me.*
Your loving mother.

P.S.

*I'm paying off the Saks bill myself. Think of it as a
birthday present. You know, you didn't have to
send me the money. I've always been generous with
you. So your payment won't go to waste, I redecor-
ated your room so it's all ready for you to come
back to.*

There was another letter enclosed with her mother's, and
it was clear her mother had opened it. This used to happen
on the rare occasions when letters came to Claire from Fred
and her mother couldn't wait to read them.

But this wasn't a letter from Fred. The return address
was Alcott and Stevens, LLP – a firm of lawyers – with a
New York address. Claire reopened the envelope.

Dear Miss Bilsop,
*I'm sorry to have to inform you of the death of
your aunt, Gertrude Bilsop Polanski. As you may
know, she was your father's only sister and had
been the sole recipient of the Bilsop estate when
your paternal grandfather died.*

*Mrs Polanski had no children and has left her
entire estate to you. I enclose a copy of her will,
but to summarize you have inherited approximately
four hundred thirty-eight thousand dollars in cash
and securities as well as the Bilsop homestead at
713 Hyland Avenue, Tottenville. Apparently, your*

*aunt had rented it out for the last two decades, but
it was on a year-by-year basis and the tenants can
be removed at the end of this calendar year.*

*In addition, there are some paintings, furniture
and jewelry that may be valuable. We could
certainly have them appraised for you by a
reputable expert.*

*Your aunt was a long-term client. Our firm
assisted her after the death of her husband and I
hope that you might entertain thoughts of our
doing the same for you at this time. As the
executor of the estate, I wait for your response.
Probate should last only a few more months.*

*Very truly yours,
John Alcott*

P.S.

*I am also forwarding a book Mrs Polanski wanted
you to have. It was published in 1888 and outlines
quite a bit about the Bilsop holdings and their
place in the community.*

Claire put down the letter and, for a moment, had no
reaction at all. Then, irrelevantly, she thought that she
could neither tell Imogen – who already thought she was
from an 'old family' – nor would she want to show Nigel
Venables that she did, indeed, 'have people'. She read the
letter again, this time more carefully. All the stuff her father
had told her, the stuff her mother called garbage, must have
been true. He had talked about his sister and she knew that
he had fought with his father long ago, back when he had
dropped out of college. She had never met her grandfather
or her Aunt Gertrude. Then she thought of the houses –
not the horrible modern ones but the beautiful old ones
the yuppies had restored – back in Tottenville. Was one of

those back on Staten Island waiting for her? And the money! It was more than she could imagine. It wasn't the lottery, but to her it was as good as one.

She looked down at the letter. So much was possible. She could, perhaps, buy a flat or at least rent one. She could stay on here at Imogen's but have the place to herself. She could apply for a working visa. It was amazing how a single piece of paper could change your life. But did she want to change her life? She certainly didn't want a house in Tottenville, even if it was on the water. Did it matter that a great, great, great grand uncle had been a gentleman farmer and a member of colonial society? Not to her.

'I'm just about done here,' Claire told Imogen. 'I'm going around the corner to say goodbye to Mrs Venables, but I wanted to give you your wedding present now.' She handed Imogen the gift she had carefully wrapped. 'I don't know if it's a polite thing to do, or if I have to wait until you're married, but . . .' she paused, 'anyway, I'd like you to have it.'

'Oh, Claire, how very kind of you. Shall we sit down right now and open it? I should, by rights, wait for Malcolm but you know how men are.' Claire wasn't entirely sure she did but she agreed and joined Imogen on the sofa. It took only a minute for Imogen to pull off the careful wrapping. 'But Claire!' she said, when she saw the little Battersea box, 'I . . . no, I really couldn't. It's so beautiful. And valuable. Do you really want to part with it?'

'I want you to have it,' Claire said. 'It would make you happy. Living here has been very, very special to me. And I'd like you to always remember me.'

Imogen impulsively hugged Claire. 'Well, it's a lovely surprise. And I have one for you. Can you just nip back here after your visit to Mrs Venables?'

Claire nodded. 'I have to anyway,' she said. 'To pick up my things.'

'Good,' Imogen told her, and went back to her somewhat ineffectual wandering around the half-packed rooms.

As Claire walked down the street that would no longer be 'hers' she thought with regret about leaving the neighborhood. There was nothing wrong with Camden but everything here was so pretty. For two hundred years, and for some buildings considerably longer, people had been looking for and finding ways to improve and beautify these houses. The boxes full of flowers were in full May bloom. Each front yard was groomed to perfection with a variety of landscaping tricks. Every balcony was covered with ivy or sported matching pairs of topiary trees in immaculate urns. Each door seemed freshly painted, all the brass shone in the spring sunshine. Even the curtains and chandeliers visible from the street seemed perfectly in keeping with the rest of the buildings and the neighborhood. Claire thought of the screen doors and jalousie windows, the cinder block walls of Tottenville and winced. But she didn't have to go back. Perhaps, if the house – the Homestead – was sold she could find something here.

What a relief to not have to return to Staten Island or Manhattan Island either. Though as different as chalk from cheese, both were wrong for her. Her decision not to marry Michael hadn't been easy, but once it was made, she hadn't had a moment of regret. She had slept well last night. She was sorry if she had hurt him but she had a feeling, after his rude leave-taking, that he would get over her soon enough. Perhaps someday a Katherine Rensselaer would be able to thank Claire for the home and family that Michael gave her.

Claire turned and saw the knitting shop from the corner. Oddly, there were people in it. Even from this distance she recognized Mrs Willis, Mrs Lyons-Hatchington, Charlotte and another woman who looked familiar from at least one class. Claire quickened her steps. She thought of the Monty Python line seemingly used by all fictional British policemen:

'What's all this, then?' When she got to the doorway she could see Mrs Venables behind the counter. She was shocked but delighted.

'Hello, Claire,' Mrs Venables said as she lifted her head from the knitting she was examining for the Countess, who huddled beside her. 'I'm having some trouble changing the wool color on this bobbin,' she admitted. 'Perhaps you could help.'

'Of course,' Claire agreed. She wanted to ask whether Mrs Venables should be there at all, and whether this was good for her but wouldn't do so in the presence of others. She smiled at the Countess. 'Here we go,' she said and deftly moved the thread around the bobbin.

'Ah, Claire, my daughter told me you would call today or tomorrow about another knitting party. But if the shop stays open, perhaps we needn't fuss about it.'

'Oh, but the shop isn't . . .'

Claire was interrupted smoothly by Mrs Venables. '. . . going anywhere,' she said pleasantly. 'Although I'm sure Claire would be delighted to run another party if you would like to entertain at home.'

Mrs Cruikshank approached the three women. 'My daughter-in-law has begun to crochet,' she said.

Claire struggled to look interested. Like many knitters, she had deep contempt for crocheting. There was no challenge to it and it was limited to three basic stitches. 'I'm not a crocheter,' Claire said.

'Nor I,' Mrs Cruikshank agreed. 'Anyway, I've never liked it.'

But, 'Now, now,' said Mrs Venables. 'I'm sure she's very good and careful. We mustn't allow our passions to rule us.' She looked up and smiled at Claire. 'Well, not all of the time,' she said and gave Claire a wicked little smile.

Claire wasn't sure what the message in the smile was. She forced herself to refrain from speaking. There was too much to ask about. The shop? It would stay open? And

Mrs Venables could work? Mrs Cruikshank, perhaps out of respect for Mrs Venables's recent illness or perhaps because of the difficulty she was having with her pattern and daughter-in-law simply shrugged.

'As you get older, you have to choose your battles. You can't fight them all.'

Mrs Venables nodded her agreement. 'You're absolutely right. It's like the shop,' she said. 'Keeping it open is necessary, but I had a pitched battle with my son.'

'Sons,' Mrs Cruikshank sighed. 'They always make a fatal decision in the women they marry.'

'Oh, I don't know,' the Countess said. 'Daughters make fatal decisions by not marrying at all.' Claire thought of Ann Fenwick, busy, busy, busy.

Mrs Venables nodded again. 'Oh, sons do the same,' she said. 'Nigel's going to be thirty-six and he still isn't married. Perhaps it's a way to keep me from ever meeting my own grandchild.'

'Believe me,' Mrs Cruikshank said, 'just because you have them doesn't mean you chance to see them. My daughter-in-law, the crocheter, makes sure that a visit once a month is sufficient, at least for her.' Then she asked for Claire's help to tie off another color. Claire, mad with impatience to know what had gone on between Mrs Venables and Nigel, managed to do it without destroying the cardigan. But when she was done and Mrs Cruikshank had gone to sit beside the Countess, Claire could no longer hold back.

'If you're leaving the shop open, how did you get Nigel to go along with it?' she burst out.

Mrs Venables shrugged and smiled airily. 'I had my way. I just declared business as usual.'

'You mean you're keeping the shop open?' Claire asked. All the women around the table nodded, smiling. 'But, but . . . how?'

'First I spoke to Mr Roberts, my physician and got his approval. But you know Nigel. It wasn't easy.'

'They're never easy,' Mrs Cruikshank said bitterly. 'But at least he's interested in your welfare.'

'So he agreed?' Claire asked, her heart beginning to beat very quickly.

'Well, not right away. I told him that I may be old, but I'm in complete control of my faculties. He took exception to that, but I was firm.' The women shook their heads in agreement.

'How did you convince him?' Claire asked.

'I asked for his objection. Was the question whether I have the strength to run the shop?' She looked at the group around her. Then she looked directly at Claire. 'I told him I didn't know, but I was sure Claire was very willing to become my partner.' She gave Claire a full-faced smile and patted her hand. The other women murmured approvingly. 'He said working wasn't the best thing for me. And I told him that sitting upstairs with nothing to do but watch the dust gather and the silver tarnish wasn't therapeutic either.'

'Good for you,' the Countess agreed.

'Didn't he try to cause a fuss then? I know my son would,' Mrs Cruikshank put in.

'Well, naturally.' Mrs Venables straightened up her head and put her hands on her hips. '"But Mother . . ."' she said in a fairly good Nigel imitation. The older women laughed, but Claire's head was too filled with excitement to join them. 'I was afraid that he needed to sell the building to organize his business affairs.' She lowered her voice and spoke only to Claire. 'I didn't want to have to remind him that the building was mine actually, not his.'

Mrs Cruikshank nodded her head. 'If I buy so much as a pair of needles they act as if I'm squandering their inheritance.'

'Well, luckily Nigel told me he didn't need any help with his business affairs. I apologized and, to tell you the truth, I was quite relieved.'

'So the shop will stay open,' the Countess said, her face wreathed in a smile.

'Well, that will depend on Claire. If she'll take me on as a partner and take over the management. I promised Nigel I'd only work three afternoons a week.'

'That seems reasonable,' Mrs Cruikshank said. 'And Claire is a good girl.' She patted Claire's arm. 'If only my son had married someone like you,' she said.

Claire could hardly believe it. To inherit money, a house, and be offered a partnership all in one day? To find out that the shop would stay open, that she would have a job doing what she loved and that people were actually grateful to her for doing it was too much. Then, 'Of course, there are some difficulties,' Mrs Venables said, and Claire's heart dropped. She should have known. 'For one thing,' Mrs Venables continued, 'she'll have to agree to take a good deal more money. And for another she'll probably have to accept a flat upstairs in lieu of some compensation.' She looked at Claire apologetically. 'Until the cash flow, or something like that, improves. And Nigel said he'd feel so much better if he knew you were within shouting distance.' She looked at the women. 'But of course, Claire might not want to be saddled with me.'

A flat! And in this neighborhood, in this very building! Mrs Venables's place on the parlor floor was very beautiful. Claire couldn't even imagine what another flat in the building would look like but . . . the possibilities of investing in the shop or renting bigger space to enlarge Knitting Kitting's inventory, having weekday evening classes or bigger weekend classes. Then there was redecorating the flat. Choosing new paint colors for the walls, new rugs to go on the beautiful wood floors, putting up new curtains and draperies, the list was endless.

'So, would you consider it, Claire?'

Then Claire remembered Mrs Patel and the baby. She had promised to help take care of the grocery and help out with the kids. But couldn't she manage to do that and the shop? Especially if she got more of Maudie's help? 'It may take me a little while to organize it,' Claire said. 'But I would be so very happy, so grateful . . .'

'Well, we'll sort that all out later, shall we?' Mrs Venables asked.

Just then the door opened and Lady Ann came in.

SEVENTY-ONE

Lady Ann kissed her mother, gave the other women a brief hello and then focused on Claire. 'Imogen told me you would still be here,' she said. 'I need you to come back to your flat.'

Surprised and curious on this day of surprises, Claire allowed Lady Ann to take her by the arm and lead her back to Imogen's. There Imogen had three glasses of wine and a large salad set out. 'Some lunch?' she asked Claire brightly as if she always prepared little meals.

Claire knew something very strange was happening. Of course, Imogen would be eager to impress Lady Ann, but when did they make this date? And why was she invited? Claire sat down on the sofa and Ann took the other seat. 'The thing is, Claire,' Imogen began, 'the thing is Lady Ann and I have discussed a book about knitting. We've been all around the houses on this and we think you would be the perfect person to write it.'

'Write a book?' Claire said. 'I can't write a book!'

'Well, that didn't stop Naomi Campbell or Ivana Trump, did it?' Ann asked and laughed.

'I've been a twit not to see it myself,' Im said. 'Ann laid it all out for me. It's brilliant!'

'Claire, you're young and attractive and you know about knitting and I could get you a lot of media coverage,' Ann said. 'We always like stories about Americans who prefer the UK to the States. It helps with our inferiority complex.'

'But . . .' Claire began to protest.

'Okay,' Imogen said. 'Here's how it would happen: I get you an editor to work with you, and you put together a book of simple patterns. We quote some celebrities and talk about the soothing contemplative aspect of knitting. You know, knitting as a kind of Zen meditation. Then you do the telly and tour.'

'Tour where?' Claire said.

'Oh, Manchester, Bristol, Edinburgh.' She and Ann laughed. 'I think I can get you a good advance,' Im continued. 'Not spectacular, but five-figures. And if it works we could do a series of books.'

'Oh, it'll work,' Ann said. 'I listen all day to people chuntering on and on. Do you have any idea of how many editors at the women's magazines owe me favors? Anyway, the truth is I already put out a punchy press release and the rags seem quite excited.'

Again, both women laughed. But Claire simply couldn't believe what she was hearing. 'I write a book and you pay me?'

'Yes. And then we go around the country – well you do – and you sign a lot of copies and you show people how to knit. What do you say?'

Claire said yes.

Nigel showed Claire the apartment the next day. 'I'd be very grateful if you'd be prepared to stay here,' Nigel said. 'So would Mother.'

Claire looked around. It was a little smaller than Mrs Venables's flat, but it had a large living room with a fireplace on one side and doors out to a little balcony on the other. There was a small kitchen, a bedroom, and – to Claire's amazement and delight – a small box room. 'I'm afraid the closet space probably isn't what you're used to,' Nigel said as if he were some apologetic estate agent. 'But

I can have one built in along that wall. And of course I'll replace the curtains. You can pick whatever kind you like.'

Claire turned to him, the glory of all that she was seeing reflected in her eyes. But, she realized, Nigel must be humiliated by this. 'Nigel, I'm very sorry if you . . .'

'Don't be sorry. I'm the one who should apologize. I was very foolish. And prejudiced. I hope you just ignored me. I don't know what I or my mother would have done without your help.'

Claire flushed. 'Oh, it would have been . . .'

'It would have been a fiasco.' He looked around. 'So, I'll have it painted, shall I? Magnolia?' Before she could answer he had turned back to her. 'The view of the back garden is very nice. Come and see it.'

They went into the empty bedroom and peered out of the window. 'It's more than a bit overgrown,' Nigel said. 'Mother used to love to keep it up but the gardener is lax.'

'Could I work on it?'

'Of course. If you like.'

Claire turned to him. 'Oh, I'd love to!'

Perhaps it was her enthusiasm, or the way the light played on the side of her face. Perhaps it was because he had been longing to do it for quite some time. But for whatever reason, Nigel Venables took Claire in his arms and, to her complete surprise, kissed her. To her even greater surprise he kissed her long and well.

SEVENTY-TWO

You might believe that Claire lived happily ever after. Of course, nobody ever does but if you'd like to believe that Claire was the exception, you're free to do it. The flat was lovely and furnished with family pieces from Claire's Aunt Gertrude, as well as the antiques that Claire bought.

You're free to imagine Claire, working away at her book in the box room that she turned into an office. You might also believe that Claire's book was a big success, and that she not only went on a national tour, signing copies in bookstores, knitting shops, and ladies' clubs all around the country, but that it was also a success in Canada and the United States. And that Leonora Atkins convinced Claire and Nigel to open knitting shops across the UK and that they prospered.

You might choose to believe that Mrs Venables lived a long time and stayed well until the very end, when she died at home, in her own bed, holding Claire's hand on one side and Nigel's on the other. You may also believe that Nigel and Claire wound up married to one another and that it was a good match, built on mutual respect, shared interests and more than a moderate amount of lust. Both the marriage and their daughter had made Mrs Venables's last years particularly happy, and she did knit a layette for her grandchild.

Whether Claire ever went back to New York, served as

maid-of-honor at Tina's wedding and made a kind of peace with her mother are, again, choices you might want to make. Along with the belief that much later Safta got her degree from Cambridge, Mrs Patel remarried and that Claire finally made it to Nice. In fact, you might feel that everything came to a fairy tale ending all because someone made a wish upon a star.

Choose that if you will, but all novels are, in a sense, fairy tales. They are pulled from the air and create the magical illusion that the characters you read about are real, are living and the lives that are described have happened. The novelist imagines and conjures but, when the narration ends, has no more idea of what happens to the characters than you, the reader, does. Fiction is so often preferable to life because, sadly, only in fiction can you write the magical incantation at the end: 'And they lived happily ever after.'

ACKNOWLEDGEMENTS

Sadly, Olivia Goldsmith died after completing *Wish Upon A Star*. Her close friend and assistant Nan Robinson remembers her:

At the time we met, Olivia lived in a historical Vermont stone house that she had renovated. She frequented a small diner in town. It was through her waitress, Etta Kennett, that Olivia and I came to work together. She asked Etta if she knew of anyone who could help with typing. Etta responded, 'I know a little girl who always has a laptop with her and works on manuscripts when she isn't driving a school bus.' With that, Olivia left a diner napkin that had her name and number on it with Etta.

When Etta gave me the napkin, I was so excited by the possibility of actually being able to give my opinion on a writer's work I called and made an appointment to meet Olivia a few weeks after she had returned from the book tour for *First Wives Club*, her huge bestseller. She told me about her work, what she expected and then sent me up to her office to 'fool around with the Mac'. When I went back downstairs to let her know I was finished, she handed me a copy of her book along with the manuscript for her second. 'Learn my style by reading and then make any comments you'd like on *Flavor*.' That's how we started working together.

The winter of '93 brought an offer from HarperCollins U.S. for a worldwide three-book deal. Olivia and I were on our usual morning beach walk in Hollywood, Florida. Olivia said she wouldn't do the deal without me. My response: 'Well, it seems like a fun thing to do.' She laughed. Obviously, I don't know how to count, do I? *Wish Upon A Star* is her eleventh novel.

Olivia was a strong believer in: 'Have pen will travel.' So we did. Paris twice, Italy three times, England at least six times, India, Wyoming, a road trip of the California coast, not to mention other places within the United States while on book tour, and for speeches and public appearances. When we weren't traveling the reward system worked for us best: hot fudge sundaes or shopping at designer outlets. As for our adventures in Hollywood – that's a whole other fairy tale. I can say that Olivia was proud to see her 'words turned into flesh' with the movie *The First Wives Club*. Having it hailed a phenomenon was a definite bonus.

As if book writing wasn't enough construction, Olivia also loved to remodel. She worked on her stone house; a classic six co-op; a three-story townhouse; two lofts and a cottage but her most challenging endeavor was *Beaver Hall* – a Georgian mansion on the Hudson River in upstate New York.

For more serious realities I have to thank her for being there when I became seriously ill four years ago before being diagnosed with multiple sclerosis.

I haven't even made a dent in thanking Olivia for all the impact she's made on my life and continues to make. If life could mimic fairy tales then I would wish upon a star for my best friend to come back so I could 'live happily ever after'.

I hope you enjoy *Wish Upon A Star* – Olivia had a love affair with London and this is a fitting tribute to it.

Nan Robinson

Uptown Girl
Olivia Goldsmith

From the bestselling author of *The First Wives Club* and *Young Wives*, a sparkling New York comedy about making plans for other people – and then tripping yourself up on them.

There's something magical about Brooklyn's Billy Nolan. It's not just that he's wickedly attractive, it's that any woman he dates and dumps (and he dates and dumps them all) immediately goes on to marry someone else.

Sassy, uptown New Yorker Kate is immune to Billy's charms – she left Brooklyn behind a long time ago, and she's not about to fall under the spell of a handsome waster from the old neighbourhood. Besides, she's dating the eminently suitable Michael. But perhaps the 'Billy effect' will work for Kate's friend, Bina, who has fallen apart because her almost-fiancé, Jack, is going away to 'explore his singleness'.

All Kate has to do is get Billy to date Bina and dump her – and then await Jack's return and watch the magic happen. It's a great plan and at first it seems to be working. But the one thing Kate hasn't considered is how Billy feels about it all . . .

'Full of wisecracks, and gossip . . . Olivia Goldsmith can keep you reading.' *Cosmopolitan*

0 00 713335 9

Bad Boy

Olivia Goldsmith

A romantic, sophisticated and wickedly funny comedy by the author of *The First Wives Club* and *Young Wives*.

Jon is Mr Perfect – handsome (in a nerdy sort of way), caring, lots of money – so why can't he get a girlfriend? Even his best friend Tracie always goes for bad boys; because women secretly love BAD. Jon's getting desperate, but Tracie can help – she can teach him the Bad Boy Rules:

Never be available
Never be predictable
Never tell them where you live . . .
. . . and most important of all, always carry a motor cycle helmet, even if you haven't got a bike

A sharp haircut, cool new clothes and a complete attitude transplant later, and Jon's the man of the moment. He can have any woman he wants, and does!

But now Tracie's not so happy . . . while her girlfriends are all fighting over the new Jon, she seems to be losing her best friend. And she's starting to wonder – has she created a monster?

'Full of wisecracks and gossip . . . Olivia Goldsmith can keep you reading'   *Cosmopolitan*

ISBN 0 00 651437 5